Happiness
for Beginners

Also by Katherine Center

The Lost Husband

Get Lucky

Everyone Is Beautiful

The Bright Side of Disaster

Happiness for Beginners

Katherine Center

St. Martin's Griffin
New York

HAPPINESS FOR BEGINNERS. Copyright © 2015 by Katherine Center. All rights reserved. Printed in the United States of America. For information, address St. Martin's Press, 175 Fifth Avenue, New York, N.Y. 10010.

Pablo Neruda's "Sonnet XXI" Copyright © 2004 City Lights Books. Reprinted by permission of City Lights Books.

www.stmartins.com

The Library of Congress Cataloging-in-Publication Data is available upon request.

ISBN 978-1-250-04730-4 (trade paperback)
ISBN 978-1-4668-4769-9 (e-book)

St. Martin's Griffin books may be purchased for educational, business, or promotional use. For information on bulk purchases, please contact the Macmillan Corporate and Premium Sales Department at 1-800-221-7945, extension 5442, or write to specialmarkets@macmillan.com.

First Edition: March 2015

10 9 8 7 6 5 4 3 2 1

For my husband, Gordon, on our twentieth year together.
Thanks for being so good at love.

Happiness for Beginners

✳

Chapter 1

If you want to put me in Hell, plunk me down in the middle of a party where I don't know anyone. If you want to be really thorough, fill the place with drunken college kids. And make sure every other one manages to spill a drink on me. Don't tell me about the party in advance, so I show up in sweatpants and ponytails. While you're at it, put a bubble-gum pink cat carrier under my arm. With a pissed-off mini dachshund inside.

Actually, don't. Because then you'll turn into my brother Duncan. And trust me: You don't want to be Duncan.

Here's what he did this time. He said he'd watch my dog, Pickle, while I was out of town for three weeks. I reminded him that she was a bit of an ankle-biter and not a huge fan of the human race. Or the canine one. Or living creatures in general. Still, Duncan swore he wanted to with such sincerity that even after knowing him for a lifetime, I said okay. He swore to devote himself to her comfort the whole time I was gone. He even teased me that he'd burn a meat-scented candle to help her feel at home.

We agreed I'd drop Pickle off the night before I left, but by the time it was time, Duncan had forgotten the whole plan as if it had never existed. Instead, he'd decided to host a "small gathering of good friends" with his roommate, Jake, bartending. Jake, for his part, had invented a drink called "the Lambada" mixed with homemade moonshine that he swore would get you laid if you even just *sniffed* it.

Suddenly a hundred people were crammed into an apartment the size of a refrigerator. And one of them was me.

The worst part wasn't even that Duncan kept doing this kind of thing. It was that I kept falling for it. And now my emotionally challenged pet had to suffer.

Duncan, as always in these moments, was nowhere to be found.

I pushed my way through to his room, which was empty. Not empty of dirty boxers on the floor, or three-week-old Chinese takeout containers, or posters with girls in bikinis—just empty of Duncan. In the corner, the recliner he'd rescued from the heavy trash was piled taller than me with dirty laundry. A six-month-old tangle of Christmas lights hung from a sad nail, flashing on and off like Vegas.

I picked my way over to the unmade bed, set Pickle's carrier down, and tilted it up to peer in at her face. Her top lip was caught on the teeth. The ears were drooping. The eyes were all betrayal.

"You don't want to live here, do you?" I said.

To my surprise, a voice behind me answered back. "I don't mind."

It was Jake. Housemate, bartender, and Duncan's best friend since tenth grade. But it took me a second to register, and not just because he was standing in a corner, somewhat out of sight. He looked different—radically different—than the last time I'd seen him. When had that been? I had no idea. Long enough for him to grow like a foot taller, and to fill out in all those good boy places, like shoulders and arms, and to get a vast improvement of a haircut that spiked up in the front. I knew it was him, of course—but he looked so unlike the person I pictured on the rare occasion that I thought of him, I couldn't help but confirm: "Jake?"

He raised a hand. "Hi, Helen."

"Were you hiding back there?"

"I wasn't hiding," he said with a frown. "I was in the nook."

"The nook?"

"Yeah," he said, turning to gesture behind him. "We turned the closet into a nook. Video games, music. I use it mostly for reading."

"You and Duncan built a nook?"

"It's awesome. It's like a spaceship in there. Want to see?"

I gave him a look: *really?* I had never liked this kid. Everything that made me crazy about Duncan? Jake made it worse. After Duncan met Jake, he did half the dishes, half the homework, and twice the dope-smoking that he'd done before. I'd hoped they'd lose touch when they went off to college, but, instead, they became housemates. For four years. Now it was the summer after their senior year—though Duncan hadn't quite graduated—and they were still living like idiots.

Apparently, Duncan didn't have time to graduate, but he had time to build a spaceship nook. No, I did not want to see it. Nope.

Jake was staring at me in the way he always stared at me when we were in the same room: mouth slightly open, as if he were not just looking at me, but *beholding* me, somehow. From anyone else, it would have been flattering.

I finally had to say something. "You cut off your ponytail."

He nodded, remembering. "Yep," he said. "Yep. Grabbed a big pair of scissors and snipped it right off. Duncan keeps it in a coffee mug on the shelf and calls it our pet."

There was a pause, while Jake kept nodding.

"Was that for graduation?" I finally asked.

"No," he said, switching to head-shaking. "That was freshman year."

That got my attention. "You've had your hair short since freshman year? Haven't I seen you since then?"

"Oh, yeah. A bunch of times."

I couldn't remember the last time I'd seen him. I'd certainly never noticed he'd cut off all that nasty hair and spiked it into a dark Speed Racer look. I guess sometimes you just get an idea of a person in your mind, and that's what you see when you look at him, no matter what.

"It could be the glasses," he offered.

I frowned.

"The new glasses," he said, tapping them. "I never wore glasses before this year."

"Oh," I said. "Right." It was becoming quite clear to me—and likely to him, too—that I'd never really looked at him before. He might have insisted he'd always worn a pirate patch, and I couldn't have argued.

"I like them," I said then.

"They're very Nixon administration," he said. "Duncan's started calling me Apollo Thirteen."

So there we had it. Haircut, hipster glasses, and the mysterious addition of all kinds of muscles. Three was a magic number after all. "Well," I said, looking away. "It's a thousand times better."

"Thanks."

Another pause.

"Are you looking for Duncan?" Jake asked then.

"Yes!" I said, and it all came back—how mad I was. "He's supposed to dog-sit for me."

"That's a dog in there?" He peered in. Pickle growled.

The music outside the bedroom seemed to get louder. "We were supposed to do a drop-off tonight," I said. "Duncan was not supposed to be hosting *Girls Gone Wild*."

Jake wrinkled his nose in apology. "He probably forgot."

"Of course he forgot," I said. "It's *Duncan*. And that's why I'm leaving. But first I want to thank him profusely for letting me down. Again."

Jake nodded like he really got it. "He's big on the offering, not so big on the actual doing."

I shook my head at my own stupidity. "I never should have agreed."

"It's hard, though," Jake said. "He really means it when he offers. You just have to train yourself to say no. I've got it on a tattoo: ALWAYS SAY NO TO DUNCAN."

I tilted my head. "Really?"

He smiled like I was adorable. "Not really. I'm kidding."

I sighed.

"Great ponytails, by the way," he added.

Pickle started barking then—loudly, over and over. "Do you know where Duncan is?" I asked.

He nodded. "He's in my room. That's why I'm here."

I shook my head. "Why aren't either of you actually *attending* your own party?"

"Um," Jake said, turning his eyes up to the ceiling to think. "Well, I'm in the middle of this great book, so I took a bartending break to see what happens next, but I'm pretty sure Duncan might be getting lucky."

I put my hand over my eyes. "Please tell me you're kidding again."

"Nope," he said. "I seem to be sexiled."

I dropped my hand to look at him.

"That's when you're exiled from your room," he explained, "because someone else is having sex there."

"I know what sexiled is," I said. "They had that word even way back when I was in college."

Jake nodded approvingly.

"Why is he in *your* room?" I asked.

Jake gestured around like it was obvious. "You can't bring a girl in here."

I scanned the bikini posters. "But yours is okay?"

He shrugged. "My filth level is lower."

I sighed again. There were very few things Duncan could be doing that I wouldn't be willing to interrupt right now, but "getting lucky" was one of them. "Can you give him a message for me?" I asked.

"Sure," Jake said. "Anything."

"Tell him he's a moron, and he can kiss my ass."

Jake nodded as he committed it to memory. "Got it."

"Don't forget," I said, as I bent down to lift Pickle's carrier.

He crossed his heart. "I won't forget," he said. "Especially the part about your ass."

Was he *flirting* with me? He was ten years younger than I was! Uppity behavior like that demanded an icy stare-down. But, in honor of the fact that he'd cut off that greasy ponytail, I let it slide.

I was at the door when he said something that stopped me. "Thanks for the ride, by the way."

I turned back with my hand still on the knob. "What ride?"

Jake looked flummoxed for a second, then frowned. "The ride?" he said. "Tomorrow?"

"I'm sorry," I said. "I'm actually going out of town tomorrow, so I can't give you a ride anywhere." Not that I would have, anyway. Had I ever given him a ride to anything? What was he thinking?

"I know," he said. "You're going to Wyoming. To go hiking. On a survival course."

"That's right," I said, surprised that Duncan had conveyed so many details correctly.

"I'm also going to Wyoming tomorrow. To go hiking—"

And then, with dread, I knew what he was going to say.

"—on the same survival course."

I set Pickle down. "I'm sorry. What?"

"We're going to the same place," he said, like it all made perfect sense. "Duncan said you wouldn't mind giving me a ride."

It didn't make sense. Why would this kid Jake be going on the same trip as me? How could the universe even let that happen? This was something I was doing for myself, on my own. A Back Country Survival Company course, no less. BCSC courses were famously hardcore, invariably grueling, and occasionally life-threatening. It was a big deal for me. It was supposed to be a spiritual journey. It was supposed to signify my bouncing back after the worst year—or six—of my life. Duncan's goofy friend could not be coming, too. He was not invited.

"But this is something I'm doing alone," I said matter-of-factly, in a mind-melding tone that always worked beautifully on the first graders in my class.

"Well," he said, "it's twelve people plus the instructor, so you won't exactly be alone."

Not a first grader, then. "But, I mean, *alone* like *on my own.*"

"On your own with eleven other people," he confirmed. "And me."

This was crazy. "How can you be coming on my trip?"

"Technically, *you* are coming on *my* trip," he said. "Duncan only knew about it because I was going."

Duncan. This was all his fault. Again. As usual. "But he never said anything about you," I said.

"I think at the time you signed up, I thought I couldn't go. But now I can." He shrugged, looking pleased.

This was not the plan. The plan, as I had fantasized for the last six months, was to drive out to Wyoming and have a brave adventure with a bunch of strangers that would totally change not just my life, but my entire personality. The plan was to set out alone into the world, conquer it, and return home a fiercer and more badass version of myself. The plan did not include anybody but me—especially not, of all people, Jake.

I made an apologetic face. "I'm so sorry," I said, like this settled things, "but I'm supposed to stay with my grandmother on the trip out."

"Grandma GiGi? She loves me."

"She couldn't," I said. My grandma GiGi didn't love anybody except me. And Duncan. On occasion.

"She does. I swear. Call her."

"I'm not going to call her. I've got things to do. On the drive back, I have to go to a bar mitzvah to see some old friends."

He nodded. "The son of your high school boyfriend and your high school best friend. Right? Why would you go to that?"

I gaped. This kid knew way too much about my life. "I'm going," I said, "because we're friends on Facebook now, and because they asked me to, and because it's not healthy to hold a grudge."

"You're friends on Facebook?"

"Yeah. Except I never, ever go on Facebook." I blinked. "Why do you even know about any of this?"

"Duncan told me," he said with a shrug. "That's fine. I don't need a ride back. Just out."

"You're not coming back?" I said.

"*Eventually* I'm coming back," he said. "But first I'm going to Baja. Like four days after the BCSC trip ends. I fly out of Denver." He paused. I guess he expected me to ask him why he was going.

I didn't.

He continued. "I snagged a research assistantship for a field study on whales."

I stared at him.

"We're going to row out to their breeding grounds in little fishing boats and study how they interact with humans."

I gave in to curiosity. "Why?"

"Because it's fascinating."

"Is it?"

"It is. The whales swim up to the boats—voluntarily. People pet them."

"Why?"

He frowned like he couldn't imagine how I could ask that question. Like I should get it. Which in truth, I did. Why would you pet a whale? *Because it wanted you to.*

"It's powerful," he said. "People cry. People burst into show tunes."

"*Show tunes?*"

"People say they are never the same again."

"I don't see what's so great about petting a whale."

He leveled his gaze at me. "Yes, you do."

"No, I really don't."

We stared each other down.

After a minute, he went on, as if that tangent about whales had somehow settled the ride-to-Wyoming question.

"So it's just the ride out. You won't even know I'm there. I'll even sit in the backseat, if you want. Or you can strap me to the roof rack. I thought about making a music mix—but then I was like, 'No way, dude, she's got her own music'—so I'll just stay out of your way and not even make a sound and we'll listen to whatever you want. Even Carly Simon, or whatever—"

"No!" I almost shouted. I felt a rising sense of panic. Here was my life, proceeding without my consent. Again. "Look, I don't know what Duncan told you, or promised you, but I'm sorry: I cannot give you a ride. You'll just have to go on a different trip."

"But it's non-refundable."

I knew that, of course. "Then you'll just have to take the bus. Or something."

Jake studied my face. "Okay," he said. "No problem."

I exhaled. "Good. Great! I'll see you in Wyoming." I bent down to grab Pickle's carrier.

"Except . . . ?" he added.

I stood back up empty-handed. "Except what?"

"Except I'm pretty short on cash," he said. "I don't think I have enough for a bus ticket."

I closed my eyes. "You're short on cash?"

He shrugged. "We went over budget on the nook."

I glanced at the nook for confirmation. Then I looked back like, *Seriously?* "What about your parents?" I asked.

"Parent," he corrected. "Just my dad."

"Can't he help you out?"

"He's in Texas," he said, shrugging like he was on Mars. "And he doesn't exactly know I'm going on this trip."

I put my hands on my hips and tried to come up with another answer. Any other answer. Down at my ankles, Pickle was whimpering.

"It's cool," he said. "I can see it doesn't work. I'll just hitch."

"You're not hitching," I said.

"No, I've done it before—"

"You are *not* hitching," I said, in my teacher voice, and it felt for a second—before I realized the opposite was true—like I'd won.

"Okay," he said, shrugging. "I'll ride with you." Then he gave me a half grin that I couldn't help noticing made a very high-caliber dimple. "If you insist."

Chapter 2

It's a thousand and one miles from Boston to Evanston, give or take. You can drive it in a day, but it's a long day. A fifteen-hour day, according to Google.

That's why I'd wanted to leave early—before the sun was up. That's why I'd wanted to get Pickle set up with Duncan the night before. If I made it home fast enough, I'd get a good visit with my grandmother. My grandmother who'd raised Duncan and me after our mother lost interest. My nothing-short-of-fabulous grandmother, who wore a bun with chopsticks in it, who I adored.

As it was, though, I had to wait for the vet to open so I could bring Pickle in for boarding.

Pickle was never happy about much, but going to the vet made her positively suicidal. As I waved a falsely cheerful good-bye, I felt a squeeze of regret and wondered if I should have left her at Duncan's place after all. But I couldn't have. That dog didn't know how lucky she was. If nothing else, the party last night had likely saved her life. If I'd left her with Duncan, I'd no doubt have returned weeks later to a desiccated pile of fur and a befuddled-looking brother, scratching his head, saying, "I *thought* she got awfully quiet."

Walking back to my Subaru after the drop-off, I realized I'd parked so hastily that I'd left one tire partway up on the curb. I hadn't even noticed at the time, but, back out front, the wonky tire was the first thing I saw. The second thing I saw was Jake, standing right next to it, holding a Starbucks coffee.

"Nice parking job," he said, handing me the cup.

"What are you doing here?" I asked.

"Thought I'd save you the trouble of picking me up."

"What if you'd missed me?"

"Well, that would have been the opposite of saving you trouble," he admitted. "But that's not what happened."

I took in the sight of him: bed-head hair, cargo pants with no belt, and a surprisingly clingy T-shirt with Snoopy on it. His duffel bag leaned against the car.

"Worried I'd skip town without you?" I asked.

That made him smile. "You bet," he said.

"I thought about it," I said.

He rummaged in his backpack and pulled out a book with a whale on the cover. "I'll read the whole time," he said. "You won't even know I'm here."

I gave him a look. "Right."

"Ready to go?"

"Not really," I said, but I unlocked the door anyway.

As I watched him shove his bag into the way back, I wondered how he'd known where to find me, but then I remembered the Pickle packet I'd assembled for Duncan, with a highlighted map to the vet's.

"Duncan showed you the packet," I said.

Jake nodded and slammed the hatchback closed. "You're very thorough."

I was. In fact, I'd truly gone overboard. Letters of explanation to the vet. Letters of explanation to Duncan. More information than anybody needed. I felt a sting of shame that swung right over to resentment at Duncan for forcing me to be that way. "When it comes to Duncan, I am."

"Want me to drive?"

"No."

No, I did not want him to drive. If it were up to me, he'd be crammed back there with his duffel, and I'd be up front, alone with all the music I'd collected for the journey: Joni Mitchell, Nina Simone, Indigo Girls. The plan had been to sing my lungs out on the drive west, to team up with everybody from Annie Lennox to James Brown and belt out every emotion in the human repertoire. And then, hopefully, by the time I hit Wyoming, to be done with them all.

Of course, I wouldn't be belting anything out in front of Jake. That's not the kind of singing you do with a stranger. Or a friend of your brother's. I glanced over at him. Driving a thousand and one miles today in songless silence while this kid played video games on his phone was not what I'd signed up for.

But there it was. Life never gives you exactly what you want. That didn't change the fact that it was time to go. We buckled up and I edged us out into the street.

"So," I said, as we joined the flow of cars. "It's one thousand and one miles from here to Evanston."

"One thousand *and one*?"

"Roughly." I nodded. "Google says it'll take fifteen hours and twenty-two minutes," I went on, glancing at the clock on the dashboard, "and it's eleven minutes after nine now, thanks to Duncan, so we won't make it in time for dinner. We should arrive at my grandma's house—"

"After midnight," he finished.

"Right," I said, giving a little sigh. I wondered if I should call and tell Grandma GiGi not to wait up. She was a night owl, but she wasn't literally nocturnal.

"I bet we can still get you there for dinner," Jake said. "A late one, anyway." I could see him thinking. "Google's assuming we're driving sixty-five miles an hour. But we'll be doing eighty or ninety, at least."

"Seventy," I corrected. "Or whatever the speed limit is."

"Okay," he said, still calculating. "You'll be driving the speed limit, and I'll be driving whatever gets us up to an average of eighty." He turned and checked the backseat. "Yup. Duncan predicted you'd pack a cooler of snacks."

I felt like I was being teased, but I wasn't quite sure about what.

"So," he went on, "we won't have to stop for meals, which'll save some time." He tilted his head back to look at the ceiling while he did the math. "Eighty miles an hour into a thousand—*and one*—is more like twelve hours. Ish. Fewer if we pee in bottles."

"Girls can't pee in bottles," I said.

He glanced over. "I bet you could. If you tried."

Was he complimenting or insulting me? I shook my head. "That's where I draw the line," I said. "At peeing in bottles."

He gave in with a nod. "Probably a good place for it."

"But the rest of the plan," I said, adding a tiny shrug as I realized it was true, "I love."

He looked pleased with himself. "Thanks."

So he had a can-do attitude. So he'd brought me a cappuccino. So he was willing to pee in a bottle to get me to my grandma's on time. Also: I had to admit the morning sunshine around us was insistently cheery. Maybe the drive wouldn't be so bad, after all. I lifted my coffee and took a sip just as he decided to strike up some more conversation:

"So," he said. "How's life without your dickhead ex-husband?"

My response was to choke on that coffee so violently that Jake had to take my cup in one hand and grab the wheel with the other.

"Sorry," he said, when I'd resumed command of the wheel. "Guess that's a tender subject."

"No," I said, defiantly pawing at my watering eyes. "It's not a tender subject."

Here, to underscore the point, I used another favorite teacher voice—the Mary Poppins. This one implied that every problem had a solution, that the world deep down made perfect, comforting, and pleasant sense, and that if you carefully maintained the right spoonful-of-sugar attitude, you might even one day find yourself traveling over London by the stem of your parasol.

The Mary Poppins was the only voice I ever used to talk about my failed marriage, and I sat up straighter to execute it properly. "The guy I happened to marry," I went on, channeling Julie Andrews so hard that I almost went British, "later turned into a raging alcoholic. When his problem began to impact our marriage, I gave him several chances to pull it together. Unfortunately for everyone, he just couldn't manage it."

In conclusion, I took a successful sip of coffee, as if to say, *End of story! Spit spot! And now I am enjoying a delicious hot beverage.*

"So you divorced him," Jake said.

"So I divorced him," I confirmed. I did not add: *After I lost our first baby at thirteen weeks pregnant. And he was nowhere to be found.*

"A year ago," he added, as if to say he was already up on all the details.

"A year ago," I confirmed. Almost to the day. And I was fine now. Ish.

"And how that's going?" he asked.

"How's what going?"

"Being single."

"Fine," I said. "Great." But I was hardly anything as adorable as "single." I was just alone.

"You're okay?" He was frowning at me.

"I'm always okay," I said.

"Nobody's always okay."

"I am," I declared. This conversation was beyond useless. Of course I wasn't okay—not "always," or, lately, "often." But even if I had wanted to discuss the infinite ways I'd felt utterly broken this year—which I frigging *did not*—Jake the bartender, inventor of "the forbidden drink of love," would be the very last person I'd turn to.

I could feel his gaze traveling along my face.

I sat up even straighter. I kept my eyes on the road. I imagined the angle of Julie Andrews's chin and lifted mine to the very spot.

"Okay," he said at last, unconvinced but willing to drop it. "If you say so."

"I do say so," I said.

"'Cause I was wondering if you might want to kill yourself."

I coughed. "Kill myself?"

"What were you thinking, anyway? Signing up for a BCSC course?"

I shook my head. "I don't know. Probably the same thing you were."

"You weren't thinking what I was," he said, as if the idea were ridiculous.

I let it slide. "I want a challenge. I want to do something really hard. I want to push myself beyond my limitations."

"Or maybe you just want to kill yourself."

I looked over. "I do not want to kill myself."

"People die on these trips all the time."

"No, they don't."

"Of all the outdoor adventure courses you could have chosen, you picked the most terrifying, the most reckless, the most lethal of them all. What's *that* about?"

"Duncan suggested it," I said.

"Duncan suggested *a* course. Not *this* course."

"He showed me the catalog."

"You never do anything Duncan suggests." Jake shook his head. "Why start now?"

It was true. But the fact that Duncan had suggested it was incidental. What got me hooked on the idea was a *People* magazine human interest story I stumbled on a few restless nights later about a guy who had lost a leg in Afghanistan and brought himself back to life by completing this very course. With one leg! He did it—and did it well enough to earn one of their prized "Certificates," which were only given out to the top three participants. The article had echoed in my head for days afterwards: "I was lost," the guy had said, "but I found myself out there."

Was I lost? Not technically. But I had lost something that I couldn't even articulate—and I'd gone far too long without finding it. Was it waiting for me in the Wyoming wilderness? Probably not. But I had to start somewhere.

Clearly, Duncan also thought I never did anything he suggested. When I'd told him I'd signed up, he'd coughed in disbelief and tried to talk me out of it, insisting a course like this was no place for someone like me. In his view, it was both pretty extreme and kind of phony. It attracted the worst of the worst. Real hard-core hikers, Duncan had argued, knew what they were doing and organized their own trips. BCSC was for hard-core wannabes. They didn't want to study the terrain or buy the proper gear or actually take the time to know what they were doing—they just wanted to sign up and do it. Which made them not just daredevils, but lazy daredevils.

I glanced at Jake. "You signed up for it, too."

"I've gone camping every year with my dad since I was three. I have tons of experience. Plus, I'm coordinated."

"You're saying I'm not coordinated?"

He tilted his head. Yes. That's what he was saying. And he wasn't wrong, either.

"I've been camping," I said at last.

"When?" he demanded.

"I drove to Colorado with my high school boyfriend."

"That's not camping. That's a slumber party. I bet you ate fluffer-nutters on white bread."

"We did not!" I said. We'd eaten beef jerky. And Oreos.

"The point is," Jake went on, "this is totally over your head."

"They took my application. They let me in."

"That's because they don't care if you die."

In truth, several people had died—or at least been maimed—on trips with this group. Duncan had Googled it hoping to convince me to do Outward Bound, instead—or something more sane and reasonable. But I didn't want sane and reasonable. I wanted crazy and unreasonable. I wanted to amaze everybody, including myself. My own personal campaign of shock and awe.

"They're under new management now," I said.

"I think they *like* it when people die," Jake said. "These guys have cornered the market on hard-core nut-job wannabes, and a clear-and-present threat of death just improves their appeal. To crazy people."

Was that me? Maybe.

I had signed about fifty waivers, declaring BCSC blameless for every possible life-threatening, or life-ending, situation I might encounter out there, including bear attacks, avalanches, hypothermia, and "fatal diarrhea."

Nothing about this course should have appealed to me. BCSC was notorious for taking the steepest slopes, following the rockiest paths, and exploring the most remote locations. Google "BCSC," and there's article after article of broken collarbones, rockslides, bear attacks, missing hikers, and hypothermia. That's how they'd become the patron saints of crazies, thrill-seekers, and people with nothing left to lose. Which, needless to say, wasn't me. I was a first-grade teacher, for Pete's sake!

I couldn't believe the tone in Jake's voice. "Why are you asking me about this? This has nothing to do with you."

"Well," he said, "it kind of does. Since I'm here."

"I didn't ask you to be here!"

He closed his mouth and looked away.

"I'm going to get a Certificate," I said.

"You think you're going to be one of the top three on this trip?" he said, in a tone like, *Come on.*

"Yes."

"Well, I don't. I think you'll be lucky to survive."

"That's because you're looking at the old me. This," I patted myself on the head, "is the former me. The me I'm *about to become* is someone else entirely. You wouldn't dare patronize her. She'd claw out your eyeballs and feed them to her dog."

"I can't wait to meet her."

"She's going to ruin your life, man."

"I don't doubt it," he said.

And despite the unabashed mockery in his voice, a quieter, raspier sound had crept in, too. One that made me wonder if he maybe, really, actually thought she would.

Chapter 3

We fell quiet as we made our way out of the city. Jake read his whale book and let me concentrate on navigating the roads and roundabouts of Boston, which are so convoluted my ex-husband Mike used to joke they were laid out by ferrets.

Ex-husband. It had taken me so long to get used to the word "husband," but "ex-husband" was taking even longer. At the thought of him, my chest got that familiar squeeze—as if all the sorrows of the past year were still in there, still collapsing inward like my own personal intergalactic black hole.

Mike. He was the reason for this crazy trip, though I wasn't fleeing him, exactly, so much as the person I'd become in the wake of our marriage. I'd met so many women this year who swore their divorces were the best things that ever happened to them. It was time—past time—to become one of those women. I needed to do something wild and brave and stupefying, though how I had settled on a survival course, I still wasn't sure.

In hindsight, it seemed far too literal.

But it was the cure I'd chosen, and I was going to try like hell to do it right.

I mentally reviewed my list of goals for the coming weeks. I'd actually taken the time to write them down on some old stationery. In my neatest print, I'd written "In the Wilderness I Plan to:" and then, below, made a bullet list with little optimistic boxes to check off:

- ☐ Find a deeper spiritual connection to nature
- ☐ Push myself beyond my physical and emotional limitations
- ☐ Rise up from my own ashes like a phoenix
- ☐ Toughen the hell up
- ☐ Become awesome
- ☐ Kick the wilderness's ass
- ☐ Earn a damned Certificate

I really, really wanted a Certificate.

I really, really wanted to be the kind of person who could dare to want a Certificate without seeming utterly ridiculous.

I really, really wanted a slip of paper that proved, at last, that I was okay.

I just wanted to be good at this. And competent. And tough. And, ultimately, just: *anybody but me.* I was tired of being a disaster. I was tired of being a trampled-on flower. I wanted to be awesome. That wasn't too much, was it?

My first act of business after registering had been to write down my goals, and I'd rifled through several storage boxes in the basement before I'd found the perfect paper to write them on: notecards from college with H E L E N • C A R P E N T E R embossed at the top. So far, having my old name back had been the best thing about getting divorced. Because guess what Mike's last name was?

"Dull." Okay, so the original old-world pronunciation had been "Dool." But even the family had given up trying to correct people.

It was amazing that I'd been willing to take a name like that. It would have been so easy to keep Carpenter. But Mike had wanted us to have the same last name, arguing that we wouldn't feel like a family otherwise. And I had wanted to feel like a family with him, truly. Isn't that a reasonable choice when you're starting a life with somebody? Try to please him and hope like heck he'll try to please you back?

Duncan had teased me about the name constantly. I'd rolled my eyes, but there was no denying that it was a downgrade. Helen Dull was a terrible name. I tried to see it as a personal challenge—to prove the name wrong in every way. In the end, I failed: Helen Dull had been a much diminished version of Helen Carpenter. Though that was hardly the name's fault. It takes a lot more than just a name to bring you down that low.

So both the list and the paper it was written on felt profound to me, even though I'd made a last-minute decision to cut my name off the top of the page for the sake of anonymity. I didn't seem to have any clothes with pockets, and so I kept the list folded up in my bra, relishing both the roughness of it against my softest skin and the vague naughtiness of using my underwear like a pocket. And that, friends, is how I set off for the wilderness: with a tribute to the person I once was, and a simple checklist for the death-defying superhero I planned to become, folded up and stuffed into my C-cup.

Right then, if I'd been alone as planned, I'd have reached in to pull out the list—if only for the pleasure of resting my eyes on it. But I wasn't alone. And somewhere near Framingham, the person keeping me from being alone finished his book, snapped it closed, and decided to strike up some more conversation.

"I liked that smile you gave me back there, by the way," he said, out of nowhere.

It startled me to hear his voice. "What smile?"

He waved in the direction of the city behind us. "Back in town. You gave me a smile."

"Did I?" I asked. "I didn't mean to."

"I know," he said. "That made it even better."

"Okay."

"Think I'll get another one?" he asked. "Because that thing was like sunshine."

He had to be up to something.

"I'm just saying. You should smile more."

"I smile all the time," I said, not smiling. "I smile constantly. From the moment I wake up until the moment I go to bed. Sometimes I get cheek cramps from smiling so much."

He knew I was joking, but he wasn't sure how much. "I can count on one hand the times I've seen you smile," he said, "including the night of your wedding."

"You only ever see me around Duncan," I said. "Who vexes me."

"I'll say," he agreed. "You're the meanest big sister I know."

"I'm not mean," I said. "In real life, I'm nice."

"If you say so."

"I rescued Pickle, didn't I? And I let people through in traffic. And I always clap really loud at plays."

"That's your version of nice? Clapping at plays?"

"That's not my *only* version of nice."

"What about nice to Duncan?" he asked. "What's your version of that?"

How had we gone from silence to this? "Are you picking a fight with me?"

"No, I'm just making conversation."

"You weren't making conversation ten minutes ago," I said.

"I wasn't finished with my book ten minutes ago."

I glanced over at the closed book on his thigh. "Don't you have another one?"

"Nope."

"So *I* have to talk about Duncan because *you* don't have anything left to read?"

"It's a long drive to Evanston."

"And you're making it longer."

"It just seems like a rich topic," he said.

"Well, it's not," I said. "It's a poor topic."

He tilted his head at me like we both knew that wasn't true. "Is it because of what happened in your family?"

I felt a sting of alarm. Did he know about that? I glanced over. "What do you mean?"

He studied me, like he wasn't sure how to put it. "The tragedy," he said at last.

The tragedy. So he knew about our family tragedy. Of course he would. He was Duncan's best friend.

"Is *what* because of our family tragedy?" I asked.

"The fact that you don't like Duncan."

With that, Jake stumbled into a restricted area. "I like Duncan!" I snapped. "And I'm not going to talk about our family tragedy with you."

"Why not?"

"Because I don't talk about it with anybody."

"Maybe you should," he said with a cheery shrug.

I tried to keep my voice un-irritated. "What are you," I demanded then, "a therapist?"

"No," Jake said. "But that's actually not a bad idea." He considered it for a minute. Then he pushed on. "So what's the deal with you guys?"

I sighed. Between "Duncan" and "the Tragedy," Duncan was no

doubt the lesser conversational evil. "The deal is," I said, "Duncan's a pain in the ass."

"Granted."

"And he makes me crazy. He doesn't make you crazy? The way he loses his keys? The way he never arrives anywhere on time? Or finishes what he starts? Or keeps a promise?"

"Not his strong suits," Jake said. "True."

"But you've been best friends for five years."

"Six."

"Why?"

Jake thought about it. "He has other good qualities."

I knew he did, of course. But I couldn't call them up at the moment. "Like?"

"Like he is hands-down the funniest person I have ever met."

I frowned. There was nothing funny about Duncan. "That can't be right," I said.

Jake shrugged. "Sometimes he makes me laugh so hard, my lunch comes out my nose. Once it was a full-length spaghetti noodle."

I pushed away that visual to scan back for a memory of Duncan making me laugh, ever. "Duncan never makes me laugh."

"That's because you're always mad at him."

"Not true! There are lots of times when I'm not mad at him. I'm not mad at him *most of the time,* in fact."

"As long as he's nowhere near you, you mean."

He had me there. "Fair enough."

He smiled. There went those dimples again.

"You seem to get along very well with him, though," I said, shifting the focus.

He shrugged. "I don't have any brothers or sisters."

"So you picked Duncan?"

"He picked me, actually."

I hadn't known that.

"He dared me," he went on. "He bet that I couldn't throw a Ping-Pong ball against the side of the gym and catch it in my mouth."

"And could you?"

"I could."

"And did you?"

"I did."

"That's how you became friends? On a dare?"

He nodded. "Sure. I can never resist a dare. Plus, he offered to teach me how to juggle."

"I didn't know Duncan could juggle."

"He can't. But by the time I figured it out, it was too late. We were already pals."

"A bromance," I said, just to see if it would irritate him.

He nodded. "Of the highest order."

"And Duncan's a good friend?"

"The best. He always defends me."

I couldn't imagine Jake needing to be defended. "Against?"

"Myself, mostly," he said, giving that half smile.

"And what do you defend Duncan against?"

Jake frowned. "Death, I suppose."

I coughed. "Death?"

"Oh," he waved, "you know. He wants to jump off a roof at three in the morning, and I suggest it might not be the best idea. Or he wants to throw a match into a box of firecrackers to see what will happen. Or he wants to stare into a flashlight until he has a seizure. That kind of thing."

"See, now," I said, "I always thought those were your ideas."

"Nope. That's all Big D."

"So you're the straight man."

He thought about it. "In terms of not getting killed, I am the straight man."

"But you're not always the straight man?"

"We take turns, I guess," he said.

He was so earnest. So thoughtful about it all. He was nothing like what I would have imagined, if I had ever thought to imagine him.

"So Duncan brings near-death experiences to the relationship—" I began.

Jake nodded. "That's his area."

"What's your area?"

He shrugged. "Everything else. Talking to girls. Swing dancing. Harmonizing. Accents."

"Why would you have to do accents?"

"I don't *have* to do them. It's just fun."

I had known so little about Jake for so many years that almost everything he said surprised me. He could do accents? He could swing dance? He could talk to girls? Who knew?

Without meaning to, I shifted into Q & A mode, asking him question after question like we were on TV. Partly, it was an offensive play to keep the focus off me. But, I must confess—I'd also suddenly become curious. As we cruised west on I-90, I gathered a whole raft of trivia about Jake. Like he was allergic to almonds and pecans, but not peanuts. He'd double majored in English and pre-med, writing his thesis on Nathaniel Hawthorne. He just got in to medical school but had decided to go see the world, instead—starting now. With Wyoming. Then, off to Baja to pet the whales. After that: The ice caves in Juneau. The Tianzi mountains of China. The ruined mines of Cornwall. The Black Forest. The Taj Mahal. The northern lights. Not necessarily in that order.

"You're taking a year off?" I asked. "Before med school?"

"Actually," he said, "I'm just not going."

"What do you mean, 'not going'?"

"Not going at all."

There he went again, surprising me. "You got into your first-choice school," I said, "but you're not going? At all?"

"That's right."

"Why on earth not?"

He looked out the window. "It just turns out not to be a great fit."

This was the vaguest answer I'd heard from him all day. "You've spent years doing coursework and prerequisites, you've taken the MCATs and gone to the trouble of applying, and you've *gotten in*—and now you decide it's not a great fit?"

"That's about right," he said, like we were done.

"But what changed?"

"I changed."

I was ready to press him for more. It was, as he himself had pointed out, a long drive to Evanston, and if he could make me talk about Duncan then I was happy to make him talk about anything I pleased. But he must really have wanted to change the subject, because before I could ask another question, he caused a diversion.

"You know what?" he said. "I need to pee." Next thing, he was rolling down the window and emptying out his half-full water bottle.

The wind came in like a roar. "What are you doing?" I shouted.

"Emptying this out," he shouted back.

"You're not going to pee into that!"

"Sure I am!"

"No, no! There's an exit right up here!"

"It's cool! I have great aim!"

"It is *not* cool!"

"But I'm fine with the bottle!"

"But I'm definitely not!"

The bottle was empty now, and he rolled his window back up. The car seemed suddenly too quiet. "I'll make a little shield with my book," he said then. "You won't even see."

"Stop!" I said. "Do not unbutton, unzip, or even think about your pants. We're pulling over!"

He shook his head. "It's a waste of time."

"But guess what?" I said—not lying, exactly. "I need to pee, too. And we need gas, so we're stopping anyway."

"Oh," he said, letting his hands fall from the top button of his pants. "I guess you've got a point there."

I veered toward the exit without even using the blinker. This, I reminded myself, was exactly the issue. This guy wasn't just a twenty-something: He was a toddler, and not even potty-trained. I had forgotten who I was dealing with for a minute there. All that talk of Nathaniel Hawthorne and medical school had obscured the essential facts: This kid was not someone I could relate to. He adored my awful brother. He had ditched medical school for no apparent reason. And he was about to unzip his pants and relieve himself into an Evian bottle. In the passenger seat of my Subaru.

Ramping off, I turned right, then right again, then stopped by a pump at the gas station. "When I said I drew the line at peeing in bottles, I meant for both of us," I said, yanking up the parking brake and turning to meet his eyes. "For this to work," I added, "you're going to have to keep your pants on."

He suppressed a smile like I was terribly funny.

"Got it?" I asked, giving in to an impulse to reach over and knock him on the forehead.

"Got it," he said, and his smile broke through. "I vow to keep my pants on," he said, offering a little salute. "Unless you command me otherwise."

Chapter 4

We made it to Grandma GiGi's before nine, surpassing all expectations.

Jake didn't want to drive at night—something to do with his new glasses—and so, after the rest stop, he took the remaining daylight shifts and kept us steady at ninety miles an hour. By the time the sun went down and I slowed us back to sixty-five, we were impressively ahead of schedule. We were so pleased with ourselves that we high-fived on arrival. In fact, we accidentally hugged.

When we knocked on Grandma GiGi's door, though, she didn't answer. I had to go hunt for the hidden key in the garden. And when we let ourselves in, instead of my white-haired grandmother in her red kimono with a glass of pinot noir in the hand with her dragonfly ring, we found a note on the kitchen table:

> *Duncan says you got a late start and won't make it for*
> *dinner. I've gone out to book club. Don't wait up!*
> *XX! GG*
> *P.S. Helen, rumple that cute boy's hair for me.*

Jake read the note over my shoulder. "I told you she loves me," he said.

"I'm not rumpling your hair," I said.

"I'll tell if you don't."

"It's self-rumpling," I said. "It doesn't need me."

Dinner—spaghetti Bolognese—was warming in the oven. A bottle of wine sat on the table.

"This is a great wine," Jake said, examining the label.

"I'm too tired for wine," I said.

"Not this one, you're not."

I rolled my eyes at Jake and plunked down into a kitchen chair. "You don't know about wine."

"I do. I took a class."

I frowned at him. "Why?"

But then I figured it out, and just as he answered, I answered, too, and we said, in unison, "To get girls."

"That's right," he said. "The same reason I learned to juggle. And took swing-dancing lessons. And read *The Beauty Myth*."

"You read *The Beauty Myth* to get girls?"

"Sure."

I put my hand over my eyes. "You used *The Beauty Myth* for evil?"

"Not for evil," he said, looking over. "For good. A whole lot of good."

"I'm going to bed," I said.

"Nope," he said. "We're having dinner." And as he said it, he carried two plates waiter-style to the back door and let himself outside. When I didn't follow, he poked his head back in. "Come on," he said.

"Where are you going?" I asked, but he was gone again.

A minute later, he came back for the wine. "We're having a picnic," he said, pulling me by the hand out the back door, across the yard, and out to the old tree house that my grandpa had built back when my mom was a kid.

I stopped at the base and looked up. At just below shoulder-height, it wasn't as tall as I remembered, but it was still taller than anything I felt like climbing.

"I'm not going up there."

The words were hardly out of my mouth when Jake brought his shoulder down to scoop me into a fireman's carry. He hoisted me up and sat me neatly on the tree house deck before I could even protest. A second later he landed beside me, handing over my plate and a glass of wine like we ate this way every night.

"You're awfully lively," I said.

"I love this tree house," he said. "Duncan and I used to spend whole weekends out here. I had my first kiss here."

"Not with Duncan, I hope."

"Leah Pearson. Redhead. I tried to French her and she bit me on the tongue."

"I like her already."

The dinner was warm, and the night was cool. Being outside in the fresh air woke me up. I picked up my wineglass, and lifted it in Jake's direction. "To biters," I said, and we clinked and sipped.

"To first kisses."

"To driving like a bat out of hell."

"To letting your little brother's pain-in-the-ass friend ride with you cross-country."

"I don't mind," I said, as I realized it was true.

We fell quiet for a few minutes while we gazed at GiGi's house. It was an actual prairie-style Frank Lloyd Wright house that my grandparents had bought for a song when it was listed as a tear-down back in the 1960s. My grandpa, who died before I was born, was an architect, and he and GiGi kept the house exactly in its original 1912 condition, except for a few kitchen and bathroom updates. GiGi had raised their four kids here before taking in Duncan and me. It had all the gravitas of a stately old home that had seen it all and then some.

I hadn't been back in a long while, and as I listened to the summer crickets, I swung my feet back and forth over the tree house ledge like a kid. The moon was out, and plenty of stars, too, and the kitchen lights made a warm glow in the windows across the yard. Even before we'd moved here for good, I'd spent lots of nights at Grandma GiGi's, and this yard held just about every connection to my childhood I had left.

"Thank you for dragging me out here," I said after a while. "I'd forgotten about this tree house."

"You know another thing I remember about being out here?"

"What?"

"You," he said. "Through your window."

"You can see into my window from here?"

"Yep."

"Did you guys watch me or something?"

"Tried to," Jake said, with a nod. "Every time you came home to visit." He took a swig of wine and added, "Not Duncan. Just me."

"Why?"

It was dark enough that our faces were mostly just collections of shadows. But he studied mine just the same. "Because I had a crush on you."

"You did?" I said. "I never knew that."

He nodded. "A bad one."

I shook my head. "But I was married."

"I know. I met you on your wedding day."

"I remember. You weren't invited."

"Duncan brought me as his date."

"Duncan did that to piss me off."

"Found that out later."

"I was mad about that for years."

"Well, it had the opposite effect on me."

"Coming to my wedding, you mean?"

"It's just a powerful thing," Jake said, "when the first time you ever lay eyes on a woman she's wearing a silk wedding gown, and a veil, and a garter. Especially when you're sixteen and new to town. And your mother's only been dead a year."

"I'm sorry," I said.

"Don't be sorry. You woke me up that day."

"If I'd known, I would have been nicer to you."

"You were nice enough."

"I probably should have discouraged you or something."

"That's not how crushes work."

"No. I guess not."

"Why did you think I gaped at you with my mouth open all the time?"

"I guess I just thought you were a mouth-breather."

"No," he said. "Crush paralysis."

Somehow, the wine bottle was almost empty. I held up my last glass in another toast. "To crushes."

"To women in wedding gowns."

"And the teenage boys who appreciate them."

We clinked again, and Jake held my gaze just a second too long before knocking the rest of his glass back in one gulp.

Back in my teenage bedroom, I slipped on an old Garfield sleep shirt from my dresser and turned down the bed. The pillow looked smooth and cool and inviting. I had just crawled in when Jake knocked on the door.

"Go away," I said. "I'm asleep."

But he cracked the door anyway and peeked in.

"Jake, it's late."

"It's ten o'clock."

"Like I said."

"I just have to ask you a question," he said, stepping in. He was fresh from the shower, wearing pajama bottoms and no shirt. I averted my eyes from his bare, collegiate torso.

"What is it? Because I'm elderly now, and old people can't drink wine without getting sleepy."

"The question is, do you want to play Scrabble?" He held out a box of travel Scrabble for me to see.

Of all things. My favorite game.

"I am way too tired to play Scrabble," I said. But he stepped closer and sat down on the bed. I let him.

I sat up, feeling weirdly naked and far too bra-less for a social call, and I pulled the covers up around my waist. "Why did you bring that?"

He lifted his eyebrows. "In case you wanted to play."

I felt a resigned sigh escaping my chest. Something about Jake seemed to wake me up. "I do actually love to play Scrabble."

"So do I," he said, and laid the box between us. He still had a few droplets of water near his collarbones.

"Are you going to put a shirt on?" I asked.

He looked up, like the thought hadn't occurred to him. "Should I?"

"Aren't you cold?" I asked, my gaze drifting to the damp locks of hair against his neck.

"Nope."

"Don't you feel kind of naked?"

"Nope."

I sighed. "Well, I feel cold and naked just looking at you."

That made him smile. Then he left me on the bed with my tiles, disappeared, and returned a second later in a T-shirt with HARVARD across it.

"That was fast," I said.

"Well," he said, "I wouldn't want you to feel cold and naked." He met my eyes for a second.

There it was again. The flirting. Was he daring me to be offended? I ignored him. "Nice shirt," I finally said.

"I thought it might intimidate you," he explained, tapping his head.

"It *might* intimidate me," I said, "if you actually went to Harvard."

"I did go to Harvard."

I gave him a *yeah, right* look.

He met my eyes and nodded. "I did, actually, go to Harvard."

I shook my head. "But Duncan went to Boston College."

"True."

"So how could you be college roommates if you didn't go to college together?"

He shrugged. "Off-campus housing."

"But why?"

"Well," he said, "I promised to be Duncan's roommate. But then he didn't get into Harvard."

"Of course he didn't get into Harvard! He was always smoking dope."

"True."

"And so were you, by the way."

He shook his head. "Not really."

"You weren't smoking dope?" I lifted one eyebrow to say, *Faker.* "All those times I came home and you were in his room and there was smoke literally billowing out from under his door, that was just Duncan?"

He shrugged. "I was doing my homework."

"He was stoned, and you were doing your homework?"

"I guess I might have been a little accidentally stoned, you know, from passive inhalation. But I still did my homework."

"But how did you get into Harvard?"

He shrugged again. "I'm really smart. And driven. And tunnel-visioned."

I looked down at my tiles.

"Are you intimidated now?" he asked.

"I'm less un-intimidated, if that's what you mean."

"Don't worry. I'll just play like a normal person."

"Great."

"Duncan and I don't allow those non-word Scrabble words when we play," he said then. "Just plain English. And we always say any word that's sexual, or can be interpreted in a sexual way, is a double word score."

I let out a laugh and rubbed my eyes. "That sounds like Duncan."

"Yeah, but it's a great rule," Jake said. "Because then you can earn points for style."

"Points for style" was one of my favorite concepts. "So," I said, thinking, "a word like 'mounds' would be double points?"

"Exactly. Perfect. A word like 'mounds' is so awesome it might even be triple." He cocked his head. "You want to play that way?"

"I'm not going to win on skill alone, brainiac."

"Are you planning to win?"

"Yes," I said.

"Do you often win?"

"Yes."

"So, you're pretty confident? Even against my T-shirt?"

"Harvard graduates aren't the only smart people in the world," I said.

"Wanna bet?"

I gave him a look.

"No, seriously," he said. "Do you want to bet?"

I looked around. "Bet what?"

I could tell from the arch of his eyebrow he was up to something.

"Maybe," he said, "if I win, you have to help me with something. And if I win, I have to help you with something."

I narrowed my eyes. "What?"

He shrugged, all innocent. "Whatever," he said. "Everybody needs help with something."

"I don't."

"I bet you'll need help with hiking," Jake said, "at some point in the coming weeks."

"What are you going to do," I asked, "carry me?"

"Possibly," he said. "If you need it. Or tie a knot you can't get. Or teach you about contour maps. There's tons of wilderness skills I could help you with. You're a total beginner."

"You're preying on my inexperience."

"I'm making myself useful."

"And what on earth could I help you with?"

"Well," he said, taking a deep breath, "actually—"

"Whatever it is," I interrupted, "I'm not doing it. I can tell from your face, I'm not doing it."

"I want you to teach me how to kiss."

"What?"

"How to kiss," he said, with a little nod, like it wasn't the craziest request in the world. "I'm a terrible kisser. Really. I need help. In a big way."

Impossible. A guy this cute could not possibly be hopeless at kissing. The whole idea was ridiculous. Finally, I said, "What makes you think I'm even qualified to do that?"

At that, he smiled. "You're qualified. I can tell."

The idea swirled through my head. "Wow. No."

"Why not?"

"Because that's crazy. That's not how you learn to kiss."

"How do you learn then?"

"By practicing. With a person you really like."

"You're a person I really like."

"With a girlfriend, Jake. You've heard of those?"

"But the idea is to get better in advance."

I could kind of see that point. For a second. Then, "Nope. Absolutely not."

"You don't want to?"

"I definitely don't want to."

"Then just win the game, and you won't have to."

He was baiting me.

"Win the game," he said, "and at some point in the next three weeks, when you are totally exhausted and overwhelmed, all you'll have to do is lift an eyebrow and I'll swoop right over and rescue you."

I shook my head in slow motion.

"Think of all those blisters you're going to have! The wet socks! The sore shoulders! Think of how tired you'll be at the end of miles of uphill switchbacks and how badly you won't want to hobble down to the icy stream to fetch water."

As he talked, my head stopped shaking on its own. My brain was smarter than to agree, but it had absorbed half a bottle of wine back at the tree house, and it wasn't operating at full capacity. I sized him up. I figured I could take him. If Duncan was his main opponent, after all, how hard could it be?

"Okay," I heard myself say, then. "I'll take that bet. But only because you're not going to win."

✳

Guess what? He won.

And he didn't even cheat. He won on skill and sexual innuendo alone.

I got seventy-four points on a beautifully placed "heaving," but he kicked my ass with "swollen" and "sticky," not to mention "bulbous" smack dab on a triple word score.

"Double or nothing," I challenged, but he raised his arms above his head in a big, yawning stretch.

"It's late," he said.

I gave him a look. "It's not even eleven."

"You almost turned in at ten!"

"And if I had, I wouldn't be in this mess."

He put away all the Scrabble tiles, set the box on the nightstand, and edged closer. "A bet's a bet," he said.

The thing was, he was cute—and now I couldn't imagine how the hell I'd missed it all these years. That dark, wavy hair in locks against his neck. Those brown puppy eyes. Those plump lips college boys have. Those bright, uniform, not-that-long-since-the-braces-came-off teeth. I can't say he wasn't appealing. If I flipped off the part of my brain that had been rolling my eyes at him since he was sixteen, he was kind of heartthrobby.

He leaned in. I held very still. He brought his face just inches from mine, and I could see his gaze brush over my lips.

But this was crazy. What were we doing? The mean-big-sister part of me had to get a word in. I put my hand against his chest. "Okay," I said, as much to myself as to him. "This is for educational purposes only."

He nodded to accept the terms.

"We're not telling Duncan, by the way," I added, with a little push to the chest for emphasis. "Ever."

"Agreed."

He leaned in again, but my hand was still in place, and I stopped him. "Who's kissing who?" I asked.

"Now you're stalling."

"I'm not."

"If you're trying to torture me, you're many years too late."

"I am trying to do this properly," I said.

"I'm kissing you, okay?" He lifted a hand and hooked it behind my neck, his fingers in my hair. But then, at the second he looked into my eyes, he hesitated. A second went by, and then another. I swear he was holding his breath. That hitch was just long enough to make me worry that he was going to chicken out. Which made me realize I didn't want him to chicken out.

"This week, sometime?" I said then, to dare him before he lost his nerve.

"Impatient, aren't you?"

I tilted my head, like, *Please. Not even close.* It felt vastly important to make that clear. Even though I was, in fact, impatient. That was need-to-know info that he wasn't getting—ever. A woman doesn't give up all her power so easily. Especially not to a twenty-two-year-old.

Plus, it's a simple fact about the friends of your little brother: You don't mess around with them. For infinite reasons. They look up to you, for one. They fantasize about you—precisely because you are unavailable. If you turned around and said, "Let's do this," they'd sprint right out of the room. But you never would—ever, ever—and they know that. You've got them in the same pimply, annoying category as your brother, and that's part of your appeal. And being completely out of their league is fun for your ego, too. Everybody wins. As long as you observe the rules.

For six years, I'd never questioned the rules. Jake rested solidly in his proper category. But, now, by total accident over the course of one single day, he didn't quite fit there anymore. Suddenly, I wasn't sure how to classify him—and he was pushing that advantage. Now, against all regulations, he was going to kiss me. And I, against all good sense, was going to let him. It was a genuine transgression. That must have been what made it so intoxicating. That, and the wine. My kid brother's best friend was about to kiss me. Worst of all, I wanted him to.

He leaned in closer.

"Okay," he said. "Here we go." His lips were almost touching mine now. His breath literally tickled.

I closed my eyes. The air in my lungs seemed to flutter.

Then, just before the moment of impact, we heard the front door slam. Then GiGi's voice, all singsongy: "Helen! You can't possibly be asleep yet!"

We froze, noses almost touching, mouths barely an inch apart.

Then Jake said, "GiGi's home."

"You think?"

I had barely said the words when there was a knock at the bedroom door.

We jumped to opposite ends of the bed and were composing ourselves as GiGi walked in.

She wore an ice-blue mandarin-collared jacket, and her hair was back in a low bun, held in place with chopsticks. She had her leopard-print glasses on tonight, too. My favorites.

She beheld us, then, for a minute, with a smile that made it clear she knew exactly what we'd been up to. Or close enough. It would be just like her to comment on it, and I fully expected her to start teasing us, but she made a choice to go the other way.

"Darling girl," she said then, swooping in for a kiss on the cheek. "You look delicious."

She turned toward Jake and reached out to ruffle his hair. "Doesn't she?"

Jake nodded without looking at me.

GiGi paused to look back and forth between the two of us. In that second, it felt like she'd figured everything out.

"Well," she said then, turning for the door, "I'm making decaf. Come join me and I'll tell you all about my X-rated book club."

"You're in an X-rated book club?" Jake asked.

GiGi paused at the door and gave us a naughty wink. "I'm the youngest member—at eighty-six. We've got to find some reason to stay alive."

It was quite a shock to suddenly find ourselves in GiGi's kitchen, getting her take on the naughty series they'd been reading—a bawdy romp through Chaucerian England.

Jake and I sat carefully at opposite ends of the kitchen table as GiGi weighed the pros and cons. "I'm very pro-sex, don't get me wrong. At my age, I'll take what I can get."

Jake and I just nodded.

"And I can forgive the lack of historical accuracy during the Maypole orgy."

Jake and I glanced sideways at each other.

"But the character development is lacking."

"That's what lost you?" I asked. "The character development?"

GiGi nodded. "And this probably makes me very old-fashioned, but I just don't get the leather and the whips."

"Your book club is reading a novel about S&M?" I asked.

"*Chaucerian* S&M?" Jake added.

GiGi nodded. "I'm the one who chose it! I admit I was curious. But now that I've read it, I feel stodgy. It just seems to me there's enough pain in the world—and not nearly enough pleasure. I guess once you've had enough kidney stones, hot candle wax on the nipples seems less appealing."

She wound up giving us the whole plot summary, and I can't say it wasn't gripping. Especially hearing words like "gag" and "bindings" from my highly refined grandmother. Before long, it was midnight. GiGi left us in the hallway as she turned off toward the master bedroom, saying, "Don't wake me in the morning. I'm sleeping in."

Jake followed me to my bedroom door—past the door to Duncan's room, where he'd be sleeping. I put my hand on my doorknob and paused. Something about the moment, despite all the overly familiar time we'd spent together that day, made me nervous, like he'd just walked me home after a date.

I expected him to say something cocky, like "You still owe me a kiss," but he didn't.

He leaned toward me the tiniest bit, like there was something he wanted to say, but he didn't say it. I felt like I was teetering on the edge of being kissed—that if I'd wanted him to, he would have. But now that I'd had time to think about it, I wasn't sure if it was a great idea. And without some kind of encouragement from me, he couldn't bring himself to do it. I was still the grown-up here. Especially in GiGi's house, where we'd spent so much time in our roles as untouchable and untouched, he couldn't make a move.

So I made one for him.

I stuck out my hand to shake. "Goodnight," I said.

He looked from my hand to my face. "Really?"

I shrugged.

He took my hand, then, but rather than shake it, he just held it for a second, turning it sideways to study it, almost. I held my breath.

When he let go, I had to cover. "Can you set Duncan's alarm for five?" I said. "Mine's broken."

"Five in the morning?"

"Big day tomorrow," I said.

He didn't fight me. "Okay," he said. "Five it is."

Next, he turned and went to put himself to bed in my brother's bedroom, which looked the same as it always had. The beer girl posters were still on the walls, the bottle cap collection still took up most of Duncan's desk, and the terrarium with the dead plants still sat by the window. This was where Jake had spent most of high school. It was where the two of them had tried to build a guillotine out of popsicle sticks, made plaster casts of their feet, and written their own video game about cannibals called BeastFeast. They'd tried to build a rainforest in Duncan's closet, and carried out endless experiments with dry ice. Oh, and let's not forget the whole summer they spent in there trying to build a working replica of R2D2 out of a trash can, a dismantled lawnmower, and an old PC.

As I watched Jake step through the doorway, I remembered who he was. The old Jake returned to my mind and blotted out the person I'd almost let kiss me. He clicked the door closed, and I turned away with a feeling of narrowly missed disaster. That's when I latched my bedroom door behind me. Keep it simple. I would sleep in my room, and Jake would sleep in Duncan's. Exactly where he belonged.

Chapter 5

We hadn't been back on the road five minutes when Jake said, "We should probably talk about last night."

"Oh," I said, leaning on the steering wheel with both hands. "Do we have to?"

"Let's just get it out in the open."

"Let's not."

"I just need to tell you that I won't hold you to it."

That caught my attention. "You won't?"

"I won't. The bet's off."

"Great," I said, feeling oddly disappointed. "Good."

"Great," he said. "That's settled."

And there it was. Settled.

After that, here's what we talked about: doughnuts, *Pulp Fiction*, best birthday parties we ever had, hidden talents, UFOs, time travel, whether politics attracts assholes from the start or turns normal people into assholes later, countries we wanted to visit, how whales breathe when they're sleeping in the ocean, childhood fears, how to make enchiladas, cats versus dogs, and global warming.

Here's what we didn't talk about: the wine we drank, the crush Jake confessed to, and the kissing we'd almost done.

At first, I thought we weren't talking about it because it was such a big deal. But as the day wore on, and Jake told me all about his Scottish father's great romance with his Texan mother, all about his favorite books (*Lord of the Rings* and *Lonesome Dove*), and all about his thesis on Nathaniel Hawthorne's shockingly naughty love letters to his wife Sophia (she had to cut whole passages out with scissors), I wondered if it had only been a big deal to me. He certainly didn't seem to be thinking about it. Maybe he was, deep down—but just faking it on the outside. Or maybe kissing wasn't the same thing in his generation that it was in mine.

Not that we'd even kissed!

But he'd wanted to. Or, at least I'd thought he wanted to. Could be it was me who wanted to. And right there was the problem, because I'd gone on this trip to become a better version of myself—and regressed. The stream-of-consciousness poem of my life—which I'd hoped to fashion into something like a nature haiku crossed with a Chuck Norris movie—had been reduced to "Does he like me? Omigod!" in the space of twenty-four hours. And that wasn't the point of this trip. When Duncan first told me about this survival course, I'd been planning a trip to Paris. I'd given up *Paris* for the wisdom of the wilderness. But I wasn't in Paris or the wilderness now. I was in middle school.

The farther we drove, the more I knew I was going to have to build up a tolerance to him. Starting immediately. I wasn't just going to drop the bet, I was going to block it out entirely. I was here for a higher purpose than shenanigans like that. I'd gone through way too much hell this past year to settle for some half-assed resurrection.

I thought of the night I'd kicked Mike out. I'd gone in for a pregnancy checkup that day, and instead of getting a little stack of ultrasound images to tape up on the fridge, I got the news that I was having a miscarriage. My body, apparently, had "shut down production," as the nurse described it, and the doc sent me home, warned me that I'd have a lot of cramping in the coming week, and instructed me to find someone to bring me tea and hot water bottles. That someone, of course, should have been Mike, who should have been there with me at the appointment. Who would have been there had he not completely forgotten to show up.

Later, I found out that he'd had a few drinks at a business lunch, goofed around at the office a little tipsy that afternoon, and then headed out to happy hour with "some coworkers." Happy hour led to late-night carousing, and he didn't make it home until after I was asleep. I drove myself home that afternoon in a blur, and, as if my body had been waiting for permission, started the miscarriage in earnest that night.

The next morning, I woke Mike to tell him what had happened and announced that I had given up on our marriage. I did it all in about ten minutes and without tears, or sorrow, or regret. That would all come later. Mike was too humbled—and too hungover—to argue. He just kept his eyes down and nodded. I was surprised, once we were separated, at how certain I was: Kicking him out was the right thing to do. Things had been so bad for so long that once he was out, I never seriously considered asking him to come back. And despite a few phone calls and logistical meetings, Mike never made a serious bid to try again. That's not to say I wasn't utterly hollowed out and lost after that. I was—and then some. But it was clear to me from that sad day forward that as bad as things were without Mike, they would truly have been worse with him.

That's what the past year had been—pendulum swings between all the panic and what-ifs that come with giving up on your life, and the wide, numb, blinking sense of shock that fills every space in between. I'm sure there were moments of relief sprinkled in there, as well, but when I think back on the year, I think of one thing: me, alone, under the fluorescent lights in the grocery store, Muzak in the background, ambient noise in the foreground, pushing a squeaky-wheeled cart full of Campbell's soup. My sad attempt at comfort food.

But I was done with fluorescent lights and Muzak. The year had gone on way too long, but it was over at last. I was ready to amaze myself, dammit! I was ready for something profound! I was ready to experience something transcendent! And Jake and his lips, no matter how mouthwatering they might be, did not qualify. Like the grown-up I was, I refused to give him even one more thought.

Until we stopped for the night.

Jake insisted on carrying both our bags. In the motel room, he dropped them with a thunk. At that, he turned to me, crossed his arms, and ruined everything.

He said, "Remember when I said the bet was off?"

"Yes."

"It's back on."

"You can't turn it back on!"

"Sure I can."

I put my hands on my hips in my most authoritative pose. "That wasn't even a real bet. You plied me with wine and spaghetti Bolognese."

"I didn't ply anybody. You plied yourself, lady."

"Regardless! I was drunk!"

"You were hardly drunk. You were tipsy at best."

"Jake," I said, acutely aware that if an almost-kiss could mess with me as much as that one had, an actual kiss could capsize me entirely, "it's really not a good idea."

"I disagree."

"It's a terrible, laughable, ridiculous idea."

"Why?"

"Because! Because you're Duncan's best friend. Because I don't even know you. Because we're headed to the middle of nowhere together tomorrow. And because you're half my age."

"Two-thirds."

"Whatever."

"I haven't heard one good reason from you yet."

"Jake," I said then, pretty sure I was lying, "I just don't want to."

That did it. He looked down. He let out a slow breath of defeat. Then he nodded. "Okay," he said. "That's a good reason."

Next, he reached down for the hem of his shirt and pulled it up, over his head, and off in one swoop. "I'm taking a shower," he said.

He did it on purpose. At that distance, I literally couldn't *not* stare at the muscles rolling and flexing on his flank as he rooted in his bag for his toiletries. Nor could I help but ogle him as his perfectly perfect male figure walked to the bathroom. He was like an Olympic diver or something—and as soon as that hit me, an image of him swan-diving off a high board in a Speedo popped into my head before I could stop it.

Good God. I gave my forehead a *pull it together* smack as Jake shut the door. But it didn't work. In fact, all I could do was stand still as my mind went carousing without permission. I was still in the exact same spot when Jake finished his shower and came out, now in the pajama pants and the Harvard shirt he'd worn the night before. His towel-dried hair made the same little damp crescents against his neck.

He shuffled right past me, climbed on his bed, and opened a book. The whale book. The only one he'd brought.

Here was the problem. I did want to kiss him. It was a 100 percent terrible idea, and I knew that for a fact, but somehow I just couldn't make myself care. I couldn't make myself care when I went to take my own shower. Or as I dried my hair. Or as I brushed my teeth and put on my sleep shirt. By the time I stepped out of the bathroom and paused at the doorway to size him up, I knew it was hopeless. And so, in the way that you watch your hand reach for a cookie your brain knows you shouldn't eat, I watched myself walk over to Jake and linger by his side.

He didn't look up.

"You're starting the same book over from the beginning," I said.

He kept his eyes on the page. "Yep."

I watched him read for a minute. Or pretend to read.

"Come here," I said, at last, letting out my own sigh of defeat.

Jake looked up, but didn't move—as if daring me to mean it.

"You better get over here before I change my mind."

At that, he snapped to attention. He dropped his book so fast it tumbled to the floor.

"We'll treat it like school," I said, shaking my head at what I was about to do. "I'll give a lecture, and you can take mental notes."

He gave me that grin of his. "I love mental notes. I'm a huge fan of mental notes."

"This is for educational purposes only."

"Also a big fan of education. I'm a straight-A student."

We stood facing each other, and, at that moment, I could not remember ever standing that close to him. I had that light-headed feeling you get after you've made a decision that will change your life. Was I seriously about to give a kissing lesson? What would I even say? I grabbed for something that sounded wise. "The thing about kissing is that it's a balance between holding on and letting go."

"That's a heck of a philosophical beginning," Jake said.

"Like with everything in life," I went on, "there's a push and pull to it. I remember kissing this boy in seventh grade who crammed his tongue in my mouth and pushed it around like a dead fish. That," I said, "was not a good kiss."

Jake nodded.

"You don't kiss like that, do you?" I asked.

He shook his head.

"Good," I said. "When you kiss someone, it's all about give and take. Getting close. Pulling away. It's not just working figure eights with your tongue. Because the push and pull mirrors the emotions."

"You've really thought about this," he said.

"I've *never* thought about this," I said. "But I'm turning out to be a savant."

He was studying me in that way of his again.

Next. "And don't just stay in one place," I added. "Explore."

His gaze drifted to my mouth. "Like from her mouth to her neck?"

"Everywhere. Her neck. Her throat. Her collarbones." I paused. "And use your teeth."

"You want me to bite her?"

"Use the teeth for contrast, I mean. Lips are soft, teeth are hard."

I could see his wheels turning as he thought about it.

Moving on. "Okay: hands. Where do they go?"

"On the boob?" He shrugged, like he knew this was wrong.

"Incorrect! Anywhere but there! The back of her neck. Or in her hair. Or against her back." I pointed at him. "Not on the boob! You've got to earn the right to go there."

He jotted it down in his Harvard-trained mind. Then he put his hands, one by one, on my hips.

"I didn't say 'hips,'" I said then, just to scold him.

He tilted his head. "I'm not kissing you yet."

"Pop quiz!" I said then. "How long is too long for kissing?"

He turned those puppy eyes to the ceiling and really thought about it. "Thirty minutes?"

"Wrong!" I said. "There is no *too long* for kissing."

"But eventually she might want to move on to other things."

"If you're doing it right, she certainly will."

"I don't want her to be frustrated."

"Frustrated is good!" I said. "Within reason."

Strangest conversation ever. We were talking about some hypo-
thetical woman in the third person when we both knew we were actually talking about me. Or, at least, me a few minutes from now. *I*
was the one I was telling him to frustrate. And explore. And bite. And
what's more, my voice was talking, but my body was *listening*. And
really, really paying attention. And turning out to be something of an
A student, as well.

Somehow, we'd closed the small distance between us. He was right
there. Inches away. I could feel the warmth of his body and the slight
stir of the air his breaths made.

"Frustration is *wanting*," I said, trying to remain teacherly. "And
wanting is always better than having."

"Always?"

I hated to break the awful truth. "Always," I said.

"Sounds like torture."

"No, no, no," I said. "Wanting without hope is torture. Wanting
with hope is anticipation."

He was staring at my mouth. "So kissing is anticipation?"

I nodded, so aware of how close he was. His T-shirt was a little
nubby, as if he'd washed it a thousand times. He smelled like soap
and peppermint. "Kissing is pure anticipation."

"What does that make the anticipation of kissing?"

But my talking voice was succumbing to my listening body. Feeling was crowding out thinking. I felt woozy from his gaze. Too woozy
to formulate an answer. "I have a lot more to say," I said, "but I can't
seem to remember what it is."

"Me neither."

There was a pause, and with it, we passed the point where words
could go. That was it. After all the frustration and wanting and torture, anticipation gave way to more anticipation.

Jake leaned in until his mouth was barely an inch away, but just when I expected him to press in and kiss me, he paused, as if he were trying to stop and savor the moment. I could feel his toothpaste-y breath against my lips, as I stood there right on the precipice. And then, at last, he lifted a hand to the back of my neck and pressed his mouth against mine. It was just as warm and firm and certain as I would have guessed. He turned out to be great at following directions. He pushed in and then pulled back. He brushed his tongue and then pulled away. He pulled tight and then relaxed. There was a great rhythm to it, like being tugged by ocean waves.

"Oh my God," I said. "You do get straight A's."

"Told ya," he said. "I've wanted to do this since the first second I saw you, by the way. All I wanted was to walk up to you and do exactly this."

"You mean, as I was walking down the aisle? To get married?"

He nodded.

"That would have been awkward," I said.

But he was serious. "I've always regretted that I didn't just do it."

"You're too young to regret anything."

"Trust me," he said. "I'm not."

Then, he was kissing me again, and in that moment, school was officially over. I didn't have anything to teach this kid. I hadn't been kissed like this in years. Or ever.

Jake nudged me back onto the bed, and I let him, laughing a little as we tried to keep kissing as we worked our way down onto the mattress. I relaxed against the pillows, kissing him back, just as breathless and just as lost. He worked over to the crook of my neck, using his teeth for contrast like the Ivy League overachiever he was. My whole body seemed to gulp every sensation down.

Through the blur, I heard myself say, "You lied to me."

He lifted up. "What?"

I looked at him. His hair was less damp now, but mussed and falling forward. His eyes were glassy. "You told me you didn't know how to kiss," I said. "You told me you were terrible."

"Oh," he said. "Sorry about that." Then he went back to my neck, making almost unbearable swirling eddies.

"I knew you were lying."

He knew I knew. He didn't even try to pretend. "I'm actually pretty good."

Was I angry that he'd lied to me? *Hell, no.*

He went on, talking into my shoulder, his voice slightly muffled. "You'd never do it for fun. You'd never do it for a dare. You'd certainly never do it because you wanted to." He worked his way back up my throat, then, and up along the curve under my chin. At last, he lifted his head. "It had to be charity. I knew you'd do it for charity."

He wasn't wrong. "You're much sneakier than I gave you credit for," I said.

He was back at my neck. "Only when I have to be."

"You didn't have to be," I said. "You just chose to be."

He lifted his head. "I had to be."

Before I could ask what that might mean, he kissed me again, until everything in my entire life seemed out of focus except for this one delicious thing. He went on, "I just wanted you. Every time I saw you, or heard about you, or saw your photo in Duncan's room."

"And now that you've got me here, how does it feel?"

"Too good to be true," he said. A second later he added, "And it's pure agony."

I didn't know what that meant, but I knew this: He did have me. If he was playing me, I was played. If this was just a teenage conquest of his friend's big sister, I was conquered. It was partly the kissing sneak-attack that had me all dazed. But it was mostly the fully earnest expression on his face. If he was acting, he was the greatest actor in the world.

Agony, he'd said. I didn't want him to feel agony. I wanted him to feel every good thing that I did.

I reached up and hooked my hands behind his neck and pulled his mouth down to mine. I wasn't playing professor anymore. I was just me, the real me, kissing him and trying to do the very best job I could. I started doing to his neck exactly what he'd done to mine. Which I knew, for sure, was the opposite of agony.

The next time he lifted his head, he seemed like he couldn't believe his eyes.

"I'm glad you tricked me into kissing you," I said.

"Me, too," he said.

"I haven't had this much fun in ages."

"Me neither."

"But you must have lots of girlfriends."

"Not lately," he said with a head shake. "Not interested."

Then I asked a question that I never would have dared to if I weren't so drunk on kisses—and if he hadn't just spent the past half hour convincing me that I already knew the answer. "But you're interested in me?"

"Yes," he said. "But you're grandfathered in."

"Jake," I said, "I really like you. How did that happen?"

His eyes roamed my face in the most grateful way. "I have no idea."

He looked at me like he was memorizing every tiny detail—the way, I imagined, a painter must look at a subject. It was pure aphrodisiac. Then an idea occurred to me: I hadn't been with anybody since Mike in all the years we'd been married, and in the years we'd dated before that, and in this whole, unbelievably long year I'd been *not married.* I suddenly wanted like crazy to be with someone, and for that someone to be Jake. I didn't care that he'd been too young to vote in the last presidential election, and I didn't care that he was Duncan's friend. I didn't care about anything at all in that moment except getting a better helping of whatever this was.

I slid a hand down and felt around for the tie on his pajamas.

He broke from the kiss to look down at me. "What are you doing?"

I looked up. "Untying your pants."

He shook his head. "You can't do that," he said. "If you get that started, I'm not sure I can stop."

"Why would you have to stop?" I asked. I'd found the knot at his waist and began working to untie it.

"Helen," he said, "we can't." He put his hand over my hand.

"Sure, we can."

"Helen. Helen—" he said. "Don't. I really did trick you. There was no way you were going to win that Scrabble game. I was on a *team*. I played in *tournaments*."

"Should I mock you about that now or later?"

"The point is, you'd lost before we began."

"So?"

"I had devious intentions. Even the whole idea of Scrabble. I knew you couldn't resist that game. Duncan told me. That's the whole reason I brought it."

"Okay, that is devious," I said. "But you did give me an out." I kissed him again.

"I'm trying to do the right thing, here."

"Don't do the right thing," I murmured into his neck just as I worked the pajama knot free. "I don't want you to do the right thing."

That's when he pressed down and kissed me so fiercely I almost lost my breath. I thought we had been kissing before, but at this moment, I realized we hadn't even started. Right thing, wrong thing. None of it mattered. I was dissolving into the moment, turning into nothing but touch and motion. Whatever had been holding him back was gone, and now we were caught in a gale-force sweep of longing. That was it. The decision was made. We were going to do the wrong thing, and there was nothing anybody could do to stop it.

Until the phone rang.

My phone. Right on the bedside table, inches away.

We froze, locked gazes, and waited for it to stop.

It stopped. But then it started up again. We waited that one out, too, stock-still except for our breathing.

When the ringing started up a third time, I had to check. Three rings is always an emergency. Or, as it turns out, an ex-husband.

I reached out to pick it up in slow motion, and we both saw Mike's name on the little screen.

"Don't answer," Jake whispered.

I shook my head. "I have to."

He rolled onto his back in defeat.

I answered. The room was quiet. Dead quiet. I put the phone to my ear. "Mike?"

"Ellie?"

I hated it when he called me Ellie.

"Can I come over?"

I sat up to hunch over the phone.

"What's wrong?" I said. "I'm out of town."

His voice had that tremble to it that he only got when he was overwhelmed. "I just took a swig of a Jack and Coke," he said.

His favorite drink. "Why are you calling me? Why aren't you calling your sponsor?"

"I can't find him. He's not answering."

I met Jake's eyes and gave him a shrug of apology. He looked away. "Hold on," I said into the phone.

I stood up and straightened out my sleep shirt to compose myself. I could feel Jake's eyes on me as I walked to the bathroom and closed the door behind me. "How much of a swig?"

"I spit it out," he said. "I was at a party and I saw a half-empty glass by the sink. Somebody else's half-gone, melted drink. I just picked it up and poured it in. But then I didn't swallow. I coughed it back out."

I put down the toilet lid and sat on it. "That's great, though, Mike. You did great."

"I don't feel great. I feel like hell."

"Where are you?"

"Walking around. I had to get out."

I leaned forward on my bare knees and tried to adjust to the change of scene. From the soft bed with Jake in a swirl of something that could only be described as *bliss* to the hard, cold, fluorescent bathroom alone in fifteen seconds. It was quite a shift. I didn't know what to tell Mike. I hadn't talked to him in months. "I think that's part of it," I said at last. "That's the process." I had no idea what the process was.

"Can't I come over for just a few minutes? I miss you."

"I told you. I'm out of town. I'm driving to Wyoming."

He paused. "Why?"

"It's a long story," I said. "I'm going hiking."

"Hiking?" he said. "Have you ever been hiking?"

"No," I said. "That's the point. I'm doing something new."

Mike let out a long sigh. "Helen. I can't believe how much I love hearing your voice."

I softened at that. I believed him. "I'm sorry you're struggling so hard."

And with that little tender moment, one of the truest ones to happen between the two of us in years, Mike did something he had never done even once the whole time we'd been married. He started to cry.

Once he started, he did not stop. He cried with abandon—with a fervor I had never heard from him. He cried like it was the first time he'd ever done it. Or like it might be the last. The force of it was paralyzing. I couldn't move under the weight of the deluge. By the time he was all cried out, I'd been stuck in that bathroom for over an hour.

What can I say? Next time your ex-husband finally decides to unleash every emotion he had pent up for six years of marriage, see how efficiently you shut him back down. Why did he pick this exact moment? Did he sense that I had somehow, just, at last, set off to become a new person beyond his grasp? Did some faint radar in his brain tell him I was about to give myself to someone else? The timing was absolutely uncanny. He couldn't have picked a better moment if he'd bugged the room.

Jake was back to reading his whale book when I finally came back out. He didn't look up.

"Must be a good one," I said, gesturing.

"I'm underlining this time," he said, holding up a pen.

I could so easily have crawled onto the bed beside him, put my mouth on his, and pulled us back into the maelstrom. We could have started up again where we left off. But an hour is a long time. Longer, even, if you're on the phone with your ex-husband. Or, in Jake's case, alone with your thoughts.

We'd both had a chance to think too much.

"So," I said, standing too far away to solicit the answer I wanted. "Should we just, like, pick up where we left off?"

Jake kept his eyes on his book.

I studied him. "You don't want to," I said.

"I do want to," he said. "You have no idea."

"Then what?"

"I should never have started this. I was being selfish."

"So be selfish," I said. "I don't care."

"You should care," he said. "You don't need another selfish man."

Of course Duncan had told him all about Mike. "Okay," I said. "It's been a rough year. Or six. Can't I do something fun now?"

"Not with me."

"You're mad that I answered the phone."

He shook his head. "No. I get why you did that."

"He doesn't mean anything to me," I said.

"Well," Jake said, "he means something to you."

"Yes," I admitted. "Of course. But I mean—" I paused. I wasn't quite sure how to phrase it. "I'm not still hung up on him."

"I know. It's not that."

"What is it then?"

"I think I've just had too much time to think."

I paced to the window and back. "So now you're saying no? You've been flirting with me since Boston, and doing badass PR for yourself, and staring at me like I was some kind of mouthwatering dessert, and now you're just going to shut it all down?"

He was doing it again. Memorizing my face.

"Jake? Are you?"

"I have to," he said.

"How fucked up are you?" I said.

But he was so serious. "You deserve someone better."

"That's not what you were saying yesterday! That's not what you were saying an hour ago!" I knew plenty of guys like that. Guys who only wanted you when they couldn't have you. Hell, I'd married one.

"I don't know how to explain," he said, sitting up.

"Wait—" I took a few steps backward. "Was this a joke?" I felt a stab of humiliation at the possibility. "Did Duncan dare you or something?" I looked around. "Were you, like, videotaping this for the Internet?"

"No!" he said. Then he rubbed his eyes. "I never thought it would work, okay? I thought you'd roll your eyes at me like you always do.

I didn't think you'd actually kiss me, or lie back on the bed like that, or look up at me like I could mean something to you. I certainly did not anticipate that crazy sleep shirt of yours. And I sure as hell never imagined what kissing you would actually feel like."

I paced around some more. Everything that had felt so exactly right a little while earlier was now the opposite. I went to the window again. There was nowhere else to go.

"You're beautiful," he said.

But I wasn't having it. I felt a burning anger roar through me. I turned around and pointed at him. "Shut up, right now! This whole thing is fucked up, and the whole point of coming here was to get *un*-fucked up. So unless you can explain to me what's going on—in simple words that a non-Scrabble champion can understand—we are done, and I mean really done, like I don't want you even talking to me."

He looked down. I couldn't read his expression. He looked . . . I don't know: anxious. Or nervous. Or overwhelmed. He stared at nothing for several minutes.

"Well?" I demanded at last. "Can you?"

He met my eyes then, but he didn't say anything.

I waited as long as a self-respecting person can wait. "Okay," I said at last. "That's it, then." I could feel the disappointment on my face, and that just made it worse. "I hope you and Duncan get a good laugh when you tell him."

"It's not like that," he said. "I'll never tell Duncan about this."

I didn't know what to do with the sadness in his voice, or the way his shoulders seemed to slump forward like his heart had been scooped out. I didn't know what to do with any of it. So I did the only thing I could think of.

"Please get off my bed," I said in my meanest big-sister voice. "I am going the hell to sleep."

Chapter 6

After that, I ignored him.

I ignored him while we slept. I ignored him as the phone rang its wake-up call. I ignored him as we brushed our teeth, checked out, and walked to the car. I ignored the hell out of him—like the tough guy I was trying to become.

It was a bright morning, and Jake offered to drive. I sat at the farthest edge of the passenger seat and leaned my head against the window. I wedged earbuds into my ears and then, even though my iPod wasn't charged, I pretended to listen to music for the next four hours as we left the motel—and civilization itself—farther behind.

Now I knew what I was dealing with. Jake only wanted me when he couldn't have me. That was a genre of man: the "I wouldn't belong to a club that would have me for a member" genre.

I knew that type.

All those years with Mike, he only loved me when I was mad. Or distracted. Or busy. He loved to *chase*, but the minute I let him *capture*, he suddenly felt smothered. I learned early on that I had to keep running to keep him interested. But after a while I got tired of running. After a while, I just wanted to be caught.

When we first met, I wasn't sure if I was interested. But Mike pulled out all the stops: flowers, dinners, love letters. After a while, I was hooked. But just about the time I'd start hoping he'd call, he'd stop calling. It was like he sensed it. Once I realized he was losing interest, I'd make a point to busy myself—with projects and friends, and sometimes other dates. But as soon as I'd manage to move him to the back burner, he'd call more often.

Of course, there were many times in between extremes when we got along great. It's just that everything we did took place within this bigger pattern, and it took me a long time to spot it. Once I did, it took me even longer to stop trying to change it. Or demanding that he change it. Or hoping a marriage counselor would change it. But some things about people just don't change. As much as I knew intellectually that it was his problem, I'd never been able to shake the feeling that there must be something wrong with me.

Was I overwhelming? Or too emotional? Or too needy? I'd never thought of myself that way before, but I guess who you are always seems normal to you because you don't know what it feels like to be anyone else.

I could see the mountains in the distance as Jake kept driving. They really did look purple, and I wondered what trick of physics made that happen. It had been an act of bravery, really, to let Jake catch me last night. In all my recent experience, being caught meant being left.

Yet, here it was, the morning after, and the facts seemed pretty plain. Jake had chased me, caught me, then looked around, wrinkled his nose, and said, "Actually, you know what? Never mind." Either I was, in actual fact, too much, or something about me attracted men who only wanted too little.

Who knew?

Who cared?

Three years of marriage counseling had taught me that this particular issue was not a resolvable one. It was lucky—*lucky, dammit*—that Jake had hit the brakes. It was one less thing to struggle with. One less thing to regret. I should be thanking him for stopping us. But I didn't feel like thanking him. I felt like punishing him for getting us started in the first place.

That was the whole morning's car ride.

By the time we pulled up to the historic wood-and-stone hunting lodge that served as the headquarters for the Back Country Survival Company, I had erected a pretty solid imaginary wall between us.

As he yanked up the parking brake, I turned toward him.

"Hey—" I said. My first word in four hours.

"Yeah?"

"Do me a favor, okay?"

He met my eyes. "Of course."

"We don't know each other."

"We don't?"

"We did not drive here together."

"We didn't?"

"And you have never stuck your tongue in my mouth."

He took that in. "That's harsh."

"I'm trying to do something important here," I said. "This is not a joke to me."

"It's not a joke to me, either."

"I came on this trip for a reason, and it wasn't to mess around with my little brother's goofy friend."

He tilted his head like that smarted a bit. "Okay."

"Whatever that was yesterday, it doesn't matter." I was frustrated that four straight hours of pretending not to give a damn hadn't worked better. I wanted so badly not to feel humiliated. And rejected. And pathetic. I'd had enough of those feelings to last a lifetime. I was supposed to be turning myself into a badass superhero—not a sniveling teenybopper. I just had to shut it all down. By whatever means necessary.

"I never really liked you," I said. Then I looked at him, dead serious, and added, "And I wish yesterday had never happened."

He looked away. "I wish it had never happened, too."

Here was something surprising. Even though I had just spoken those exact words with no feeling at all, the sound of them boomeranging back at me really stung. I made my voice falsely bright. "Great. I agree. So let's do that."

He frowned. "Do what?"

"Pretend it never happened."

He tried to read my expression. "That's what you really want?"

"What I really want is for you to not be here. And to never have been here."

He shrugged.

"Right. So I'll take the next best thing. Strangers."

"But we're not strangers."

So true. "Nobody knows that but us."

"You want to pretend to be strangers?"

I nodded. "I want to pretend so hard that we almost believe it."

He took a deep breath and then looked into my eyes, as if trying to decide something about me. "I'll pretend for you, Helen," he said at last. "But there's no way I'm going to believe it."

His intensity flustered me a little. "Okay," I said. "That works." Then I wasn't sure what to do next. I stuck my hand out. "I guess this is good-bye, then."

He looked at my hand a second before he took it. We shook.

"Good-bye," he said, without looking up. He let himself out of the car. And then, just like that, we were strangers.

Jake turned out to be good at pretending. At check-in, he stood an anonymous distance behind me. When I climbed the stairs to take my stuff to my room, he did not watch me go. I didn't see him again until the orientation meeting that afternoon, where I sat near the back, and he took a seat right up front like he didn't even know I was there.

Good, I thought. *Perfect.*

But nothing felt good or perfect. As I watched the room fill up, I felt more and more out of place. It was all college kids, which, as I thought about it, made sense. Who else has this kind of time off in the summer? Or ever? As one tall, lanky, coltish twenty-year-old after another appeared in the doorway, the sameness of them smacked me in the face. They wore the same kind of T-shirts—all with Greek letters commemorating some party or another—and the same kind of nylon shorts, and sneakers in some shade of neon. They wore the same kind of lip gloss and applied their eyeliner the same way. They were all the same shade of tan. Their shoulder-length hair was all blow-dried straight in the same shape. All only slight variations on the same twenty-year-old theme.

It was ridiculous, of course, to think they were all the same. As the weeks wore on, I'd come to see them all as distinctly different, no matter how hard they tried to match. But that didn't do me any good at the time.

There seemed to be only two kinds of people gathering for the trip: all of them, and me. Pale me. Freckled me. Wavy hair a cross between red and brown twisted in a knot at the back me. I had on black yoga pants, of all things, and plain black flip-flops, and a cute little batik-print halter top from Old Navy. I had liked that shirt very much when I bought it, and when I packed it, and even when I put it on that morning. Now it felt like the thing that was going to keep me from fitting in. That is, until a mental list of all the other things that were going to keep me from fitting in started to write itself in my head: my age, my divorce, the fact that each of my toenails was painted a different rainbow color. I was nothing like these kids. I was doomed.

Where were the grown-ups? The guys having midlife crises? The stockbrokers with lumberjack fantasies? The carpool moms with something to prove to their personal trainers? I had expected another adult or two, at least. But they weren't on this trip. This trip was one big frat party. We might as well have had a keg.

I want to state for the record that, at thirty-two, I was hardly "old." Thirty-two isn't "old." It's just adult. A pretty nice age, actually. I'd never disliked being thirty-two.

Until now.

Surrounded by nothing but college kids, I decided I wasn't a huge fan of college kids. They were far too confident for my taste—far too proud of themselves. They were the Self-Esteem Generation, and they were all *awesome*. Where was the doubt? The angst? The self-hatred?

I couldn't literally be the oldest person on this trip. I kept waiting for the instructor to come in. Surely he—or she—would be an adult, right? Some grizzled old leathery mountain guy with a flannel shirt, and a trick knee, and a scar from a bear fight under his beard? I would have loved an instructor like that: a wise and comforting Grizzly Adams type.

But that's not what I got. At three P.M. on the dot, a high schooler appeared in the doorway and eyed the room without coming in. Nobody noticed him but me. I watched him there for several minutes before deciding to pipe up and direct him to the Junior School meeting across the hall—just as he introduced himself as our instructor.

I gaped. He couldn't be a day over sixteen. Not with that little wispy goatee and overgrown frame that didn't even have its muscles yet. He was stringy, pale, and a little pimply, with oily hair and a home-knitted stocking cap the color of beets. I would have pegged him for a video game programmer, easy, or a movie theater concession stand worker, or even a misfit paperboy. But not—*not*—the person who was going to lead me through the greatest journey of my life.

His voice was as stringy as his facial hair. "Listen up, people," he said. "It's time to get schooled."

I couldn't help it. I raised my hand.

"It's not time for questions," he said.

"Are you the instructor?" I asked.

He pointed to a patch on his backpack strap. "Is this an instructor's patch?"

"I don't know," I said. "Is it?"

"It is," he said, "and I am."

"How old are you?" I asked. It just popped out.

He stood up straighter. "Old enough," he said.

But he wasn't. He really wasn't. I felt a tingle of alarm.

He turned to the room. "I'm Beckett," he said. "And for the next three weeks, I am your only link to survival."

He crossed his arms and squinted as that sank in, then said, "I'm about to introduce myself—and our program, and the wilderness—to you. But I want you guys to go first." He sat down in an empty chair and leaned forward, instructing us all to volunteer our names, ages, and what, exactly, had brought us here.

It felt like a big question, that last one. What exactly had brought me here? I was still wrestling with that question. I didn't know how to answer it for myself, much less a clump of overconfident kids.

He waited for volunteers. Finally, a J. Crew model in a tank top raised her hand—showing a total absence of upper-arm fat. This one, I noticed, was a little different from her peers. She had long blond hair and wore no makeup. Of course, she was so striking she didn't need makeup, but even just that little variation was enough to get my attention. "I'm Windy," she said. "And I'm here because my older brother did the same trip five years ago, and he said it changed his life. Not that my life needs changing!"

Beckett nodded. "How old are you, Windy?"

"Twenty-one."

That was all Beckett wanted, it turned out. I had overthought it again. He didn't need our life stories, or our hopes and dreams. Just name, age, and a one-sentence summary. In a way, that was easier— and much harder. Windy looked like she expected more questions, but Beckett was on to the next volunteer: a tall guy with a backward baseball cap. "I'm Mason," he said. "I'm a junior at the University of North Carolina, I'm taking this course for college credit, and I'm hoping for a near-death experience."

"How many of you are here for credit?" Beckett asked then. Just about every hand went up. Another reason for so many college kids: It's much harder for grown-ups to get credit for anything.

"I'm Kaylee," a girl piped up next, as the hands went back down. "I'm a sophomore at Auburn, and I'm a Pi Phi, and I'm hoping to come back a total hardbody."

They'd set the tone, then. One by one, the kids jumped in, using that same template. Name, year, university, Greek affiliation, and a ten-words-or-less goal for the trip. They were all sophomores and juniors. They all went to big Southern universities. The boys were all hoping for a narrow escape from death, while the girls all, universally, hoped that three brutal weeks in the wilderness would send them home skinnier. Everybody was here for a stupid reason.

Everybody, that is, except me, and I guess that girl Windy, too. And possibly Jake. Though it occurred to me I didn't really have any idea why he was here.

I hung back. My life did not fit into that template, and I dreaded having to announce it publicly to the group. I figured I'd wait to see what Jake said, and maybe crib a little from him. But Jake wasn't volunteering, either. He seemed to be waiting for me.

When every single person had taken a turn but the two of us, Beckett looked back and forth and said, "Well? Who's next?"

Jake pointed at me. "She is."

Everybody turned in my direction—the guys in their LIFE IS GOOD T-shirts and leather, and sharks' teeth necklaces, the girls with their unnaturally tan faces and lip gloss. I surveyed the group. They were not, to say the least, what I'd been expecting. It's possible I'd been in denial, given everything Duncan had insisted about the type of people who'd sign up for a course like this, but I'd expected crunchy-granola hippies. And nature freaks. Shoppers at Whole Foods. Readers of *Outside* magazine. Hemp enthusiasts. Athletes. Perhaps a poet or two. Instead, I was surrounded by the kids you see at spring break on reality TV. Terrifying prototypical teenagers, self-centered and heartless in the way you only are before life has shoved you down and sat on your head for a while.

My turn. *Who was I? Why was I here?*

Time ticked. They stared.

At last, I forced out some words—any words. "I'm Helen," I said. "I don't go to college. Anymore, I mean. I graduated already—years ago. I went to Vassar, though, back when I was your age, but I wasn't in a sorority or anything because we didn't have them there." I'd lost these kids already. I was from another planet. "I'm thirty-two," I went on, digging myself deeper, "and my life sort of fell apart last year."

They were blinking at me as if they literally had no idea what it might mean for someone's life to fall apart. But that couldn't be right. Everyone, no matter how carefully they do their eyeliner, knows something about disappointment, or loss. That said, the older you get, the *more* you know about those things. Maybe it wasn't that they didn't know anything—maybe it was just that they didn't know *enough*.

Something about those blank looks pushed me forward and made me want to force them to get it, even though, of course, that just goes against the physics of human life: People can't understand things before they can understand them.

"I got divorced, actually," I heard myself say. "We'd been trying to start a family, but that went off the rails."

My gaze flickered past Jake, who shook his head imperceptibly as if to say, *Abort! Abort!*

But I couldn't. I couldn't find a stopping place. They were all so quiet. I'd stunned them, and not in a good way, and my mouth refused to shut down until it had stumbled upon some kind of redemption.

"I remember in high school," I went on, turning my own volume down to match the quiet in the room, "I had this crazy crush on a boy who was completely out of my league. He was handsome like a Greek god, and I was just a plain old slightly awkward mortal. I had no business liking him, but he'd helped me up one time when I'd tripped on the stairs, and I couldn't let it go. One day in study hall, as I stole glances at him, I decided that I was going to kiss him at graduation. It was three years away, but I made this solemn vow to myself. And I wasn't going to do it because I thought it would make him suddenly fall in love with me. I was going to do it for me. As a gift to myself. Because I refused to swoon so achingly over him for so long without ever getting even one thing out of it. I pictured it over and over. I planned out different forms of attack. And guess what?" My gaze had fallen to the floor and I didn't look up or wait for an answer. "Graduation came, and I never did it. I didn't chicken out, exactly. I just realized that day that the reality of it would spoil the fantasy. And I *preferred* the fantasy. And guess what else? I ran into him about a year ago at the gas station, and I didn't even say hello." I looked up, at last. "You can't understand this yet, but that's most of life: breaking your own promises to yourself."

With that, I hit bottom. My attempt at redemption—to say something wise and useful for them—ended with the kind of silence you give the crazy cat lady after she tells you about the time Mr. Mittens ate a cockroach. I guess if the only person you ever process things with is your mean little rat-tailed dog, it's all bound to come out sideways sometimes.

That was all I needed, apparently: a crushingly awkward silence and a sudden 3-D glimpse of myself through the group's eyes. I had to lose all hope, and it released me, somehow. "So that's why I'm here, I guess," I said at last. "To get stronger and toughen up. To care less. To rise up from the ashes of my existence like a really badass phoenix and give life the finger, at last."

After an overly long beat, Beckett turned to Jake. "Okay," he said, stretching out the "ay" sound in a *that-was-totally-bananas* tone. "And what about you?"

We all turned toward Jake. That's when I got a look at him for the first time, in context, and noticed that he really didn't look like the rest of the guys. They were all wearing baseball caps, and cargo shorts, and Patagonia shirts. Despite individual variations of size and coloring and hair length, they were all somehow *alike*—the boy versions of all the girls in the room. But not Jake—in his red vintage Hawaiian shirt, and frayed khakis and flip-flops. He wore a tattered canvas fisherman's hat with a home-tied fishing fly pinned to it that should have made him look like a total goofball. But it didn't somehow. Perhaps it was the implied power of all his muscles. Or the hipster glasses that gave him a Cary Grant–like star presence. Or maybe the goofiness of that Gilligan hat proved beyond a doubt that he truly didn't care what anybody thought of him. But the whole room, including me, was thinking the same thing at the same time: *This guy is going to be the boss.*

Jake gave the entire group a big, flirty grin. "Why am I here?" Then he pointed at me with his thumb, and spoke these words: "What she said."

The whole room burst out in a loud, tension-relieving laugh. Even I laughed for a minute. Until I realized none of us were laughing *with* me.

"Actually," Jake said then, as everybody fell quiet. "Seriously." He looked around. "I agree with the redhead." He squinted at me a little. "Or the strawberry-blond-head." The remaining laughing died down, and a few kids glanced over in my direction. "What's-her-name's not wrong. Life *is* going to kick the hell out of all of us. Everybody here. Me included. And I think I'm here to learn to survive it. And take it like a man. Or maybe learn to kick back a little." He turned his eyes toward me. "Like her." With that, maybe even just that one look, he saved me. "Oh, and my name's Jake, by the way," he added. "And I didn't go to Vassar. But I did just graduate from Harvard."

A second silence hit the room—but this was one of awe. In that moment, Jake became our official alpha dog. Theirs, because he was cool, and confident, and hip, and friendly, and had just graduated—which essentially made him a senior. And mine, too. Because even after I'd been as mean to him as I could all day, he still went to the trouble of rescuing me.

Beckett, though, didn't want Jake to be our alpha dog. He stood as fast as he could to snatch back his position as leader, and, when Jake sat back down, Beckett demanded in a voice that sounded suddenly deeper, "Does anybody know where we are?"

The kids all kind of looked around. Did anybody *not* know where we were?

"More importantly," Beckett went on, now that he had our attention, "does anybody know where we're going?"

"The wilderness," a guy said.

"The backcountry," offered another.

"The middle of nowhere," said a third.

"Are we going to Disneyland?" Beckett asked the group, looking around.

"No," everybody said now, getting in the groove.

"That's right," Beckett agreed. "We are going to the opposite of Disneyland. We're going to the Absaroka mountains. Not pronounced the way it's spelled, by the way. Say it with me: 'Ab-SOAR-kas.'"

"Ab-soar-kas," we all said.

"One of the steepest, wildest, most bloodthirsty ranges in the U.S. It will chew you up and spit you out like cherry pits. This is not kid stuff, kids. If you have any hope of surviving," he paused here for emphasis, "you will follow my rules to the letter."

I wondered if any of that was true, or if he was just trying to get back on top.

"This afternoon, we'll go to Outfitting for any gear you still need. After that we'll go to the Pantry to fill our packs, and then, after a good supper—I recommend the Mexican place on State Street—you will enjoy your last shower, and take your last shit on a toilet, and curl up for your last night in a bed."

Beckett looked delighted to bear this news. "You are about to get pummeled on a daily basis. We're not going to the Four Seasons, people. Motel 6 will look like a luxury cruise when I'm done with you. You want to know where we're going? To a land with no toilet paper." He nodded, pleased at the shocked expressions. "That's right. For the next three weeks, you're going to be wiping your ass with a pinecone. You're going to get absolutely filthy. There are no showers out there, friends. No shampoo, no deodorant, no Axe hair gel. You're going to look like hell and smell like a skunk. I don't know who you think you are or why you think you can do this trip. Maybe you think you're amazing. Maybe you think you're a tough guy. But I'll tell you something: The only tough guy in the Absarokas is Mother Nature, and she is going to drag your ass up and down the block."

I glanced around the room. The kids were thrilled with the idea of an ass kicking.

Beckett pulled out a sample backpack and started showing us how to pack.

"Here's how we live in the Absarokas," he went on. "We don't take anything—*anything*—we don't need. Every ounce counts when you carry your whole life on your back. You'll have a toothbrush, two ounces of toothpaste, and a plastic bag to spit into. You're permitted sunscreen and ChapStick and a comb. You are not permitted: makeup, lotion, jewelry, or electronics of any kind. And guess what? We leave nothing but footprints. Everything we pack in, we pack out. Ladies, if it's your time of the month—"

"Gross!" one of the guys shouted.

"You'll keep your used feminine supplies double-bagged and bring them back with you. *Pack it in, pack it out.* You cannot flick your used lady-products into the woods and get away with it. Leaving tampons on the trail is grounds for expulsion."

Was this a problem? Did the women on these trips just fling their old tampons all around the forest? Did we need to cover this in the opening monologue? I really had not thought this trip through. I hadn't foreseen that we wouldn't bathe for three weeks. Or that we wouldn't be allowed to bring deodorant. Or the whole "wiping with a pinecone" situation. As my chest seized up with anxiety about the horrific wrong turn I had just made by coming here, I tried, at the same time, to give silent thanks for the fact that, at the very least, it wasn't going to be my time of the month.

What the hell had I been thinking? I wasn't a hiker! I wasn't out-doorsy! My favorite things in the world were soft beds, good books, and big cups of coffee. I did not want to have my ass kicked—by Mother Nature or anyone else.

How had I not figured this out before? This trip was the very last thing on earth I wanted to do. I suddenly felt a lurch of despair in my stomach. I should have gone to Paris in a jaunty hat and taken a cooking class! How on earth had I picked Bigfoot for my role model over Julia Child?

I looked around the room to see if anybody else was panicking. But those kids—those dumb kids—were enraptured. The scarier Beckett got, the more they loved it.

"You can bring one small camera if it fits in this pocket," he said, pointing at a zipper on his daypack. "You are permitted one extra T-shirt, one extra set of socks, and one extra pair of underpants. You are required to bring a notebook to serve as your journal, and you may bring one book only for entertainment. You'll be issued anything you need at Outfitting. You'll pack your bags yourself, using our system, but don't even think about trying to sneak in shampoo or deodorant." He glared at all of us, but the women in particular. "That's wasting space and adding weight. If I find it in your pack, I will make you eat it."

Next, he pulled out a map and pointed at a green area with a bunch of wiggly lines like fingerprints on top of it. "Over the next three weeks, we will traverse this range." He traced a route with a ballpoint pen. "We'll sleep in tent groups of four and hike together every day. We'll rise with the sun and travel six to twelve miles a day, some of them vertical miles. You will be exhausted. You may well have blisters. You will hate yourself and everyone around you. That's okay. Too bad. When we get to camp, you'll set up your sleeping tarps first, then your kitchens. There'll be a lot of farting on this trip, people. It's funny and hilarious. Get over it. Dehydrated food does that to you. Think of it as jet propulsion."

This guy was dead serious.

"This is not Hiking for Beginners, people," he said, looking around at the group. "Man up and deal with it."

It wasn't? It wasn't hiking for beginners? Yes, it was! "Actually, it *is* hiking for beginners," I blurted out. "It's listed as a beginners course. In the catalog."

For a second, he blinked like he hadn't realized that. Then he gave me a look. "You know what I mean."

Actually, no I didn't.

"Okay," he said next, clapping his hands together as if he'd covered everything there was to cover. "That's it for now. Any questions?"

That big guy Mason raised his hand. "What do we do with our poo?" he asked. "Do we pack that out in plastic bags, as well?"

Beckett's face got serious. "Yes. You'll keep that in your pack with your kitchen supplies."

Our *kitchen supplies*? The room held its breath.

"I'm kidding!" Beckett burst out with a head shake, after the longest minute ever. "No. You don't pack out your feces. Fecal matter is biodegradable. You'll dig a cat hole with a stick, do your business, sprinkle some dirt on top, stir it up, then cover it. Mother Nature will do the rest."

"Do our business?" a girl asked. "Like, out in the forest?"

"No," Beckett answered. "We helicopter you back to base camp every time you need to go."

There it was. We had ourselves a comedian. A sarcastic, pubescent, wilderness comedian.

Beckett looked around for other questions. I, personally, had a thousand, but I'd be damned if I'd ask them—or ever speak again for the rest of my life. When no other hands went up, Beckett slapped his palms on his thighs and stood up.

"Okay then," he said, surveying the group one final time with a wicked smile. "Let the games begin."

Chapter 7

At Outfitting, I tried on several pairs of boots. Beckett said it was best to rent them unless you had your own well-broken-in pair, which I didn't, of course. The rental pairs were certainly well broken in—by other people's stinky feet. The boots had been gelled so often with water repellent they were crusty. The laces were fraying. And every single pair rubbed me wrong in some different spot.

I snagged a side-of-the-eye glance at Jake. He was helping that blond girl Windy try on boots. I saw him yank her laces tight, then I heard her burble a delighted squeak before I looked away. In that moment, I had a vision of the next three weeks of my life: I was going to make myself miserable on this trip by being overly serious and overly self-conscious and overly self-critical. And Jake was going to make me even more miserable by being the pure opposite of all those things.

They loved him. We'd been here two hours, and he was already the king of the group. He was just one of those guys, it turned out, who always had something funny to say. Plus, he was confident without being pompous. He was interested without being anxious. He was laid-back without being a slacker. He had something for everyone.

The hard-core guys could talk hard-core hiking with him. The sorority girls could ask him to adjust their pack straps. He was infinitely likable. To everybody. Except me.

I was fully aware how crazy it was, but the more they liked him, the less I did. This was supposed to be my trip! It was like he'd taken it over, somehow, and squeezed me out. We were enemies now, after all, if only in my mind. We were like the broken-up couple whose friends had to choose sides. Except we had never been a couple, and there were no sides left because everybody had already chosen him.

There it was. If he was happy, I had to be unhappy. If he fit in, I had to be left out. Especially since I still wasn't talking to him. If he was the person everybody was gathered around, I didn't have any place to stand.

At the Pantry, we measured and bagged up ten days' worth of dehydrated food, as well as mixtures of spices and dehydrated milk, lemonade, and cocoa. We got the glorious, unbelievable news that butter can last for weeks unrefrigerated without going rancid, and the same was true of cheese. Each cook group would carry its own cheddar wheel so thick it had to be cut with a wire, and enough butter to last until the re-ration at the midway point. Apparently, someone was going to ride up into the mountains halfway through with a full load of replenishments on a caravan of donkeys.

"Donkeys?" that guy Mason asked.

"No cars. No ATVs. Just living, breathing nature."

"What happens if we run out of food before that?"

Beckett shrugged. "Then we eat each other."

There was a limit for the packs based on each person's size, and yes—they weighed us one by one on a scale and called out the results. The big guys carried more than the small girls, which is why they got the gas cookstoves and the giant wheel of cheese. My own pack weighed in at seventy-nine pounds, which seemed like plenty.

I was issued flour, dehydrated milk, a bag of homemade granola, and hot chocolate.

Packs full, we practiced putting them on. You can't just hoist a pack that heavy straight up to your back from the ground. You have to kneel down like you're proposing marriage, pull your pack up onto the shelf of your thigh, then wriggle it around onto your back. Beckett had us practice. I took it very slow, worrying that I might drop it, or strain something, or otherwise humiliate myself. Because the only ways I knew how to shake off embarrassment were: (a) to leave the room, or (b) to laugh it off with a friend. Since I couldn't leave, and I had no friends, the stakes were pretty high.

I would have expected to have a simple but clear education about the wilderness by the time we finished our orientation. The basics, at least. But Beckett, for all his posturing, talked in scribbles. He gave lines of information with gaping spaces in between, and after listening to him for five straight hours, all I knew for sure was that dandelions were edible, singing on the trail would keep the bears away, and we had to drop iodine in our water bottles every single time we filled up or risk an intestinal infection called Giardia that would have us "spewing out of both ends."

When Beckett dismissed us for dinner with instructions to meet at the lodge entrance at six the next morning, I couldn't shake the feeling that we had only a tiny fraction of the information we were going to need.

I asked him about it on the way out the door, but he said, "It's all in the handouts."

"The two handouts?" I asked.

"Don't worry so much."

"I feel under-educated."

"We do experiential learning here. You'll learn as you go."

"But what if there's some information I need before I have it?"

"You'll figure it out."

"What if I don't?"

"Then you'll die," Beckett said with a shrug. "And I'll use my one stick of dynamite to make it look like an avalanche."

I took my journal with me to the Mexican place on State Street for supper, thinking I'd sit quietly with a bowl of guacamole and jot down some pre-journey deep thoughts. But as I approached the hostess's podium, I heard a loud wave of laughter in the back. When my eyes followed the sound, I saw every single member of our hiking group, including Beckett, cozied up for dinner at two pushed-together tables, well into their meal.

I looked away so fast I spun halfway around. Then I peeked back to see if they'd noticed me. They hadn't.

I felt like I was crashing a party I hadn't been invited to. Like I was stalking them, or tagging after them, or trying to be friends with a group that wasn't friends with me. Except they weren't friends. We were all strangers, dammit. How had they formed a south-of-the-border drinking club in the half-a-day since we'd all met?

Maybe I should have joined them. That's no doubt what Jake would have done—just bounded over like a chocolate Lab with a wagging tail to slip into the pack. But I wasn't a chocolate Lab. In fact, in that moment, I was Pickle: a mangy-looking mini dachshund with a tail that never wagged and a foul temper. Maybe that's why we got along so well.

Pickle was, of course, quite literally, a bitch. And though I would not have called myself a bitch, I certainly admired that about her. There are women who describe themselves as bitches—often proudly—on T-shirts, say, or bumper stickers. I've noticed them for years around town: Sweet Bitch, Sexy Bitch, Crazy Bitch, Alpha Bitch,

Yoga Bitch, Bitch on Board, Bitch on Wheels, Bitch on a Broomstick. Pronouncements like that caught my eye because I actually didn't get it. Why would you put that on your car? Or across your boobs on a T-shirt? What were you trying to say about yourself? Was it a beware-of-dog warning to let the world know how tough you were? Because I couldn't help thinking that if you were tough enough to fit into the "bitch" category, you probably didn't need to bedazzle it in rhinestones across the butt of your shorts.

Pickle certainly didn't need a sign. One look at Pickle's little pinched-up, pointy face, with that one lip always caught on her teeth, and you knew not to mess with her. That was the kind of toughness I wanted, especially in that moment. The kind you didn't have to de-clare.

The principal at my school had a poster of Chuck Norris jokes hanging in his office. I'd read that poster a thousand times since he'd put it up, and it always reminded me of Pickle: "Chuck Norris doesn't call the wrong number. You answer the wrong phone." "When Chuck Norris does division, there are no remainders." "Superman wears Chuck Norris pajamas."

I'd read the poster so many times, I'd just about memorized it. And even though I knew the jokes were, in fact, *jokes,* I had somehow come away with a bizarre affection for Chuck Norris—and, also, for the idea of toughness in general.

So, tonight, I decided to see this experience of standing ignored in a Mariachi-themed entryway as a teachable moment. Had the group left me out on purpose, or just forgotten me? Did it even matter? I felt like I had exactly two choices: slump my shoulders in defeat, or stand up taller in defiance. What would Chuck Norris do?

Another roar of laughter from the group at the back. One of the girls stood up and started looping an imaginary lasso above her head while the rest of them cheered her on.

That was fine. I wasn't here to make friends. I was here to do the opposite of that, actually. I'd spent my whole life way too tender. This was good for me. It was time to learn how to not give a shit. Plus, the last thing I needed, I told myself, was to get plastered on tequila the night before I set off into the wilderness. Hungover is no way to start a journey of self-discovery.

What would Chuck Norris do? Hell, what would *Pickle* do—aside from biting everybody's ankles? The answer was easy. She'd find another restaurant and go eat her own damn dinner.

But there was a reason Beckett had recommended the Mexican place on State Street: It was the only restaurant in town. Other than the Chinese restaurant with the wagon wheel out front that called itself the Golden Corral Chinese Buffet and BBQ, which was closed on Thursdays, of all the luck.

In the end, I assembled my dinner from the gas station snack shop under the influence of two opposing motivations: to load up on healthy fuel so I could start this new journey in tip-top condition, and to consume all the nastiest junk food I could get my hands on in case it was my last chance. That's how I wound up out on a park bench at sunset, balancing my "dinner" on my thighs: a bag of sunflower seeds, some peppered beef jerky, a bottle of spring water—and a Coke, a Hershey bar, and a Whoopie Pie for dessert.

I forced myself to appreciate my surroundings. The town had a classic Western profile of square storefronts facing each other across a wide main drag. Off in the distance, mountains. All of this was topped off by a sunset so wild and fiery and breathtaking it just had to be showing off.

At the sight of it, I reached into my bra for my list of self-improvements. It was time for a pep talk, and there was nobody to give it but me. I'd come to the wrong place, that much was clear. But so what? I'd made wrong choices before. Wasn't that what I was here for? To outdo everybody's expectations—especially my own? So what if I was the last person anybody would ever bet on. I was going to earn a Certificate. I might not be the best outdoors-woman in the world, but I could certainly out-hike a batch of hungover college kids. They were too young to understand the stakes. They lived on the mistaken assumption that their lives mattered, that life was essentially fair, that it was all going to wind up happy in the end. I knew what they didn't— that everything you care about will disappear, that deserving a happy life doesn't mean you get one, and that there really is no one in the entire world you can count on but yourself. I had the edge that disappointment gives you. I had the advantage of life experience. I might be eating Whoopie Pies for dinner, but at least I knew how very pathetic that was.

That was me on the precipice of my Big Journey: all alone with a lap full of junk food and an open notebook with one useless quote written on the page: "If at first you don't succeed, you're not Chuck Norris." I was funneling sunflower seeds into my mouth and worrying over just how uninspired I felt, when my phone rang.

I fumbled around to find it in my bag and barely caught it in time. Mike.

I didn't even say hello. Just, "You're calling me again?"

"Actually," Mike said, "you're the one who called me."

"I did not."

"You did. You pocket-dialed me. I've been listening to the inside of your purse for ten minutes."

I just had to double-check. "I pocket-dialed you?"

"About ten minutes ago. It happens a lot, actually."

"It does?"

"Maybe once or twice a month."

"What do you do about it?"

"I shout, 'Hey! You're pocket-dialing me!' But you never hear me."

"Then, what?"

"Then I give up and listen for a while before I hang up."

"You *listen*?" I said. "Can you hear anything?"

"Well, on a good day, I can hear everything."

"But that's eavesdropping! That's morally wrong," I said, wondering what on earth he'd heard me say.

"Hey!" he said. "You're the one calling me."

"Not on purpose!"

"Nonetheless."

"Have I ever said anything—" I started.

"Incriminating?" he finished.

I nodded into the phone.

"Nah," he said. "It's always just grocery checkers. Or your hairdresser. Or your pet. Sounds like you got a dog that eats your furniture."

I nodded again. "A mini dachshund. She's terrible."

"Get rid of it. Life's too short."

"Why didn't you tell me I'd been pocket-dialing you?"

"I didn't think you'd want to hear from me before."

"But now you think I do?"

"I hope so," he said. "Plus I want to thank you for yesterday. For being so kind."

"It was nothing."

"It wasn't nothing to me."

I opened a bag of potato chips, and several spilled on my lap.

"I take it you haven't left yet," he went on.

"Correct," I said, crunching the chips.

"Are you sure you're up for this?"

"No," I said, the honesty of the word fluttering over me like a breeze. "But there's no turning back now."

"Sure there is," Mike said. "There's always turning back."

"I'm not so sure that's true."

"Duncan seems genuinely concerned about your safety on this trip."

"You talked to Duncan?"

"He says these guys are notorious for killing people. They recruit the dumbest possible thrill-seekers and then don't supervise them."

"They're under new management."

"There are many excellent survival courses out there," Mike said, like he had any authority to judge. "This isn't one of them."

"Guess you read about the bear attack."

"No, but I did read about the rappelling accident. And the rockslide. And the guy who died from hypothermia."

"I'll be fine," I said, wondering if that was true.

"Why are you doing this?"

"If you survive, they might give you a Certificate."

"Do you hear yourself talking?"

"I want that Certificate."

"The thing is," Mike said, "you're not exactly a jock."

He wasn't wrong, but I resented the comment anyway. "I've been training for this for months," I said, more irritated than I needed to be. "I've been running three miles every morning."

"This is not a little jog around the neighborhood—"

"A *three-mile* jog," I corrected.

"The fact that you're impressed with three miles proves my point. Seriously."

"That's not funny."

"I'm not joking."

"Don't tell me I can't do this," I said.

"Helen, you can't change who you are."

"Sure I can."

"It's just not like you to do stuff like this."

"It didn't *used to be* like me," I said then, "back when you knew me. But I've turned myself into an animal now. A bloodthirsty animal."

"Why?"

"You don't want me to answer that." I was regretting picking up the phone. Sometimes *anybody* really isn't better than *nobody*.

"Helen," Mike said then, "you don't have to do this."

"I do, actually. I really do."

"I want you to come home."

"I'm not coming home. I made a plan, and I'm following through."

"No," Mike said. "I mean, come home to me."

I dropped the phone into my lap. And stared at it a second before I picked it back up.

"Are you still there?" Mike was asking. "Did I lose you?"

"I'm still here," I said, but I wasn't sure I meant it.

"I mean it, Ellie. I really do."

"I never liked it when you called me Ellie."

"Hang up and come home. It's crazy that we're apart."

It took a second to assemble a response. "We're not just apart, Mike. We're *divorced*. It's been a *year*. People don't get un-divorced. We signed papers, we officially ended it in every possible way."

"I know, and I get that, and from a certain perspective it seems a little crazy—"

"From any perspective, it seems a lot crazy."

"We made the choice we had to make at the time. But I'm better now. It took a hell of a wake-up call, but I pulled it together."

"It wasn't a wake-up call. It was a legal document."

My phone beeped. The battery was dying.

"I'm telling you," Mike said. "I'm like the old me—but better. I can be good for you now, Ellie."

I leaned my head back. It was just so perfectly like him to say the exact words I'd always longed to hear—but to wait until it was solidly too late.

He went on. "I've been dating constantly for the past six months—and guess what? Nobody can compare to you."

"You've been dating constantly?" I asked.

"Haven't you?" he said. "Toby said you'd been on some dates."

"One. With a Belgian insurance adjuster. I don't think it counts."

"There's been nobody else? Really?"

Of course, there had been somebody. A vastly inappropriate somebody Mike himself had interrupted me with. Mike and Jake knew each other, of course, from many Thanksgivings and New Year's Eve parties at Grandma GiGi's, and I could have shocked the hell out of him if I'd said something about it right then, which was tempting. But I didn't. Partly because Mike and I really weren't close enough anymore to share anything that private. Partly because I wasn't sure myself if messing around with Jake had been kind of awesome or totally pathetic. And partly—though I never would have admitted this, even to myself—because something about that almost-night with Jake had cracked open a place so tender in my heart I knew I had no choice but to stand twenty-four-hour guard in front of it.

"I've had lots, *and lots,* of opportunities," I said, "but I've been in a healing period."

"I get that," Mike said.

My phone battery beeped again.

"Come home," Mike said then. "Why do you always have to be so hard on yourself?"

I hesitated. This was exactly our pattern, of course. Certain people in life—and not even always ones who deserve it—can just unlock all your doors, somehow. Even if you change the locks or hide the keys. And Mike had always been one of those people for me.

Until right now. It was time to be a tough guy. It was time to bare the fangs of my inner bloodthirsty beast. It was time to not just say *No*, but *Hell, no*.

I took a breath to do it, at last—but then, as if on cue, the battery died.

"Mike?" I said, even though I knew he was gone.

There was no answer.

It wasn't his fault, and I knew that. But I went ahead and added it to my long list of disappointments. That damned ex-husband. He never let me win.

I chewed the rest of my dinner in slow motion. I can't say that Mike's proposition didn't rattle me. If it had come a year ago, or even six months, I might have had a softer heart toward him. But it was too late now. *Chuck Norris can slam a revolving door.*

I had an empty Coke can and two cheeks full of my last bite of Whoopie Pie and was just about to pack up and head back to the lodge, when the group—my group—came ambling up the sidewalk toward the hotel, tipsy.

They were all best friends already, in the way Mexican beer and salsa can make you friends. Windy, the one who kept flirting with Jake, called out to me on the approach. "We're going up to the roof to play Truth or Dare!" she said. "Want to come?"

Before I could think better of it, I slipped into Pickle mode with a sarcastic, "Seriously?"

The tone was way too mean, but she wasn't listening, anyway, because just then, one of the guys grabbed her from behind in a tickle, just like in a wine cooler commercial.

I hated them all already.

I tried to assess Jake without looking directly at him. Was he drunk, too? Was he going up to the roof, too? I stood up at the idea, and when

I did, the wrappers from my shameful and tragic dinner fell to the ground. Busted. Dammit. But before I'd even bent down, there was Jake, at my feet, gathering them up. He stood, and stepped closer without meeting my eyes, and just when I thought he was going to hand me the whole pile of trash, he gently, almost tenderly, pulled one last thing—the Coke can—from my grasp and walked the bundle back to the trash bin at the corner.

I watched him, and I wasn't the only one. The whole group was waiting for him to come back, as if there was nowhere to go without him. As he turned back toward everyone, somebody shouted, "Move it, J-Dog!" and Jake ramped his walk up to a trot.

J-Dog? He was already "J-Dog."

Suddenly, I wanted a nickname. I wanted to be the kind of person that people gave nicknames to. How would my life be different if they all suddenly started calling me H-Dog? Okay, H-Dog didn't work— but *something?* I tried to remember if I'd ever had a good nickname. Duncan had about fifty for me, but they didn't count because I hated them all: *Helena, Helenita, Holla, Sis, Sistah, Sister Sledge, Sister Mister, Big Mama, Crazy Lady, La Loca, La Locita, Lena, Lane, Fast Lane.* He also thought I looked like an armadillo when I got mad, which gave rise to a whole cornucopia of irritating names, including *Dillo* and the dreaded *Dildo.* But nicknames I liked? I couldn't come up with one. Mike had sometimes called me *Mrs. Dull* after we got married, with no self-deprecating awareness at all, which kind of made my skin crawl, even though I never said that to him. After a while, he settled on Ellie, which never really fit me, somehow, but was a slight improvement. And Grandma GiGi called me *Darling,* but she called everybody *Darling.*

Oh, well. It was fine. I liked the name Helen.

I watched J-Dog jog back to the group. Somehow, he even made disposing of trash cool. Beckett would not have approved of that

Whoopie Pie: the nuclear chemicals it was made with, the plastic it was wrapped in, the trucking industry that had brought it here from the factory in Kansas, or wherever. He could so easily have used me as an example to everyone—a consciousness-raising cautionary tale of bad food and littering. As it was, though, Jake had those wrappers hidden at the bottom of the trash before Beckett even noticed I was there.

I wasn't going up to the roof. I wasn't going to sit around up there watching a bunch of goofy kids play a goofy game. But just after Jake turned around, for no reason I could explain, I had this funny little spark of hope that he might tell them all to go on without him and stay here, instead, with me.

Which he didn't. Of course.

Jake was going up to the roof to drink beers at sunset and be his easy-going, optimistic self in the way you only can when you're twenty-two. And of course I was going to stay here alone. There was no other way it could play out.

Except for this: As Jake caught back up to everyone, he veered for the spot between the group and me, and I wondered just for a second if he might reach out, somehow, or find a way to brush against me as he went by. I allowed myself to hope for it just the tiniest bit— for the welcome human contact, for the acknowledgment that I was even here, for somebody out in this wild, empty land to have the slightest idea who I was.

But I shouldn't have let myself hope like that. Jake walked right on by without even a glance my way. Just exactly like a total stranger. The one I had ordered him to be.

Chapter 8

I was still half asleep when we boarded the bus the next morning—an old school bus that had been repainted green with the BCSC logo.

I chose a seat near the front and purposely sat right next to the aisle so nobody could sit beside me. Or, at least, so I could tell myself that's why nobody sat beside me. But then a skinny guy named Hugh wedged himself past me and sat down without even making eye contact. I stared at him until he asked, already seated, "Is this seat taken?"

"No."

"It is now."

I looked past him, out the window, even though it was still too dark to see.

"You were hilarious yesterday, by the way," he said.

"I was hilarious?"

He nodded. "The sad kind of hilarious."

I frowned. "Thank you."

"You're my new favorite person here."

"I am?" Something about his voice made it sound like everything he said actually meant the opposite.

He leaned in. "I had no idea this course would be such a frat party." I smiled. "Me, neither."

As the kids loaded on one by one, Hugh leaned into me and whispered insults about each one, zeroing in immediately on everybody's most ridiculous and vulnerable traits: the ankle tattoo that said BFFs, the muffin top, the fake tans. He was sharp, I gave him that. And maybe a little mean. But I wasn't in a position to be picky.

The conversation on the bus was boisterous and cheery—all the kids raring to start their near-death and slimming adventures. I was the only person, as far as I could tell, who was terrified and subdued. Adrenaline prickled in my veins. I tried hard not to notice the way Jake was leading the frivolity, but, of course, the harder you try not to notice a thing, the more it becomes center stage in your mind. Especially when that thing is a person in the seat right behind yours.

The first topic for the morning was everybody's One Book. I guess it did say a lot about a person: If you could only have one book for three weeks, what book would it be? Most of the boys had brought thrillers, and they all agreed to trade. The girls showed more variety. One brought the Bible. One brought a workout manual. One brought a cupcake cookbook, of all things. One brought her favorite book from childhood, *Anne of Green Gables,* for the literary equivalent of comfort food. Windy brought a psychology textbook for a summer class she was taking.

She was also in the seat behind me—with Jake, by the way, who she had yanked in as he passed. "What book did you bring?" she asked me.

I turned around to find the whole bus looking at me. Waiting.

"I didn't bring a book," I said.

"She forgot her book!" one of the boys shouted, like it was hilarious.

"I didn't forget it," I said. "I chose not to bring a book."

Another incomprehensible statement from me. One guy scratched his neck.

"I just wanted to, you know, really *be here* and soak up every single moment," I said, realizing as I said it how stupid the idea sounded. "I didn't want to miss anything." Just saying the words made me want to go right home and miss *everything*.

I turned back around and faced away, but Windy leaned over after me.

"I'm Windy, by the way," she said.

"I remember that from yesterday," I said.

"But with an 'i.' "

It wasn't computing. "With an 'i'?"

"It's not 'Wendy,' like in *Peter Pan*. It's 'Windy,' like"—here, she waved her arms around—"*whoosh, whoosh*."

"Oh," I said.

"Guess what my little sister's name is?" she said then, and before I could guess, she said, "Stormy."

"With an 'o'?" I couldn't help it.

"Yep," Windy said, all cheer. "We're from California."

She waited a second, to see if I'd add anything else, which I didn't, and so, at last, she rejoined the bigger conversation, and I was forgotten. My seatmate had fallen fast asleep, and I sat still with my hands folded on my lap. I could have pretended to listen, but I didn't feel like it. I didn't see how they could all be so nonchalant in the face of what we were about to do. Mike's words "you're not exactly a jock" ricocheted around in my head as we followed the winding two-lane highway farther from civilization. Soon we were cutting through angles of pushed-up earth and zooming past striped rock sediments.

The colors were so different here. On the East Coast, the rocks were all shades of gray, but here the earth was red and purple and orange, and the greenery was sparser, and the earth was sandier. I watched it blur by out the window, and I decided it was the change of colors, more than anything, that made me feel so very far from home.

When Beckett stood with his clipboard to start making announcements, he opened with: "It's all uphill hiking today, people. The whole day. Every step. Let's get focused." I gave him my full attention and even pulled out my journal to take notes. Focused, I could do. A whole day of uphill hiking? I wasn't so sure.

I wrote feverishly as Beckett gave us the plan for the day. We'd hike as a group of twelve, plus Beckett—splitting into our tent groups of four each afternoon as we reached our camps. We'd cook and sleep in our tent groups, and reconvene in the morning to hike together.

"So we get to sleep in tents?" a girl asked.

"Weren't you at Outfitting?" Beckett asked. "Did anybody here receive a tent?"

The girl looked around.

"No," Beckett answered. "There are no tents. We sleep under tarps."

"Why do they call it a tent group, then?" she asked.

Beckett looked up toward the heavens, like he'd had all he could take, and then said, "That's just what they call them."

Beckett read the names of the tent groups. As soon as I crossed my fingers and thought *Not Jake,* I immediately overthought it and wondered if I should wish *for* him, instead. He was clearly the nicest person here, after all. But he was also Jake. Who I both wanted to be near and couldn't bear to be near. Of course, making that "not Jake" wish wouldn't necessarily lead to a "not Jake" tent situation. Sometimes I wondered if stating a preference to the universe just dared it to mess with me. It might have been a smarter idea, at this point, to try some reverse psychology.

Either way, Jake wound up in the first group, and I found myself in the last—with that guy Mason, and the girl Windy, and that sandy-haired boy who sat next to me on the bus, Hugh.

Tent groups settled, Beckett gave us his rules of the trail, including nonnegotiable commands to hydrate at every rest stop, to wear sunscreen, and to pay attention to our feet. "If you feel a hot spot rubbing inside your boot," he said, "do not wait. Stop the group and deal with it. Blisters can become totally debilitating out here. At home, you get a blister, you curl up in front of the TV until it's better. Here, you walk five miles in agony." He looked around. "Got it?"

"Got it," the group said.

"Pop quiz! What do you do if you feel a hot spot?"

"Deal with it!"

I wrote that in my notebook. *Hot Spot = Deal With It.* But there was a chill of fear in my chest. I'd been so pleased with my three-mile-a-day jog. But it was on pavement—and flat pavement at that. I'd never in my life spent an entire day hiking uphill. What if I truly couldn't do this? What if I could only get halfway up whatever I needed to climb? What if I was the weakest link? Looking around, it seemed not just possible but likely. Forget earning a Certificate! What a delusional idea. I'd be lucky just to finish. Who was I to think that I could change my whole life just by announcing things were going to be different? I'd always been one of those kids who was picked last at PE and who came in last around the track. Before doing a Mile Swim at summer camp, I'd cried myself to sleep.

The top half of the bus window was open, and the wind cut in and fluttered my hair. I leaned my head against the seat back. Of course, in adult life, nobody forces you to swim a mile or run a track. You can escape all that. Unless, of course—for some reason you cannot honestly even fathom—you sign yourself back up.

We reached the trailhead and piled off the bus. It was literally the end of the road. From this point on, it was nothing but foot trails leading off in different directions marked by wooden signs with yellow writing. The pine trees stood tall, and you couldn't just see them, and smell them, but you could also feel them—a silent presence all around. This was it; I would walk into that forest today and wouldn't walk out again for three weeks.

Our packs were all strapped onto the roof, and Beckett climbed up top with a rope and some carabiners to lower them down. But before we had a chance to put them on, Beckett said, "Don't saddle up yet, people. Time to pee."

I looked around for a bathroom.

"Where?" the tent girl finally asked.

"Out there!" he said, gesturing to the woods. "Go find a place! Scatter! Welcome to the giant, free-for-all toilet of the wilderness."

We scattered. I walked until I couldn't see or hear anybody, thinking all the while this would be an easy way to get very lost. As I squatted, and tried not to splatter on my boots, I thought about how guys really had it better than girls in so many ways. Of course, the idea of boys peeing made me think of Jake, and how he'd almost peed in my car. It seemed like a hundred years ago now, but part of me wanted to be back in that car, and badly. Driving, I knew how to do.

All the guys were back before I was—in fact, most of them hadn't even left, just turned their backs and peed where they stood. The girls, of course, took longer, and by the time we returned, the guys were gunning to go. I found my pack again—it was the only green-and-orange one—and I kneeled carefully to put it on. I'd managed fine the day before, but this time, with all the boys tapping their watches and shouting, "Come on, ladies!" I must have rushed it a bit. Also, if I'm totally honest, I was so frightened at that moment, so humbled in the face of the four hours of uphill climbing I was about to do, so viscerally terrified at the prospect of the path that literally lay before me, that my whole body, I swear to God, was trembling. So, as I twisted around to hoist my pack up into place, the true weight of the pack hit harder than it had the day before, and my knees buckled under me.

I caught myself, but not before my knee dipped down to slice itself on a rock.

It hurt. I made an "oof" noise, but I slid my pack on anyway and tried to stand at attention. I bit my lip to keep from cursing. Blood ran down my leg. I didn't look, but I could feel the wetness. Oh, well. What would Chuck Norris do? Treat it like a scratch and keep going.

We were lining up to start hiking at last, and I could feel the blood soaking my sock, when Beckett noticed my knee.

"Hold up!" he said. "What the hell happened to you?"

I shook my head. "I'm fine."

"You're not fine," Beckett said, his tone all irritation. "How did you do that to yourself? We haven't even started yet."

"I slipped while putting on my pack."

"Who's got the medical kit?" Beckett called to the group.

"I'm fine, really," I said.

"I've got it," came a voice from behind. Jake's voice.

"Let's just go," I pleaded to Beckett.

"You ignore a cut like that," Beckett said, pointing at me like I was trying to be naughty, "before you know it, you've got an infection so bad you've got to be evacuated by helicopter. Or worse. Packs off, people," he shouted to the group. "We've got an injury."

Some of the guys at the back hadn't realized what was going on. "What?" Mason shouted. "We haven't even started yet!"

Beckett pointed at me. "She slipped putting on her pack!"

I stared at the ground as the guys in the back groaned with irritation.

When I looked up, Jake was in front of me. He was wearing what he'd be wearing every day for the next three weeks: dark green cargo shorts, a rich blue baseball tee with a navy collar, a blue plaid Western overshirt with pearl snaps, that crazy Gilligan hat with the fishing fly, and those heavy-rimmed gray glasses—now secured around the back of his head with a neoprene camo strap.

His eyes were kind. "Take off your pack," he said.

I sat on a nearby rock, and he poured hydrogen peroxide over the cut, whistling at the size of it. As we watched it bubble, he said, "That's pretty deep. Right on the kneecap, too. If we were in town, I'd send you for stitches."

"But we're not."

"No," he agreed. "You'll be okay, though," he said, looking up. "You'll just have a scar. Think of it as a wilderness tattoo."

Here he was again, being nice to me.

Under any other circumstances, we'd be nowhere near each other right now. I'd be off nursing my bruised ego, and he'd be off doing whatever it was he did. Instead, he was kneeling before me, asking me all kinds of questions about my body and touching the skin all around my knee in the most tender way.

I closed my eyes. "Why do you have the medical kit?"

"Because I'm an EMT."

"Of course you are."

His hands seemed awfully steady and sure of themselves. I sat completely rigid while he cut the Band-Aids into shapes and built a little scaffolding to help protect the cut while still allowing my knee to bend.

"Can we go yet?" Mason shouted in our direction.

"In a minute," Jake replied, taking his time. Then, before he helped me up, he pulled out a roll of duct tape from his pack, ripped a piece off with his teeth, and covered the whole bandage with it. "What's that?" I asked.

He frowned to say *duh*. "Duct tape."

At last we set off. I insisted on putting my pack on by myself again—still nervous, but this time distracted by the pain—and when we were all buckled, we started off, single file. I was relieved to get on the trail at last. The trek across this range might turn out to be torture, but at least every step I took was one less that lay ahead of me.

Did I just say I was relieved to get on the trail? That was true. For about ten minutes.

Then, those gross old rented boots started rubbing my feet. In several places. At first, I thought I was imagining it, but after a half hour, it was clearly happening: I was getting blisters. On the first day.

So I ignored them. I didn't want to be that girl who complains and makes everybody wait.

With blisters or without, I was still going to be one of the slowest hikers there. We'd barely started when I lost sight of the person in front of me, and then got passed, one by one, by almost everybody in the group. By the time we took our first break for water and snacks, about two hours in, I could not deny that there were only two girls slower than me. It probably would have been a great time to pull Jake off and surreptitiously tend to my hot spots, but I just didn't want to. Nobody else was getting blisters! As stupid as it was, I ignored them. I couldn't be slow *and* blistered. Slow was bad enough. Beckett lectured us about sticking together on the trail, and how we were only as fast as our weakest links. When he said the words, "weakest links," he pointed right at me and the two girls at the back.

"I know it sucks to go slow," Beckett said to the guys, "and you may feel that these out-of-shape girls are hampering you. But teamwork is a wilderness skill, too. Remember that."

I wanted to believe that Beckett was more clueless than mean. But some of the other boys were both clueless and mean. And juvenile. And asinine. By lunchtime, I knew that guy Mason was going to be trouble, because he constantly picked on everybody and sniffed out weaknesses. When a guy named Ron asked one too many questions about how to read a topographical map, he nicknamed him "Mapron," his own variation on "moron." After Hugh tripped on a branch, Mason made sure to pelt branches at him at every stop, saying "Don't trip!" He'd insulted every girl in the group before lunchtime as well, passing them all one by one as we hiked, and saying, "Move it, heifers. Real hiker coming through." He was a meanness overachiever. It almost made me glad to be way at the back.

The trail had stayed flat-ish for about half a mile, and then, as promised, it started to incline. At first, the angle was like a ramp, but pretty soon, it was more like we were climbing stairs. This was the moment that separated the boys from the girls, which was another clear insult from nature. The shorter girls had shorter legs. We had to take more steps than those tall boys to cover the same distance. The hiking group settled itself into this configuration: tall boys up front, medium-sized people in the middle, short girls at the way back. I'm five foot four, and though I don't think of myself as short, it appeared that the Absarokas definitely did.

"Straighten your leg with each step," Beckett shouted back at us. "Then you're using your bones to support your weight instead of your muscles."

I did as I was told, but I was still out of breath.

The girls behind me didn't mind being last. Their names were Kaylee and Tracy, but they looked so much alike no one could remember who was who. They belonged to the same sorority, it turned out, and so they referred to themselves as Sisters. It was clear within the first hour of hiking what their schtick was: They were girly. They squealed at bugs. They wouldn't sit on mossy logs. They complained loudly about the injustice of being forced to leave all their makeup behind. I couldn't imagine what on earth they were doing here. They were an even worse match for this program than I was.

"I don't care what Beckett says," I overheard one say. "I *will* be washing my hair."

She'd snuck in shampoo, she confessed, despite the fact that on the bus ride out, just that very morning, Beckett had reminded us again that soap of any kind was verboten—and he'd expressly forbidden bathing in streams. Just the bacteria on our bodies, he'd told us in no uncertain terms, was enough to disrupt the ecosystems of the rivers. Shampoo would be lethal to the native algae and bacteria in the waterways, which would then be lethal to the fish that ate those things, and lethal to the birds and predators that fed on the fish—and on up the food chain.

"Seriously," one of the Sisters had said to Beckett during that lecture. "One girl having one shampoo will bring the whole wilderness to its knees?"

"Look at the rest of the world," Beckett said. "What do you think?"

"I think I don't want to smell like a skunk," the Sister said.

"You can wash your body," Beckett said. "You just can't do it in a stream. And you can't use any soap."

Somebody asked, "What do we wash our dishes with if we don't have any soap?"

"Dirt," Beckett answered, and nobody knew if he was joking.

Having to hike at the slow end with these girls was literally adding insult to injury. I'd come here for nature. I'd come here to be transformed. And yet for that whole first day of hiking, I listened to celebrity gossip, tales of intra-sorority injustice, and diet tips. The air was thinner here, up in the mountains, and we were all panting some as we pushed relentlessly uphill. The Sisters were out of breath, too, but they didn't let it stop them. One had just finished an all-grapefruit and laxative cleanse, which had cured her acne but given her a seizure, and the other—I swear I'm not exaggerating—spent a solid hour enumerating the benefits of juicing, and listing every fruit, vegetable, or meat that could be put in a blender for any reason.

It had not occurred to me that there could be something worse than being dead last. But those girls gave dead last a run for its money.

Much to my thighs' relief, we stopped to set up camp midafternoon so Beckett could instruct us in proper tarp-hanging techniques, teach us how to light and use our kerosene stoves, and demonstrate a "bear hang."

"Anybody know what a bear hang is?" Beckett asked.

We'd convened as a group in a clearing full of wildflowers for our first wilderness survival "class." I had my journal out, taking furious notes—my inner A student refusing to accept defeat—but nobody else seemed to be writing.

Mason raised his hand. "You have to hang your food at night between two trees so the bears don't eat it."

"Correct," Beckett said. "And why would that be bad?"

Mason frowned. "'Cause you don't want the bears to get your food, dude."

Hugh added, "And you don't want to give the bears a reason to come to your camp."

"That's right," Beckett said. "We also don't want bears to become dependent on humans for their sustenance." Something about the way he said it made me suspect that he was more concerned for the bears—and fish, and algae—than the humans.

"Who wants to be our first bear hang volunteer?" Beckett asked.

Nobody raised a hand. I looked around and was pleased to see that everybody looked about as dead tired as I felt. Finally, Jake raised his hand. "I'll do it," he said.

"Good man," Beckett said.

After dinner, we combined all our food together in one big nylon bag. Then we followed Beckett and Jake as they scouted a spot.

I'd taken careful notes on the bear hang. It wasn't just enough to hang your food from a branch. Bears were smart enough to figure that out. You had to climb a tree with one end of a rope while another person climbed another tree with the other end, and then tie that rope from tree to tree, attach your food bag to it, and then pull it to the middle point between the two trees. Bears were awesome, but they weren't tightrope walkers.

"Watch," Beckett said, "and pay attention."

It was starting to get dark now. Setting up tarps and cooking dinner had taken us, as Beckett had pointed out, "way too long." As Beckett and Jake started to climb their trees, I wondered about Jake's night vision. But it didn't seem to hold him back. In fact, the bear hang wasn't supposed to be a race, but as Beckett noticed how quickly and easily Jake was pulling himself up, hand-over-hand through the tree branches, Beckett started to do the same. And people were cheering.

Hugh came to stand next to me, and said, "My money's on Jake."

I sighed. "Mine, too."

We both watched, arms crossed, mouths open. I'm not sure if Hugh was marveling at the sight, but I sure was. There really didn't seem to be anything Jake couldn't do.

Jake and Beckett stopped midway up, tied their ropes with special knots around the trees' trunks, and then Beckett attached the food bag with a carabiner to the rope and slid it out to the middle. It slowed at the halfway point, then stopped. Everybody cheered, even me, and then Beckett and Jake shifted into reverse to climb back down.

It hadn't been that dark when they started, but in the twenty minutes that had elapsed, day had tipped over into night. It might have been the darkness. Or maybe it was just bad luck. But somehow, halfway down, Jake missed a branch or lost his footing. There was a fast, unnatural rustle as he dropped the final six or so feet to the ground that made me gasp when I heard it. He landed on his feet, but he held stock-still for a few very long seconds. He was really hurt, I thought.

But, then, he raised his arms over his head in victory and turned to the group, which erupted in cheers. With that one gesture, he rewrote the moment. He hadn't fallen—he had won the race. The nonexistent race. And he wasn't hurt, he was victorious. I stared in awe. Only Jake could make falling out of a tree into something awesome.

That night, I lay my sleeping bag under the tarp next to Windy—and as far away from Mason as I could get.

I was way too tired to change into the T-shirt and shorts that were my designated pj's for the trip, but Beckett had warned us that we absolutely could not sleep in the shirts we'd hiked in that day. They might feel dry now, he said, but they retained sweat and moisture, and if we didn't change into different clothes, we'd shiver all night.

It was my first experience changing clothes while lying down in a sleeping bag, and let's just say that my tired muscles weren't exactly up to it.

"You look like a ferret," Windy said, shining her flashlight on me. "A ferret with convulsions."

"That's about how I feel," I said.

Windy turned on her side to give watching me her full attention. When I finally pulled my clothes from the day out of the bag and tossed them on top of my pack, she said, "So, no book, huh?"

"Kind of regretting that now," I said. "My fantasy of this trip was a little—"

"Off target?"

I nodded. "Yeah."

"I'll let you borrow my book, if you want," Windy said.

"Your textbook?"

"It's very fascinating."

"I'm sure it is," I said, not meaning it.

"It's for my Positive Psychology seminar."

"Are you a psychology major?"

She nodded. "Double, actually—in psych and sociology." Then she looked up and smiled. "I'm going to be a pet psychologist."

I coughed a little. "For real?"

"Actually, a dog psychologist."

"That's a job?"

Windy nodded. "A lucrative one."

"I have a dog," I said.

"Don't tell me," she said, squinting. "A cocker spaniel."

"No," I said.

Windy looked surprised to get it wrong. "A labradoodle?"

I shook my head.

"I'm usually really good at this," she said, squinting again. "Havanese!" she declared at last. "National dog of Cuba."

"Nope."

"I give up."

"A dachshund," I said. "A partly bald, wire-haired dachshund that's fat as a tick and hates everybody, including me."

Windy frowned. "I wouldn't have pegged you for a dachshund person."

"She's an ankle-biter, too," I said. "And she'll eat literally anything.

Toilet paper rolls, sponges, lady products. She's been to the vet for swallowing popsicle sticks, barrettes, Sharpies. She has no sense of self-preservation. And she has a skin disease," I added. "Her tail is all hairless, like a rat. She looks terrible."

"I bet," Windy said.

"I put the medicine on, but she licks it off and then it gives her diarrhea. All over my seagrass rug." I shook my head. "So many other rugs in the house, but she chooses the seagrass."

I shined my flashlight on Windy's face, which was compressed into a sympathetic frown. "Sometimes they have a favorite place to be sick."

"She chews the furniture, the rugs, and the electric cords. She hates all dogs and all humans. She lunges and growls at everybody who comes into my apartment and everybody who walks by. I have to wait to walk her until all the other people and pets have gone to bed. And you have to guard your ankles at all times. She's totally vicious. She's a dog piranha."

"Not good," Windy said.

"I thought getting a dog would get me out more. You know, that I'd visit with the neighbors on walks in the evenings. Go to the dog park. Befriend the world of dog lovers. But, actually, it's the opposite. It's isolating. She's so bloodthirsty, I just have to keep her in all the time—and I feel guilty for going out."

Windy wrinkled her nose. "Not fun."

"She makes my life a living hell," I said. "She's the worst pet in the world."

Windy read my face, and then broke into a smile. "But it's too late now."

"That's right," I said. "It's too late. Because I already love her."

Windy was still smiling as she shook her head. "Isn't love awful?"

I shouldn't have gone on and on like I did—but Windy was such a good listener, asking question after question, that it all came tumbling out. How I'd become obsessed with the idea of getting a dog, and how I'd gone to Petfinder.com every night for months and months, scrolling through the rescue dogs listed there, looking at their pictures, their videos, their personality profiles. I'd wanted something fluffy and adorable and sociable and hypoallergenic, and I'd scoured the poodle mixes ad nauseam. Windy's guesses hadn't been that far off: I bookmarked endless labradoodles, cockapoos, golden doodles, malti-poos, schnoodles. I'd made lists of traits for my ideal dog and done searches by color, fur style, temperament, age, and proximity of foster home to my apartment. I'd danced right up to the edge of getting several different ones—all of them blond and fluffy with bright eyes and little smiley dog mouths.

Finally, one night, I was ready. I'd found the perfect pet. I'd e-mailed one of the rescue groups to make an offer on a smiley yellow pup named Lola, and filled out an application and been accepted, and set a date to go out and meet her later in the week, and I was finally, finally going to take the plunge at last—when somebody abandoned Pickle by tying her to a street post on the sidewalk in front of my building.

The first time I saw her, with that mottled fur and skin tail, I thought she was a possum.

As soon as it was clear she was a dog, it was also clear she'd been abandoned. And mistreated beyond belief. Her fur was matted, her skin was scabbed over, she was covered in fleas. She didn't bark at me—or anyone—that day. All her fight was gone.

I couldn't leave her out there like that. I found a vet clinic with late hours and took her in. It turned out she had a broken leg, too. It was going to be three hundred dollars to fix it.

"What if I can't afford that?" I asked.

The vet looked at Pickle, then back at me. "Then probably the kindest thing would be to put her down."

I paid the three hundred dollars. And with that, she was mine.

As she recovered her strength, she also recovered her abiding hatred for all living creatures. In theory, I admired her moxie, but in practice she was a grade-A pain in the ass.

"It sounds like she's got some post-traumatic stress disorder," Windy said then.

"We're talking about a dog, of course," I pointed out.

"Whoever tied her up to that pole outside your apartment really did a number on her. The defense strategies she developed when her life was unsafe made sense at the time—but now she can't let them go."

"We're going to psychoanalyze my dog?"

"Hello? That's what I do."

"Well," I said, "she's unfixable. I called in a trainer—at seventy bucks an hour—and he gave me a whole program, and I followed it to the letter for months, and it didn't work."

"Did he tell you to become an alpha?"

"Yes."

"And why do you think it didn't work?"

"Because Pickle is the alpha," I said. "She's way meaner than I am."

"Wrong!" Windy said. "It didn't work because he told you to be the wrong kind of alpha."

I couldn't imagine what that meant.

"All popular thinking about dogs is based on wolf packs," Windy said then. "But dogs are not wolves. A wolf is a wild animal. A dog is a domesticated animal. Wolves want to be with other wolves, but dogs want to be with people."

"Not my dog," I said.

Windy went on. "Humans have always hated wolves. Every culture has myths about the Big Bad Wolf, and in every place where humans and wolves have tried to coexist, the wolves have been exterminated."

"Is that true?"

"So how did one of the most hated animal foes of the human race give rise to Man's Best Friend?"

I wasn't sure if it was a rhetorical question. I was about to attempt an answer, when Windy went on: "Dogs evolved from wolves. Wolves hung around the outskirts of human settlements—for the food scraps, mostly. But the ones who were too aggressive got killed. Only the ones who got along with people—who were friendly enough and nonaggressive—survived to reproduce."

"So you're saying it was 'survival of the friendliest'?"

"Exactly! Research backs it up. The leaders of wolf packs may be the most aggressive and dominant, but the leaders of dog packs are invariably the dogs with the most friends." I couldn't help but think of Jake in that moment. Friendly Jake, who had emerged as the clear alpha of our little group, despite all of Beckett's protests.

"Dogs have friends?" I said. My dog certainly didn't have any friends.

"That's what I'm saying," Windy said. "Whatever horrible things happened to Pickle, she's given up on everybody."

I felt tears in my eyes. I knew, of course, that Pickle had been in a bad situation before me, but I'd never tried to imagine *how* bad. What had those former owners done to her?

I said, "So she thinks of all humans as out to get her?"

"Probably."

"I'm not out to get her."

"I think she knows that. Did you say she sleeps with you?"

"It's the only time she's not mad," I said.

"So she must trust you to some degree."

"I rescued her," I said. "Do you think she knows that?"

"She definitely knows."

I felt the need to defend her. "I kind of like her toughness. Nobody messes with her."

"But she's afraid for no reason. Nobody was going to mess with her in the first place. Nowadays, anyway."

"True."

"She's lost the ability to trust."

"So how do I fix her?"

"You're going to have to teach her not to be afraid. You're going to have to convince her that she's safe."

"But how?"

"Well," she said, like she was still thinking, "you're going to have to retrain her neurobiology. Which will take a serious effort for a long time. And it may not work. How old is she?"

"They think she's about three, but they don't know for sure." She looked a thousand.

"It'll be worth it, then."

"Do you think she can be fixed?"

"I think she can be *helped*."

We lay there in silence for a few minutes as an image popped into my head of Pickle hiding behind the toilet, baring her teeth at me as I held out a treat and said, "Come on! Let's retrain your neurobiology!"

Then Windy asked, "Is she your only family?"

"Yes," I said. Then: "No! I have a brother. And a grandmother. And an ex-husband." It seemed like a pretty sad list, even to me. I could have gone on: "And a father, and a stepmother, and two half siblings in California who I never see. And a mother I'm estranged from." Something about Windy made me want to go ahead and say it all—to talk about my parents, and what had happened, and the Tragedy that had spun all our lives off on unexpected, distant, isolated paths.

Windy had such a kind face and such a patient way of listening that I almost just took a deep breath and exhaled the whole story. Almost. But I caught myself. It was far too bleak for a campfire chat.

Who would want to hear a story that sad? I didn't even want to hear it myself.

"And I have lots of friends," I said then, as if I'd never hesitated. "Teacher friends from school. We have a Chick Flick Movie Nite once a month, and we've been learning to crochet."

Windy nodded, like *That's nice.*

"But Pickle," I concluded at last, bringing us full circle, "is by far my closest companion."

Pickle truly had been my friend this year. My mean, irritable, homely dear friend. If she hadn't waddled into my bedroom every night, skinned tail wagging, beady eyes fixed on me until she guilt-tripped me into picking her up and setting her on the bed, I might have collapsed from loneliness. I'd saved her, but she'd saved me right back. Despite all her flaws, Pickle was—in the right context, under the right circumstances, on a quiet night when you were very lucky— surprisingly good at love.

Chapter 9

I woke up sore, and puffy-eyed, and stiff. My thighs hurt. My calves hurt. My back and shoulders hurt. My knee throbbed. I had bruises forming on my hips where the pack belt sat. And the blisters I had ignored the whole day before? Like I'd been splashed with acid.

I hobbled over to Jake's camp in my flip-flops—pausing only to throw on my fleece jacket. I showed up while his group was cooking breakfast, and he was pouring everybody coffee through a strainer.

He glanced up as I approached, and I felt this crazy jolt inside my rib cage at the eye contact. I don't know if he felt it too, but he looked back down fast, and didn't look up again until he was done pouring. He took his time, and I had no choice but to notice the beginnings of a beard on his face and neck. No razors. All the guys would end up with beards, Beckett had told us. I'd always been a fan of the five-o'clock shadow. And Saturday morning stubble. It made men look rugged, somehow. It made Jake look older and more mature—more like somebody I could be infatuated with.

I bent forward to massage that thought out of my head.

That's when he turned to me. "Altitude headache?"

I looked up. "Actually," I said, realizing I did have a slight one, "yes."

He nodded, stepping toward me, all EMT business. "Extra water today. If it gets worse, you can have Tylenol."

"Okay."

He started to turn back, like we were done.

"Um," I said then. "Also? Could you help me with my bandage?"

As his tent group looked on, he squinted in apology. "I'm sorry. I forgot your name."

I gave him a look. "Helen," I said.

"Ellen?"

I flared my nostrils. "Helen," I said. "With an 'H.'"

"Right," he said. "Sorry. Well, let's grab the first-aid kit, Helen-with-an-H. I'm Jake, again, by the way. Coffee?" He held out the pot, as if I might slurp directly from it.

"No, thank you." I wanted to repeat his name wrong, too, but there's not really another name that sounds like Jake. What would I say? *Rake? Flake?*

I put my hands in my pockets and took the high road. "Thank you for your help, Jake."

He led me over to a fallen log so I could sit.

This was something I'd already noticed about the wilderness: the fallen tree trunks everywhere. It was the life cycle of a tree, of course—to grow, live, die, and fall—but you never saw anything like that in the city. Dead trees were cut down and removed precisely so they didn't fall. Here, still-standing dead trees were called "widow-makers." "Don't set up camp within reach of a widow-maker," Beckett had said the night before. "One good gust of wind, and that thing's going down."

He wasn't exaggerating. There was evidence of it all around—dead logs everywhere, especially lying across our trails. At first, I'd found it a great pleasure to step on them—willing to go to the trouble of climbing up so that I could enjoy literally one second of the relief of going back down. Stepping on those trees had been my favorite part of hiking that first day, until Beckett called me out at a rest stop. "You guys haven't seen Ellen doing this," he'd started off, pointing at me to make sure everybody knew who he was talking about, "because she's all the way at the back. But she's been stepping on the logs that lie across the path."

"It's Helen," I corrected. "With an H."

But he was making his point. "Who wants to tell her why she can't do that?"

Jake shouted out the answer. "Some of them are rotten," he said, meeting my eyes. "They can't support your weight. Your foot will crash right through."

"That's right," Beckett said. "That's a broken leg and an emergency evacuation, right there."

"Sorry," I said, shrugging.

Beckett pointed at me. "Don't do it again."

"I won't," I said, pouting like a naughty child, and not saying what I wanted to: This is exactly the type of information I would've wanted *before* we set out into the wilderness.

So, this morning, as Jake gestured at the dead log, I hesitated.

He knew what I was thinking. "You can sit on it," he said. "Your butt is much, much wider than your foot—"

"Thank you," I said.

"So it distributes the weight more evenly. Plus you don't have your pack on, so you weigh less right now."

I sat. And I didn't crash through.

"And anyway," he went on, "you can't really break your butt."

"Just watch me," I said.

He turned to the medical kit, and I couldn't tell if he was stifling a smile.

He pulled off the old bandage on my knee and examined the cut. The scab was about an inch long, and so dark it was almost black. The skin around it looked bruised now, too.

"It looks worse," I said.

"No, it's good," he said. "That's a great scab."

"A *great* scab?"

"And the bruising's to be expected. I don't see any signs of infection. Nice job."

"You're the one who bandaged me."

"I was talking to myself," he said.

"I have to confess something else to you," I said then. "I may have some blisters."

"Actual blisters?" Jake asked.

I nodded.

"That can't be right," Jake said. "I saw you taking notes during Beckett's Beware of Blisters lecture on the bus."

I nodded. I knew how we were supposed to handle blisters. I gave a little shrug.

"Okay," Jake said, looking down. "Show me."

I stuck out my feet for him to examine a total of four red, bloody, pissed-off-looking welts—two on each foot.

Jake let out a whistle.

When he looked up, he was dead serious. "Why didn't you tell me about these?"

"I didn't want to stop the group again."

"During a rest break?"

I just shrugged.

"I know we're strangers," he said. "But you have to let me help you."

I gave a little salute of capitulation, and waited while he worked on the blisters in the same tender way as the cut. Except this time, he lifted both my feet up and laid them across his thighs for a work surface.

That's when I noticed he was in a short-sleeve T-shirt. "Aren't you cold?" I asked then. The temp was in the fifties. Why wasn't he wearing a jacket?

"Yep," he said, pouring hydrogen peroxide over the spots.

"Why don't you have your jacket on?"

"You showed up before I had a chance to get dressed."

"So it's my fault?"

"No, I—" He paused to unwrap a pack of moleskin. "I just didn't want to make you wait."

"Go get your jacket!"

"I'm almost done."

"You literally have goose bumps." As I looked him over for confirmation, I saw a dark red scrape and a bruise under his arm.

"What happened to your arm?" I asked, but as I said the words, I knew. "That's from yesterday!"

"I'm fine," he said, still working on my blisters, not looking up.

"I knew it!" I said. "I knew it hurt when you fell out of that tree."

"I didn't fall. I scrambled down fast."

"So fast that you fell."

He sucked in his bottom lip for a second. "Fine. I fell."

"Can I take a look at your arm?"

"No."

"But it might need some—"

"Some what? It's just a bruise." He was done with the bandages. I took my feet back and slipped them into my flip-flops.

"You can give me hell for a couple of blisters, but I can't say anything when you fall out of a tree?"

"Pretty much."

"Was it too dark for you?" I asked then.

"What? No!"

"I mean, like the night blindness. I worried about that when you were climbing. That you might miss a branch or something. Is that what happened? You didn't see the branch?"

He stared at me while I talked, suddenly concentrating hard. Then he leaned in closer, and said, "I just slipped. That's all." Then he looked right into my eyes. "Please don't mention the night blindness to anyone. Okay?"

"Okay," I said. "Why not?"

"Because we're strangers," he said. "So there's no way you could possibly know."

I nodded. "Good point."

"And also," he added, "because I didn't exactly pass the medical."

"What?"

He shrugged.

"How can you be here if you didn't pass the medical?"

"I have a friend in med school who faked my report."

I didn't know what to say. I shook my head. "Why?"

He shrugged again. "So I could come on the trip."

"But it's dangerous!"

"Crossing the street is dangerous. Going swimming is dangerous. Eating a hamburger is dangerous."

"Not the same!"

He lowered his voice to a whisper. "We don't hike at night. I'll be fine."

There was no way I'd confess to the shiver of anxiety I felt right then at the prospect of him not being fine. But I did feel it. Maybe we were strangers now. Maybe he'd ruined my trip in ten different ways.

But the fact remained whether I liked it or not: He was my favorite person here.

I shook my head at him. "What were you thinking?" I whispered back.

He looked down then, and said in a voice I could barely hear, "I just really needed to come out here and do this."

And how could I argue with that?

Jake forced me to take off my boots and let him check the blister bandages at every stop. When Beckett saw the state of things with my feet, he said, "You have got to be kidding me. Weren't you paying attention during Beware of Blisters?"

"She wasn't just paying attention," Jake said, readjusting the bandages. "She was *taking notes.*"

Beckett looked flattered. "You took notes?"

I nodded.

"So how did you let yourself get like this?"

I took a breath. "I just felt I'd delayed the group one too many times yesterday."

Beckett nodded. "Well, that's certainly true." He watched Jake working on my feet for a minute, before calling everybody over to make an example of me. Again. "Listen up, people. This is what happens when you ignore my instructions. Ellen's got four blisters—ugly mofos—on her feet from one day of hiking."

"It's Helen, actually," I corrected again. "With an H."

Beckett squinted at me like I was trying to pull a fast one. "Helen?"

Then Hugh shouted, from off to the side, "With an H!"

I nodded to confirm.

"Okay," Beckett went on. "Do not be a *Helen.* If you feel a hot spot—like I explained in detail on the bus yesterday—deal with it. Right away."

Looking back, I often think this was the moment that crystallized me into Beckett's What Not to Do Girl, though it might have started earlier. From that point on, I became Beckett's go-to example for doing things wrong, and over the following week alone, he'd point out my hiking stride, the placement of the pack on my hips, the amount of water I drank during rest stops, my knot-tying, my cooking, my attitude, my sense of humor, and my understanding of the basic physics of the natural world as being wrong, wrong, wrong. I had nightmares that started with the phrase, "Okay, people, gather round," and ended with, "Don't be a Helen." He had my name right at last, but he was using it all wrong.

At one point, after a particularly humiliating teachable moment, I approached Beckett and said, "You know, I do a lot better when people point out the things I'm doing *right*."

"Do something right," he said then, "and I will."

The best thing about that first week on the trail was Windy. After our Pickle conversation that first night, she started seeking me out. She even took to falling back to hike with me, which was truly remarkable because she could have left every single person in our hiking group for dead. She was that good.

The first time I looked up from the trail to see her hiking right in front of me, I couldn't imagine what she was doing there.

"Why are you back here?" I asked. "You should be up front."

"With Mason and his minions?" she said. "No, thanks."

I was kind of predisposed not to like Windy because she was so very perfect, and there's always something so exhausting about perfect people. She was long and lean without an ounce of cellulite anywhere—that ideal adolescent-boy-with-boobs look that girls are always striving for. She never seemed overwhelmed or anxious. She took everything in stride—as I supposed I might have if I were that pretty, that fit, and that pleasant. She had Marcia Brady–style long hair: classic, flax-colored, and so long she could literally tie it in a knot. My own hair just got frizzier and more dreadlocked as the days passed. But Windy stayed chic with her nape-of-the-neck, hand-tied chignon, seeming only to get more and more lovely as the rest of us devolved into filth.

She was the only person on this trip who'd been nice to me consistently, and I felt grateful enough when she hung back to hike with me that the little hitch of shyness I often felt around new people kicked in. We walked in silence for a good while as I got more and more nervous that she was going to get bored and return to the front. Then I called up the advice that Grandma GiGi always gave me for meeting new people: Ask them about themselves.

"Ask them what?" I once asked.

GiGi had shrugged. "Where they're from, what they do for fun, hobbies, favorite books, favorite actors, pets. Anything. Everything."

"Isn't that kind of nosy?" I'd asked.

She shook her head. "People are always their own favorite topics," she said. "It's the only thing they're experts on."

It was great advice and it always worked. When I remembered to use it. More often than not, though, I forgot. Being nervous made my brain go blank. But this time, like magic, I remembered.

"Hey," I called up to her. "Tell me about being a pet psychologist."

"An *aspiring* pet psychologist."

"Do you need a degree for that?" I asked.

"If you want to be really good at it, you do."

"Do you want to be really good at it?"

"Of course," she said. "I want to be really good at everything."

As I walked behind her, watching her calf muscles flex and release, I decided they were just exactly the perfect human shape for calves—and for legs in general, really. I felt an impulse to tell her how much I admired them. After all, if someone were admiring me, I'd want to know. But I couldn't figure out how to bring it up. What would I say? "Great gams, by the way"? It might have pleased her, but it might just as easily have creeped her out.

"Tell me about your summer reading," I called up from behind.

"It's for this class I'm taking on the positive psychology movement."

"What's that?"

"It's the study of happiness."

"They teach that in college?"

"They do," she said. "Psychology always used to focus on problems. You know: neuroses, pathologies, disorders. The idea was to analyze the effed-up parts of human life so you could cure them."

"Sure," I said. "I get that."

"But there's this new theory that we should look at what people do right. Figure out how happy, well-adjusted people do things."

"That's what your textbook is about?"

She nodded. "The question is, what are they doing right?"

"What *are* they doing right?" Suddenly, I really wanted to know.

"Lots of things. That's why it takes a whole textbook."

"Okay. For example?"

"Well, for example, happy people are more likely to register joy than unhappy people. So if you take two people who have experienced a day of, say, fifty percent good things and fifty percent bad things, an unhappy person would remember more of the bad."

"Kind of that glass-half-empty thing."

"But it's not just attitude. It's genuinely connected to memory. It's like, for unhappy people, if you ask them at the end of the day what they remember, it's the bad stuff. But they aren't ignoring the good memories, they just didn't retain them."

"Is that brain wiring?" I asked, trying to figure out which type I was.

"It is brain wiring," Windy said. "But brain wiring appears to be something you can alter. They've done these experiments where they have people practice remembering the good stuff. And guess what? It works."

I thought about that.

"The more you register good things," she went on, "the more you will think about and remember good things. And since all you really have left of the past is what you remember—"

"It changes the story of your life."

Windy turned around to nod. "Exactly. Every night, you write down three good things that happened to you that day."

"And *presto*? You're happy?"

"Kind of," Windy said. "Like, what are three good things that have happened to you today?"

"I don't think I can come up with three."

"Maybe you just don't remember them."

"Oh," I said. "I think they'd stand out."

"Try. It doesn't have to be winning the lottery. Just little things. A moment you enjoyed. A gentle breeze that felt good."

I thought for a long time. It wasn't until Windy said, "Hello? You still back there?" that something hit me. "I was glad that you came back to hike with me," I said.

"See! That's good! One down!"

"The oatmeal this morning was slightly less rubbery than the oatmeal yesterday."

"That one's less good," Windy said. "Dig deep!"

I sighed. "Okay," I said. And then, like the lights had just flipped on, I suddenly thought of something real. "I love that feeling, first thing in the morning, when you're still in your sleeping bag and your body's toasty warm but your face is cold from the night mountain air."

"Genius!" Windy said. "You're a natural."

"What about you?" I asked. "What good things will you remember about this day?"

"So far?" she asked. "The cowboy coffee we boiled on the stove. The sound of the wind rustling those pine branches overhead. The mossy smell of the woods. A little forget-me-not that was growing on the stream bank. That good, snug feeling when you settle your pack on your back and snap the hip belt. The crisp feeling in the air. The sound of the stream. The heart-shaped stone I found this morning near our tarp. The burn in my muscles as we go uphill. The quiet pat-pat noise our boots make on the trail. That crazy red bird that flew past a few minutes ago."

"You're too good," I said. "You're freaking me out."

"I've just had more practice," she said. "You can be just like me."

"Probably not *just* like you," I said. I was fairly certain, at this point, I was stuck being me.

"I told myself before this trip that I would appreciate everything," she said. "It's my battle cry: *Appreciate Everything.*"

I wondered what my battle cry would be right now. *Ask Me if I Care? Leave Me Alone? Talk to the Fist?* "I want a battle cry," I said.

"I'll share mine with you, if you like."

"I'm going to try for an original," I said, "but thanks."

"There's another good thing that I'm going to remember about this day," Windy said then.

"What?"

Windy paused for a second. "The amazing, delicious, all-consuming crush I've got." She turned around to wiggle her eyebrows at me without missing a step.

"You have a crush?" I said. "Already? We only just got here."

"It was an obsession-at-first-sight kind of thing," she said.

"Who?" I asked.

"Can't you guess?"

I could, actually. I knew exactly who any—and possibly *every*—girl on this trip would get a crush on. But I held out hope that I was wrong. "Beckett!" I said.

"Ick! No!"

"Not Mason, or any of his minions."

"Not Mason or the minions."

"Hugh?" I asked hopefully.

"I think he might be g-a-y," she said, in a stage whisper, although there was enough space between us and everyone else that nobody would have heard her, anyway.

"Well," I said, wishing there were some way to *eject* from this conversation. "I can't think of anybody else."

"Seriously? You can't?"

I pretended to think about it. "Nope."

She slowed down to let me catch up side by side, and then she leaned in, still hiking, and whispered, "Jake."

"Who's that?" I said, feeling transparent even as I did.

"You know Jake! He's the EMT. He fixed your knee! And your blisters!"

"Oh!" I said. "I thought his name was Jack."

"Isn't he dreamy?" she said, letting me fall behind her again.

"I don't know," I said. "I guess."

"He's the cutest guy here!" she said, daring me to challenge her.

"If you say so."

"Can you think of anybody cuter?"

I shook my head. "They all just look like second graders to me."

"Can I tell you about the moment we met?"

"Um. Okay."

"I was climbing the stairs that first day at the lodge, and I dropped my duffel bag. It rolled down the stairs, and when I started to go after it, there he was. He'd *caught* it. And he brought it up to me. As he handed it over, I thought, 'This is the man I'm going to marry.'"

Holy hell.

"You know what I mean?" she went on. "When you see someone, and you just *know* you love them?"

"I don't think that's how it works," I said, trying to be the voice of reason. "I think love has to grow out of knowing someone really well. It takes time."

"Not for me," Windy said.

"I think what you're talking about is infatuation," I said.

"Did you know that he can juggle? And swing dance? And do a Scottish accent?"

"He told you all that on the steps?"

"No. On the bus."

"That's right."

"I got a lot out of him during Truth or Dare. He kept trying for Truth. But we forced him into Dares."

"What kind of Dares?"

"Daring ones." She turned around and did the eyebrows again. "It kind of turned into a feeding frenzy."

A feeding frenzy? What were they feeding on? "What happened?"

"I'm sworn to secrecy," she said. "Sorry. What happens on the roof stays on the roof."

What?! I wanted to shout. *What happened on the roof?*

Windy walked on a minute, no doubt enjoying the pleasant tap of her boots striking the trail.

Then I said, "I still don't think you can love that guy Jack if you've only known him two days."

"Jake."

"Whatever. It takes more than a game of Truth or Dare to spark real love," I said. "No matter what happened on the roof."

Windy turned around and gave me the most blissed-out grin I'd ever seen. "You only think that," she said, "because you weren't there."

Chapter 10

As the week wore on, we got our sea legs. We got used to the weight of our packs, and the dehydrated food, and the pinecones. We adjusted to the altitude and got better at breathing. We crossed our first icy river, and saw a moose across a valley. The men grew beards and the women grew out their leg hair. We had classes most nights after dinner—on the constellations, on map-reading skills, on how to, say, identify the differences between the tracks of black bears and those of grizzlies. We climbed our first pass, one called "U-Turn" because, apparently, it was common for hikers to arrive, glimpse the terrain ahead, and turn around.

But not us. We were building momentum. We were getting into it.

I also found a solution to my didn't-bring-a-book problem. Beckett had the official BCSC handbook in his pack, and he let me borrow it. I read it cover to cover in two days. Then I read it again. Then I went back and took notes. It had a whole section on Certificates, and how to earn them. It felt a little bit like cheating to read the list, but Beckett insisted that anybody was free to read it—just nobody else had asked. I found the book comforting. It made it seem like earning a

Certificate wouldn't be impossible. The handbook stressed that it wasn't necessarily the toughest people who earned them—or the fastest—but the people who tried the hardest. And that was something I knew I could do. Trying, I was good at. Even if succeeding was a different story.

We fell into a daily rhythm: wake up at six, get dressed, make breakfast, meet to plan the day, strike camp, and head out by nine. No lunch—we just noshed on trail food along the way. Hike until around two or three in the afternoon, stop, and set up camp again in the late afternoon. We always camped near water. It was the one thing we couldn't do without. Then, dinner by five, and bed by seven, and nobody even thought about staying up late. We were exhausted by bedtime. Nine P.M. was "hiker midnight."

My cut and blisters healed up nicely, thanks to Jake's bossy attention. Beckett continued to use me as his prime example of what *not* to do. I thought I could build up a tolerance to it, but I never did. There were so many other people doing things wrong, but he never called them out. Just me. My posture was too stiff. My sunglasses weren't UV protected. My personal items were stowed incorrectly.

Aside from me, the group was bonding. Somehow, in such a short time, most people had acquired nicknames. Apparently, every guy in the group had a thing for Windy, and so she had become "Heartbreaker," or "HB" for short. There were even "Heartbreaker points." If she sat next to you, it was twenty points. If she talked to you, it was fifty points. If you managed to get a glimpse of some high-value body part, it was a hundred points. Everybody knew about it. The boys called the points out! If Windy tripped, for example, and stumbled into one of them, he'd shout, "Body contact! A thousand points!"

Windy thought it was mildly funny, but she didn't seem to notice it much. I guess she was used to that kind of thing by now, after a lifetime of being amazing.

But even less amazing people wound up with nicknames. They evolved quickly and easily. The Sisters became "Sister One" and "Sister Two," which turned into "Uno" and "Dosie." The girl in the shorts with *Go Gators!* appliquéd over the butt had earned herself the nickname "Caboose," and the best chef in the whole group had become "Cookie." As for the boys, Mason, who had never learned how to slow down and hike with the rest of us, became "Flash," as in "Wait up, Flash!" And the big guys had become "Hound Dog," "Caveman," and "Vegas." Even Hugh, who never talked—except to me—had become "Huey Lewis."

In fact, everybody had a nickname. Every single person. Except me. I was just Helen—or, just as often, "Ellen."

A good nickname should say something about who you are. It hints at something profound. Or maybe it's just funny. But it's meaningful, no matter what. It shows that you are *known*, that you have an identity other people recognize. But not me, apparently. I had the opposite of a nickname. They couldn't even get my actual name right. It made me mad to think about it. I could have been snatched up by a hawk and carried away and nobody would have noticed.

It was the kind of thing I could really stew about. We had three uneventful days of hiking after I noticed the nickname situation, and I could easily have fixated on it every step of the route. But I kept thinking about what Windy had said. "The things you think about determine the things you think about"—meaning the more you focus on something, the more likely your brain is to focus on it.

So I made a choice not to focus on it, and to work, instead, on appreciating all the wonders the wilderness had to offer. Like the hidden waterfall we came across. And the elk scat we saw near the stream. And the salmon that flipped itself up out of a creek before disappearing back into the water. And the crazy sunset where we'd counted eight different colors. And the fact that my face had finally become so dirty that it didn't feel dirty anymore.

Despite everything, and even though it wasn't perfect, I was really starting to feel at home in the wilderness. In my lopsided way. And I also got the hang of pretending Jake wasn't there. Except, of course, for the time I tripped sideways over a fallen branch walking back up a creek bed one night after dinner. The incline was so steep that I knew that if I didn't catch myself, there'd be no way to stop myself tumbling all the way to the bottom, smacking my head on bread-loaf-sized rock after rock. I'd land in a mangled pulp and have no choice but to die.

But I didn't fall, and I didn't die, because an arm reached out, cinched my waist, and pulled me back, and when I angled around to gush thanks at whoever had saved me, it turned out to be Jake.

His face was all irritation. "Dammit, Helen—be careful! Could you try not to kill yourself for five straight minutes?" He let go so sharply it felt like a push.

Where was all that anger coming from? Aren't you supposed to be nice to someone who almost just died? I straightened up to regain my balance. "I was being careful," I insisted. I could still feel the memory of his arm around my middle.

He turned away. "No you weren't."

"Yes I was."

"No," he turned back. "And every time you do something stupid, I have to save you."

"So don't save me!" I said, angry now, too, just because he was. But he had already started walking away.

That stopped him, and he turned back around with a glare.

I stood my ground. "You don't have to save me."

But he just shook his head, and took in the sight of me head to toe for a long minute before saying, "Yes, I really do," and then walking away.

✳

One night, after a post-supper Basic First Aid class, Beckett made an announcement.

"I'm kind of going off-book here," he said. "But I'm breaking us up tomorrow."

Everybody looked around. What did that mean?

I'd just spent the last half hour taking first-aid notes on every injury or disaster that could befall us—from broken legs with bones sticking out to icy river drownings, so I guess my head was primed to worry, but something about Beckett leaving us to hike alone didn't sit right with me. There certainly wasn't anything about splitting up for day hikes in the manual I'd memorized. Not, at least, until the very end.

But Beckett was insistent. We needed a change. "You guys follow me like ducklings. You all suck at map skills. You'll never master them before the Solos unless you get some practice."

The Solos were the grand finale of the trip—the big event that would test our abilities to use everything we'd just learned. During the Solos, we'd go out for an overnight in groups of four with nothing to protect us but our new skills. Beckett used the idea of "the Solos" quite often to scare us into paying attention. It worked.

"So," he said. "Tomorrow, we'll split up. We're hiking the same trail, but leaving thirty minutes apart, so you're not just mindlessly following me." In truth, we were mindlessly following *Jake*. But nobody pointed that out to Beckett.

"Are we hiking in our tent groups?" I asked.

"Good question, Ellen. No. I will put the fastest four together"—here, Beckett gestured at the four tallest guys—"and then the next four"—he gestured at a group that included both Windy and Jake—"and then the next four"—me, the Sisters, and Hugh. "Fastest group first, slowest group last, so there's no traffic jam."

"Who are you hiking with?" Mason asked.

"I might take a day with the guys up front."

Something about it seemed fishy to me. I couldn't shake the feeling that Beckett was tired of going slow and just wanted a day when he could fly along the trail with the fast guys. But he showed us the route, and it didn't look too confusing. He was right that nobody had been working very hard on map skills. Beckett had held three Mad Maps sessions, and people kept dozing off, reading their books hidden behind daypacks, and asking to go to the bathroom. I, myself, paid attention and took copious notes—partly because I didn't know how to take a class and not lean forward in the front row like a Type-A nut job, but also because I found I liked looking at contour maps. Everybody else seemed to see squiggly lines and patches of color. But I for some reason looked down and saw it all in 3-D. It was, without a doubt, the only thing in the course that came naturally to me. That said, I didn't make a big deal of it. It was too easy to just follow along in line like everybody else.

That night, in my sleeping bag, waiting to fall asleep, the prospect of Beckett leaving us behind for a whole day to hike with the fast guys pricked a feeling of alarm in my chest. I had a knack for reading maps, yes—but I hadn't actually used them in the real wilderness. Disaster scenarios ran through my head like they were on a loop. But I talked myself out of worrying. After all, it was hiking three simple miles—on a trail, in a fairly straight line, on flat terrain. How hard could that be?

The next morning, before he headed out with the first group, Beckett spotted a piece of litter.

"Hold up, guys," he said, raising his palms in a "halt" gesture.

He crossed the campsite and squatted to examine it.

"Seriously folks?" he said. "Litter?"

He slid off his pack in one smooth motion, keeping his eyes on the white square. Then reached out, picked it up, and held it in a pinch like it was a dead thing.

All our eyes drifted to the white square. It did seem jarringly out of place with its surroundings, I thought, and just on the heels of that thought, I had another: That litter was mine. It was the list of goals I'd been carrying around in my bra.

"Beckett—" I said, starting toward him.

"How many times have we talked about respecting nature? How many times have we talked about leaving no trace? And yet, you people leave a constant trail of detritus behind you like you haven't heard a word I've said."

He unfolded the paper.

I was about to say that it was mine—that I hadn't *littered*, I had just *lost* it.

But before I could say anything, he started reading the list. Out loud. "*To gasp at the raw power and beauty of nature. To fall to my knees in awe of the magic of the world. To become a part of something so much larger than myself.*" The big guys did some laughing and some snorting. But Beckett was dead serious. "Does somebody want to claim this?"

I held perfectly still. Not anymore, I didn't. I gave silent thanks that I'd had the good sense to cut my name off the top long before this journey even started.

"What do I keep telling you guys? What did I say on the very first day?"

Mason was enjoying this. "Littering will not be tolerated."

"What else did I say? In our very first lecture on protecting Mother Nature? What did I tell you would happen if I saw you guys littering?"

Everybody looked around. Finally, Dosie gave it a go. "You would go insane?"

"That's right! That's exactly what I said. *If you want to see me go insane, throw a piece of litter on the ground.*" He pulled out the propane lighter we used for the cookstoves. "Well, I guess you wanted to see me go insane. And that's fine! You asked for it, you got it."

He held up the lighter in one hand, and my list of self-improvements in the other. He clicked the flame on. "Anybody want to claim it now?"

Nope.

And without speaking another word, he lit it on fire.

We stared at the flame. Beckett let it burn down almost to his fingers, then he dropped it, stamped out the fire with his boot, picked up the remaining corner of paper, and stuck it in his pocket.

"The world is not your garbage dump, people," Beckett said. He looked around. We all just stared at him like he was completely bananas.

"Do it again," he said, "and I will scorch the earth." Then he whistled for the first group of hikers like a pack of dogs and led them off down the trail.

It wasn't until after they were out of sight that the rest of us let out a long, collective breath. Hugh came over to stand next to me, and we watched them hike away. "Scorching the earth sounds counterproductive," he said.

I smiled at him.

"I love when he sets things on fire," Hugh said. "It's totally hot."

I gave a little laugh. "Literally."

Hugh decided he was going to go "find the bathroom" before we set off, and he left me kicking at the pile of ashes.

A few minutes later, Jake came up.

"He is actually crazy, that guy Beckett," Jake said.

I shrugged.

"That was your list, wasn't it? The one you kept in your bra?"

How did he know that? I just shrugged. "Time for a new list, any-way."

"Is it?" he asked.

I looked up. "Windy's been teaching me how to be happy."

That caught his interest. "She is?"

"Apparently, there's a lot of list-making involved."

"She's something, isn't she?"

"Oh, man," I said. "I just love her."

Jake nodded. "Anyway, I brought you a present. To replace your lost list." He held out a folded piece of paper.

"What is it?"

"It's a poem."

"You wrote a poem?"

"No. It's Pablo Neruda. My favorite poem by my favorite poet."

"You had it in your pack?"

He shook his head with a little half smile. "I keep it in my pocket. Though I'd keep it in my bra if I had one."

"You don't want it anymore?"

"I want you to have it. On one condition."

"What's that?"

"That you don't read it."

I frowned. "I can only have it if I don't read it?"

"It's private. Between Pablo and me."

"What good is a gift-poem if I can't read it?"

Jake shrugged and held out the piece of paper. "Wouldn't want that bra of yours to be empty."

Again with the flirting.

"Promise you won't read it," he said, "and it's yours."

"I won't read it." In truth, I didn't even want it, but I was too sur-prised by the turn of events to marshal a protest. What did it mean for a boy to give you a poem you weren't allowed to read? I had no idea.

He started to walk away. "Anyway. Sometimes it's just nice to have something to hold on to."

"What are you going to hold on to?" I called after him.

But he just shrugged. "I'll think of something."

I missed Windy immediately. Hugh had become a pal of mine, but he wasn't much of a talker. All attempts at conversation fizzled, despite my efforts. It left me with no escape from Uno and Dosie as they prattled on and on, like a talk show I couldn't turn off. They sang pop songs; they fantasized about shampoos and facial scrub; they debated endlessly about whether or not they were skinnier now; and they gossiped about everybody in our hiking group.

As we walked, Hugh fell in with the girls' gossip, eventually taking the lead up front, and I fell to my old standby position of dead last.

To give them credit, I did learn a lot that morning. Mostly about the boys. Beckett had been recently dumped, as had Mason, but all the other guys were off the market, including Hugh, who they were sure was gay. "You're gay, right?" one of the girls called up to Hugh.

"Yep," he called back, without missing a step. "But single."

"So, on the market—" Dosie said.

"Just not *our* market," Uno finished.

It was decided that Mason was too juvenile, and Beckett was too crazy. So that left them in the unthinkable situation of having no romantic prospects. They lamented this at great length, revisiting the possibility of Mason over and over, since he was, after all, handsome. If only he'd turn around that backward baseball cap.

I was just wondering about Jake, and why he was on the unavailable list, when Hugh piped up. "What about J-Dog? He's not seeing anyone."

The girls let out long sighs. "It's tragic," Dosie said.

My ears perked up. What was tragic? Had he revealed something during Truth or Dare? Did these girls know something about Jake that I didn't?

Hugh didn't hold back. "What's tragic?"

"Well," Dosie said, "he is the best kisser in this entire group—"

"Amen to that," said Uno.

Had they *all* kissed him? What the hell had happened on that roof?

"But he's taken."

Taken?

"Taken?" Hugh asked.

My breathing deepened. What had he told them? Had he told them he was taken so they would lay off? Was he just saying that because he'd sworn off women, or whatever his deal was? Or did he actually think of himself as taken? Because—and here was the first time I'd admitted this, even to myself—*I* felt taken. By Jake. Even after all these ridiculous Being Strangers shenanigans. Even though I'd basically spent the past week fully ignoring him. Even though it was now looking like he was some kind of Truth or Dare kissing maniac. There wasn't any way around it.

This was not what I'd come here for. I was not here to get wrapped up in some teenage-style romance. I was here for the power and beauty of nature. I was here to connect with something larger than myself. I was here for transformation, dammit! Toughness! Fierceness! Strength! But who was I kidding? Those things weren't on offer here, anyway. That wasn't to disparage the wilderness, which was truly awe-inspiring—but it *was* to disparage everything else about this shallow, juvenile, mean-spirited, show-offy, deeply disappointing trip.

Had Jake said he was taken? Was he still flashing back to that night in the hotel as often as I was? I was dreaming about it, both awake and asleep. The memory of it had lodged in some central hub of my brain, so that almost everything I thought about sparked some association of that night with him. Brushing my teeth reminded me of how I'd brushed my teeth at the hotel with Jake. Going to sleep reminded me of going to sleep at the hotel across from Jake. Seeing people with books reminded me of the book Jake had been reading when I walked over to proposition him. And on and on. I couldn't escape it. And maybe that wasn't even a bad thing.

My heart gave a little shimmy at the thought of it. I didn't have to turn into Chuck Norris. Or Pickle. I could meet Windy the aspiring dog psychologist and learn how to be happy, instead. Maybe, just maybe, I'd let Jake go ahead and join me.

But the girls were still talking. "Taken," they confirmed in unison.

"Who is he taken by?" Hugh wanted to know.

For a second there, I really did expect them to say something like, "Oh, some mystery woman back at home. He's been in love with her for ages." I was gearing up for a poker face, ready to deny all, when Dosie said, "Windy. Of course."

"He's taken with Windy?" I said.

"She's liked him this whole time, and now he likes her back."

"How do you know that?" I asked.

"We have our methods."

I was ready to argue with them, but then Hugh jumped in with, "Perfect. They're perfect for each other."

"Perfect seems a bit strong," I said.

Hugh lifted his eyebrows. "He's articulate, and so is she. He's handsome in that all-American way, and she's—well, let's face it, she's *gorgeous*. Sorry, ladies. You really couldn't invent a better couple.

They're both lean, and tan, and thoughtful. They have great calves. Great teeth. And he's got that *jawline*. Do not get me started on the jawline."

So it hit me: It wasn't that Hugh was quiet, exactly. We just hadn't stumbled on a topic he liked. Until now.

"They both love sailing," Uno piped up.

"And they both have family summer homes in Maine."

"And they both like sheepdogs."

"And waffle fries."

"And neither one likes French food."

"And they're our two best bear-hangers."

"Wow," I said then. "The two best bear-hangers! Why aren't they married already?"

"Good question," Hugh said. "We'll have to check in about that tonight."

Actually, we would not check in about it that night. Because, as we walked along, Hugh did something he wasn't supposed to. Something *none of us* were supposed to. Maybe he was distracted. Maybe he forgot. Maybe Beckett had given us so many warnings about so many catastrophic things that he'd begun to seem like he was crying wolf. Whatever the reason, the fact remained: Hugh was stepping on tree trunks. And as Beckett had warned us, if you stepped on enough of them, one was bound to be rotten.

We'd come to a section of the trail that was lousy with fallen trees across the path. It was a sunnier, thinned-out patch of forest, too, as if something—a flood, maybe, or a drought—had hit this spot hard, and now the bodies of the trees that had succumbed still lay where they fell.

At the back of the line, I wondered what had killed them all.

But Hugh and the Sisters didn't notice. They were planning Jake and Windy's boho-style wilderness wedding, swooning over every mental picture.

"He'd be so handsome in a tux," Uno said.

"He won't wear a tux," Hugh declared, stepping up on a trunk and then back down.

"Not like an Al's Formal Wear tux," Uno persisted, behind him, coming to the same trunk and straddling over it, like we'd been told. "Like a shawl-collar tux. A Cary Grant tux."

"No," Hugh said, stepping up on the next trunk. "He's too awesome for a tux. He'll wear a brown vest with a loose tie and his sleeves rolled up to the elbows."

"A loose bow tie?"

"A loose long tie," Hugh corrected, stepping up on the next trunk, then down.

"I kind of like bow ties," Dosie said.

"If he wants a bow tie, he'll wear it with suspenders. Not a tux. But if he knows what's good for him, he'll wear a long tie. With a Windsor knot."

"Why does it matter what kind of knot?" Uno asked.

Hugh stepped up on another trunk. "Why does *anything* matter?"

The truth is, I *saw* him stepping on those trunks, just as I saw the Sisters straddling behind him, and as I hurdled over them, myself. I saw him, but I never once thought to correct him. Who was I to tell Hugh what to do? He was making his choices, and the rest of us were making ours. I just didn't realize yet how tangled together all our choices were.

Looking back, I'd wish over and over that I'd been feeling just a tiny bit bossier that day.

I glanced up at Hugh just as it happened, in fact.

I can see it all in slo-mo in my memory: He steps up on the next log, and in the half second that it would have taken to swing his other foot forward, the surface crumbles beneath his foot and he loses his balance, pitching forward and landing across a second one—this one not rotten at all—just ahead of him.

Hugh screamed like I have never heard anybody scream—in a way that seemed to shock the forest into silence. Then he fell silent and crumpled. He just lay collapsed over that second log in an upside-down V, pinned down by his pack.

I had my own pack off in seconds, trying to remember our first-aid class. But then I froze.

You didn't move a head injury—but what about a leg injury? *First things first*, I kept thinking. But what were the first things? I had to pick something. The Sisters were utterly still, watching in shock as the moment unfolded. Somebody had to be in charge, and it looked like that somebody was going to be me.

Get his pack off, I decided. I unlatched his shoulder straps, but then, when I worked my hands under his hips to unbuckle his hip belt, Hugh woke up, screaming. "No, no! Don't!"

I did it anyway.

His pack tumbled forward to the ground.

"Okay," I said, stepping back, breathless. "Can you stand up?"

He pushed against the trunk with both hands for about one second before seizing in pain. "No."

Here was the problem: He was the smallest of the guys, but he was still a lot bigger than I was. I pointed at the Sisters. "Take off your packs," I said. "We have to move him."

"No!" Hugh shouted.

His head was upside-down. "We can't leave you like this," I said.

"Do not touch me!" Hugh said.

"Are you supposed to move injured people?" one of the Sisters asked, frowning at Hugh, but taking her pack off, anyway.

"I don't know," I said. "But I do know we can't leave him bent in half like this."

The girls nodded. They were with me.

"You two take the shoulders," I said. "I'll get the bottom half. We're just going to flip him like a pancake and set him right there." I pointed to a log-less part of the trail. Each girl took a shoulder, and I wrapped both arms around Hugh's thighs—him screaming all the while. "On three!" I shouted. "One! Two! Three!"

I thought my eardrums would pop when we lifted him, he screamed so loud. And holy cow, was he heavy. But adrenaline saw us through, and we did manage to flip him back in one fairly coordinated motion to lay him as gently as possible on the flat ground.

Halfway through, Hugh stopped screaming. He'd passed out again.

"That must hurt like hell," Dosie said.

I grabbed that moment to press my hands against his thigh and his hip. I wasn't sure what I was even feeling for. Bones sticking out? Huge lumps of pooling blood? Not only did I have no idea what I was looking for, I had no idea what I would do when I found it, either. But I didn't find anything. Just a regular-feeling leg. Maybe it wasn't so bad.

That's when one of the sisters, who had stepped back, said, "Does it look like one of his legs is longer than the other?"

I stood up to look. Yes. It did.

"That can't be good," the other sister said.

But Hugh was coming back to consciousness. "Hush," I told them. I turned to Hugh. "Can you hear me?"

"Fucking fuck," Hugh said.

"I guess you're conscious."

"Something's broken," he said. "I heard a crack."

"Can you move your leg at all?" I asked.

He shook his head.

"You're not even going to try?"

"I am trying," he said, and we both watched the leg. Completely still.

"Okay," I said. "So maybe a broken leg. Or hip. Or pelvis." I went in to push on his rib cage. He screamed again. "Or possibly ribs."

Hugh closed his eyes, panting.

"What were you doing stepping on those dead trees, anyway?" I said, rooting through my pack for the Tylenol, which was the strongest painkiller we had. "Didn't you see Beckett humiliate me about that on the first day?"

"He's such a worrywart," Hugh said.

"Well, now we know why."

I made him take the Tylenol, even though he almost choked on it.

Hugh did not look good. The color was gone from his face. And even though his skin felt cold, tiny beads of sweat covered his face. "He's going into shock," I said.

"Wouldn't you be?" Uno said.

"Who's going for help?" I asked.

"You are," they said together.

I didn't argue. Even though I was the most competent person there, that wasn't saying much. I grabbed the map and debated whether I should take my entire big backpack, or just my daypack. I decided that even though I could move faster with less, if I got lost or injured or attacked by a bear—which didn't seem impossible—I'd do better with more. I hoisted on the big pack and was snapping it onto my hips when the girls stopped me.

"What do we do?" they asked.

I shook my head. "I don't know." But they were almost as pale as

Hugh himself, and I knew I had to say *something.* "Keep him hydrated. Keep him warm. Hold his hand." I handed them the little medical pack with our remaining Tylenol. "Keep a log of everything you notice. Talk to him. Cheer him up. Plan the wedding."

I started back on the trail, but Dosie followed me and grabbed my hand. "What if he dies?" she whispered.

I shook my head with a confidence that I did not feel. "He's not going to die."

She still had my hand.

I squeezed it. "Be brave," I said. "I'll come back with help."

She stood on the trail and watched me go, but I hadn't gotten far when I started noticing that the trail I was walking on didn't look anything like what I'd pictured in my head the last time I'd studied the map. Of course, that was way back before we started analyzing how in love with Windy Jake was. I guess I'd found that discussion more distracting than I'd realized, because it suddenly hit me that we'd been angling down a ravine when we should have been walking a flat, straight stretch. I stopped and opened the map to check the route. And, just like in class with Beckett, I could see in 3-D what the trail I was supposed to be following should look like. And I could see just as clearly that the place where I stood bore no resemblance.

We were going the wrong way, I suddenly knew—and we had been for a while, which happened a lot on this hike. Trail markers were much more infrequent this far back in the wilderness, and far less noticeable, than they probably should have been. After all, where else would markers be nearly as vital but way back in the deepest wilderness?

I would register a complaint with the Park Service when we got home. If we lived.

I turned around and booked it back the other way, passing the Sisters and Hugh as I went.

"We were headed the wrong way," I called out cheerily, using my Mary Poppins voice.

The girls looked stricken.

"Back ASAP!" I called, without slowing as I went by. "Possibly tomorrow!" I added, when I was too far past them for anyone to have the energy to come after me.

Twenty minutes later, I was rounding the fork and starting down the right path.

Next, all I had to do was catch up to the other two groups. Which took hours.

Because the hike was such a straight shot on relatively level ground, Beckett had gone ahead and added a little more mileage. He had intended for the first group to get to camp around one in the afternoon, and for the slower group—mine—to straggle in around three. But we'd lost at least a half hour just getting Hugh stabilized. Not to mention the time it had taken me to settle the Sisters—who were freaking out, to say the least—or the half-hour-long detour while I followed the wrong path, or the forty minutes it took me to get back to the right path. I won't lie: I was tired. But slowing down wasn't really an option, so I literally pretended that I was a steam engine, imagining my arms as those metal bars that spin the wheels. Crazy as it sounds, it helped. All I had to do was stay steady and continue down the track. I'd catch up at some point.

"Some point" turned out to be six o'clock at night. The other groups were eating dinner when I finally chugged into camp, and when Beckett saw me, he stood up and rushed over. Jake stood, too, and, despite all the important life-and-death business I had going on at that moment, the sight of him, even all the way across the camp, had a physical effect on me. I once flipped a light switch that must have been leaking a little bit of current, and when I touched it, an electrical flutter penetrated my fingers. Not enough to hurt—just enough to get 100 percent of my attention. That's exactly what this feeling reminded me of—an electrical current: a cross between a zap and a flutter. But this was much more powerful than that—powerful enough that I had to look down to break the connection. I couldn't look at him. It was too much.

What *was* that? It happened a lot on this trip with Jake. I remembered the feeling well from crushes I'd had when I was younger, but it had been years since I'd felt it. Why was it so physical? How could a pair of eyes twenty feet away have a visceral effect on another person's body? Was it just nervousness? Or, today, emotional exhaustion from dealing with Hugh? Or maybe some intensified variation on that phenomenon that happens when someone's looking at you, and you just *feel* it, and you turn right toward them? I've always wondered if that was some leftover herd animal instinct from the mists of time. Of course, humans weren't ever herd animals. We were predators. But even predators have to know on some level what it feels like to be prey.

"Where the hell have you been?" Beckett asked.

"We missed a fork on the map," I said, "and it took us a little time to figure it out."

"Where's the rest of your group?"

"Hugh fell, and he's injured."

Beckett looked up to locate Jake, who was still standing at attention, watching us. "J-Dog," he shouted, and signaled him over. Then he turned back to me. "Fell?"

"He stepped up on a fallen tree trunk. His foot broke through and he lost his balance, and then he landed on another fallen tree just a couple of feet ahead."

"I told you guys not to do that! Didn't I?"

I nodded. "You did."

Jake joined us at that point, and now that I'd had a minute to talk myself into it, I could force myself to meet his eyes.

"It happened fast," I said, "but I think he might have landed with all his weight on his left hip."

"It's just the left side?" Jake asked.

"As far as I can tell," I answered.

Jake and Beckett looked at each other like this was not good. So I agreed. "It's not good," I said. "I think he's in shock."

Then Jake shifted into serious EMT fact-gathering mode. "Was he conscious?" he asked.

"Yes," I said. "Mostly. Though he passed out when we moved him."

"Why did you move him?"

"He was bent over that second log with his head upside down. It didn't seem like a good idea to leave him that way."

Jake nodded. "Good call." Then he asked if Hugh could move the leg at all, and I said no. He asked if Hugh had been panting or spitting up blood, and I said no. Then he asked a whole bunch of questions I didn't know the answers to. What was his pulse? (I hadn't thought to take it). Could he wiggle his toes? (I hadn't checked or even thought to take off his boots). What was his capillary refill? (I didn't even know what that was).

"I'm sorry I don't have better information for you," I said.

"How did he look when you left?"

"Pale. Clammy. Bad."

Jake looked at Beckett. "We need to get him out."

"Tonight?"

"Sooner is always better than later."

Was Jake really thinking of trying to find our lost hiking group in the middle of the night? What did he think we'd do—hold his hand and lead him there? The stars weren't even out. Even people who could see would be stumbling into trees.

But Beckett looked at the sky and shook his head. "It's too dark.

If they were on the trail, I'd say go for it, but they're off it somewhere, and we don't know where."

I knew where, but I didn't say anything. Was I protecting Jake over helping Hugh?

"We can't start an evac until the morning, anyway. An hour or so won't make a difference."

With that, it was decided. We'd wait to leave until dawn. "Bunk in with Windy's group tonight," Beckett told me.

Then he gathered the group together, clapped his hands for everybody's attention, and filled them in. "This is serious, people, and this is not a drill. We will be doing an evac tomorrow. No breakfast in the morning. We will strike camp by 5 A.M.—no food, no coffee— and head out. You can all fuel up at the site while Jake and I tend to Hugh. Be sure to save us something to eat." Then he looked around, surveying our faces. "Tomorrow's going to be a bitch, folks. Hit the sack right now, and soak up every ounce of rest you can."

Our tent group was already set up and had to move their bags over to make space for me under the tarp. I would have gone for the other side—the side farthest from Jake—but the group made space by parting in the middle, and I wound up right next to him.

Everybody begged for more details as I wriggled into my pj's inside my bag, but I wasn't feeling talkative. I didn't give them much to work with, and pretty soon, they took Beckett's advice, curled up, and conked out. Except for me. I couldn't relax. I lay flat on my back trying to massage my palms into relaxing. It was so dark, the tarp ceiling above me could just as well have been the sky. I couldn't stop thinking about Hugh there by the side of the trail, his face so gray. I'd done the best I could—with my one page of first-aid notes. It wasn't nearly enough, and I knew it. It was a strange, lonely feeling.

"You did good, you know," Jake said then, his voice right near my ear. He'd been quiet for so long, it seemed impossible that he was still awake.

But I was glad he was. I closed my eyes. "I'm afraid Hugh's going to die."

"Don't think about that," he said. "We'll do everything we can. He'll probably be fine."

"Probably?"

"It's possible the Sisters might talk him to death."

I laughed a little bit. "I had no idea what to do," I said. "I had one page of notes to go on."

"That's more than anybody else would have had."

"Except you."

"Yeah, but I'm in the industry."

"And now he's there. And we're here. And I can't sleep." I was genuinely rattled.

"You need to sleep, though," Jake said. "Tomorrow's going to be brutal."

But I didn't close my eyes. Instead, I said, "Shouldn't Beckett have come to find us? When we didn't show up in the afternoon? Shouldn't he have known something was wrong?"

"He'd decided to go back and look for you after dinner."

"After dinner?"

"He wanted to 'fuel up' first, and he didn't seem too worried. I think he just expected your group to—"

"Suck?"

"Dawdle." He gave me a little smile. "But you're right. He's not exactly a trained professional."

"How old do you think he is?"

"If I didn't know you had to be twenty-one, I'd say seventeen."

"I'd say fifteen."

"He's not elderly, that's for sure."

"But he does surprise me sometimes."

"You know," Jake said, rolling onto his side to face me, "while we were waiting for you guys tonight, Beckett had us do the most touchy-feely exercise ever. He even apologized for how touchy-feely it was. But he said he'd done this on his first-ever BCSC course, and it had always stuck with him."

I rolled onto my side to face him, too. I kept my voice low, so as not to wake the others. "What was it?"

"He said, 'Think of somebody who loved you. Or loves you. Somebody who is rooting for you. Who believes in you. Who would be willing to suffer for you.'"

"Beckett said that?"

Jake nodded. "He said that there will come a day when things are so hopeless that the only way we'll get through will be to turn to our person, whoever it is, in our heads—so we can draw strength from them to keep going."

I studied him. "Are you telling me this now because tomorrow is going to be one of those days?"

He nodded. "That, and you seem pretty shaky. You might want to get ahold of your person."

"Who's your person?" I asked.

No hesitation. "My mom."

"Not your dad?"

"My dad's great," he said. "But he's not my mom." Then he turned to me. "Who's your person?"

No hesitation, either. "My brother," I said.

Jake lifted his eyebrows. "Duncan?" he asked. "Really?"

And here was a moment when I could have faked it. I could have just said, "Yes, Duncan," and no one would have been the wiser but me. But it wasn't Duncan. It was my other brother, the one I never talked about. And yet suddenly, out of nowhere, with this twenty-two-year-old guy, I'd just brought him up.

It could have been the quiet of the night, with the two of us lying on our sides so close to each other—the only ones awake in the whole crowd—that made it feel like the right time for sharing secrets. Or the fact that we were already whispering. I didn't know. But I did know this: I could lie to him right now, or I could tell the truth—and for some reason, suddenly, telling the truth didn't seem so bad.

"No, not Duncan," I said then, in what felt like slow motion. "My other brother."

Jake nodded like that's what he'd expected. "The brother you lost."

"That's right. The brother I lost. Nathan."

I looked over. Jake met my eyes.

"Do you know about him?" I was never sure how much Jake knew about anything.

He gave a little shrug. "Just that you were very close. And he died the year before Duncan was born."

"That's right. He's the *reason* Duncan was born, actually."

"He was killed in an accident, right?"

"He drowned." As I said the words, that familiar feeling of sorrow filled up my lungs.

I could have stopped there, but for some reason I didn't understand, I wanted to keep going. I sat up crisscross then, making sure to stay close and keep my voice down. "We were at my parents' friends' lake house. The adults were all drinking and having a good time. We were with a big batch of kids, and we were supposed to be watching a movie, but Nathan wanted to go to the marina instead and run around on the docks. He begged me to take him, but I didn't want to, and so without telling us, he went on his own. I just wanted to watch the movie—and you know what's funny? I can't even remember what movie it was. You'd think a detail like that would be seared into your memory, but it's lost. Sometimes I lie in bed and stare at the fan, trying to remember. Now and again, I think about getting in touch with the other kids who were there that night to ask if anyone else remembers. But then I don't. How do you call a total stranger after twenty years and ask a question like that? You can't. So I'll never know. It will be one of the great unanswered questions of my life."

Jake took a minute to sit up himself, crossing his legs just like mine so that our knees touched.

"Be quiet," I whispered, glancing at the blanket of sleeping people around us. "You'll wake them."

"Are you kidding?" he whispered back, glancing around. "An air horn wouldn't wake them."

I gave a little smile, and looked down at my hands in my lap.

After a minute, Jake said, "It wasn't your fault, you know."

I looked away. "Of course it was my fault. I was the big sister."

"You didn't do anything wrong."

"I should have gone with him."

"What were you—nine years old?"

I nodded. I knew what Jake was trying to say. I realized that it was complicated, and that siblings aren't the same as parents, and that I should have forgiven myself long ago. But there was no changing any of it, and even though I knew that no regret was strong enough to change the past, I still kept hanging on to it. Somehow, it seemed like the only decent thing to do.

"I'm sorry," Jake said in a quiet voice.

"After it happened, my mother became frantic. She was frantic at the lake looking for him. Even after they found him in the water, she stayed frantic. It was like she couldn't stop looking. She woke up night after night and paced around the house. Two months later, she was pregnant."

"On purpose?"

I nodded. "I think so. Trying to replace him. But the thing was, he was irreplaceable."

Jake gave a little half smile. "And that's how the world wound up with Duncan."

"Some brothers and sisters don't get along," I went on. "But Nathan and I were real, genuine friends. He was a year younger, but it didn't matter. We fought, but we always made up. We palled around together. We built forts. We went exploring. We drew each other pictures. We stood up for each other."

"So, basically, exactly the opposite of you and Duncan."

I shrugged. "I don't know what my mother was thinking. Before we knew it, there was this new baby—this colicky, stuck-pig-sounding baby—screaming its head off twenty-four/seven in the house. New babies have got to be tough on a family under the best of circumstances but Duncan was unbearable. So my father disappeared into his job. My mother had been working part time as a librarian, but she quit to deal with the baby—which was the opposite of what she needed. She got trapped in our sad house with an inconsolable infant. And I—"

Here, I paused.

"You?" Jake prompted.

I shrugged. "I just got forgotten."

Jake leaned in a little closer.

"My parents separated within a year," I went on. "My dad moved to San Diego and got remarried. I hardly ever see him now. And for two years after that my mom stayed in Evanston in our house and tried to raise Duncan and me on her own, but she just couldn't hack it. It was a nice house in a nice part of town, but there wasn't enough money—or maybe she just couldn't manage it all. We got yellow bills. They kept turning off the water and the power and it would take her days to get it back on. There were piles of laundry everywhere—so many, you couldn't tell dirty from clean. She cried all the time and forgot to make dinner. She forgot to pay the lawn guy so many times, he just stopped coming, and our grass grew like three feet tall. The pool in our backyard sprouted a sheet of algae. I tried to pick up the slack: I folded the clothes and taught myself to heat up soup and make grilled cheeses, but one morning, not long after I turned thirteen, she drove us across town to Grandma GiGi's and left us there."

"It's lucky Grandma GiGi is so awesome."

I gave a nod. "That part was lucky."

"Do you ever see your mom now?"

I looked out at the night shadows. "Every now and then, we go to coffee, and she tells me about her job while I nod and nod. She's a graphic designer–slash–yoga instructor now, and when she asks me how I am, I tell her I'm great."

"Because you're always great."

"That's right."

"She wasn't at your wedding, was she?"

I shook my head.

"Was your dad?"

I nodded. "I did invite my dad. I was less mad at him, I guess, though I'm not sure why. Maybe my expectations were lower."

"But he didn't give you away, did he?"

I shook my head. I hadn't wanted him to walk me down the aisle. "I gave myself away."

"I remember."

I took a deep breath. "So, you see, I lost everybody."

In a quiet voice, Jake said, "Not Duncan."

I looked over.

"You didn't lose Duncan. He loves you. Actually, 'love' is not a big enough word. He *adores* you. You barely tolerate him, but he would give you the skin off his back."

"I don't want the skin off his back."

Jake gave a tiny shrug. "The point remains."

I took a long breath and thought about everything I'd just told him. Then I said something that I must have always known, but I had never articulated until that moment: "I guess I haven't forgiven him for not being Nathan." It was surreal to hear myself say the words.

Jake looked over at me. "That sounds about right." Then he went on. "But he didn't ask to be born. He was pulled into that shit-storm the same way you were. By accident."

It had all seemed so clear when I was ten: *Duncan was the problem.* I buried my guilt about Nathan's death and blamed Duncan for everything. He arrived and my father disappeared, my mother got crazier, and I got completely ignored. He went from being a colicky baby to an exhausting toddler to a mischievous kid. Grandma GiGi loved us, but her tolerance for children was low, and so I wound up babysitting constantly from the age of thirteen until I left for college. Once I was gone, I was just so relieved to be on my own, I never rethought it. I never went back to take another look. It happened, I'd survived it all, moved away, and now I was completely fine. Except that I happened to have a particularly annoying younger brother who I couldn't stand to be around. And that was all his fault.

But here, talking to Jake, I hovered back over the story of my life from a different angle. For the first time, I saw Duncan as a motherless child, starving for attention, even from me, and doing anything— even stealing Grandma GiGi's car at the age of eight—to get it. I saw my mother as absolutely blinded with grief, and guilt, and regret— blaming herself for what happened, ripped apart with no idea of how to put herself back together—and my father, too, burying his sorrows in work, totally unable to help my mother, buckling under the weight of it all. I might have left, too, if I'd had the option. But I didn't. I had to stay, and the only person in the world who could have made it better was the one person who was truly gone.

Jake was watching me as I thought about it. I met his eyes. "It's a lot to think about," he said. "It'll keep your brain nice and busy during the evac tomorrow."

The evac. Right. "What time is it?" I asked.

"Nine o'clock," Jake said. "Hiker midnight."

"I guess we should get to sleep."

Jake rolled to settle on his side again, facing me. I followed suit and did the same. Lying side by side and face-to-face, we held each other's gaze for a good while before I said, "Thank you, by the way."

"What for?"

I didn't know how to enumerate it all. For staying up with me when I was feeling sad. For taking care of my blisters. For having my back over and over when Beckett went after me. For taking care of Duncan and being his friend. I shook my head. "For everything."

I was ready for that to be the last word—to end the day just like that, with gratitude. I closed my eyes.

But then Jake said, "Helen?"

I opened them again.

"There's something I've been wanting to say to you."

Oh, God. "Okay."

"I'm genuinely sorry about—" He paused for a second. "About the kissing thing."

I gave him a look. "What kissing thing?"

"I'd just gotten some bad news," Jake went on. "And I was reeling from it. I'm still reeling, actually."

I waited.

"I just wasn't making great decisions, is all."

"What kind of bad news?"

"The bad kind."

"You're not going to tell me? I just gave you my whole life story, and you're not going to tell me?"

"Actually, I got the bad news last fall, but then, for a while, I hoped that it might not be so bad, after all—but then it turned out it was. Is. And I'd known that for sure for about three days before we wound up in that motel together."

Was he trying to say that he'd only kissed me for comfort? Or as a distraction from bad news?

"Tell me."

He studied me like he was considering it, but then he shook his head.

"Well, that's just mean," I said. "You brought it up."

"But only as part of my apology."

"I didn't ask you for an apology."

"You didn't have to ask. I owed you one."

"You didn't owe me anything."

"I just want you to know that if my life were different—if it were *better*—that night would have shaken down very differently."

What did that even mean? I wanted to ask him, but it seemed way too vulnerable to admit that I cared. "It doesn't matter," I said. "It was a thousand years ago."

"It was last week."

"Well. It's been a long week. And you've been awfully busy in the interim."

He frowned.

"The Sisters talk," I said. "I know all about what you've been up to with *every single girl* on this trip." I hadn't realized I was so very jealous until I spoke the words.

"That was a game."

"Did you actually kiss every single girl here?" I asked.

"I don't know."

"Did you kiss enough of them that you lost count?"

"It was a *game*."

"Kind of like Scrabble is a game?"

"It was different."

I wanted it to be different. I wanted it to be different so badly in that moment that it terrified me. And in response to the terror, I did the only thing I could think of. I said, "Whatever. I really don't care." It was the full opposite of how I felt, and it felt so good to even pretend not to care, that I ran with it—hard—by adding this: "While you were playing Truth or Dare, I got a phone call."

He took the bait. "What kind of phone call?"

"The kind where your ex-husband announces he's pulled himself together and you're the only good thing that's ever happened to him. And he begs you to come home."

Jake lifted up on his elbows to try to read my expression. "Come home and do what? Annul your divorce?"

"I don't know," I said. "Date, maybe."

"Date?" he said. "You can't date your ex-husband."

"Why not?"

"It's going in reverse!"

"At least it's going somewhere."

He took a breath. "What did you answer?"

"I guess I'll tell you about my answer when you tell me about your bad news."

"That's not fair."

"Life's not fair."

Jake studied my face for a minute. "Helen, you can't—"

"I can do anything I want," I said. And then, before he could reply, I rolled over in my sleeping bag to face the other way.

Chapter 11

Beckett woke us at four thirty, and we struck camp in silent darkness. I managed to trip three times—over a tarp wire, a rock, and a broken branch—before the sun even thought about rising.

Putting on our packs to head out, I expected Beckett to take the big guys and Jake ahead to get moving fast and leave the rest of us to follow as best we could. But that's not what happened.

"Helen," Beckett said, pointing me toward the front. "Lead the way."

"*What?*" Mason turned toward us. "We'll never get there."

"She administered care to Hugh. She set up the Sisters for the night. She got herself un-lost and found her way back to us. She is the leader."

"But she's the slowest hiker in the group."

I raised a finger. "I am the *third*-slowest hiker, actually."

"Beckett—" Mason started.

But Beckett pointed at him. "Not another word. Hike at the end today. Go to the back."

I wasn't sure how I felt about being the leader. I'd already marked Hugh's location on the map, and they'd certainly get there a lot faster if they sent the big guys ahead, so it seemed like a waste of precious time to prove a slightly unimportant point. It would waste even more time to argue, though, so I stepped to the front of the line and started walking. Windy fell in behind me, and Jake behind her. Beckett hiked at the back to keep an eye on the big guys.

We made great time. The idea of Hugh in mortal peril doubled my speed. Plus, it's amazing how somebody calling you slow can make you fast. It felt good to move with such focus and purpose. I guess I'd gotten stronger without realizing it. Sometimes things like that sneak up on you.

Nobody talked at first. Unlike other hikes, where everyone sang and talked and made lots of noise, this hike was eerily quiet. My brain kept flipping back to the previous day. When I challenged myself to find three good things, they came to mind in seconds: I'd used my severely limited first-aid training to help Hugh. I'd put my 3-D map-reading skills to real-world use. And I'd had a landmark moment about my relationship with my brother—in fact, my entire life. Not bad for one of my worst days on record.

Of course, my instinct was to look back at the bad things, too. The unpleasantness of being stuck at the back with the Sisters and their gossip. The horror of watching Hugh's foot collapse into that log and the subsequent panic of not knowing what to do—and not wanting to do the wrong thing. The terror of having it all depend on me. The frustration of realizing that we were literally on the wrong trail and headed the wrong way.

But there was a pleasure to figuring out the trail problem, as well. That felt good, there was no denying it.

What felt less good was this idea of Windy and Jake together. I confess that's where my mind drifted, unless I consciously steered it away. The problem was, they *would* be great together. It *was* a perfect match. I couldn't even root against them. Except for one problem: As sad, and hopeless, and cougarish as it might be, I wanted Jake for myself.

Were the Sisters right? Was Jake taken by Windy? Did he like her? Was I totally forgotten—as I had demanded to be? Barely over a week ago, he'd seemed fully, entirely smitten with me. But maybe he was a faker, and that was just something he did to girls: use trumped-up longing to get them to do things they never ordinarily would. I had to admit it was powerful stuff. Girls always wanted to believe in love. Girls always wanted to feel seen, and admired, and wanted. Even girls who knew better. Like me.

Or maybe he really liked me, back at the time—before he knew Windy existed and before he knew he could have me. Maybe now whatever it was he thought he felt for me had been eclipsed by lovely feelings for the lovely Windy. Could I really blame him?

But there it was. Whether he was a scheming seducer or not, I knew him well enough after a week on this trip to know that in all other respects he was a good guy. Despite all my best efforts, it was time to call it: I liked him. I just liked him. As much as it clearly fell into the Bad Things category, I was amazed to find—and Windy would have been so proud—that I could pull a genuine Good Thing from it, too. Because on that morning, during that silent hike, I confessed a whole cascade of things to myself: Whenever Jake touched my knee to replace my bandages, or stood up for me with Beckett, or looked away when I glanced at him, I got this crazy jolt of anxious pleasure. Even though I felt plenty of misery when I, say, found out he was destined to marry Windy and have a hundred photogenic and kind-hearted children, I had to give those feelings credit, too. They were something different from the numbness I'd felt so solidly for the past year. Or longer. The word that kept surfacing in my head was *alive.*

I was working hard to feel grateful for the opportunity for heart-break and all the *aliveness* it would bring when I realized that Jake and Windy had broken the morning's quiet and were chatting with each other.

"So the *pleasure* system," Windy was saying, "is modulated by neurotransmitters called opioids. They help us enjoy the good things in our lives and tune out discomfort. But the system of *desire* is governed by dopamine, which makes you antsy and itchy with longing."

"So they kind of cancel each other out," Jake said, following her thinking closely.

"That's right. When desire is high, pleasure and satisfaction are low. They're, like, at opposite ends of a seesaw."

I had no idea what they were even talking about, but I heard myself jump in, anyway. "Is that why some men only want women they can't have? Because they confuse pleasure for desire?"

"Yes," Windy called up. "Probably. It always seems to come back to neurotransmitters."

"Can't they take something for that?" I asked.

"Not really. People can get hooked on longing, though. They wind up liking the wanting more than the having."

"Exactly!" I said. "Is that fixable?"

Windy thought for a minute before answering. "Well," she said, "there's a lot more neurological plasticity in the brain than we used to believe. In theory, anything's possible. But that's in theory. The most important thing to remember is that getting what you want doesn't make you happy."

"It doesn't?" I asked.

"Not for long. Happiness is more about appreciation than acquisition."

"Oh," I said. That stumped me a little. I'd always assumed that getting what you wanted was *the definition* of being happy. Guess I'd kinda jumped in over my head, here.

When there were no more questions from me, Windy turned her

attention back to Jake. "So, anyway, that's when I decided to become a Buddhist. Freshman year at Barnard."

"That's awesome," Jake said. "I keep meaning to become a Buddhist."

"It's not that hard," Windy said. "I can teach you."

"Sure," Jake said. "Great."

Windy went to Barnard? And was a Buddhist? That was the thing about her—she was full of surprises. She was never dull. And she was very much, unapologetically, her own person. I couldn't even dislike her.

"Maybe next time we have a Zero Day," Windy suggested, "I could give you a lesson."

"It's a date," Jake said.

Or maybe, actually, I could dislike her—just a tiny bit.

It took us three hours to get back to Hugh. He was alert when we arrived, and sipping soup the Sisters had made for him.

Jake went right to work, cutting Hugh's pants and socks off with shears to assess the situation, and he sent Windy and the big guys to go find him a branch of some kind to use for a splint.

"You're going to splint his leg?" Mason asked.

Jake shook his head. "I'm going to splint his whole body."

Beckett herded the rest of us a few feet away to start preparing for the evac. He divided us into two groups. He pointed at three people who had packs with external aluminum frames and told them to empty them out. When the packs were empty, he told the owners to redistribute their belongings into the remaining packs. Then he started dismantling the frames.

"What are you doing?" I asked.

"Making a litter for Hugh."

We had flat, nylon ropes called lashes with us, and Beckett used several to weave around the three frames. Lashed together, they made a litter shape, and a woven surface for Hugh to lie on. When Beckett was done, he spread a sleeping bag over it for padding, and then lay down on top. "Not bad," he said, looking at me from the ground. "It's no featherbed, but it'll do."

Over breakfast, Jake reported on Hugh's condition. He was bruised black from his waist to his knee, he could not bend his leg at all, and the one-leg-looking-longer-than-the-other problem made Jake suspect that Hugh might have both fractured and dislocated his hip. But he was conscious, which was great. Jake turned his eyes to me in front of the whole group. "He said Helen is his hero."

"You got something right, girl," Beckett said. "Way to go."

Beckett took over from there, detailing the plan: Half the group—six of us—would carry the litter. The other half would shuttle all the backpacks up ahead in groups. Apparently I was helping to carry the litter. So was Jake.

We were going to make our way to the closest trailhead—about three miles away—to meet the ambulance that'd take Hugh to the hospital.

"We're just going to drop him at the trailhead and keep moving?" Mason asked.

Beckett shook his head. "A BCSC administrator will meet us at the trailhead. She'll take it from there."

It was nine thirty in the morning. It was time to get moving. Three miles didn't seem so far, I thought to myself. Maybe today wouldn't be so bad.

But that's when Beckett turned around to say one last thing to the group. "This is going to be the longest day of your lives, people. No matter how miserable you are, remember that it's ten times worse for Hugh. It's a good thing we did our little exercise in inner strength last night. Now's the time to call up those people who love you. You're going to need 'em.''

It all seemed a little dramatic to me. Beckett always did seem a little dramatic. And yet, he had a way of being right, too. I walked over to help get Hugh onto the litter. The guys were gathered around him, ready to pick him up and position him on top. They looked menacing, even to me. Jake instructed them all to slide their hands underneath Hugh "like spatulas."

"Is it going to hurt?" Hugh asked.

Jake nodded. "Sorry, pal. Like hell." He looked at the guys. "Ready?"

"Wait!" Hugh shouted.

They waited.

But he was just stalling. I read the terror on his face so plainly that I moved in—cut between Jake and Mason—and grabbed his hand. "Squeeze my hand," I instructed, just as Jake capitalized on the distraction and shouted, "One-two-three! Lift!"

I have never in my life heard anybody scream like Hugh did in that moment. If agony could speak, that's what it would say. When he stopped, I realized that he'd passed out again.

We zipped him into his sleeping bag for warmth and protection. Then we lashed him to the litter—tight, so he wouldn't slide around. "He'd be screaming now, too," Jake said, "if he were conscious."

Just like that, it was time to go. "Let's move," Beckett said, as we, the litter bearers, took our places around the edge of the frame. I had assumed that we'd raise Hugh up to our shoulders, kind of like pallbearers, but Beckett told us to lift him hip-height and carry him with our arms extended straight down. "Easier for you," Beckett said, "and safer for him."

"Safer?" I asked.

"In case we drop him." Then, off my look: "Which we won't."

Beckett had tied six lashes around the edge so that we could hold on to the frame with our interior hand but pull the lash around and up over our shoulders with the other. "Wrap the end of the lash around like this," he said, demonstrating, "and straighten your elbow."

"*That'll help*," I thought. "*But not much.*"

The minute Beckett said, "Lift on three . . . one, two, THREE," and I felt the real weight of what we'd be carrying for the next three miles, both uphill and down, my muscles were like, "Nope! Set it down."

But I didn't. Because no one else did, and because there wasn't any other choice.

"He's way too scrawny to be this heavy," Mason said then.

"You have to add in the weight of the frames. And the sleeping bags."

"He's probably about one eighty," Beckett said. "Add the frames, and I'd guess two hundred. Maybe more."

"So that should only be thirty pounds each. Ish."

"That's not that bad."

But it was that bad. Before we'd even made it back to the fork of the original trail, my shoulders felt seared where the lash dug into them—and my hand was throbbing and purple where I'd wrapped the end around. Beckett had predicted that it would take us most of the day to get to the trailhead, because the pack shuttlers would literally be running the distance twice—once with their own packs, and once with a pack of one of the litter carriers. We, of course, would be moving slow—both for Hugh's sake and for ours. It was, without a doubt, the most physically grueling thing I'd ever asked my body to do.

Think about something else, I tried to command myself. Beckett had advised us to call up our person. Someone who loved you, he'd said. I tried to picture Nathan standing up ahead, cheering me on like a marathon spectator. But it was too hard, not to mention too silly. I didn't have any energy left over for imagination, and I couldn't believe Beckett had suggested it—if anything, trying to do two things at once just made both harder.

But that's when Jake started something I wouldn't have expected. A military cadence.

We'd lurched into shaky motion along the trail, pushing and pulling in our different ways against the litter, bumbling and yanking and struggling, when Jake's voice rang out so loud and strong it startled us into alignment.

As smooth and certain as any sergeant calling cadence you've ever seen in a movie, Jake just started up: "Left! Left! Left, right, left!"

And the guys, out of nowhere, went ahead and answered the call, repeating back on the beat. How did they know to do that?

Next, Jake launched into the "lyrics" of it, if that's what you call them: "My back aches, my shoes too tight, I'm tossing-turning every night."

And the boys all followed, not missing a step. As their voices fell into rhythm, their feet did, too.

Jake went back to another "left, right, left" verse, then continued on to the next line, which turned out to be the refrain: "I don't know quite what to say. That girl just takes me all the way."

At that, he glanced back at me, saw I wasn't answering the call, and said, "You're part of this unit, Helen-with-an-H."

The boys were already answering. So I joined in, too.

He had us. It turned out to be a cadence that alternated between "left, right, left," descriptions of how terrible life was, and that returning refrain about the girl in a syncopated rhythm that somehow made carrying Hugh's dead weight through the forest feel almost like dancing.

I liked the verses about misery the best:

My car's broke, my TV's dead, I just woke up in a stranger's bed.
My dog bites, my tires all flat, it just don't get no worse than that.
My head's bald, my lady's gone, got nothing left but a dumb ol'
song.

I don't know how standard the song was, or where Jake learned it, but after a bit he definitely started making up words to fit the day:

No lattes, no takeout food, we've only got this heavy dude.
My boots hurt, my blister's sore, I just can't take it anymore.
My pits stink, this trail is steep, why can't the Rangers
bring a Jeep?

I couldn't imagine how Jake could do that. He did not exactly give off a military vibe. But I loved it. Was I still in physical despair? You bet. But did Jake somehow manage to make things a whole lot better? He really did.

Near the end, we woke Hugh, who blinked a few times, listened to us for a minute, and then announced, "I'm in Hell."

"You don't know the half of it, brother," Mason said from right next to his head. "I've got the farts something fierce."

"Jet propulsion," Beckett said, and everybody—even Hugh—laughed a little.

"Oh, God, it hurts to laugh," Hugh said, then. "Don't say anything funny."

"No fart jokes," Beckett said, and Hugh laughed again.

"It's either laugh," one of the big guys said, "or cry."

"Or neither," Hugh suggested. "How about neither?"

✳

Beckett was exactly right. We didn't make it to the trailhead until three in the afternoon. For a minute, during Jake's cadence, it looked like we might beat Beckett's prediction and make it by two. But then we hit a slick patch of trail from a flash summer shower. The ground was drenched and each step we took slid partway downhill in the mud, more like working out on a StairMaster than walking. Halfway through that, just after pausing for lunch, we came to a river crossing. Rivers always swell during the day, as snow from the mountaintops melts in the warm summer air. This one was mid-thigh height on the boys— hip-height on me. It would have been tricky on our own, the icy currents pushing and tugging at our legs with every step, but it was even harder keeping Hugh's litter high enough to stay clear of the water.

"That's it, folks," Beckett encouraged, as we worked our way across. "Let's not add hypothermia to Hugh's list of ailments." It took twenty minutes to cross, and by the time we made it, the skin on my legs was bright red from the cold, and my shoulders—both—were cramping so badly they felt like fire.

On the other bank, we set Hugh down, awake, and I bent over at the waist to shake my arms around to loosen the tension. It didn't work.

When I stood up, Jake was next to me. "Do this," he said, bending my arm up and then down.

I stared at him.

"It's your shoulders, right?"

I nodded.

"Okay," he said. "This'll help."

I let him do it. I was too tired to refuse. In all my life, I'd never been so tired. I was past the point of protesting anything. I wondered if Jake was going to give me hell about the popped blisters all over my palms. But then I looked at his own hands, and they were the same. Everyone else, too. Even Beckett.

As if he could read my thoughts, Hugh said, "Thank you. For evac-ing me. By the way."

Some of the guys had laid themselves out on the riverbank. Some were studying what Jake was doing to my shoulders and trying to copy. They all made murmurs of "No problem, man."

Except for Beckett. "I've had a question in my head all day long," he announced, and as we all turned to give him our attention, he shook his head. "Is anybody in this group ever in their lives going to step on a fallen log again?"

When we made it to the trailhead, the BCSC administrator had not made it yet. Nor had the ambulance. Beckett decided that some of us would stay with Hugh, and the rest of the group would go on ahead and start setting up camp and making dinner. Beckett announced that Jake, the EMT, should stay. I should stay, too, Beckett said, "Because Hugh likes you the best."

I looked over at Hugh. "Do you?"

He smiled at me and winked. "I don't really like anybody," he said. "But I like you better than most."

That was something.

"I'll need one more volunteer," Beckett said.

Windy's hand shot up like lightning. Which was funny, because nobody else even raised one.

"And Windy's the lucky winner," Beckett said.

"Yes," Windy cheered, turning that raised hand into a fist pump.

The trailhead was quite a sight. Unlike the one where we'd been dropped off, this one had a bathroom, and vending machines, and electrical hookups—which meant there were camper vans all around, families grilling burgers, and grandmas in muumuus.

And litter. Lots of litter. The minute we arrived, it was all I could see. Twinkie wrappers, beer cans, and empty potato chip bags everywhere. After a solid week in the pristine wilderness, it was shocking. What was wrong with people? Beckett had seemed so psychotic to me the other day, burning my list of self-improvements. But as I looked around the trailhead, I got it. Who the hell were these people, trespassing on the wilderness and making a mess? I wanted to set fire to every piece of trash I saw. Possibly every human being, too.

Jake and Beckett decided to leave Hugh strapped into the litter. We were to dismantle it once the ambulance arrived and carry the frames, along with our daypacks, to the campsite. They would move a half mile back into the wilderness—away from the circus of the trailhead—and we would meet up with them once Hugh was gone. Before the group left us, one of the Sisters asked if she could go use the indoor toilets.

"Hell, no," Beckett said. "Go shit in the woods like a real hiker."

I confess: He was growing on me.

We'd set Hugh down under an empty lean-to, and there we waited for the ambulance to arrive. After all the hauling ass we'd done to get him here, it seemed incalculably rude for the ambulance to make him wait any longer. Hadn't he been through enough? I fed Hugh some crackers, and then, when he fell asleep, I announced to Windy and Jake that I was going to nap, too. I lay down to rest my head on my daypack, close my eyes, and drift off for a few minutes.

But I couldn't sleep. I was exhausted, yes, after staying up way too late talking to Jake the night before. I wanted literally nothing more than to sink into a black, numbing state of unconsciousness, but everything hurt too much. Instead, with no other choice, I listened to Windy and Jake chat as they sat together on a nearby picnic table.

Windy was telling Jake all about a Russian scientist who had domesticated wild foxes in secret, and it was actually pretty fascinating stuff, and for a while there I couldn't help but enjoy my eavesdropping—until Windy ran out of things to say about foxes and said, out of nowhere: "Jake. Kiss me."

Jake didn't seem all that surprised. "Now?"

"Now."

"Do you really think it's the best time?"

"I think it's the perfect time."

My eyes had popped open, and I couldn't seem to close them again. I should have given them some privacy, at least. But it was like rubbernecking at an accident, and I literally couldn't look away, no matter how traumatizing I knew the sight would be. They were facing the direction of the road, at least, and so there was little chance of them turning around to see me. But I couldn't have looked away if I'd tried.

"Don't you think we're kind of too filthy?" Jake asked.

She shook her head. "Our mouths are the only clean parts we've got."

She had a point. Tooth-brushing was just about the only hygienic behavior allowed.

"You don't care that I literally smell like a skunk?"

"Not really."

"We're doing this now, then?"

He was stalling, I thought, as Windy said, "Yep."

This couldn't really happen, could it? I know the Sisters had said that Jake liked Windy, but I hadn't truly believed them. Deep down, I'd held tight to the idea that it was me he was taken by. That all this other stuff was just misunderstandings and twenty-something shenanigans. My dumb, stubborn heart just kept insisting there was something genuine going on between us, even if nobody knew what it was.

Until now. Now, he leaned in close and pressed his mouth against hers, and at the moment of impact a crazy thing happened to me: For a second, I couldn't breathe. It was time to take a breath, but I couldn't make it happen. It was like I was drowning in plain air. It wasn't until I looked away that I could breathe again. When I glanced back over at them, I was terrified that, in my panic, I might have made some gasping noise that would have the two of them staring at me. But I hadn't—or if I had, they hadn't heard it. I might as well not have been there at all.

And so, they *locked lips, sucked face, made out,* and *smooched.* For the longest few minutes in the history of time.

Once I'd glanced back, I could not look away.

"Now that's too bad," a voice said then.

I startled. It was Hugh. Awake, and watching them, too.

"I always thought, deep down, that you were the one he really liked."

I frowned at him. "That's not what you said yesterday."

"I was just messing around," Hugh said. I gave him a sip of water, and he added, "Hey, I'm sorry about all this."

"Me, too. Just don't die, okay?"

Hugh gave me a little grin. "Right back atcha."

When I dared to glance back over toward the picnic table, Jake and Windy had wrapped things up. Just past them, an ambulance rounded a corner and pulled into view. The sirens weren't on, but the lights flashed, and the driver gave a little "woop" as he pulled to a stop in front of our lean-to.

Jake hopped down from the picnic table and walked out to meet the two paramedics and the BCSC administrator, who stepped out of the passenger seat and ran around to get a look at Hugh. She had a taut ponytail and aviator glasses.

"This'll make the papers," she said. "How did it happen?" she asked Jake, who looked, I suppose, the most in charge.

Jake turned to me. I stood up and walked over. "He stepped on a fallen log," I said, "but it was rotten, and he fell."

"Didn't your instructor tell you not to do that?"

"Several times," I said.

The administrator closed her eyes and sighed. "So we're not liable."

"His dad is a lawyer, though," Jake said, nodding at Hugh. "So I'd get him fixed up real good."

"Thanks," she said, like he'd given her a great tip, as he stepped away to meet the paramedics and fill them in.

It took a long time to get Hugh off our homemade litter and into the truck. Everything we'd done, they had to redo properly. I stayed right by Hugh's side, even though they wouldn't let me touch him. Once he was finally secured on their gurney, I pushed my way close to him, anyway, and gave him a little kiss. "Be brave," I told him.

"Always," he said. He was a little breathless from the pain, but he met my eyes and then glanced over at Jake. "You too."

"I'd promise to come see you in the hospital when we get back," I said, "but I don't think you'll still be there."

"Nah," he said. "I'll be at Miami Beach by then."

"Take good care of yourself," I said, giving his hand a squeeze.

"I will if you will," he said, squeezing back.

I let go as they loaded him up, and waved until they were out of sight.

"Hell of an exit," Jake said to me, when I turned around.

But all I could think about was how the mouth making those words had just been all over Windy. I looked down at the ground. I couldn't talk to that mouth.

The hike back to the others felt much longer than a half mile.

My full-out exhaustion was only made worse by the fact that Windy

didn't seem tired at all. She and Jake hiked up ahead while I fell farther behind. How could she not be tired? My hands were throbbing. My
neck and shoulders felt like glass. I'd somehow gotten sunburned.
My boots felt like iron blocks riveted to my feet.

But there was Windy, up ahead, walking with a ponytail that
bobbed behind her like she was prancing. She bounced. She skipped.
She trotted up to say things to Jake, things I could not hear. But I
could hear the giggles. And I could hear the smacking noise her hand
made on his shoulder when she swatted him for his shocking retorts.
I felt a thousand years old.

Jake kept stopping to let me catch up. "You don't have to wait for
me," I said, every time I saw them. "Just go ahead."

"We're not leaving you behind," Windy said, meaning to be kind,
but wielding that little pronoun "we" like a knife.

"I really don't care," I said, wishing more than anything for exactly that: to be left behind.

"But we do," Windy said, and tried to give me a hug.

I ducked away. "Let's not stop. I don't want to rest. If I stop, I won't
start again."

"You look pretty awful," Jake said.

Fuck you, I wanted to say. But I just kept shuffling along, instead.

So this was it. Whatever Jake's bad news was—if there was, in
fact, any—it was enough to keep him from getting involved with me,
but not enough to keep him from Windy.

Instead of ignoring me, as any other thoughtlessly in love couple
would have done, they purposely hiked slower so we could all be together. Like assholes. There I was, left to walk right alongside them
and contemplate the hot mess that had become of my life. It occurred
to me that that should have been one of my good things—that I had
at least traded one kind of heartbreak for another on this trip. At the

very least, it wasn't the same old sorrow that had dogged me all year. I tried to order myself to count that as a blessing. But I wasn't taking orders very well right then.

Jake and Windy. Could I blame him, really? If I were choosing between Windy—so nice, so cheery, so hopeful, a dog lover and a literal *student of happiness*—and my grumpy, disillusioned, jaded, thirty-two-year-old butt, there was really no contest. That wasn't Jake's fault. In fact, if it was anyone's it was mine.

This was the problem: I saw so many good, kind, worthy things in him—though, granted, it had taken me six years to figure it out— and I found him so *lovable,* that I wanted him to find me lovable, too. But that wasn't Jake's job. It wasn't even fair to ask of him. This was something I had to prove to myself.

Yeah, right. That would work. I'd get right on that.

Up ahead, Windy and Jake were engaged in conversation. He asked her how she got interested in positive psychology.

"It was after my mom had breast cancer, after she got better," she said. "My little sister started smoking and drinking and getting in trouble. I was really trying to find a way to help her . . . but in the process I helped myself."

"Did you need help?" Jake asked.

"I wasn't breaking the rules," Windy said. "I was, like, following them too well. I was trying to be perfect at everything. You know, to have the best grades, and letter in every sport, and star in all the plays."

"Did you manage to do that?"

"I did," Windy said. "But I was miserable. I started having a little trouble with anorexia, after that. And I just had this moment when I thought to myself: *This is it. This is going to be my life if I don't change it.*"

Oh, God. That girl just wouldn't let me hate her.

We were coming up on the camp. We could see flashes of Patagonia jackets up through the trees.

This was the halfway point of the trip. It was just as far to go back as it was to go forward. Something about that idea made me want to try again—even harder—to be a better person. So Jake and Windy had kissed. So he liked her better. I wasn't going to resent her for it. I wasn't going to waste time being bitter. I was going to grow from this experience and become a better person. I liked Windy. I was *rooting* for Windy. She'd had a tough time of it and she'd pulled herself together. She was an inspiration, dammit! She was exactly the inspiration I'd come here looking to find. She hadn't gone all Chuck Norris on the world when things got tough. She hadn't turned herself into a skin-tailed dachshund. She'd found a way to be brave in love, and to take care of herself as well as others. Was I going to punish her for being nice? Or resent her for being kind-hearted? Or hate her for being a better person than me? *This is going to be my life if I don't change it.*

No. I was going to drag myself back to camp. And I was going to give Windy a hug and wish her well. Jake, too. And I was going to take a deep breath, shut the hell up, and do, at last, what I came here to do.

Chapter 12

The next day should have been a Zero Day, since you always follow a really tough day of hiking with a day of rest, but Beckett didn't want to take a Zero Day so close to the trailhead and the people camping there, who he referred to as "the Ding Dongs." He was itching to get us back deeper into the wilderness, far away from the affronts of civilization, and he had the perfect spot in mind—a place called Painted Meadow. It was a three-day hike from here, he explained, but it was the most beautiful spot in the whole range, so it would totally be worth it.

I looked around at our bedraggled group. Everybody who'd been on litter duty had blistered hands and hunched, sore shoulders. The pack-shuttlers didn't look much better, with their scratched-up legs and bleary eyes. Not one person was sitting up straight.

"Aren't you supposed to rest after a tough day of hiking, Boss?" Mason asked.

"You don't even know what a tough day is," Beckett said.

And so, we pushed on. If all went according to plan, we'd arrive at Painted Meadow just in time for the summer solstice. We'd take our Zero Day, rest and recharge, and have a solstice party. That night would also mark the end of our second week out, and the time when we'd turn our sights to gearing up for the grand finale of the trip—the Solos.

But I couldn't even think about the Solos. All I could do, for the next three days, was put one foot in front of the other. I didn't just *want* a rest, I *needed* one, and I thought Beckett was dead wrong to push us so hard. Wasn't he the one always lecturing us to take care of ourselves out on the trail? I didn't understand his thinking, and I confess I didn't entirely trust him to be in charge, but there it was. He was the Boss. He called the shots, and he had the nickname to prove it.

Speaking of nicknames, it was on the first morning of this endless three-day hike to Painted Meadow that I finally got one of my own: "Holdup." As in, "What's the holdup?"

I was so tired on that first day after Hugh's evac, and so generally demoralized, that I couldn't get motivated for hiking, even as I dragged myself along the trail after the others. *I want an evac,* I kept thinking, wishing Hugh were here so I could give him hell for causing all that trouble.

Little things were bugging me. I'd get something in my boot. Or my pack would feel crooked. I kept stopping to adjust things. My ponytail needed reworking. My hat was too tight. Beckett was hiking at the back that day, and every time I stopped, or even slowed down, he'd shout, "What's the holdup?"

"Sorry!" I'd call back. "Just fixing a wedgie!" Or whatever.

By midday, I'd been christened. He didn't even have to ask anymore. Whatever it was, he already knew it was nonsense. "Holdup, get moving!" he'd shout. Or, "This is not a rest stop, Holdup!"

That afternoon, as we stopped to set up camp, Beckett reminded us as a group to fill our water bottles. "Camel up, people! Tomorrow's another hot day!" Then he turned in front of everybody and pointed at me. "Holdup, that means you!"

That was it. It stuck. They loved it. The guys, especially, enjoyed coming up to me for no reason to say, "What's the holdup, Holdup?"

So I got my wish for a nickname—but, as so often happens with wishes, it wasn't at all what I'd hoped for.

"You could think of it differently," Windy suggested. "You could make it a tough-guy thing, like, 'This is a holdup.'" She made her hands into pistols and pointed them at me. Then she made shooting noises: "*Pew! Pew!*"

"But we all know that's not what it is," I said. "I'm not a bandit. I'm just a terrible hiker."

"People are forgetful," Windy said.

"Not that forgetful."

"What if," she started, in a run-with-me-on-this tone, "every time Caveman comes up to you and says 'What's the holdup, Holdup?' you turn around and shoot at him?" She demonstrated again, "*Pew! Pew!*" Then she spun her guns around and set them back in their holsters.

I thought about it. "I could never pull that off," I said.

"I bet you could."

I shook my head and wrinkled my nose, like, *Not really.*

"Can I do it, then?" she asked. "Just to see? Just for an experiment?"

I shrugged. "Sure."

From that point on, Windy never said my nickname again without turning her hands into pistols. Sometimes she'd fire them into the air like Yosemite Sam, shouting, "Anybody seen Holdup?" Sometimes she'd pull them out of her imaginary holsters, point them hip-level at people, and say, "Where's my girl Holdup?" Sometimes she'd straighten one arm and look down the barrel at somebody, and say, "Go get Holdup for me."

And here's the thing: It worked. Before we even reached Painted Meadow, Windy had turned me into a gunslinger. I became the Annie Oakley of our hiking group. People were throwing every Old West metaphor they could think of at me. When I served dinner one night, it was, "Nice grub, Holdup." When I helped with the bear hang, it was amid shouts of, "Yeehaw, Holdup! Rope that sucker!" If I moved slow in the morning, Mason would walk by and call out, "Git along, Holdup! We're movin' out!" When we had to scramble up an extra-steep section of trail, and I managed to make it all the way without pausing, Beckett called out, "That's the way, Holdup! Use your spurs!"

Pretty soon, Windy wasn't the only one slinging imaginary guns when she talked about—or to—me. Vegas would pass me on his way down to the kitchen, point at me with two finger guns, nod a greeting, and say, "Holdup." When Caveman caught my eye, he'd point his two fingers at me and say *"Pew! Pew!"* And Jake, a.k.a. J-Dog—and lately a.k.a. Archer, for some reason I couldn't fathom—used a finger gun to tip his imaginary ten-gallon hat.

"Why do they call you Archer?" I asked him the last morning before we reached Painted Meadow.

He dropped his shoulders. "Seriously?"

"Seriously," I said. "Do you, like, shoot bows and arrows?"

He shook his head. "'Archer' is my last name. How is it possible you don't know that?"

That didn't seem right. "It's your last name? I thought your last name was—" But then I couldn't think of anything—because I'd never had any idea what his last name was, or had any interest in finding out.

"Archer," Jake filled in. "Jacob Samuel Archer."

"Jacob *'J-Dog'* Samuel Archer."

"Yeah," he said, with a head shake, "that's not my best nickname."

He had others. Of course. "What could be better than J-Dog?"

He looked up. "My dad calls me 'Doc.' Then there's 'Big J,' 'J-Money,' 'Jaegermeister,' 'Cash,' 'Bonkers,' 'Ranger,' 'Matrix,' 'Half-Nelson,' 'Club Med,' 'Hawk,' 'Honey Badger.'"

"People call you Honey Badger?"

"Only very special people."

"*Honey Badger*? Seriously?"

"Don't let the sweet name fool you. The honey badger is utterly vicious."

"What does Duncan call you?" I asked.

Jake thought about it. "Too many to list. He's a nickname genius. He's probably got a hundred."

"Like?"

"Anything. He'll call me anything that pops into his head. 'Crab-walker,' 'Soda Can,' 'Big Daddy,' 'Mighty Max.' He was the inventor of 'Naked Jake.'"

"Because you were naked?" I asked. "Or because 'naked' kind of rhymes with 'Jake'?"

"Both."

"What do you call Duncan?" I asked.

Jake sighed and shook his head. "So many. Never 'Duncan,' that's for sure. 'Dunk,' 'Dunkers,' 'Dunkin Donut,' 'D-Train,' 'D-Bag,' 'D-lite,' 'Chuck,' 'Charles.'"

"Why Charles?"

Jake shrugged. "Because it's not his name."

I nodded. "So, basically, any word or non-word in the English language can function as a nickname for any reason at all."

He nodded, like we were done, but then he added, "We do have a default though."

"What's that?"

"Bro."

That was kind of sweet.

But then Jake shook his head. "Actually, no. That just devolves into 'Bra,' 'Brew,' 'Brewsky,' 'Beer Can,' 'Beer Ball,' 'Boner.'"

He came to a stop, then, waiting for what I'd say.

A month before this moment—even two weeks before—I would have shook my head like they were idiots. But now I had a new appreciation for nicknames. And for Duncan, as it happened. And for Jake, as well. It occurred to me that every single one of those names was some basic, goofy substitute for "friend." And I felt so grateful, then, that Duncan had Jake. That they had each other.

"He's lucky to have you," I said.

"He is lucky," Jake said. Then he made his finger into a pistol, pointed it at me, and said, "But I'm luckier."

Beckett wasn't wrong about Painted Meadow. It was, after all, breathtaking. It was better than he had described, and better than I even would've imagined before I saw it for myself. It was a perfect place to spend a Zero Day and have a summer solstice party, and once we were there, I was glad we'd pushed ahead. Sort of.

Here's what greeted us as we rounded the trail and Beckett shouted, "This is it, people!" A sunny green meadow with calf-height grass and wildflowers bowing and fluttering in the breeze. White butterflies. Above, a brilliant blue sky with cotton clouds. On every side, mountain peaks, cradling up around us. The air was cool, but the sun was warm. As each of us stepped into the meadow, we stopped still at the sight. We couldn't keep walking and behold it at the same time.

"You were right," I said to Beckett, as he stopped beside me. "It is like a painted meadow."

"Yeah," he said, "but that's not why they call it Painted Meadow."

I looked over.

"This was the site of a Shoshone massacre," Beckett said. "So many people were killed, the meadow was painted with blood."

"I didn't realize the Shoshone were so bloodthirsty," I said, looking around.

But Beckett gave me a look. "They weren't," he said. "The Shoshone were the ones who were massacred."

"Oh."

Beckett turned to the group. "There's a stream at the east edge," he said. "We'll pitch camp there. And they say this place is haunted, so be on your best behavior." Then he looked around with a big smile, and, for what felt like the first time, I genuinely liked him. "Welcome to my favorite place in the Absarokas."

My first act of business there was to exchange my boots for flip-flops. Just that one act—and taking off my pack—made me feel a hundred pounds lighter. My blisters were healed now, and the sight of the tender new pink skin where they'd been made me feel strangely optimistic. There was business to take care of that afternoon—setting up camp, making dinner—but the prospect of a whole, luxurious day ahead with nothing whatsoever to do made everything else seem easy. I smiled at everybody. I closed my eyes when the breeze blew over me and tried to drink the feeling in through my skin. I paused to look around at all the colors of flowers in the field: magenta, baby blue, butter yellow.

This, I thought. This made it all worth it. This place was the reason I'd come here, and this feeling of awe was exactly what I'd been looking for. It made all the humiliations and injuries and blisters and loneliness worth it.

Cooking dinner was bliss. Falling asleep that night was bliss. And the next day was bliss, too—at least at first.

We woke as usual, made our coffee, ate breakfast, and tidied up our camps. But instead of lining up for more marching through even more mountains, we were free. The morning was cold, but as the sun rose, it warmed my skin, and I had my sweater off by ten. For the rest of the day, I did nothing. Delicious nothing. Some of the big guys went exploring, and Vegas and Jake went to practice their fly-fishing in the stream. Some of the girls decided to "do laundry," which meant scooping up river water and walking it to the farthest, driest side of the meadow, pouring it over their salt-caked socks and T-shirts, and wringing them out a few times before setting them on a rock to bake in the sun.

I watched them work, but I didn't join. We were way past the point of trying to get clean. Instead, I laid myself on my own rock to bake in the sun. Later, I might go looking for wildflowers, press a few into my journal—an Indian paintbrush, a touch-me-not, and a coreopsis— and try to identify others using a booklet Mason lent me. I might help Windy collect dandelions and miner's lettuce for a salad for our solstice dinner. I might cheer for the boys when they brought back three (Beckett's limit) fish to fry up for dinner.

But that morning, all I wanted to do was nothing. I lay melted on my sun-warmed rock. Massacre or no, today, in the warm sunshine, this place was exactly what I'd always seen when I pictured heaven: sunshine, wildflowers, a meadow—and air as clear as water, and just as cool. As strange as it sounds, here, of all places, I felt profoundly close to my lost brother—like I was near him, somehow. I could imagine him in this field. I could see his eight-year-old self with his knobby knees and red sneakers skittering through the long grass or angling down to the riverbank to see what the big guys were up to. He would love it here. He could almost be here, just out of sight somewhere. If I pretended hard enough, it was sort of like he was.

The idea of it filled my eyes with tears. But I was okay. There was too much beauty around me, and too much tranquility, to feel truly sad. I never really felt tranquil, ever—and yet here, under the warming sun, what choice did I have? I had a day of rest, a gentle breeze, and I was lying so limp across a rock that I was practically boneless. And that thought reminded me of a poem I loved to read to my first graders: "The Ballad of the Boneless Chicken." I smiled at the memory and realized that now, every time I read that poem, I'd remember this day, this boneless moment on this big rock, and for that reason, I'd always carry the memory. Really, I had no option but to be happy.

And then some of the girls came to join me. Uno, Dosie, and Caboose.

They'd finished up their washing, and sat on my rock to warm up and dry out.

Dosie said, "Hey, Holdup. You look plum tuckered."

I was. In a good way. "Yep," I said. "Rode hard and put away wet."

They lay down and arranged themselves all around me on the rock, following my sun-soaking lead, and I felt so pleased they were there. I'd gotten so used to being alone over the past year, it still shocked me when I wasn't. I was glad to see them. I was glad to have company.

At first, they yammered about pleasant things—the no-bake cookies we were going to make for the party, the best way to stretch out a tight hamstring, the M&M Uno had found forgotten in her daypack. I enjoyed listening to them and found myself thinking of them like chirpy little songbirds. It surprised me, but I couldn't help deciding they were fun to have around. Until Caboose said, "Let's plan the wedding."

"We think they should have it here," Uno said.

"Who?" I asked, not opening my eyes.

"J-Dog and Heartbreaker," they all said, together.

Had I just been feeling *tranquil*? I sat up.

"We think they should get married in this meadow," Uno said.

"Since this is the place," Dosie finished, "where they're going to get engaged."

I shook my head. "What are you talking about?"

"I have it on good authority," Uno said, "that J-Dog is going to propose marriage to Heartbreaker here. Tonight. During the summer solstice party. In this meadow."

But this was *my* meadow! Mine and Nathan's. I had been happy here, dammit—for like a full five minutes. "Can we use real names, please?" I said.

"It'll have to be a Buddhist ceremony," Uno said, "because HB practices Buddhism."

"What's Buddhism?" Caboose asked.

No. It wasn't possible that anybody didn't know that.

"An ancient Native American religion," Uno answered, with authority.

Make that two people.

I shook my head. "Nobody is getting engaged today. That's totally just wrong."

"Trust me," Uno said. "I'm never wrong."

Could she seriously think that about herself? "You're dead wrong about Buddhism," I said.

"Okay," she said, shrugging. "But I'm never wrong about L-U-V."

"Apparently," Dosie said, "they sleep cuddled up next to each other every night."

They weren't even in the same tent group! "Where are you kids getting all this?" I asked.

"I can't reveal my sources," Dosie said.

I felt a crazy panic I couldn't explain. "First of all," I said then, "they're, like, in preschool. And second of all, they've known each other a week."

"Two weeks, actually—as of today," said Uno.

"Sometimes, you just *know,*" said Dosie.

"Haven't you heard of love at first sight?" Caboose demanded.

"We are all way too disgusting for anybody to fall in love," I declared. "They haven't even changed underpants since the first day they met."

"Gross," Dosie said, opening her eyes to squint at me.

"People do not meet and get engaged in a week," I insisted.

"*Two* weeks."

"Actually," Caboose offered, raising her hand like she was in school, "my parents did."

"When it's right, it's right," Uno said.

"When it's fate, it's fate," Dosie agreed.

I took a deep breath, held up my hands in a *stop* gesture, and said, "Okay." I couldn't stop them planning the wedding, but I didn't have to stay and listen. I stood up and faked a stretch. "Have fun party planning. I'm going to take a walk."

"You don't want to brainstorm?" Dosie said.

"Maybe I'll work on a sample wildflower bouquet."

"Awesome," Uno said, and I nodded like I agreed.

Heading out into the meadow, *my meadow,* I took a second to steady myself. This was nonsense. Literally nonsense. Five minutes of tranquility? That was all I got? A glimpse of heaven just to watch it turn into love-at-first-sight wedding hell? The irony was not lost on me that being here was robbing me of the tranquility I'd specifically come here to find. And the only two people I could have talked to about how miserable I was were the exact two people who were making me miserable.

I pretended to pick flowers for a long while, and then made my way to the stream bank to follow it back up toward camp. I thought I might ask to borrow Windy's book on happiness. But when I got there, I spotted the two of them, J-Dog and Heartbreaker, sitting knees-to-knees by the campsite, eyes closed in meditation as Windy taught Jake all about the Native American art of Buddhism. For their up-coming nuptials.

Knees-to-knees. That was how *I* had sat with Jake!

Oh, God. I was genuinely losing my mind.

Then, I noticed Beckett was nearby, and I was alarmingly happy to see him. "Hey, Boss," I said, turning his way. "Give me something to do."

He looked up. "Anything?"

I nodded. "Anything."

So he let me inventory and reorganize the first-aid kit, sort and consolidate the food packs, darn a ripped tarp, and help him work a splinter out of his right thumb.

"I like your work ethic today, Holdup," Beckett said then. "This is Certificate-worthy behavior."

I hate to admit those words were motivating, but they were. "What's next?" I asked.

Beckett sucked on his thumb. "Go collect dandelions for a salad for tonight," he said, gesturing back toward the meadow. Then he glanced the other direction. "I'd send you that way for blackberries, but I don't want to interrupt the lovebirds."

Three Good Things. What were three good things about today? Actually, even as grumpy as I now was, I could name plenty more than three. Easily. I'd woken under our blue tarp to the sound of the creek running by. I'd made a terrific batch of morning coffee, if I did say so myself. I'd had a whole morning of freedom. I'd rested. I'd sunned myself on a hot rock with all the abandon of a gecko. I'd felt a hun-dred breezes. I'd stood in a field of wildflowers. I'd seen a cloud in the shape of a heart. I'd helped Beckett get that splinter out. And I'd literally had a glimpse of heaven—and felt a closeness to the person I missed most in the world that I hadn't experienced in years.

A pretty remarkable day, all in all. Even if, at the moment, I happened to be ever so slightly miserable.

As I made my way around the field, picking dandelions for real now instead of wildflowers for pretend, I tried to construct a plan to be less miserable. At the beginning of this trip, I'd wanted to learn how to be so tough that I was untouchable, but instead I'd gone the other way: I'd become all-emotions-all-the-time. Well, maybe that wasn't entirely a bad thing, since at least I wasn't numb anymore. And shifting my heartbreak from Mike to Jake seemed like an improvement—surely a not-even-boyfriend I'd made out with on one night would be easier to get over than a bona fide husband I'd been married to for six years. You'd think so, anyway. "Be brave," Hugh had said. And Windy had said, "*Having* doesn't make you happy: *appreciating* does." Maybe not having what I wanted would force me to appreciate what I did have. It was possible, at least. All I could do was try. Even just trying, I decided, could be an act of bravery in itself.

So, salad picked, I went back to our tarp for a refreshing nap, and by the time I woke up, it was late afternoon and dinner prep had already started. All the tent groups had pooled their cookstoves together for the party. Windy was pouring fruit punch powder into everybody's water bottles and calling it mojitos. Somebody had collected blackberries and added them to the dandelions. Vegas had amazed everyone by making a very palatable salad dressing out of Dijon spice and powdered milk. The three fish had been cleaned and seasoned with dried oregano and garlic pepper, and Cookie was grilling them with all the attention of a master chef.

I rubbed my eyes, fixed my ponytail, brushed my teeth, and headed down to join them.

I would find a way to enjoy this party; I had earned the right to enjoy it. I would not let anybody's marriage proposal to anybody depress the hell out of me. There was a lot more to life than who was or was not marrying whom. *Getting what you want doesn't make you happy.* I hadn't understood Windy when she'd said it at first, but now it made sense.

I worked out a strategy. I would focus on the food first, and savor the hell out of each bite. I'd sit next to Beckett, who I was actually growing fond of. I would participate wholeheartedly in whatever goofy rituals he wanted us to do. I would immerse myself in the moment, fully, without holding anything back. If we sang, I'd sing. If we danced, I'd dance. I'd saturate my brain with such an overabundance of gratitude for every little joy around me that I wouldn't have any room for envy, or loneliness, or sorrow. And if J-Dog did, after all, propose marriage to Heartbreaker two weeks after meeting her—and two weeks and one day after messing around with me—I'd be too insulated by happiness to even care.

The fish smelled mouthwatering as it cooked, and it tasted even better. I let my tongue caress every mouthful, savoring the smoky juice. When Jake came over with his dinner and sat next to me, I popped up and moved over next to Beckett. Jake frowned a little as if to say, *That was weird,* but then Windy came to take my place, and all was forgotten. As we ate, we toasted the fishermen in the group and gave thanks for the fish. I also gave silent thanks for the existence of butter in the world, and the fact that it was so well suited to long camping trips.

We all ate together in a big circle around the burners, which served as a campfire. We sang bawdy songs. Vegas turned out to be a drummer in a college band back in Memphis, and he got all the minions playing Run-DMC rhythms with rocks and sticks. Once that was going, the kids started to dance. They were drunk on plain Kool-Aid somehow, or maybe drunk on exhaustion, or drunk on the good life. I steered my eyes away from the sight of Jake and Windy sitting two by two. Caboose turned out to be quite a singer, and she busted out with a song called the "Cupid Shuffle," which every single person there could sing along to. (And which I had never even heard before.) Apparently, it had its own line dance, and the kids all popped up to do it.

That's when Beckett pulled me up to join, and when I protested that I didn't know the dance, Beckett said, "Shut the hell up, Holdup. It's easy."

He wasn't wrong, it turned out. That dance was so easy that a group of goofballs could do it with no music, twenty miles from civilization, under the stars—me, Uno, Dosie, Cookie, and Beckett, dancing in the grass like we'd been friends forever. The fact that I was participating at all was surprising, but it was even more surprising that my plan worked. I had so much fun I forgot to be unhappy. I even forgot to be careful not to look over at Jake and Windy.

That's when I accidentally did. Just as Caboose and the drummers took a break and the dancing broke apart, before I'd found a new distraction, I forgot to resist the gravitational force of glancing at the two of them—and I discovered quite by accident that they were gone.

I looked around. They weren't dancing. They weren't warming up by the cookstoves. They weren't anywhere that I could see. It gave me a jolt of anxiety because there really wasn't anywhere else to go. They couldn't exactly wander to a bar down the street. There was nothing else to do but stay here—except, possibly, the one thing people sneak off in the woods for.

I told myself not to stand there like an idiot looking around for them, but I did it anyway. That's when I saw something else—something even more interesting than the absence of Jake and Windy.

Snowflakes.

Chapter 13

H ey!" I said. "Hey! Snow!"

Everybody stopped to stare at me.

I shook my head and pointed at the air. "Snow!" I said again. That's when they saw it.

Sure enough. Snow. Plump, ethereal snowflakes, smack-dab on the summer solstice. Fluttering down, backlit by the campstoves' flames.

"Um," Mason said. "Isn't it summer?"

"I *thought* it felt really cold tonight!" Cookie said, delighted to be right.

We all turned to Beckett, but he was just as amazed as the rest of us.

"What do we do, Boss?" Caveman asked.

Beckett turned to us with an *I don't know* expression on his face, but then, taking in the sight of the ten people who needed him to have a plan, I watched him turn his brain to the task of making something up.

"Okay, people," he said, getting into character. "There's no doubt we've got a snow situation." With that, he started barking orders to everybody. We were to clean up the party site, but keep the stoves burning and boil water for hot cocoa—but he wanted us to melt a spoonful of butter into each cup we drank. "I don't care if it's gross," he said. "You'll need the calories to keep yourselves warm through the night." We pulled out the cheese and cut off hunks to eat. We retied the tarps to make one large cover so we could consolidate warmth by bunking together. We put on our pj's, but then Beckett had us layer our outerwear on top of it—wind jackets included. Anything that wasn't wet, we put on—from mittens and extra socks to the little fleece head-and-neck coverings they called balaclavas. Then we all piled into our sleeping bags like a middle school slumber party.

I was hell-bent on finding a place to sleep as far from Jake and Windy as possible, but there was a lot of jockeying for position. In the end, I wound up sandwiched between Vegas and Caveman, the two loudest snorers in the group, and as awful as that was, I thought, at least it was better than my worst-case scenario. That's when I felt knuckles rapping on my scalp like it was a door, and when I arched back to look, Jake's face was six inches away. His sleeping bag was head-to-head with mine.

He waved. "Sweet dreams."

Windy was right next to him. She waved too.

"Don't be jealous," I said, gesturing to the big guys on either side of me. "And no trading."

"That's right, Holdup," Vegas said, with a note of affection in his voice. "Just think of us as your personal hot water bottles."

The next morning, when I opened my eyes, the blue vinyl of the tarp was about an inch from my nose. We had tied it low, but not *that* low. It had sunk at least three feet during the night under the weight of the snowfall. I lifted my hand to touch it, and it was heavy and dense, like a water balloon. I gave it a push and, over by the edge of the tarp, some snow slid off the side. I was the first person awake. I lifted my feet, still in the bag, and gave the tarp a kick, which caused another avalanche off the same spot. Each time I knocked some snow off, the tarp got lighter and rose a little farther from my face.

I kicked until it was high enough for me to sit up and look around, waking everybody around me in the process. I saw a tapestry of sleeping bags, and, beyond it, a forest as white as Narnia. We were in the exact same spot we'd been in before, but the grassy meadow and the wildflowers and the warm rocks where we'd sunned ourselves the day before were all gone. Every single thing that had not been sheltered by the tarp that night was solid, pure white. It was a summer winter wonderland.

The morning was surreal. We cooked breakfast without any sense of how the day would play out. Maybe it goes without saying, but there was no weather forecast; there was no way to know what to expect. We just had to watch the sky to make our best guess. Beckett wanted to stay put if it was going to keep snowing. If it warmed up, he thought we should move to a lower elevation. We lingered around camp, in a state of limbo, waiting to figure it out.

By noon, the sky was clear, and it was warmer. Beckett announced we'd do a short three-mile hike to a place called Elk Ridge, which had a better wind block in case the temperatures plunged again.

We hiked all afternoon. It was slow going—not because the snow was that deep or physically hard to manage, but because we literally didn't know where the trail was. Beckett stopped us every ten minutes to double-check positions and landmarks. Before we left, he'd gone over the route on the map with me and had me double-checking our position as we hiked. We hadn't been moving long before I realized it was actually warming up. The snow seemed to notice it too, because the ground was turning to slush under our feet.

It took the rest of the day to cover those three miles to Elk Ridge, and by the time we arrived it was already dark and most of the beautiful snow was gone.

The next morning, after breakfast, Beckett pointed out to us that we were starting our third and final week of the trip. "This is it, folks," he said. "Next stop: grand finale." By "grand finale," he meant the Solos. Before the week was out, he would send us in three separate groups out on our own to survive for twenty-four hours. He had us make a list of the four people we'd most like to have with us in our groups.

"Take this seriously, people," he cautioned, raising half an eyebrow. "And be careful who you wish for."

I took it seriously. I would have loved to hike with Windy, but I felt sure that she'd put Jake on her list—and that Jake, in turn, would put her on his—and I did not want to spend my final days in the Absarokas engaged in *will-they-won't-they* theorizing like a teenage girl. One basic fact was clear: I needed to get the hell away from both of them.

Other than that, I didn't care who I Soloed with. Truly.

In the end, I wrote down, *Anybody but Jake*, circled it twice, folded up my slip of paper, and turned it in.

When Beckett had collected them all, he stuffed them into the pocket of his daypack and said he'd take a couple of days to review our requests and assemble the groups.

In the meantime, we'd work our way to a section of the range where the trail split into three roughly equivalent paths—each path for a different Solo group. When we got there, after reviewing our maps and strategies, he'd turn us loose for twenty-four hours and cross his fingers. During that time, we'd have to find our way, find water, pitch and strike our camps, and make good decisions over and over again. "This is what you're here for, people. This is what you've been working toward. The Solos. Sink or swim. Kill or be killed. Eat or be eaten."

Then he grinned and waggled his eyebrows. "But not quite yet. Not today. Today, we're just hiking a totally brutal pass called Devil's Crotch."

Three days later, after supper, Beckett gathered us all to announce the groups for the Solos.

"Remember when I asked you to tell me who you wanted in your group?" he asked.

We nodded.

"Well, I forgot to mention one thing. I don't care." He lifted his hands, in a what-were-you-thinking shrug. "I don't care who you like or who you don't like—who you have a crush on—who you dream about in your sleeping bag. Doesn't matter. This is not about having fun. It's certainly one of the few things in life that's not about sex. This is survival, folks. I've matched you up not with *who you want*— but with *who you need*. To survive. Skills. Remember those? You came here to learn wilderness skills? Some of you have paid close attention, even taken notes"—here, he paused to point a finger gun right at me—"others of you have wasted your time—and mine. But this is the moment that's either going to make you or break you."

He reached into his daypack and pulled out his list. "These are the groups. They are nonnegotiable. Do not come to me and tell me you don't like Vegas or that Flash farts in his sleep. I don't care! Maybe Dosie makes fun of you behind your back, or maybe Heartbreaker won't give you the time of day. Too bad! These lists are for your safety and survival. You will make the most of them, and you will be grateful for the opportunity."

I crossed my fingers. *Not Jake*, I chanted in my head. *Not Jake, not Jake, not Jake.*

"Jake!" Beckett called out then. "You will Solo with . . ." He checked his list again. "Flash, Dosie, and Calamity Jane."

I looked around. Calamity Jane? Who was that? Then I realized Beckett was pointing at me with another finger pistol. "That's you, Holdup," he said. "New nickname. Get used to it. *Pew.*"

Windy turned out to be with Caveman, Hound Dog, and Caboose.

She was at my side before Beckett had even finished reading off the rest of the names. "You're with Jake?" she asked. "You got Jake?"

"I didn't *ask* for him," I said.

"Trade ya?"

I shrugged. "Sure."

Windy grabbed my hand and pulled me over to Beckett.

"Can we trade places?" she asked. "In the Solo groups?"

Beckett tilted his head, like, *Seriously?* "No."

"But I thought you didn't care," Windy said.

"I don't care who *you* want in your group. I do care who *I* want in your group."

Windy crossed her arms in front of her and tried to stare Beckett down. Then, at last, when it didn't work, she flipped that long sheet of yellow hair, and marched away. It was the most juvenile gesture I'd ever seen from her.

Now it was my turn to stare Beckett down. I crossed my own arms. "I put 'anyone but Jake' on my list."

"I know," Beckett said. "And then you got Jake."

"It's not funny."

"It's a little funny."

"You gave me Jake because I asked not to have him?"

He tilted his head. "Not exactly."

I lowered my voice and leaned in. "Hey. Unlike you, I do not come to the wilderness every summer. This is a once-in-a-lifetime thing for me. I have never been here before, and I will never be here again—or anywhere even similar—and even though I am totally and completely out of my element, I am trying like crazy to make it count."

"I know," Beckett said, nodding. "I can tell."

"I've done everything you ask. I've obeyed every rule. If you said, 'Go get water,' I got water. If you said, 'Carry the litter,' I carried the litter. I never said no. I never held back. I've given this trip every single thing I had."

"I know that, too," Beckett said, his voice quieter now.

"And there was one—*one*—person I wanted to avoid during the very last week I will ever spend in these mountains. Why the hell did you put me with Jake?"

Beckett took a breath, then, and let it out.

He took a step closer and leaned in toward my ear. "I gave you Jake because you're headstrong and accident prone, and he's our medic and I trust him to patch you up. I gave you Jake because you're the best map reader we've got, and he's damn near blind. And I gave you Jake because you absolutely never believe in yourself—and he finds a way to believe in you every damn day."

He gave me Jake. And now it was my job to be grateful for the opportunity.

The morning of, Beckett went over each group's route with them on the map. Then we all literally waved good-bye, turned in three separate directions, and started hiking.

With luck, we'd all see each other again the next afternoon. And by luck, I meant: not getting crushed by a falling widow-maker, not stumbling on a hungry bear, not suffocating under an avalanche, not running out of water, not drowning in an icy river, not choking on a hunk of cheese at dinner, not accidentally setting someone on fire with the cookstove, not getting lost, and not giving up entirely and just sitting down to die.

All possibilities.

Beckett had given me the shocking news that I was the best map reader in the group, but he hadn't given that news to Flash, a.k.a. Mason, a.k.a. the Meanie of the Mountains. I had built a fairly peaceful relationship with Mason since we'd been out, mainly by staying out of his way, but people who crossed him always regretted it in the end. Even if they got their way in the moment, he'd find a way to punish them later by, say, pointing out to the group when they had food in their teeth. Or stalking them when they'd walked out alone to go poop and growling like a bear once their pants were down. Or—keeping it simple—just tripping them along the trail. He had a real talent for humiliation and cruelty, and I could not imagine what had inspired Beckett to put Flash, who was incapable of slowing down, in a group with Dosie, who was incapable of speeding up. On the surface, it seemed like a recipe for disaster, but after the insight smackdown Beckett had offered up the night before, I chose to give him the benefit of the doubt.

That said, as we started hiking, Mason literally lifted the map out of my hands, and said, "I'll take that, thanks."

I didn't fight him. He seemed like a competent hiker, although I wouldn't know for sure, since he was always far out of sight on the trail. I didn't need to be a big shot, and I didn't need to assert my map prowess. I knew I was good—now, suddenly—and that was more than plenty.

There wasn't a lot of wiggle room to our hiking order. Mason took the distant lead, pausing every twenty minutes or so to wait for the rest of us like a restless bull. Dosie took the back, shouting every five minutes or so, "Hold up, Holdup!" when she lost sight of me. And

Jake and I walked at about the same pace—a pleasant, conversational pace—together.

"So," Jake said. "How are you liking the wilderness?"

"In my whole life put together, I've never done as many scary things as in the past two point five weeks."

"But you've survived."

"So far," I agreed. "And fear is a hell of a lot less scary than it used to be."

"Now you're fearless."

"No," I said. "But I'm fearless-*er*."

"Like Chuck Norris."

"What?"

"Like all those jokes about Chuck Norris being so fearless. You know, like, 'Chuck Norris doesn't take showers. He takes bloodbaths.'"

"How do you know about those Chuck Norris jokes?"

"Everybody knows about those Chuck Norris jokes."

"I didn't. Until recently. Ish."

"You're a girl."

"My whole journal is filled with Chuck Norris jokes," I said. "He was totally my role model coming out here. I was like, *What would Chuck Norris do?*"

Jake shrugged. "Guess I'm more like, *What would Bill Murray do?*"

"But that's just it!" I said. "I came out here trying to learn how to be tough and mean, but then I went the other way."

"Now you're soft and sweet?"

"No," I said. "Not the opposite way. Just another way."

"So who's your role model now?"

"I don't know," I said. "Maybe Annie Oakley."

Jake raised a finger pistol and shot it into the air. I made a mental note to thank Windy for that nickname makeover.

It was nice to hang out with Jake again. I'd been avoiding him so desperately ever since the evac that I'd forgotten how fun he was to talk to. We joked around so much, in fact, that we failed to pay attention to where we were going. For most of the morning, that was all right, but sometime around noon, it became apparent that we weren't on the right trail. According to Beckett, our group was supposed to go around the contour of a hill—but at a certain point, as we caught up with Flash, who was literally tapping his boot as he waited for Dosie to catch up, he made a confession.

"Looks like the trail kind of disappears here," Flash said, gesturing ahead at an absence of trail.

"Disappears?" Jake said.

"The trail can't disappear," I said. I looked around. We had been hiking for quite a while under the deep shade of some pine trees. There wasn't a lot of undergrowth here. The ground was just sandy dirt, which meant that the trail, even if it were there, might be hard to see.

Something hit me, then. "Why are we going over a hill?" I asked Flash. "Our route wasn't supposed to go over a hill."

"You're just noticing that now?" he asked. He turned to share a chuckle with Jake when he saw that Jake, too, was just noticing that now. He shrugged. "We're taking a shortcut."

"We're not supposed to take a shortcut, Mason," I said.

"Nobody said not to."

Jake said, "Actually, Beckett said not to."

I squeezed my eyes closed. "When did we leave the trail?"

Mason thought about it. "Two—maybe three—hours back."

"Hours?" I said.

Just then, Dosie came ambling up. "This hill is steep," she said, winded.

I was still gaping at Flash. "You just led us off the marked path, onto a random shortcut, without bothering to mention it?" I asked.

"I figured if you weren't cool with it, you'd say something."

"We weren't paying attention!" I said.

"Well, that's rule number one, right there," Mason said.

What can I say? He had me.

"I thought it was so obvious," Mason said. He pulled the map out of his pocket and showed the oxbow shape of the trail, curving around the half-circle edge of a hill. "Rather than walk all this way," he traced the distance around with his finger, "why not just cut across?"

"Because there's no trail!" I said.

"But there was a trail! I followed a trail."

"A deer trail," I said, "or an elk trail. Moose, maybe. Not a *human* trail! Not a National Park trail."

This was the moment for Flash to say, *Wow, I'm a complete idiot,* and beg our forgiveness. But, instead, somehow, he flipped it the other way. "Why weren't you guys paying attention?"

Because we were talking! Because we were flirting! Because Jake is so frigging funny, and he was telling me Chuck Norris jokes, and I cannot remember the last time somebody made me laugh! "Because," I said to Mason, putting a hand on my hip for authority, "you were supposed to be the leader!"

"Keep your pants on," Mason said. "We'll just turn around and go back."

But when we all turned around, there was nothing to go back to. There were lots of little animal trails, crisscrossing each other through the dry dirt. No big, simple, obvious trail like the ones we knew.

"That's it," Mason said, pointing southeast.

"That's definitely not it," I said. "We came from the southwest."

"I thought we came from over there," Dosie said, pointing due west.

I let out a sigh. "Give me the map," I said.

Mason handed it over.

"You know you've got it upside down, right?" I said.

Mason blinked. "Do I?"

"Mason," I said. "Tell me you're kidding."

But his eyes widened just a bit, and he shook his head very slowly.

I pulled my compass out of my pocket. "Okay," I said. "This is north." Then I rotated the map 180 degrees until the arrow for "north" on the map matched the arrow on my compass. "And now the map is oriented properly."

Mason let out a long whistle.

Had he slept through map-reading class? I'd be the first to admit that contour wilderness maps required a certain sense for spatial relationships and weren't everyone's thing—but lining up two arrows seemed pretty basic.

"You took us left when we should have been going right," I said.

"And," Dosie added, "you took us off the trail."

"Okay, okay," I said. "Here's what we know. The trail goes between this hill"—I circled one with my finger—"and that hill." I circled the other. "We've been going up this hill. So if we go back down, we should, at some point, hit the trail."

"What if we don't?" Dosie asked.

"I think we will," I said.

"What if—"

"Dosie!" Flash shouted. "Not helping!"

"Let's check water bottles," I said. We were all about the same: two-thirds gone.

"That's the biggest worry," Jake said. "Water."

"The trail crosses a stream down here," I said, pointing, "so if we can get back to it, we can camp right there."

"If?" Dosie said.

"Sorry—" I said. "*When.*"

We started making our way back down the hill. I held my compass out to keep us on a straight line, which was easier under the trees than it was once the trees thinned out and the underbrush was thicker. After an hour, we were truly bushwhacking, and everybody's legs were scratched and bloody. We'd all taken a few stumbles, but Jake had fallen the most, and his arms and face had scratches, too. It was tempting to avoid the brush by following the animal trails that zigzagged around us, but we didn't want to get off course. Adversity kept us close together, and we hiked as a unified group of four.

"What happens if we don't find water tonight?" Dosie asked.

"Then we'll find it tomorrow," I said.

"How long can the human body go without fresh water?" Dosie asked.

"Three days," Jake answered. "Well, two days before the hallucinations set in, anyway."

"Jake—" I said.

"It's the rule of threes," Jake said, like it was just empirically interesting. "You can go three minutes without air. Three days without water. And three weeks without food."

"Not helping," Mason finished.

"Haven't people died on these trips before?" Dosie asked next.

"They're under new management," Jake and I said, in unison.

It took a total of four hours before we hit the trail again. But oh, God, was it glorious to see it. Breathless and bleeding, we all hugged anyway. We were saved.

Except. We'd backtracked a bit coming down the hill and rejoined the trail in a spot we'd already passed. If the map was correct, and if I was reading it right, it was still a good mile to the stream crossing— and it was already five in the afternoon.

It took us another hour to hike that last mile. And when we reached the stream crossing at last, we realized something I hadn't noticed on the map. A stream did cross the trail, just as I'd insisted, but the stream was at the bottom of a steep ravine. A hundred feet down, or so. The trail actually used a terrifyingly rickety rope bridge to cross it, like something out of a spaghetti Western.

We walked to the point where the rope bridge met the trail, and peered over. And it occurred to me suddenly that the creek bed, after all this, might be dry. I crossed my fingers. We looked down. Way below, it was wet.

I closed my eyes. "Thank God," I said.

Jake gave me a high five. "It's going to be a bitch to get to," he said, "but it's there."

And so, we set up camp. On closer inspection, there was a footpath down to the creek. Jake offered to take all four water bottles and a cookpot down to load up at the stream, though, looking back, why we gave the guy with Coke-bottle glasses that job I can't imagine. Dosie started dinner, and Mason and I went to set up the tarp.

When the tarp was ready, I went back to the kitchen to find that Jake still hadn't come back with the water. We were starting to lose the light, now, too.

Something was wrong. I just knew. "I bet it's hard to climb that ravine with an open pot of water," I announced to the rest of the group, even though nobody was paying attention. "I'll go help Jake out."

The path to the water was steep, and bumpy, and counterintuitive. You often had to go up to go down or sideways to go forward. Also, probably half of the big rocks that I stepped on in the path were wobbly. The farther along I got, the more I started to worry that I would find Jake unconscious at the bottom of the trail, splayed out on the rocky riverbank.

I made it to the bottom before I found him. He wasn't unconscious, but he did look like he'd fallen. He was on his hands and knees, panting and frantic. When he heard me, he looked up, but didn't see me. His eyes were red, like he'd been crying. "Don't come any closer!" he said. "I've lost my glasses."

I took a few steps closer.

"Stop!" he shouted. "You'll step on them!" His face was all agony.

"I won't step on them," I said. "They're not a contact lens."

"I'm serious! Stop!"

"Okay," I said. He was serious. Seriously freaking out. I switched into teacher mode and infused my voice with calm. "I'll help you. We'll find them."

He shook his head. He wasn't listening. "I'm telling you. They're lost."

"We'll find them," I repeated, sinking to my knees and starting to crawl across the beach toward him. "I'm going slow," I said. "I'm crawling. We'll find them."

He was breathing like he'd just sprinted a marathon.

"Take a deep breath," I said. "Slow down."

He nodded and tried to slow down.

I kept crawling toward him.

"It's Helen, by the way," I said.

"I know that."

"But you can't see."

"I can see. It's just blurry. Anyway, I know your voice. And your gait."

"My gait?"

"It's very distinctive."

"Are you hurt?" I asked, still crawling closer.

"Not much."

"I'm going to help you."

"Okay."

"Deep, slow breaths."

He did a few of those and, while he was at it, I reached him. As soon as I was in arms' distance, he grabbed me and pulled me the last couple of feet like a drowning man grabs at a life preserver. He put his arms around me crushingly tight and pressed his face into the nook between my neck and my shoulder. The air pushed and pulled against me as he panted exactly the way you do when you're terrified of something. I couldn't imagine what he had to be terrified of, but in that moment it didn't matter.

I slid my hands up and down his back, patting and soothing the best I could. "It's okay," I said, over and over. "I'm going to help you."

We stayed like that for a good while, the sky fading, the evening air losing its warmth. As I held on to him, his breathing slowed and settled.

After a while, I said, "I thought you had a strap to keep your glasses on."

"I did. But we used it to hold Caveman's boot together when it came apart on a day hike."

"There was nothing else you could've used?"

"Not at the moment."

I shook my head. "Always the hero."

"I'm so stupid," he said then, into my neck.

"You're not stupid," I said. "You just lost your glasses."

"I shouldn't even be here," he said.

I thought about how he'd faked his medical report. "Well," I said, "that might be true, actually."

He leaned back a little, and looked down at his hands. "Do you remember how I signed up for this trip—but then I canceled? And then I signed up again?"

"Sort of," I said. Not really.

"I canceled because I was having trouble with my eyes. And after several exams and a bunch of tests, it turned out that I have an inherited vision disorder that can't be fixed."

"You mean like the night blindness?"

"That's part of it."

I waited.

"Over the next few years," he said then, still looking down, "I am going to lose—" Here, he took a deep breath, hitching at the height, and let it deflate slowly before he finished: "—my sight."

All I could do was echo. "Lose your sight?"

"I have a thing called retinitis pigmentosa," he said.

"That does not sound good."

He shook his head. "You have these receptors in your eyes. Cones and rods. The rods are around the edges. They're in charge of peripheral vision and dim light."

He paused to make sure I was following.

"Okay," I said.

"The cones process color and detail."

"Okay."

"When you have this thing like I do—it's inherited—your rods and cones start to die."

I shook my head like that was impossible. "Die?"

"One by one, they go out."

"Why?"

He shrugged. "They make the wrong kind of protein. It's all very scientific. They basically just stop working, one at a time. Most people who have it are legally blind by forty."

"But you won't be!" Legally blind? By *forty*?

"No," he agreed. "For me, it'll be much sooner."

"Sooner?" I was like a denial parrot.

"My receptors seem to be dying very quickly."

I could feel my heart beating fast in my chest. It was that feeling you get in an emergency when you have to figure out what to do. But there was nothing to do.

"It started with the night blindness—just a little, at first. Two years ago. That was the rods. I ignored it junior year. But by the start of senior year, when I couldn't read to study, I went to the doc."

"And got glasses."

He nodded. "That's the cones."

"So what do you do? What's the treatment?"

"There is no treatment."

There was no treatment? "This is the twenty-first century," I said. "There's a treatment for everything. Even things that don't need treating."

He shrugged. "Not this."

"People don't just go blind!" I tried to imagine Jake, of all people, unable to see. What about that wry grin he was always giving people? I loved that wry grin. How was he supposed to give that grin if he couldn't see the person he was giving it to?

"Vitamin A is supposed to help some," he said. "So I take supplements. Some studies indicate fish oil might not be a bad idea."

"Fish oil and carrots? That's the best they can do? Who's your doctor—Bugs Bunny?"

"There is an experimental gene therapy," he said then. "A nine-year-old boy did it and he could see the blackboard at school afterward. A girl did it and saw fireflies for the first time."

"Why aren't you doing that? Right now?"

"It's not a treatment. It's an experiment."

"But if these kids got some, you should get some, too."

"It's not a cup of lemonade. It's an experimental gene therapy."

"But there's got to be—"

"There isn't!"

I fell quiet.

"I've spent the past year using my pre-med–trained brain to rake through every available piece of information. If you never believe anything else I say, believe this: All I can do is wait for the light to go out."

I put my hand over my mouth. He really wasn't kidding. This impossibly capable, utterly independent guy was losing his sight. He knew it, and he knew there was nothing he could do about it, and he'd carried that knowledge every step we'd hiked on this whole trip, here in the middle of nowhere with a bunch of yahoos, listening with compassion as they—*as I*—complained about popped blisters and being misunderstood and generally took every single one of our blessings for granted.

His eyes were dying. What was he facing? What would his life be like when all the light was gone? How would he even pick out his clothes in the morning? How would he buy his groceries? Or get from his house to his job? Or find a book to read? I couldn't think of a future less suited to the person fated for it. He'd given up medical school—for what? How on earth would he keep that fearsome brain of his busy in the dark?

My thoughts spun. I thought of all the beautiful things that were going to disappear: twinkling lights, bonfires, late-afternoon sunshine, shadows, fluttering leaves, rain clouds, smiles. I thought of all the things he'd never even see. He'd never know what his children looked like—or his grandchildren. He'd only ever hear their voices. The idea of it was enough to pull all the air out of my lungs. I felt them deflate.

"You're killing me," I said at last.

And there came the wry grin. "Don't say that."

"That's why you faked your medical report."

He shook his head. "Stupid."

"And that's why you aren't going to med school."

"That's right."

"Why didn't you just tell me?"

He shook his head. "I didn't know how to talk about it."

"Does your dad know?"

"Yes."

"That's why he didn't want you coming here?"

"That's why he doesn't know I'm here at all."

"You lied to your dad? Where does he think you are?"

"A Buddhist meditation retreat in the Berkshires."

"Good thing you met Windy and she taught you to meditate."

"That will come in handy."

"What does he think?"

"My dad? He thinks what he always thinks. That if he pretends nothing is wrong, then nothing will be."

"He's in denial?"

Jake pretended to think about it. "Yeah. When you look up 'denial,' there's a picture of my dad."

"I didn't think that was a real thing."

"His nickname for me is 'Doc.' When he looks at me, he literally sees the person he's always intended me to be."

"But he'll adjust, right?"

Jake frowned for how to explain it. "My dad has only ever been willing to have one kind of son. The high-achieving, hard-working, valedictorian kind."

"Tell me you weren't valedictorian."

He shrugged, like, *Sorry.* "But now everything's different."

I shook my head as I took it all in. "That's why you can't drive in the dark?"

He nodded. "And also why I was so squirrelly, too, in the hotel room."

I looked down.

He went on. "I'm not really myself these days."

Just then, it started to rain a little—just a sprinkle.

"I hate that I can't really see you right now," he said then.

"I bet you can," I said. "If you try."

He lifted his eyes, then, and I could tell he wasn't sure what I meant.

So I took one of his hands—a scratched, callused, dirt-caked hand—and I pressed it against my face. He lifted the other one, then, to touch the other side, and then he moved his hands all around, touching my jaw, my cheekbones, my eyebrows, my nose. He closed his eyes, lost and concentrating. The feel of it, the intimacy of it, made my breath shudder.

"There you are," he said, at last.

"Here I am."

I studied his face while he concentrated on mine. "You have the best beard of the group, by the way," I said.

"Yeah?"

"The bushiest, at any rate."

"Oh, yeah. The men in my family can grow a beard in like a day."

"That's something," I said.

"It's a blessing and a curse."

"I can imagine."

"I grew a handlebar mustache junior year and waxed it into points."

"Beckett's beard makes him look like a rat," I said.

"And Vegas looks like he's been eating a caramel apple."

"But you," I said. "You have, like, a thick black forest of beard. In the right light, it's almost glossy. You definitely win the beard prize. You're like the Brawny paper towel guy."

"I don't think he has a beard."

"Well," I said. "If he did."

He smiled for a second at that, but then the smile faded. Dropping his hands, he said, "I can't believe I lost my fucking glasses."

It sparked me to action. We were losing the light. "I'm going to find them." I pointed at him. "Stay here." Then I shifted back to my hands and knees to start crawling again, and right as I did, we both heard a snap. I looked down. I'd been kneeling over them the whole time.

"Found 'em," I said.

"For real?" he asked.

"Yes," I said, picking up the two pieces.

"Did they snap in half?" he asked, peering for the answer.

"No, actually," I said. "One of the arms just came off. Is that what they're called? Arms?"

"But the lenses are okay?"

I put the lenses in his hand, and he wiped them with his shirt and popped them right up onto his face. "Oh, God, there you are," he said, and he clamped me into another full-body hug.

I hugged back.

Then, without warning, he pulled back just a little, brushed that glossy beard past my cheek, and without asking or even thinking about asking, he shifted that hug into a kiss.

The kissing we'd done in the motel was like a peck on the cheek compared to this. This was like nothing else—a driven, anxious, ravenous kiss, and he brought his hands up into my hair to keep me close. It felt like a last kiss, somehow. Like a farewell kiss. One that eclipsed everything around it. Some kisses are dares—and some are just truth.

I don't know how he could press so much longing and so much determination into one stolen moment, but there, on our knees, in the rain, the two of us possibly the dirtiest people to kiss since caveman times, he did. It was like nobody else even existed. I couldn't have pulled away if I'd wanted to. By the way, I didn't want to. His mouth was warm, and his arms were absolutely clutching me to him. It was utterly different now. Because now I knew him. He wasn't a stranger, or just some friend of my brother's. He was Jake. Jake, who had a hundred nicknames. Jake, who made everything funnier. Jake, who found something to like in everybody.

Jake, who was dating Windy.

As I remembered that, I pushed back. "That's not a great idea," I said.

He looked away. "I'm sorry."

I was still a little breathless. "Don't be."

"I shouldn't have done that."

He shouldn't have. Not cool. *Not cool.* But I wasn't mad. How could I be? Even the best of us could have a flash of stupidity in a moment of sorrow. No matter how much I didn't want to be the kind of girl who would do something like that to a friend, I cut myself some slack, because I truly hadn't seen it coming. I cut Jake some slack, too.

"That never happened," I said then. "Okay?"

"Okay," he said. Then he added, "We do a lot of things that never happened."

I thought about Windy. Were they together? Was she his girlfriend? Had we just cheated on the nicest person ever? For all our sakes, I hoped not. But I sure as hell wasn't going to ask.

"You know what?" I said. "You've had a tough day. I won't tell if you won't."

Jake gave me a sad smile. "I won't."

"Done, then," I said. "Easy. It's erased." Even though, of course, it wasn't.

We helped each other up, and then gathered up the water bottles.

"Sorry I broke your glasses," I said, as we started across the rocks to the path.

"Nah," Jake said, sliding the broken glasses arm into his pocket. "It's nothing a little duct tape can't fix."

✳

That night, after a terrible dinner of rehydrated vegetables, boiled water, flour, and salt, we went wordlessly to bed and slept as if the world didn't even exist.

For a few hours. Until we were awakened by some rutting elk. Some very loud, very nearby, very randy elk. Or so we figured out later—right about the time I learned that elk are not exactly Bambi. Elk are like the buffalo of the deer world. Some of them weigh nine hundred pounds. Of course, I didn't know anything about elk at the time. All I knew was that something incomprehensibly large—and obscenely close—was making huge, insistent, otherworldly noises in the darkness. And when I say "close," I mean five feet away. Possibly four.

We all woke instantly at the first sound. It was a long, high-pitched, eerie squeal that echoed through the valley and pierced my brain. It sounded like a banshee. One banshee at first. Then two. Then, at last, maybe five or six. All shrieking like nothing I'd ever heard and clomping around way too close to our tarp. I have never felt such paralyzing fear in my life. I could not have moved—even blinked—for anything. If those beasts had wanted to trample me, I would have been too frozen to even run. Fortunately, it turned out that elk are really all about other elk when they make sounds like that. The calls lasted at least twenty endless minutes, at which point the elk either found each other or gave up. All became quiet again.

"What the hell was that?" I asked, when my terror had melted enough to speak.

"Elk," Jake said.

"Mating elk," Flash added.

"They're not actually mating," Jake said. "They're bugling. It must be rutting season."

"Did you seriously just say that?" Dosie asked.

"I've done a lot of camping," Jake said.

"What's 'bugling'?" I asked.

"Mating calls," Jake said. "Which are not the same thing as mating *sounds*."

"How do you know they were bugling?"

"Because that's what it sounds like."

"Didn't sound like any mating calls I've ever heard," Dosie said.

"Maybe you're just not doing it right," Flash said.

We listened for another minute. "Do we think they're done?"

"They may go on all night," Jake said.

There was really nothing else to do at that point but try to fall back asleep, keep our ears open, and hope we didn't get trampled to death—or eaten, for that matter, or rutted with. While we waited, Dosie and Flash fell back asleep. But I didn't. Lying there, I felt pretty sure that I'd never sleep again.

"You awake?" Jake whispered after a while.

"Yep," I said.

"Me, too."

"I intuited that."

"Are you scared?"

"Fully, no-holds-barred petrified."

"Does it help if I remind you that elk are vegetarians?"

"Not really."

He was quiet for a minute after that. We stared up at the ceiling of the tarp. After a while, he said, "We wind up sleeping together a lot, you and me."

I turned toward him. "In a manner of speaking."

"It's like the universe keeps throwing us together."

"More like pelting us at each other."

Jake was quiet for a second. Then he said, "Sorry about today, by the way."

"What do you mean, 'sorry'?"

"I know you're working hard to be happy these days. I don't want to make you sad."

He had made me sad. But I shrugged. "I don't think trying to be happy means you can never be sad," I said. "Right?"

Jake agreed with a nod. "Right."

"It's sadness that gives happiness its meaning."

"That sounds pretty wise."

"Doesn't it? I think I learned it from Windy."

"No. That one's all you."

"Anyway," I said, keeping my voice low. "It was a privilege to help you out. And break your glasses."

"Three cheers for duct tape."

"I want you to know, I am very sorry about your eyes," I said.

"Yeah," he said. His voice was very quiet, then. "I think mostly I just don't want to be alone."

"You couldn't be," I said. "Don't you see how people follow you around?"

"But I won't be myself."

"You will be," I said.

I wanted to say, *Maybe it won't be so bad. Maybe you'll be more than yourself, somehow. If anybody can find something good in all this, it's you.* But I didn't know how to say any of that without sounding flip. Or ignorant. Or Pollyanna-ish. Instead, after a bit, I said, "So you faked your medical forms, huh?"

"Yep."

"Why?"

"Partly because I'd always wanted to come out here and do this, and I wasn't going to let my eyes stop me. Partly because it was easy. And partly because you signed up."

"Me?"

"Yeah."

"You came because of me?"

"Not entirely. But, yes."

"Why?"

"Because it seemed not just possible, but *likely*, that you'd get yourself killed out here."

"And you thought you could save me?"

"No, probably not. I just didn't want you to die alone."

I took that in.

"Duncan thought about coming, too," Jake pointed out. "You know, like, as my wingman."

"But?"

"But he's totally out of shape. Besides, there would have been nobody to watch Pickle."

"Has Duncan known all along?"

"Yup. And he really did have genuine plans to be the best dog-sitter ever," Jake said.

"But then he had the best party ever, instead."

"My fault," Jake said. "I should have helped him stay focused."

"See, now," I said, "that's not your job. He should be able to handle his own shit."

"Yeah, but he'd had a rough week," Jake said, as if we both knew what that meant.

But I didn't. I shook my head at him, like *What?*

"Because of Florida," Jake said, like that ought to jog my memory.

I shook my head again. Had Duncan gone to Florida? What would he be doing there?

Jake frowned. "Florida," he said, slower.

Another shake.

"You never met Florida? Duncan's girlfriend? Of two years?"

"Duncan went out with a girl named *Florida*?"

"How is it possible you don't know this?"

I shrugged.

"He was crazy in love. He thought she was The One."

"He thought a girl named Florida was the one?"

"You would have liked her," Jake said. "She was a Fulbright scholar."

"Named *Florida*?"

"But she dumped him. He asked her to move in, and she was like: *Nope. Shut it down.* That was three days before the party."

"Why did she dump him?"

"Standard Duncan stuff. Too juvenile. Too messy. Too forgetful. Girls really hate all that."

"Yeah," I said, in defense of my gender. "Because it's super annoying."

"I don't see why they can't look for the good stuff," Jake said. "He's loyal. He's good-hearted. He's funny as hell."

I continued Jake's list. "He's filthy. He's disorganized. He smells like a gym sock."

Jake studied my face for a minute. "You're going to start seeing him with kinder eyes. I know you are."

"I am?"

"Yep," Jake said, nodding. "Once I show you how to see him the way I do, you won't go back." He nestled down into his bag. "Especially when I can't see at all anymore. You'll have to see all his goodness for both of us."

It was kind of a low blow, but maybe he'd earned it. I let the notion sink in for a minute. Then something occurred to me. "Is that why you're going off after this? To go see all those sights?"

"Yep. I have a master list of things I want to see."

"Exotic things," I said, thinking back to the places he'd named on the drive out.

"Some exotic, some not. I'd like to see my childhood home again. And there's a merry-go-round at a park my grandma used to take me to. I've been thinking I should maybe go to Texas and look through all my dad's historic photographs of my great-grandparents and aunts and uncles. And there are things I want to *do* on the list, as well."

I turned on my side to face him.

"I'd like to go scuba diving. I'd like to drive a race car. I'd like to ride the world's scariest roller coaster."

"You'd like to pet a whale."

He nodded, pleased to be reminded. "That was lucky. I applied for that research assistantship on a whim. I literally saw the posting on a bulletin board in the student center and thought, 'Cool.' But ever since I actually got the job, I've been thinking it might be—"

"Destiny."

"Well, I was going to say, 'a possible new direction.'"

"I could totally see you as a whale researcher," I said.

"I've been thinking about it. The professor I'm going to work for, she brings an underwater microphone and records their sounds. Whales have a highly evolved language that works like sonar. They have special neurons called spindle cells. Humans have them, too, and they're linked with self-awareness, and compassion, and language. Except whales have had them about fifteen million years longer than we have." He thought for a second. "I might make a career out of trying to decipher what they say."

"Wouldn't it be amazing if whales turned out to be smarter than us?"

"I suspect they are."

"And you can be the guy to figure out just how much."

He squinted a little, like he was thinking about it. "I'll just have to see how this internship goes," he said. Then he grinned. "Meanwhile, you'll be rocking it out at that bar mitzvah."

Oh, God. I'd forgotten. I'd been dreading it ever since they invited me. But now it was looming, suddenly, not that far away.

"Why did you agree to do that, again?" Jake asked.

"Because they asked me to. And I wanted to prove that I wasn't mad anymore."

"Mad about what?"

"I thought you knew that story already."

He shook his head. "Just parts."

"Well," I said, "my high school boyfriend cheated on me with my best friend. Then he dumped me at the prom, where he took my corsage back. I had to catch a ride home with this scrawny guy who'd gone stag, and he made me listen to 'Bohemian Rhapsody' and tried to put his tongue in my ear."

"He took your corsage back?"

"A year later, my now-ex-BFF got accidentally pregnant and so they decided to get married. At nineteen. She converted to Judaism for him. Everybody thought they had ruined their lives, but they're still together. He's an accountant, and they've had two more kids. I'm not sure if that means they're happy, but I don't think they're more unhappy than anybody else. They look happy on Facebook, anyway."

Jake had closed his eyes. "Everybody looks happy on Facebook."

"I lost my virginity to him, you know."

Jake opened his eyes and looked over.

"His mom worked for Planned Parenthood, of all things," I went on. "He got a box of condoms, and we filled them up like water balloons—just to kind of get in the groove." The memory of that night appeared in my mind—still so sharp after all these years. "Then we got naked and climbed into his bed and fumbled through. We had no idea what we were doing. He had a Beatles poster on his ceiling, and I remember feeling like they were watching us."

"Which poster?" Jake asked.

"Sergeant Pepper's," I said.

Jake smiled. "Igniting, of course, a lifelong marching band fetish for you."

I nodded, like *Of course.* "Marching bands and walrus mustaches." Jake stroked his beard.

It was good to remember that night now, in the face of the looming bar mitzvah: The memory of it was something I hadn't realized I'd held on to so tenderly. It had been fun. We had been friends. I suspected not that many women could look back on their first time so fondly, and I decided right then that I'd always be grateful for that one night, if nothing else.

"His mom worked for Planned Parenthood and he still knocked your friend up?"

I looked over. "Yep."

"He was an idiot."

"It was probably just a birth control malfunction."

"Not for knocking her up. For cheating on you in the first place."

Hearing that felt surprisingly good. I turned to meet Jake's eyes. "Thanks."

"Anybody who takes that kind of luck for granted deserves what he gets."

I rubbed my eyes. "He got what he wanted."

But Jake shook his head. "Nope."

I frowned. "*Nope?*"

Jake shrugged. "Because you're that kind of girl."

"What kind?"

"The kind you never get over."

I looked away.

Jake didn't. "And now he's invited you to the bastard's bar mitzvah."

"I don't think people say 'bastard' anymore."

"You know what I mean."

"I think the baby wasn't even technically a bastard, either, because of the shotgun wedding."

"And you agreed to go."

I nodded. "But then, as soon as I did, I regretted it."

"Why?"

"Because now I have to *go*."

Jake took a long, assessing look at me. "You're going to surprise yourself and have a great time," he declared. "I dare you to steal the ice sculpture."

"All I want to do," I said, "is go back to GiGi's and watch bad television and take like three showers a day and eat ice cream straight from the carton. I don't want to put on heels, or Spanx, or an underwire bra."

Jake yawned. "I hear you, sister."

I yawned, too. We'd talked too long. My elk-induced adrenaline had dissipated without my noticing it, and by the time it hit me that I was tired, I was so far past tired, I was downright sleepy. I looked over, my eyes only half open. "Maybe that was too much information about my underthings."

"No such thing," he said, closing his eyes.

I yawned again and settled down farther into my bag, and thought about how I really, really did not want to go to that bar mitzvah.

"Come with me to Baja," he suggested then, like he was reading my mind. "That's a legitimate excuse."

"I love that idea," I said, trying it on for size as I sank toward sleep. *I'm sorry. I can't make it, after all. It's spawning season for the gray whales.*

The second day of our Solo was as easy as the first day had been hard.

Packing up that morning, it was clear that we'd set up camp in Elk-ville. There were squished-down ovals of trampled grass all around our campsite. We'd spent the night surrounded by sleeping beasts the size of flying saucers. But there was no sign of them now.

"Early risers," Flash said, surveying the scene.

Dosie and Jake proclaimed me the leader that day, and Flash didn't argue. "Take us back to the barn, Holdup," Flash said, as we clicked on our packs.

And so I led us back. Easy. It helped a lot to have the map right side up. But I didn't say that. It also helped that I had this magical, totally-useless-in-the-real-world map-reading ability. I led us with complete confidence. We stayed on the trail, we stuck together, and the only difficulty at all came at the very start of the hike when we had no choice but to cross that rickety bridge—which was far more difficult for Jake, in his duct-taped glasses, than for the rest of us. The bridge creaked and swayed and the bottom dropped out of my stomach more times than I could count before we all made it safely to the other side.

We were the first group to make it back, and as we told Beckett our tale, he shook his head. "I can't believe you people. Wasn't *anybody* paying attention?" Then he added, "Besides Calamity Jane?"

I couldn't help it. I lifted up my finger guns and blew the smoke off the barrels.

It turned out every group had a near-death experience to report. Cookie's group had a bear sighting, a mosquito infestation, and a twisted ankle. Windy's group had been swept away during a swollen river crossing, leading to plenty of near-drowning, CPR, and hypothermia. Looking around, it seemed like a miracle that we were all still alive—assuming, of course, that Hugh was.

Nobody had said it out loud yet, but once we'd made it through the Solos, there was nothing else to distract us: This was our last night.

It was a bittersweet feeling sharpened by opposites. We all, including me, wanted to go home exactly as badly as we wanted to stay. That night, we talked incessantly about the things we couldn't wait to get back to (pizza, french fries, TV, showers, Charmin) and the things we never wanted to do again (eat rehydrated food, dig a cat hole, carry a full-grown man three miles through the woods). But it was an overly loud, overly boisterous strategy: staving off sadness by insisting you didn't care.

Our last order of business before we turned in for the night was to cast our votes for Certificate winners. Beckett took this very seriously. It was a secret, fully democratic process, and everybody got one ballot—except for Beckett, who got an extra. "Everybody gets one vote and one vote only," he said. "Unless you're me. Then you get two." We were expected to consider our hiking buddies without prejudice and to take into account the ways they'd evolved during our time here. "You are not the same idiots you were when you arrived that first day," Beckett said. "Remember that."

Our criteria were supposed to be: leadership, compassion, commitment, and virtue. The people who had consistently demonstrated these qualities were the only ones who could hope to go home with Certificates. "Take it seriously, people," Beckett warned. "It's not about the biggest or the fastest. Who paid attention? Who cherished every moment? Who helped out the most? Who went for water when no one else would?"

"Can we vote for ourselves?" Flash asked.

Beckett lifted his eyebrow a hair. "It's fair to say that if you're the type of person who'd vote for himself, that's the only vote you're likely to get."

"What if we can't decide?" Dosie asked.

"It's not that hard," Beckett said. "In fact, it's not hard at all. I know who both my votes are going to. There's one obvious winner here."

The kids all bent their heads to their ballots. That's when Beckett raised his eyes to mine. Then he pointed his finger at me and pulled the trigger.

Chapter 14

The last morning, we woke like any other, made coffee, packed up, struck camp—and then said good-bye to the wilderness. Beckett had us observe a full minute of silence at sunrise in honor of Mother Nature. Then he had us hold hands while he said a farewell prayer.

"All-knowing Mother," he said, with his head bowed. "I'm sorry human beings are such a blight. I'm sorry we litter your earth and choke the fish in your oceans with plastic grocery sacks. We have been given incomprehensible beauty on this earth, but we don't see it. We walk around angry and blind and ungrateful. I wish we were better, our dumb human race, but I don't have much hope that we ever will be. The best I can do today is say: Thank you for this world of miracles. We will try to be more grateful. And less ridiculous."

On the first day, or even during the first week, I would have been looking out of the side of my eyes, like *Is this dude for real?* But now, as he came to a close, I started to clap. Everybody else started to clap, too, and shout things like, "Go, Boss! Tell it like it is!"

"Pipe down!" Beckett said, but he was smiling.

That was it. We hoisted up our packs for the very last time and snapped them in place. We assembled for the very last time in our well-worn grooves in the line. Everything was just the same as it had been all along, except each minute had a bittersweet tint because it was the *last time*. It was Flash's last chance to moon Vegas. It was Beckett's last chance to shout, "Move it out, people!" It was the Sisters' last chance to straggle along at the back, gossiping.

All morning, the kids had been talking about "next year," and making plans to come back and do it over again, in a way that made me saddest of all. Because I knew that they wouldn't. A year is an eternity, and they'd never come back. Life would get in the way. Maybe one or two would come back once or twice over the next few years, but it would never be this group again, in this place, with these circumstances. This was a moment in time that was already lost.

I would certainly never come back—but not because I'd never want to. Only because that's how life is. It moves too fast—faster and faster the older you get, no matter how much you'd like to slow it down.

Jake lingered the longest before putting on his pack. After the prayer, as everybody hugged and cried and exchanged numbers, Jake stood off at the edge of the clearing, soaking in the light from that sunrise. Even as we started to hike away, Jake kept turning back for one more look.

Then we were in the trees, following a trail the sunrise hadn't reached yet. Within the hour, we arrived at the final trailhead. The old green-and-white BCSC bus was waiting for us, door open. There was nothing left to do but get on.

Three weeks is not that long in the big picture. But humans are never that great at the big picture, and after three weeks of never going faster than a walking pace, riding on that bus at forty miles an hour felt like a roller coaster. We *oohed* and *ahhed* over every hill and around every curve. Some folks literally put their arms up. It was thrilling and terrifying and awful.

When we'd gotten on, I took a seat behind the Sisters, who would spend the entire hour-long ride back to the lodge talking about who they'd nominated for Certificates and who they thought everybody else had voted for. Windy sat next to me, and when she heard Dosie say, "I think Hugh should get a posthumous Certificate," she rolled her eyes.

"You know that means 'dead,' right?" Windy said.

"Oh," Dosie said, never embarrassed to be wrong. "What is it when you get an award for something you didn't do?"

"Honorary," I called up.

"Okay." She nodded. "One of those for Hugh."

As for the other two Certificates, Uno and Dosie were divided. Jake was a shoo-in, but Uno wanted the second to go to Caveman, who had kissed her during the summer solstice party.

"First," Dosie said, "he was cheating on his girlfriend when he gave you that kiss. Second, kissing is not a wilderness skill."

"But it was a really great kiss," Uno said.

"No," Dosie declared. "It should go to a girl." She looked around the bus at the candidates, then turned toward Windy and me. "I nominate Holdup," she said. "For trying the hardest." Then her eyes jumped to Windy. "And HB for being the prettiest."

Never mind that her math was all wrong and her criteria were bananas. I wanted one to go to Windy, as well. And she absolutely was the prettiest. As well as the nicest. And the wisest.

"Who are your picks?" Uno said, leaning toward us on her elbows.

"I pick Jake," I said, "for being an awesome EMT, and for wearing that goofy Gilligan hat the whole time."

Windy raised her hand. "Second that."

"I pick Windy. For working hard, believing in people, being a great listener, managing to be both gorgeous and really, really nice, and for keeping elegance alive on the trail by tying her hair into that fantastic chignon."

With that, Windy leaned in and gave me a big hug and kiss on the cheek, saying, "Thanks, friend."

Dosie nodded. "Then Hugh, right? Posthumously?"

I shook my head. "I'm not sure Hugh should get an honorary Certificate," I said. "He knew he wasn't supposed to step on those logs."

Uno and Dosie turned to each other, delighted, like, *Oh, snap!* Then Dosie made her fingers into cat claws and made a mean meow.

"I like Hugh," I said. "I hope he's doing great—but I don't think he should get a pity Certificate."

"Who, then?" Dosie asked.

I hesitated. I couldn't nominate myself. Maybe Flash and I could nominate each other.

Windy didn't hesitate, though. "*You,*" she said, poking me with a gun finger.

"She can't nominate herself!"

"I'm nominating her," Windy said. "She saved Hugh! She's a map-reading ninja! She always took notes during Beckett's lectures."

"Thank you," I said to Windy.

"You're a shoo-in, Holdup," Windy said.

Back at the lodge, I took the longest shower of my life—but only after peeling off the clothes I'd been wearing for weeks and throwing them in the trash.

The lodge was prepared. I guess they'd seen large busloads of filthy people drive up pretty often, because there were plenty of showers and endless hot water. I felt a little guilty wasting water but then I decided the twenty showers I'd just skipped in a row had earned me a few extra minutes. Or thirty.

I washed my hair four times. And conditioned it twice. And combed the tangles out. I scrubbed every inch of my body. All while standing under the most glorious spray of hot steamy water in the history of the world.

There was a banquet that night, and the girls gussied up. It was like they were seeking revenge for all the product deprivation they'd been forced to endure. Every room in the girls' wing of the corridor overflowed with beauty activities: girls with blow-dryers, girls working curling irons, girls blinking on mascara, girls squirting fruit-scented body spray. So much applied femininity! It was fascinating to see them transformed. They looked different, for sure, but in the end, I'm not sure they looked better. Instead of ponytails and ChapStick, they suddenly had poofy hair and cat-eye liner. I kind of missed the faces I was used to.

I confess to a little mascara, myself, and a dab of lip gloss—but I didn't want to go overboard. I tied my hair back in two low ponytails and slipped into a light, fluttery sundress I'd brought. The younger girls were excited about makeup and looking different, but I was excited about wearing something light and fluttery and *feeling* different. Just the difference between my three-pound boots and the flip-flops I'd put on felt like an entire universe.

I let Dosie paint my nails with little dotted flowers, and while she was working, she said, "I like your hair like that." Then she tilted her head toward me and said, "You know, you're prettier than I gave you credit for."

"Oh," I said, not sure how to respond. "You're nicer than I gave you credit for."

She looked up in surprise, and I wrinkled my nose at her. Then she smiled and went back to work.

Windy showed up before dinner in jeans and a halter top, with her hair in her trademark chignon. She pointed at me from the doorway, and then crooked her finger. "I need you," she said.

I followed her down the hall to her room. "I have something for you," she said, then. When we arrived, she pointed at the bed, and there was a little daisy chain. "It's for your hair tonight," she said. "For when you win your Certificate."

"Did you make this?" I said.

She nodded. "The meadow out back is covered in daisies." She lifted it onto my head and tucked it into place. "If you dry it just right, it'll keep forever."

"How do you dry it?"

"Actually, I can't remember."

"We're going to keep in touch, right?" I asked then.

She nodded. "I can be your personal Pickle consultant."

"Perfect," I said. "Actually, you are the only person from this trip I expect to keep in touch with."

"Except for Jake."

"Jake?"

"Since he's your brother's friend."

"Oh," I said. "Did he mention that to you?"

"Yeah," she said, "he kinda did." Then she realized she might be getting him in trouble. "But I didn't tell anyone! Swear to God!"

"That's fine," I said. "It was a dumb secret, anyway."

The "banquet" was pizza from Pizza Hut, imported from the next town over, which is what everybody had been discussing, craving, and fantasizing about since day one. Not the fanciest food, but the old ballroom of the lodge had windows that overlooked the lake and bulb lights strung all around the ceiling, and so it felt fancy, even still.

As the boys arrived, one by one, with all their beards shaved away (except for Beckett, who had left a stringy version of a Yosemite Sam), they almost looked more altered than the girls. We were a fine-looking bunch that night, I had to admit. Once we'd scrubbed three weeks' worth of sweat, dirt, grit, sand, and muck off our bodies, all that sunshine and fresh air could shine through. We were tan, fresh-smelling, clean, and healthy, if also a little blistered and callused. I had never felt so happy to be clean. Beckett had the Steve Miller Band playing over the speaker system, and Vegas and Caveman had spiked the lemonade with vodka. It was a heck of a party.

Jake was the last to arrive, not that I was counting, and he rounded the doorway just as Windy was pulling me toward it to go look for him. He was less than five feet away as it happened, and right as he looked up I could have sworn his gaze hit me first before jumping over to Windy. And here's something else I could have sworn. At the moment he saw me, I thought I heard him say, "Whoa."

But that couldn't have been right. It must have been someone scooting a chair, or Beckett messing with the microphone. I just wasn't the type of person to inspire a word like that from a guy. I inspired other words, maybe. Words like, "Careful!" Or "Are you going to eat that?"

Still, my brain would circle back to that moment over and over for the rest of the night, unable to let it go, even as I doubted it more and more. I even indulged in the paranoid fear that it might have been *me* who said "Whoa." But my heart, at least, thought it knew what happened: Jake had seen me in that moment, and something he'd seen had surprised him, and possibly impressed him, and no matter how self-doubting I insisted on being, it was too real to deny.

Of course, in that same moment, I felt the exact same things. Jake arrived at the party—so overwhelmingly appealing in his red Mexican guayabera shirt and frayed khakis and flip-flops—that I felt the impact of the sight of him as a visceral shudder in my body. He was tan, and clean-shaven, and he'd gotten his hair cut. He'd found some-body to fix his glasses, too—and so now he looked just like the guy I'd driven out here with, but better, and he was using those newly re-paired glasses to focus all his attention on Windy.

It was too much. My only option was to walk away. I didn't even excuse myself. I just turned and headed out. I don't even know if they noticed.

Outside, on the deck that overlooked the lake, I took some deep breaths. So what? *So what?* I was proud of myself, dammit. I had done exactly what I'd hoped to do on this trip. I'd triumphed. I'd arrived. I'd signed up for a hell of a challenge, and I had kicked its ass for once instead of the other way around.

On top of that, I'd managed a paradigm shift. I had found things to like about everybody on this trip even though I started out think-ing I'd hate them all. And I had made at least one real friend—a friend who had taught me to look for what I wanted in a different place. Af-ter a year of talking to almost no one but Pickle and feeling a con-stant, unfulfilled longing for some kind of happiness almost like it was a prize I could win, I had finally come to understand that not getting what you want is actually the trick to it all. Because not get-ting what you want forces you to appreciate what you already have.

I finally got that if you were always in a state of longing you could never truly get satisfied, and that insight hit me just as a veritable tidal wave of longing for Jake crashed over and swirled all around me—and maybe it had to get that bad before I could really under-stand. But alone by the lake, all I could do was lean down, press my head against the railing, and wait for the feeling to pass.

This was good for me, I decided. Maybe my heart had needed a little jolt, anyway—just to get itself pumping again.

I willed myself to bounce back. Life is going to knock you down over and over, I reminded myself, and the best you can do is learn to get back up. I was going to head home tomorrow morning with a Certificate—proof positive that I was not defeated. That was something. That was really something.

Behind me, I heard the Steve Miller Band go quiet. Then a tapping sound on the speakers, as Beckett said, "Is this thing on?" too loud and too close, followed by a squeal of reverb.

I guessed that was my cue to go back inside.

I slipped in and found a spot next to the stone fireplace. Jake and Windy were standing together, but I kept my eyes on the stage.

Beckett held the mic up again, this time a little more gingerly, and said, "Hooray for another BCSC successful trip! No drownings! No decapitations! All right!"

The room cheered.

"Hope you guys are liking the pizza."

The room cheered again.

"We're going to present Certificates now, while everybody's still sober."

Another cheer.

"After that the night is yours to squander however you like!"

More cheering.

"One quick announcement: You'll be glad to hear that Hugh is still alive."

The room went crazy.

"It was both a fractured and dislocated hip—so, pretty uncomfortable there—but it looks like he's going to make a full recovery. Martha at the front desk has his address, if you want to stay in touch."

"Huey Lewis!" Caveman shouted.

More cheering.

"Now," Beckett continued, "for the grand finale of our time here. Drum roll, please," and Vegas and Hound Dog obliged. "As you guys know, BCSC awards Certificates of Merit to the three finest students in every course. We're not necessarily looking for the biggest or the strongest, here. We're looking for the students who give it their best shot every time; the ones who pay attention; the ones who have made our trip a better experience just by their presence. You all voted for your top choices by secret ballot, and the three people we will honor tonight will go on to great things. Past recipients of BCSC Certificates now run corporations, lead expeditions, and generally rule the world. These are the Navy SEALs of the wilderness, people!"

Another cheer.

"Martha from the front desk has tallied the votes, and she's ready to announce the results. And so, I present: Martha!"

A leathery, no-nonsense, sixty-something lady joined Beckett at the mic and leaned in. "I'm here to announce this June's Absaroka Course Certificate recipients." She unfolded a piece of paper and put on her reading glasses.

She squinted. "The first recipient is—"

Beckett did a drum roll on the pizza table. I felt a sting of nervousness.

"Jacob Samuel Archer."

The room cheered and clapped. Windy grabbed Jake and hugged him. The guys shouted, "J-Dog!" and "Jaegermeister!" and, for some reason, "Juice!!"

Jake walked up and took a bow.

Martha handed him a Certificate, but she also had a medal on a red ribbon for him, like we were at the Olympics. He bowed his head as she placed it around his neck.

Martha stepped back to the mic. "The second recipient is—"

Another drum roll.

"Windy Anne Sky!"

I cheered with everybody, but I also thought, *Windy Sky? So her sister was Stormy Sky?* Oh, California.

Windy loped up to the mic and almost knocked Martha over with her big hug. She got her Certificate and her medal, and then she turned around, hugged Jake, and planted a kiss right on his lips.

I looked away.

"And our third and final recipient," Martha went on, "and a real crowd favorite—"

Final drum roll.

Windy pointed her guns at me from the stage. "Pew! Pew!"

"Hugh Edmund Davenport!"

The crowd goes wild.

I lifted my eyebrows, contracted my cheeks into a smile, and jumped up and down, shouting "Go, Hugh!" Just like everybody else.

"Now," Martha said, when the cheering quieted a bit, "for obvious reasons, we'll have to mail Mr. Davenport's Certificate to him. Congratulations to everybody. Great job!"

But her voice was muted. The cheering and the jostling and the partying were muted, too. What had just happened? Had they really given it to Hugh? Jake was a shoo-in: no surprise there. And Windy was irresistible. And maybe the cranky, judgmental, stand-offish person I'd been at the start of this thing couldn't have beaten out Hugh, but that was the old me. The new me had bonded with these kids, hadn't she? I wasn't Helen—or even Ellen—anymore. I was Holdup! I had finger guns! I could read maps like a ninja! I had at last won Beckett's respect and become his hand-picked choice above everybody. Hadn't I?

But none of that got me up on the stage. I looked around. This is how it was, and there was no changing things: Me down here in the crowd, getting jostled between Vegas and Caveman as they body-slammed each other in celebration. And Jake and Windy—Olympians of beauty and niceness—on the stage with their medals and their Certificates, afloat on adoration.

Windy stared at me from the stage, a little stricken. She lifted her arms in a shrug to me, like, *What the hell just happened?*

I felt a sting in my chest, but I shrugged back, like, *Doesn't matter! I'm okay!* So Hugh had gotten the sympathy vote. He'd certainly been through the ringer. Then I made a shooing motion at her with my hands, like, *Go! Be happy.*

She shook her head at me, like, *I can't be happy if you got screwed.*

So I gave her a *such is life* shrug and then waved my hand bye-bye, like, *I'm outta here. Enjoy your night.*

And she waved back, like, *I totally get it.*

As the big guys started chanting "Speech! Speech! Speech!" I skulked my way back toward the side door to escape unnoticed. Which worked pretty well, except that I paused a second too long next to the Sisters as they ogled Jake and Windy up on the stage.

"Oh my God!" Dosie was saying. "Aren't they the cutest?"

Uno agreed wholeheartedly. "They're like the Kennedys of the backpacking world."

On the heels of that, I literally bumped into Beckett as I stepped away, and turning to apologize, I got this from him: "Should've been you, kiddo. You got both my votes—no contest. They only picked Windy 'cause she's prettier."

I drew in a deep breath and turned to take one last panorama of this micro-section of my life. Then I called it: *Time to go the hell home.*

I managed to make it through the lobby to the base of the big stairs without getting stopped again, and I thought I was in the clear until I heard Jake's voice behind me. "Helen! Hold up!"

I took a deep breath, held it, and turned around.

He was jogging toward me with that great form he had, medal bouncing the tiniest bit against his chest.

"Great shirt," I said.

"I can't believe you didn't get it," he said.

I was still holding my breath. "Not a big deal."

"You were robbed!"

"I'm happy for you all," I said. "You're Navy SEALs of the wilderness now. Even Hugh."

He gave me a look. "He knew better than to step on that log."

I gave Jake a smile and little shrug, like, *Okay, that's true.*

Jake looked around. "Are you—leaving?"

"Yeah," I said, trying so hard to sound casual that I sounded strangled instead. "Thought I'd turn in."

"Sure." He nodded. "Long drive tomorrow."

I nodded. "Very long. And I'm not going to stop."

"What—between here and GiGi's?"

"I figure it's fifteen hours, if I speed."

"But you don't speed."

"Sometimes I do."

"What if you fall asleep at the wheel?"

"They've invented this great thing called coffee. I'll be fine."

"But why race back?"

"I'm just ready to go home." And as I said the words, I realized how true they were.

"About that," he said then. "I know you don't want me to hitch to Denver."

I held perfectly still. That was right. I did not want him to hitch anywhere. Hadn't there been enough made-for-TV movies about the dangers of hitching? Did we really have to go over it again? Or maybe we weren't going to go over it. Maybe he was working up to asking me to give him a ride. Which, as soon as the thought hit me, I knew I'd love to do. Even just the idea of it was enough to ease my aching heart. We could snack on chocolate and listen to music and psychoanalyze all the crazy kids from this trip. I'd love to hear his take on Beckett. Plus, I had some dirt on the Sisters I knew would make him laugh. Just then, from the depths of my memory, I remembered a middle-of-the-night conversation where he'd invited me, half asleep, to come with him to Baja. He'd been kidding about that, of course. Probably. But it added fuel to my fire. The idea of going anywhere with him was so appealing, in fact, that even before he asked any question at all, I just went ahead and said, "Yes."

Jake frowned. "'Yes' what?"

"Yes, I'll drive you to Denver so you can catch your flight to the whale lagoon. Or whatever."

He stared at me with his mouth open. "You will?"

"Yes."

He shook his head a little. "But it's the wrong way for you. You'll miss the bar mitzvah."

I shrugged. "I can miss it."

"But then they'll think you chickened out."

"I don't really care."

Suddenly, the conversation felt way too naked. It seemed far too likely that the next question he'd ask me would be *why*. And then what would I say? In a gust of fear, I covered: "If you hitch, you'll be murdered and cut into tiny pieces. If you're murdered, Duncan's life will be ruined, and if his life is ruined, then he'll make sure mine is, too."

Jake blinked at me.

"It's a domino." I shrugged.

"But, that's what I was about to say," Jake said. "I don't have to hitch. I found a ride."

I raised my eyebrows like a happy person would. "Oh! Great!"

"Turns out, Windy's parents have another vacation house in Crested Butte. She's renting a car in Riverton and driving out tomorrow."

Arguably, I fixated on the wrong information first. "Windy's parents have two vacation homes?"

Jake shrugged.

Then I hit the crux of it. "Windy is giving you a ride to Denver?"

Jake nodded, trying to read my face.

I brightened under the scrutiny. "Fantastic," I said. "Then I'm off the hook."

I confess I'd been holding out hope that it had all been a freakish misunderstanding. That despite everything everybody had said over and over, Windy and Jake might not be destined for each other, after all. That, somehow, despite every impossibility, this night, this trip—my life—could rewrite itself in front of my eyes.

Until those words.

Jake was going to the Rockies. With Windy. And I was going to a bar mitzvah. Alone.

I just nodded. It was all I could do.

He stuffed his hands in his pockets.

"Well," I said, feeling like the oxygen was draining out of the hallway. "Look me up when you get back. I'd love to hear about those whales."

"Definitely," he said. It was time for him to go back to the party. But he didn't leave. "Bet it'll be a relief to have your car to yourself, huh?"

I manufactured another smile. "Yes. Yep. I can bust out all my Abba albums."

He nodded toward the party. "Beckett's about to DJ. I think he's got some Abba."

Was it an invitation? I just shook my head.

"Well," he said then, looking down. "Thanks for the ride out, anyway. I had a great time."

"Me, too."

"And I'm glad you didn't get killed in the wilderness."

I nodded. "Right back atcha."

"And sorry about all the kissing."

"No apology necessary." I was starting to get woozy. I told myself to breathe. He was about to go to the Rockies, and I didn't know when I would see him again, and my life had apparently turned into a John Denver song. It felt in this moment like there ought to be something I could say here to change the course of things, but I had no idea what.

I went ahead and took one last, good look at Jake—to soak in the sight of him all clean-shaven and tan in that pressed cotton shirt. A mental picture. A keepsake.

He looked up and we locked eyes—and I felt it again: that pulsing, electrical flutter in my rib cage. For a second, I wondered if he felt it, too. He seemed to be holding his breath as much as I was.

He took a step closer. "Helen—"

But that's when the banquet room doors burst open with a *whap!* and Mason and the minions came running out—buzzed on spiked lemonade and the thrill of civilization. They came right for Jake, and almost as soon as he'd turned his head, they ratcheted him up onto their shoulders.

"Woooo!" the minions were all shouting.

"Where're you going, Prom King?" Mason said. "We're not done with you yet!"

Through the open doors, I could see they'd put Windy up on a chair on the banquet table—and an empty chair waited for Jake.

With that, they carried him off, the minions chanting "Prom King! Prom King!" Jake turned back like he might try to shout something to me—but then the doors swung closed behind them, and they were gone.

I stood still for several minutes, looking around, hoping against hope that Jake might come back out. But he didn't. When it was too pathetic to stand there any longer, I turned and walked myself back up the steps—trying like hell to think of Three Good Things for the day, but not coming up with even one.

Chapter 15

I left that night and made it back to Grandma GiGi's by the next. No, I did not do all fifteen hours without stopping—and yes, I stayed in the same motel where Jake and I had stayed on the drive out, coincidentally, in the exact same room we'd had before. And, yes: I felt so alone against the contrast of those memories that I could barely sleep.

At bedtime, I lay in Jake's old bed, in the solid hotel-room blackness, wondering if this was what *his* blackness would look like, when it finally arrived. With the heavy hotel curtains closed and all the lights off, the darkness was as thick as cotton. I opened my eyes as wide as I could against it, straining for any sliver of light, but nothing changed. It made me feel closer to Jake in a way to lie there like that and imagine that I was seeing through his future eyes. It was a stupid game, but one I couldn't stop playing, and after far too long—An hour? Two?—of waiting for sleep, the ache to talk to him finally got so strong that I fumbled around in my purse until I found my phone, found his number, and hit SEND.

I was thinking I'd confess it all. Who cared if it was embarrassing? Who cared if he'd found someone better? I couldn't keep it all in any longer.

But then I hit END before it even rang.

It was too humiliating to call him. This wasn't some kid I'd never see again. This was Duncan's best friend. I would know this guy— and see him at Thanksgiving, Christmas, New Year's, and Duncan's birthday—for possibly the rest of my life. Mistakes I made with Jake would last forever. And I'd already made plenty.

I convinced myself to wait until daylight. If I still wanted to call him in the morning, I'd call him in the morning. Never call anybody you have a crush on after ten P.M. *Crushes for Beginners*.

So, I didn't call. I just lay in the darkness and thought about how brave he was, and how good he was at making the best of things. At last, I just gave in and let myself miss him, and the feel of his hands, and the warmth and pressure of his body, and the way that something about his gaze made me feel profoundly, heartbreakingly *not alone*.

Until, at last, alone in his motel bed, I fell asleep.

By the time I made it home to GiGi's the next evening, just in time for supper, I was groggy, overcaffeinated, and hoarse from far too many Aretha Franklin songs.

When I tried to set my purse down on the kitchen table, I caught the edge instead, and all the contents—lipstick, wallet, crappy cell phone—hit the ground in a splatter.

GiGi was cooking. She turned at the sound, and smiled to see me. "You're back already?"

"I'm back," I said, squatting down behind the table to pick up my mess.

Guess what else was in that purse? Jake's poem from my bra. I probably should have burned it with the rest of my filthy things. I'd promised not to read it, but now that it was all finally over, that funny little promise didn't seem to mean much anymore. So, without asking myself permission or even hesitating, there on GiGi's kitchen floor I unfolded the paper and read it.

I don't know what I was expecting but it was exactly what Jake had said it was. A Pablo Neruda poem. Actually, just an excerpt. But it was enough to make me clasp my hand over my mouth as I read.

> *Only do not forget, if I wake up crying,*
> *it's only because in my dream I'm a lost child,*
> *hunting through the leaves of the night for your hands.*

GiGi came looking for me behind the table. "You okay?" she asked, when she found me.

"Not really," I said, folding the poem up and sliding it back into my bra where it belonged.

I stood and came over for a hug.

She pulled away to get a good look at me. "Darling, you're gorgeous."

"Hardly."

"You *are*. That mountain air did something to you. You're radiant."

"I don't feel radiant."

But she didn't let it go. She had a way of speaking the truth that was as exhausting as it was inspiring. "Something happened to you. You're different."

"A lot of things happened to me," I said. "I almost got killed about ten times."

"I mean, something good happened to you."

I nodded. "Good things and bad things, both."

"Tell me the good things," she said, turning back to pull her salmon out of the oven.

I was good at good things by now. It was easy. "I saw beauty I'd never even imagined. I faced impossible challenges and survived. I let people surprise me. I lived through a snowstorm. I made a real friend. I revised the framework of my life."

She nodded in approval. "Lots of good things."

"And something else," I said. "I saw Nathan."

She had moved on to tossing a salad, but she stopped, turned, and looked at me.

"Or—I almost saw him," I said. "I remembered him, at least. I remembered him more clearly than I have in years."

"Well," GiGi said, her expression an exact mixture of happy and sad, "that is something."

I told her all about it. I wasn't trying to avoid talking about Jake by telling her about sensing Nathan in Painted Meadow, but it occurred to me over dinner, as she asked me all about the trip, that it might do the trick. Seeing Nathan could, potentially, explain whatever she was intuiting about my aura. That was plausible, at least. I'd found a way, at last, to mend the hole he'd left in my life. A healing moment like that could certainly change a girl.

GiGi filled our wineglasses and said, then, in a way that sounded like we were bringing our conversation to a close, "I thought this camping thing was literally the worst idea you've ever had. But it looks like you really made something of it."

"I tried to." I nodded, thinking we were done.

I didn't want her to read my heart like a map. I didn't even want to read it myself. I was just about to launch a new topic when she beat me to it. "And? So? Tell me about Jake."

I made a poker face as I lifted my wineglass. "Jake's good," I said.

She tilted her head. "Did he irritate the hell out of you on the trip?"

"No," I said, shrugging. "He was very helpful."

"Did he follow you like a puppy?"

I hadn't realized she was quite so clear on our dynamic. "I asked him to keep his distance," I said.

"And he managed it?"

I nodded. "He managed it very well."

"I'm glad," she said. "Maybe he's gotten over you."

Something about those words made me look down. I stabbed at my salad.

GiGi stopped chewing. And right then, she knew. She set down her fork and stared at me until I looked up. "Well?" she asked.

"'Well' what?"

"Did you fall in love with him?"

I coughed a little. "Was I supposed to fall in love with him?"

She shrugged. "Why not?"

"He's a teenager."

She looked at me over her glasses. "He's hardly a teenager."

She had me there. "He's ten years younger than I am."

"I was ten years younger than Grandpa," she said, "and we had a great time."

"That's different," I said. "He was a man."

Now she raised an eyebrow. Just one. "Don't be such a church lady. You know that doesn't matter."

I did know it didn't matter. I'd known that all along. I bent my head, squeezed my tired eyes closed, and rubbed them.

GiGi watched me. "Are we going to talk about something real, or are we going to keep making excuses? Because I could be watching *The Golden Girls* right now."

"Fine," I said, squaring off. "I fell in love with him. I fell stupidly in love with him."

"Now we're getting somewhere," GiGi said, leaning back in her chair.

That would have been a good moment to stop. But I went the other way. After weeks of holding it in, at last, I let it all out. "I fell in love with his hair, and his beard, and the way his eyes crinkle when he smiles, and his goofy Hawaiian shirts, and his can-do attitude, and the way he applies Band-Aids. I fell in love with the way he's read every book in the world. How he listens when you talk and remembers what you say. How he knows every fact in existence about the ocean and the creatures that live in it. I fell in love with his forearms, and his calf muscles, and the way his front two teeth are just a little longer than the others. And the dimples. And the way he sings. And the way he watches me, and pays attention in a way that guys never, ever do and seems to get something essential about me that I don't even get myself." When I paused, I was a little breathless. "Is that what you wanted to hear?"

GiGi gave me a contented smile. "Wonderful."

I gave a sharp sigh. "Not wonderful."

"How the hell did he finally make that happen, anyway?"

"Actually, he kissed me."

"He kissed you?"

"Yes. We had a bet. And I lost. And so he kissed me."

"I bet he's a terrific kisser."

"He is."

GiGi watched me as I thought about it.

"Anyway," I said. "Then we were interrupted. By Mike."

"Mike who?" GiGi said.

"Mike, my ex-husband."

She squinted like she'd forgotten him. "Oh. Him."

"He was having a bad night."

"I didn't know you were still in touch."

"I wasn't," I said. "Until then. Once the mood was broken, Jake said we should stop. Then I got mad at him—and so I told him not to talk to me anymore and I tried to ignore him for the rest of the trip."

GiGi nodded like that was all very reasonable. "And were you able to?"

I sighed. "Yes. Sort of. Not really. And then he kissed me again."

"Interesting."

"But really, right from the beginning, the damage was done."

"Doesn't sound like damage to me."

"He sabotaged my healing process!"

"I'm sure he didn't mean to, darling."

"Doesn't matter."

"It matters a little."

"He was selfish," I said. "He admitted as much. And he ruined everything. Twice!"

"Not everything. You gained some wilderness skills."

"I don't care about wilderness skills!"

"Well," she said. "That's progress."

"He messed with my head."

"And your heart, it sounds like."

"That, too."

"Good thing the heart is so resilient."

"Mine's not."

"Oh, sweetheart," she said, pausing to meet my eyes. "It is."

I took a sip of wine.

"And how could you blame him?" she said, shaking her head. "He's been so in love with you for so long."

I swallowed. "He told you that?"

"He didn't have to. It was plain to see. Every holiday meal. If you were in the kitchen mashing potatoes, he was in the kitchen washing dishes. If you had to run out to the market for something, he'd offer to go with. You'd say, 'I don't need your help to carry a bag of cran-berries,' but he'd insist on going, nonetheless. He switched the place cards every year to sit next to you."

"I thought that was you."

"No. But I was rooting for him. He was so charmingly, obviously lovesick."

"It wasn't obvious to me."

"You weren't paying attention."

I reached up to rub my shoulder.

"And then!" GiGi went on. "For him to get you alone on a car ride! And you're single now! It's a wonder he didn't eat you alive like the Big Bad Wolf."

"GiGi!"

"It sounds like he was a perfect gentleman."

"Not exactly perfect."

"Poor thing," she said. "Now you've ruined his life."

"He ruined mine!" I said. "He got over me. On the trip. He's moved on now—already. With someone else."

"So that's why you're angry."

"No!" I said. "I'm angry because I did not get what I wanted. I wanted to transcend all these dumb human shenanigans. I wanted to do something amazing! I wanted to be transformed! I wanted to be fully immersed!"

"Sounds like you were pretty immersed to me."

"That's not what I mean."

"All I'll say is this: You were a ghost of a person when you left. Now, you're flesh and blood again."

"It was the hiking! And the mountain air! And the sunshine!"

"If you say so."

"I'm telling you, he likes somebody else now."

"I don't believe that for a second."

"He's gone to Colorado with her. She's amazing."

"So are you."

"I'm really not."

"You don't give yourself enough credit. Or Jake, either." Gigi paused then, holding her fork in the air. "Do you remember when he brought that blond girl to Thanksgiving? What was her name? Pippi? Piper?"

"No," I said.

"This was a couple of years ago. You were still married. And that girl what's-her-name was lovely! And charming! And guess what?"

"What?"

"He still switched the place cards."

I held my breath until I couldn't anymore. "This is a disaster."

She took a sip of wine. "Love is always a disaster, darling. That's what makes it fun."

"I was mean to him. I ran him off."

She shook her head. "You've been mean to him for years."

A thought occurred to me. "Maybe he has a thing for mean women. Maybe he can only like me if I'm mean."

Now GiGi smiled like I was terribly funny. "He doesn't like you because you're mean," she said. "He likes you in spite of it."

"We don't know that. He could be completely messed up."

She met my eyes. "But he isn't."

No. He wasn't.

"He just likes you. He's always liked you. He sees all the good things about you. He has that gift—those wonderful, loving eyes."

"GiGi," I said then, breaking Jake's confidence, but unable to stop myself. "He's losing his sight."

I thought I'd have to go on and explain all about the rods and cones to make it all clear, but she held up her hand. "I know."

I frowned. "How do you know?"

"Duncan told me. He tells me everything."

Duncan told her *everything*?

"Jake will still have that vision, you know," she said then. "Even if he can't see."

I nodded. She was right, of course.

"It's his heart he sees with, sweetheart."

At those words, my eyes stung with tears. I wiped them away fast, but too late. More followed. Thinking of Jake and what he was facing, and how he was facing it, made me feel ashamed. My troubles looked awfully small in comparison. I was self-pitying and self-centered and self-indulgent. No wonder he'd gone to the mountains. No wonder at all.

"I'm sorry," I said.

"Don't be," she said. "I always like you best when you're a mess."

"You do?"

She nodded, and said in a softer voice, "You're going to be okay."

But "okay" seemed far away. "I'm not sure I know how."

GiGi leaned across the table to take both my hands. "You never liked the boys who liked you. You know that about yourself, right?"

I shook my head.

"You always ignored the boys who liked you in favor of the ones who didn't."

"That's not true!"

"What about Dave from high school? He left you for your best friend."

"He liked me!"

"But not enough. And you had that cute little poet boy who wrote you all those sonnets, but what did you do?"

"I ignored him."

"That's right. And the same thing in college when you had to choose between the rugby player and that boy with the stupid little car."

"A Dodge Dart."

"You should have gone for the Dart! He adored you. But what did you do, instead?"

"I went to rugby games."

"Exactly." She nodded. "It was like you only wanted the ones who didn't want you. Like you needed the challenge of getting their attention."

She wasn't wrong. "And then I married Mike. The alcoholic."

GiGi nodded. "Who loved you—"

"But loved drinking more."

GiGi nodded again.

She was right. I let it sink in. "Why didn't you ever point this out before?"

She shook her head. "You can't tell people their lives."

I shut my eyes. "Because they have to figure it out themselves."

"That's right," GiGi said. "And now you have."

"But too late."

"You broke a pattern," she said. "That's something. Maybe you lost Jake. Maybe he'll never come back. Maybe he'll marry this girl and have a hundred babies—"

"That's enough of that."

"But it's okay. He taught you something. He taught you how to let somebody love you a little bit. That lesson right there is enough to change your life."

Something about that idea brought a fresh sting of tears. Maybe she was right. Maybe I would change my life, and maybe I would get better at love, and maybe by the time the next person came along, I'd finally get it right at last. But I didn't want the next person. I just wanted Jake.

I let out a little laugh. Then I wiped my eyes with the hem of my T-shirt. "It doesn't matter. I just have to get through the bar mitzvah, go home, see my dog, pick myself up, and start a new-and-improved life." The prospect of it all seemed awfully bleak. So, after a minute, I added, "Maybe I'll take some dancing lessons."

GiGi nodded. "That's a brilliant idea, darling," she said, as if that one idea would solve everything. "You were always a fantastic dancer."

We let that idea sit with us in the room for a while as I digested all the things we'd just talked about. At last, after a long pause, I said, "Duncan tells you everything, huh?"

"Everything," she said, with a little eye roll. "Far more than I want to know."

"Do you think it makes you like him more than you would otherwise? Or less?"

"More," she said. "Certainly more."

"I'm not sure I'd have that same response."

"You'll get there," she said. "Keep working on it." Then she met my eyes and said, "He's always better at trying than succeeding."

"That's a family trait."

She smiled. "Keep that in mind when he shows you the cooler."

I frowned. "What cooler?"

But she just shook her head and stood to take her plate to the sink. "I am not at liberty to say."

The next morning, I woke up late. GiGi was in the kitchen, making coffee, barely awake herself. This was the bar mitzvah day. My day to face the future and the past at the same event. I had to get a haircut, assemble an outfit, and figure out a way to convince everybody— including myself—that, despite all the facts that argued otherwise, my life had turned out well.

I should have hopped up, showered, and headed out for errands. But I really just wanted to lounge around in my robe.

GiGi eyed me as we drank our coffee.

"Let me paint you," she said, at last.

I wrinkled my nose. "I don't want to be painted."

"Yes," she insisted. "You will curl up on the green sofa and tell me more about your trip, and I will capture *you in love*." She gestured at my aura.

"More like me in agony."

"Same thing."

What can I say? When your eighty-three-year-old grandmother wants to paint your portrait, you let her.

She kept all her paints and brushes and easels on the sun porch. She'd painted my portrait often when I was a kid, but then, after we came to live with her, she did it less. I guess kid-free grandmas have more time for projects like that. One exception was the portrait she did of me before my wedding, in my bridal gown, which hung above her fireplace. I loved that portrait best of all. She'd captured me exactly, but somehow made me much prettier than I was in real life. I'd asked her to give it to me many times, but she wouldn't.

So I sat on her green velvet couch on the sun porch, sipped my coffee, and told her all about the wilderness, and what I learned in the mountains. I told her about the blizzard, and Hugh's evac, and getting lost on the Solo. I told her about wiping with pinecones and smelling like a skunk. I told her that I'd been terrified and shy at the beginning, but I'd found a way to make some friends. I'd surprised myself. I'd been brave in all kinds of ways.

"You've always been brave," she said. "You were my brave one."

"I was?"

She nodded. "And Duncan was my scaredy-cat. Just like your mom."

I frowned. "My mom was a scaredy-cat?"

GiGi nodded. "She was terrified of everything. Still is."

"But she's a yoga instructor!"

GiGi nodded. "I think that helps. She does seem to find that soothing."

I had never once thought of my mother as a "scaredy-cat." "I don't think of her as scared," I said.

"Well, children can't see their parents clearly until they grow up."

"What is she scared of?"

"Oh, everything, just about. Dogs. People. Life."

I took a breath. "Is that why she gave us up?"

GiGi held very still, and moved only her eyes to look over at me. "In part, I suppose."

Then I said, "On the trip, Jake was asking me about what happened that day. I told him we were too much for her. She dropped us with you and never came back. But he didn't think that could be the whole story."

"Jake's a smart boy."

"So that's not the whole story?"

"Is there any story in the world that can be told in two sentences?"

We all knew what happened—the basics, anyway—but I suddenly realized I was fuzzy on the details. "Tell me," I said.

"Well," GiGi said, carefully continuing to paint, "she did drop you off for a sleepover with me that day. I don't know if she intended to come back or not. I've often wondered what was going through her head as she said good-bye to you."

"She said she'd see us in the morning."

"Yes, she did. But I think she knew she wouldn't. She lingered over the two of you a little too long."

"Did you know she wouldn't be back?"

"No! I was going to make you pancakes in the morning, drop you off at home, and then head out to a sitting."

"So what happened?"

"Well, she drove away. I fed the two of you spaghetti and then it was time for bed. But your brother had forgotten his blankie. What did he call that thing?"

"Softie."

"That's right! He'd forgotten Softie. When he realized it was bedtime, and he didn't have it, he wailed like a widow at a wake."

"I remember," I said. He was three then. He had those striped, footed pajamas.

"I kept thinking he would give up and conk out, but after about an hour and a half, you came up to me like the little caregiver you were and said, 'You'd better go home and get it, GiGi. Or he'll be up all night.'"

"I don't think of myself as a caregiver," I said.

"You were for Duncan," she said. "Your mom was struggling so hard back then. Duncan was in so many ways like a motherless child. But you stepped in. You changed his diapers. You put him to bed. You rocked him."

"I don't remember any of that. I only remember resenting him."

"I'm sure you did resent him! You never asked for that responsibility! But you tried your best, anyway. You knew too much was missing, and you gave everything you could."

"What was she thinking, having another baby?"

"I have asked myself that a thousand times. Your father was already halfway out the door before Duncan even arrived."

GiGi was still painting. She still had that expression she always wore when she worked—like she was half in the world, and half in the painting—but now we'd come to the precipice. GiGi took a good look at what she'd painted so far, and then she dropped her brush in a jar of water. She took off her smock, came to sit beside me on the green sofa, and took my hand.

"This must be important," I said, "if you're putting your brush down."

"That night," she went on, "your brother had frazzled my nerves with all the crying. When you told me to go home and get Softie, I was glad for the break. I drove over to get it and let myself in. That's when I found your mom."

"What do you mean, 'found' her?"

GiGi squeezed my hands a little tighter. "She had taken a bottle of painkillers and crawled into bed with Nathan's teddy bear."

I pressed my free hand to my mouth.

"I found her in time, and that's all you need to know about that. When I got home from the hospital at four in the morning, you were asleep on the sofa in your clothes, and your brother was tucked in his bed like an angel. I don't know how you managed without Softie, but you did."

I had to say the words out loud. "She tried to kill herself."

GiGi nodded, but barely. "After that, I found a place for her where she could try to get better. But 'better' is a tricky term. She stayed six months. But even after she came home, she was too fragile to take you back. I convinced her to sell the house and start a new life as best she could. She found a nice little apartment, but a one-bedroom was all she could afford. She talked endlessly about getting you two back, and I played along, but the truth is, you were better off here. And she was better off there."

I realized I was shaking. "You never told us."

"It wasn't my story to tell."

"It was! It was our story. Our whole family."

"Would you really want me to have come straight home and told you? You, with the world on your shoulders? You, with your father gone, still grieving Nathan so badly? Imagine that little girl asleep on the sofa in her sneakers. Would you want me to walk into that living room, wake her up, and tell her what really happened?"

I shook my head.

"I would never have put that on you."

"But later?" I asked then. "When we were older?"

She shook her head. "She asked me not to."

It seemed incomprehensible to me. So much would have been different if she'd told us the truth. "Why?" I whispered.

"She was ashamed, I think."

"I thought she didn't want us."

GiGi pulled me in and put her arms around me. "Better that than the truth."

But I wasn't sure it was better.

She held me for a long time before she added, "I always felt like the two of you sensed something was wrong that night. Maybe it was only coincidence. But the truth is, the two of you made sure I went back over there. I can't see it any other way. You saved her."

At lunchtime, GiGi made a mushroom and chive frittata. I sat at her table in my favorite chair and let my brain revolve around everything she'd said. I had to revise the entire story of my life. It was one thing to be the child of a mother who didn't want you, but it was another thing entirely to be the child of a mother who couldn't keep you.

"Maybe I'll give Mom a call while I'm in town," I said at last.

"I bet she'd like that."

"Can I tell her that you told me?"

"Yes. I always warned her that I'd tell you if you asked."

"Do you think she'll be angry?"

GiGi turned to shake her head. "I think she'll be relieved."

"*I'm* relieved," I said. There had been a great question at the center of my life that I didn't even know was there. Now it was answered. Of course, answers always raise more questions, too. But now, at least, I knew what to ask. And who. As it all sank in, I felt my body relax, as if I'd been bracing, somehow, for years, without even knowing it.

"It explains a lot, doesn't it?" GiGi said.

I nodded, but then I wasn't sure what I was nodding about.

"Like why you have so much trouble letting people love you."

I stopped nodding. Did I?

"Maybe you just decided—so long ago that you don't even remember—that it made more sense to be alone."

"But I hate being alone," I said.

GiGi reached over to smooth my hair. "Exactly."

After lunch, I forced myself to get on the ball. I had toenails to paint, elbows to moisturize, hair to trim. There was a lot of deferred maintenance, to say the least. The bar mitzvah was looming at the end of the day, and I couldn't imagine how on earth I'd agreed to go. But I moved through the day like a robot, crossing things off my to-do list. By the time I got all the grunt work done, GiGi had gone upstairs for her siesta, and it was time to get ready.

But "ready" sounds easier than it is. As I showered, I felt full of dread. It's a tricky thing, dressing for an occasion like this particular one. As a rule, when you haven't seen the boyfriend who dumped you for your best friend in fourteen years, it's best to look hot, if at all possible. But I'd never been an obviously pretty kind of person. When I looked pretty, it was usually in a kind of subtle way, not in a hit-you-over-the-head "hot" way, which, really, had forced me to be interesting, instead. Which was fine. I was old enough now, and had seen enough lives unfold, to know it's always better to be an interesting girl than a hot one.

Except on a night like this. On a night like this, I would have gladly given up all my "interesting" for "hot." I'd brought a suitcase full of clothes to choose from, knowing that I'd need lots of options for this moment, and I tried on everything at least twice before I settled on a little pink '50s-style sleeveless shirt dress and white strappy heels. I put my hair into two ponytails, and then I twisted them around into buns and stole two of GiGi's mini chopsticks for decoration. Makeup-wise, I went for it: thick, retro liner on the top lids, mascara, and dark red lipstick.

I was ready way too early. I had overestimated how long it would take to make myself presentable, and now I'd have to pace around until it was time to go. I stared myself down in the mirror. Did I look like I was trying too hard? I wanted to seem fabulous, but effortlessly so. If you have to try to be fabulous, it doesn't count. I wanted to seem as unlike my scruffy high school self as possible. To make it clear to everybody how distantly I had left those days behind. I might have been a frizzy-haired, sandals-wearing, forgettable hippie back when we'd all known each other before, but I wasn't that girl anymore. I was no longer the kind of girl you'd cheat on and leave for someone else. I'd grown up to be amazing, dammit! I'd grown up to be the kind of girl you never get over.

I was trying to decide if I should brush-and-floss one more time for good measure when the doorbell rang. In the seconds before running downstairs to answer, I decided it had to be Jake. He'd come back for me! He'd somehow magically sensed how great this outfit was, politely ended things with Windy with no hard feelings, and hitched a ride here! As I walked toward the front hall, I felt a little guilty at the prospect. I wouldn't want to break Windy's heart. But, even still, I could feel little electrical flashes of anticipation sparking around my body, and I held my breath as I pulled the door open.

But it wasn't Jake.

It was Duncan.

He held a large Igloo cooler in both hands, leaning back to counter-balance its weight. I was just about to ask him about it when he spoke.

"Hey," he said, tilting his head. "You look hot."

A thousand points for Duncan. "I do not," I said. But I smiled.

He shrugged. "Have it your way."

I shook my head. "What are you doing here?"

"Coming for a visit."

"What's in the cooler?"

"Just some stuff."

"Why did you ring the bell?"

"I lost my key."

And here was a moment when, at any other time in our lives, I would have rolled my eyes and said, "Of course you did." But this time, I didn't. I just nodded, which felt like a sign of personal growth.

I stepped back to let him through.

He crossed the threshold and set the cooler down in the foyer with an "Oof!" and ducked back out to grab his duffel bag. Then he turned and made his face bright and cheery. "Hey, Sis!" he said, next, pulling me into a hug. "How was the wilderness?"

"Good," I said, nodding.

"Did you see any bears?"

"Not really."

"Were you almost killed?"

"Several times."

"Did Jake get you to fall in love with him?"

"Hell, no."

I looked him over, in his cargo pants and baggy T-shirt. I chose not to wonder how long it had been since those clothes had been washed. I chose not to fixate on the fact that he'd just dropped all his stuff in GiGi's entryway as if the servants would be along any moment to pick up after him. Instead, I said, "It's good to see you."

"It is?"

"I thought about you a lot on the trip," I said.

"You did?"

"How are you doing about Florida?"

He frowned for a second, until he figured out that Jake must have told me about her. "I'm okay," he said. "I've been stalking her just the tiniest bit at the restaurant where she works. But not in a creepy way. Just in a sad way."

I could have said, *Is there a difference?* But I didn't.

"She was way out of my league."

"That's what Jake said."

"How is Jake?" Duncan asked then, brightening at the prospect of a better topic.

"I think he's good," I said, as if the subject didn't interest me much. "He went to Colorado with a really cute girl."

Jake frowned. "That's weird."

"Why?"

"Jake doesn't like cute girls. He likes you."

"Thanks."

"He's always been that way. It's like an affliction."

"Well," I said. "Now he's cured."

"Shoulda sent you two into the backwoods years ago."

He was trying to make me laugh, but instead I just sighed.

"So," Duncan said, after a pause, "he didn't get hurt or anything?"

It was a question about his vision. Duncan knew, but he didn't know if I knew. "Do you mean his sight?"

"So you know?" Duncan asked.

I nodded. "And you do, too."

"Of course I know. He's my best friend."

"But you didn't tell me."

He seemed genuinely puzzled. "Why would I tell you?"

It was a good point. A month ago, I wouldn't have cared much.

"So he did okay?" Duncan asked. "He didn't get maimed?"

"He lost his glasses at one point," I said. "Then I broke them. But we duct-taped them back together."

He nodded. "Big fan of duct tape."

It was strange to see Duncan again after weeks of Jake touting all his good points, but it was even stranger now that I knew what GiGi had told me about our mom. Somehow, even though it didn't change anything, it changed everything. I'd been vacillating all day over telling Duncan. Part of me thought he should never have to know, and another just-as-vocal part thought we both should have known all along. Suddenly, the vacillating stopped: I just knew I needed to tell him, and—standing in our childhood hallway in the only home Duncan even remembered—the words were out as soon as I felt the impulse to speak them. I was almost as shocked to hear them as he was.

"Mom tried to kill herself," I said then.

He went white. "What?"

"Not today!" I said. "When we were kids."

He stared.

"The day she left us here and didn't come back? It was because she tried to kill herself."

"I don't remember that day."

"I do."

"GiGi told you this?"

I nodded.

"Today?"

I nodded.

"Why today?"

"Because I asked her."

Duncan ran his hands through his hair. "I always thought Mom left because I was such a little shit."

"But that's just it!" I said. "By being a little shit, you saved her!"

He frowned.

"She forgot to pack Softie. You wailed so bad for so long about it that GiGi finally went home to get it for you. That's when she found Mom. She'd taken pills. She was curled up with Nathan's teddy bear."

Duncan squeezed his eyes shut, then opened them and said, "That's why she never came back?"

I nodded.

"I think I liked it better when it was all my fault."

"It was never all your fault." As I said it, I realized it was true.

"I thought she just didn't like us."

"Puts things in a different light, doesn't it?"

It felt comforting, somehow, to know that we'd both carried the same wrong story of our lives—that I hadn't been the only one. That's when it sank in: No matter how alone I'd felt all those years, Duncan had been right there with me. We'd been alone together.

We talked about it for a while longer, standing there in the entry hall, combing through the information I had. He was surprised GiGi hadn't given me more details, but I said I wouldn't have wanted them. "Sometimes," I said, "the big picture is enough."

In the end, he asked if he could come with me when I went to see our mom, and I told him I'd be hugely grateful for company.

"Sorry to throw this at you when you've just walked in," I said.

He put his hands in his pockets. "It makes me feel weirdly better, somehow."

I nodded. I got that. "And worse, too."

"Yep," he agreed. "Much worse."

As the topic wound down, both our eyes started drifting over toward the cooler.

Finally, I had to ask. "What *is* in the cooler?" I asked. "GiGi told me not to be mad."

Duncan pointed at me. "I definitely need to tell you. But I need to pee first. And get a soda from the fridge."

I shrugged. "Okay."

"So weird to need to pee and be thirsty at the same time," he said, as he walked away. "You'd think those things would cancel each other out."

"I guess so," I said, thinking about it.

Then he stopped and turned back. "Just promise me you won't look inside the cooler."

"Is it something for me?"

"In a way."

"I promise I won't look inside."

"Great," Duncan said. Then he doubled back to grab his duffel and set it on top of the cooler, as if it might provide a barrier, just in case.

"Go to the bathroom!" I said.

While he was gone, I waited in the hallway. What would GiGi have been talking about? What would Duncan have brought me in that thing? Cold beer—but some awful kind? A seafood dinner from my favorite restaurant in the North End—but no longer safe to eat? A tub of my favorite ice cream, but melted? It had to be some kind of food-related welcome-back treat gone awry, right? I took a moment to appreciate him. He was much sweeter than I gave him credit for.

He came back, walking and glugging a Coke at the same time.

"Duncan, I'm very touched that you tried to bring me a—"

But he held up his hand to stop me. Then he let out a foghorn-like belch. "Sorry," he said. "Carbonation."

I did not want to be a bitchy big sister anymore. But my arms just kind of crossed themselves.

"Listen," Duncan said. "About the cooler—"

"Yes. I want to thank—"

He stepped over next to it. "It's kind of a good-news-bad-news situation. Except . . ."

I looked down at it. "Except?"

"Except there is no good news."

"Oh."

"I meant to tell you right away. But then you hit me with the Mom thing."

"Just say it. Waiting never makes anything better."

"Right," he said. But then he didn't say it. He took a breath, but no words came out.

I checked my watch. "I've actually got somewhere to be, so—"

"It's about Pickle!" he burst out then.

My eyes went wide. "My dog Pickle?"

He took a deep breath, looked up, and said, "She's dead! She died."

All I could do was stare.

"She got very sick," he went on, like he'd rehearsed his speech. "And then she died."

My brain spun. How does a dog die at the vet?

"She had a thing called 'torsion,'" he went on. "Actually, the technical term is GDV, 'gastric dilation volvulus.' Their stomachs flip over, and fill up with gas, and they basically implode. It's common in big dogs with deep chests."

I was shaking my head. "But she's a small dog with a narrow chest!"

Duncan nodded. "It's also common in dachshunds."

I couldn't fit the pieces together. "Couldn't they do anything for her?"

Duncan shook his head. "It's lethal if you don't catch it within an hour."

My voice was rising. "But why didn't they catch it?"

I registered Duncan's expression. He wasn't kidding. Gone was the Coke-belching brother who'd just walked in. Now his expression was contorted with worry. "This is the part where you hate me." At the words, tears spilled over and down his cheeks. "She wasn't at the vet."

"She *was* at the vet," I insisted. "I checked her in."

"Yes." Duncan nodded, his voice quiet. "But then I checked her out."

My eyes went wide. "You checked her out?"

"I didn't want her to spend a month in a cage! I wanted to bring her home and teach her tricks and take good care of her like you'd asked me to. I was going to surprise you! I was going to come through for once. And we had a great time! I got her a jangly tag for her collar with her name in rhinestones! She ate my *Catcher in the Rye*! And I taught her a trick! I taught her how to shake!"

"She already knew how to shake," I said.

That threw him off. "We were pals, I'm telling you! She was happy with me. But then one day, I came home and found her panting."

"Came home from where?"

"From work! I got a job."

"Doing what?"

He scratched the back of his neck. "Ironically, I got a job at the vet."

"What vet?"

"Pickle's vet! When I was there signing her out, they had a sign posted for a tech. I applied, and got hired, and I've been working there ever since. I'm good at it."

"You were at Pickle's vet's office while she was dying in your apartment?"

Duncan closed his eyes, and more tears spilled over. Then he pushed on, "When I found her, I couldn't drive her back because my car had a boot on it from a parking spot mishap, and so I got on my bike with her cradled in one arm and rode the twenty-two blocks back to work. We were almost hit by a bus. And the whole time, I was talking to her, and saying, 'All we have to do is just get you to Doc Sampson. He'll fix you right up. You're going to be fine.' But by the time I got there, it was too late. She died in my arms."

I was crying now, too.

"She slept with me every night," he said. "She burrowed under my Budweiser blanket."

"She loved to burrow," I said.

After a minute, Duncan whispered, "I'm so sorry."

"You killed my dog."

"I tried to save her! I'd have given anything to save her!"

"But she died."

"She was a great dog," Duncan said.

"She was a horrible dog," I corrected.

"Not to me," he said, barely able to get the words out. "I loved that little rat-faced pooch."

And in that moment, I knew that he did. I stepped close and grabbed him into a hug. "Me too," I said. And right then, on that crazy afternoon, for what felt like the first time in our lives, we had something good in common.

It wasn't until later, at the kitchen table, after we'd raided GiGi's pantry for Oreos, that I thought to ask him what all this had to do with the cooler.

"You haven't guessed?" he asked. He had a milk mustache.

I shook my head.

"It's Pickle."

I almost dropped my glass. "What?!"

He nodded, all earnest. "I brought her to you."

"Pickle?" I said, still catching up. "Is in the Igloo cooler?"

Duncan nodded.

I rounded the kitchen corner back to the entryway to stare at it. "How long has she been in there?"

"Five days."

"Five days!"

"Don't worry," he said. "She's on ice."

I looked back and forth between the cooler and Duncan.

"And she's in a Hefty bag."

"You put her in a Hefty bag?"

Duncan nodded. "Duct taped her up nice and tight."

"What is it with boys and duct tape?" Then the most irrational thought popped into my head and spilled out of my mouth. "But she'll suffocate!"

Duncan made his voice gentle. "Helen, she can't suffocate. She's already dead."

But then I thought about that story I'd heard about Martha Washington when I was a kid—how they'd dug up her coffin and found fingernail scratches on the lid. "Maybe she wasn't fully dead. Maybe you killed her twice!"

Duncan was sympathetic to my state. He shook his head. "She was dead."

"She could've been just unconscious—you know—with a really slow heartbeat."

But Duncan shook his head. "Trust me. You could hit a baseball with that dog when I put her in that bag. She's dead."

And so, it was official. There was no more fighting it. Pickle, the worst pet in the world—and also my very favorite—was dead.

I didn't know what else to do but head for the back door.

"Where are you going?" Duncan asked.

I stopped and looked back. "To bury her," I said. "Get the cooler."

❋

That's how I wound up digging a grave in my grandma's backyard in a pink party dress and heels. Duncan stood beside me, clutching the duct-taped mummy of Pickle's body in his arms, his face shiny with tears. His shirt was wet from ice water where he held her. If we'd had any sense, Duncan, in his dirty sneakers, would have dug the grave. But we didn't.

We picked a spot right next to where we'd buried our childhood bulldog, Lambchop. The idea was to put the two close together so they could be friends in Heaven.

I was about halfway through the digging, with a big pile of black soil next to me, when Duncan said, "Don't hit Porkchop."

I paused and turned to him. "*Lamb*chop."

"That's what I said."

"You said *Pork*chop."

"Didn't."

"Do you even remember Lambchop?"

"Sure. Of course. He was a bulldog."

"*She* was a bulldog."

"And she died by swallowing a tree branch as long as her entire body."

No corrections there. That was true.

By the time the hole was deep enough, one of my hair buns had come unpinned and my strappy heels were broken and smeared with mud. Duncan kneeled to set the little package of our friend into the hole, and while he backfilled the dirt, I kicked off my broken shoes and ran up to my room to grab the daisy chain that Windy had made me. I laid it over the grave. We said a few words of parting, and Duncan put his arm around my shoulders as we made our way back up to the house.

It wasn't until we were back in the kitchen that I realized Duncan had a six-pack of beers in his other hand. He set it on the counter and then pulled a can out to offer it to me.

But then it hit me: "Tell me that six-pack wasn't in the cooler, too," I said.

He froze with his fingers on the pop-top. "What?"

"Nope." I pointed at the door. "Take it outside."

"A day like this, and I can't have a beer?"

"Not one covered in dead dog juice," I said, turning to the sink to scrub the mud off my hands.

"She was in a Hefty bag."

"Outside!" I ordered, in my bossiest big-sis voice. "Now!"

Duncan obeyed.

When he came back in, I said, "You can have a beer at the bar mitzvah."

"What bar mitzvah?" he asked.

I turned to look at him. "You can't walk in here with my mummified dog and still expect me to go to my high school boyfriend's love-child's bar mitzvah by myself!"

He shook his head in submission. "No."

"Go find something to wear," I said.

Duncan started toward his room. "What do you wear when you're crashing a bar mitzvah?"

"Something nice!" I shouted. "With a tie!" Then I lifted a bare, muddy foot into the sink to wash that off, too.

Once I was cleaned up, I had to wash off all my smeary makeup, put an ice pack over my puffy face for a few minutes, and start over. My dress had a few flicks of mud, but it was still passable. My heels, I threw in the trash, and so I wound up in a pair of red ballet flats. I had just repinned my bun and redrawn my eyeliner when Duncan came into my room. He'd scrounged up a skinny black tie, the black tux pants he'd worn at my wedding (now two inches too short), and a white oxford that had been part of his school uniform. He looked like a waiter, but I said, "You look very handsome."

Had I ever said anything that nice to him before? He seemed to blink in surprise. "Thank you," he said, "and right back atcha. You look like a piece of candy."

I turned toward the mirror, and glared at my puffy, splotchy face. "Actually," I said, "I look so terrible right now, I'm thinking about ditching."

"You can't ditch," Duncan said. "If you ditch now, they'll think you chickened out."

Jake had said the same thing.

"They'll think you never recovered from high school."

"Are you saying I have to go?"

Duncan gave a shrug, like, *Pretty much.* "You may feel terrible," he said, "but you don't look terrible. How you can dig a grave one minute and look so great the next, I'll never know."

That got me. The sweetness of it made me laugh.

"What?" Duncan asked.

I stood up, ready to go. "Come here," I said, and I put my arms around him for our second hug that day—and also that decade. "Thanks for the pep talk."

He hugged me back, stiffly. "I thought you'd hate me forever after you knew about Pickle."

I didn't hate him. If anything, it was the opposite. Which was weird. A month ago, I would have pummeled him senseless over all this. A month ago, I would have held up this dog-in-the-Hefty-bag situation as definitive proof that I had a useless, hopeless, terminally irritating little brother that I would never be able to relate to, or care about, or like. But a month can be a long time. Before, what I saw were all the ways Duncan kept *failing*. But now, at last, I knew too much about him—and even, in fact, too much about myself—to think of him so obtusely. What I saw now were all the ways he was *trying*. And I could so relate to that. It made all the difference.

"You did your best," I said. "I know you did. Now let's go kick some thirteen-year-old ass."

Chapter 16

The first person—literally the first face—I saw as we walked into the top-floor ballroom of Chicago's historic Mercer hotel was David "Dave-O" Hoffman. First boyfriend, first sex, and first—but not last—agonizing heartbreak. I am pleased to report that in the fourteen years since I'd seen him, he'd gone bald as a walnut. No wonder his Facebook profile photo was a headshot of Scooby-Doo.

He stood right near the door in an oversized suit, greeting guests and looking far more middle-aged than any ex-boyfriend of mine had a right to. I walked right up to him and waved. "Hi, Dave."

He turned, stuck out his hand, and said "Hello!" in such a loud and overly cheerful way that he clearly had no idea who I was.

"It's Helen," I said, touching my hand to my collarbone. "Carpenter. From high school."

I saw the recognition come over him. "Helen!" And then, as if the words escaped on their own: "You got better looking!"

"You got bald," I shot back, as fast as a reflex. Oops! Too mean! Unnecessary! "Sorry."

Dave stood up straighter. "In some cultures, baldness is a sign of virility."

I gave an overacted nod of enthusiasm. "Yes! I've definitely heard that. Good point."

Dave's turn. But he didn't say anything. Just held his breath, deciding where to take the conversation from there. At last, he went with, "How are you?"

"Great," I said. "I'm great. Better than great." I turned to Duncan. "What's a word for 'better than great'?"

Duncan made his voice about an octave lower and said, in a Spanish accent, "*Excellenté.*"

I turned back to Dave. "I'm *excellenté.*"

Now it was all coming back to him. He wrinkled his nose. "Heard about your divorce."

"Did you?" I said, sinking a little. I guess I'd asked for it with the bald thing. "Well," I heard myself say then, "I'm completely over that. In fact, my ex just called the other week and begged me to come back to him. But I said no. Actually, my cell phone died before I got a chance to say no, and then I had to go into the wilderness for a while, so I haven't technically said the word—but I *will* emphatically say no at the next opportunity."

Duncan leaned in to catch my eye. "Did he?"

I nodded.

"He begged you to come back?"

I nodded.

"You know Jake and I will chain you up before we let you go back to that asshole."

At that, Dave turned to Duncan and said, "Who's this?"

"This is my brother, Duncan," I said.

Duncan waved and said, "Hey, Dave-O."

Dave burst out with a laugh. "Oh!" he said. "I was thinking he was your boyfriend. Like it was a *Harold and Maude* thing."

I wanted to smack him and say, *What am I? Ninety years old?* But I said, "Nope! Just my kid brother."

Dave frowned. "I don't remember you having a kid brother."

"He would have been a baby back then."

"Actually, I was eight," Duncan said.

"Hey," Dave said then, turning fully back to me, as if something were just occurring to him. "I've always wanted to apologize for being such a dick to you in high school."

That took me aback. "You have?"

"I can't believe I took your corsage back."

"That's your takeaway?" I said. "The corsage?"

Dave smiled. "Okay." He shrugged. "I can't believe I did all the rest of it, either."

"You should have known better! Your mom worked for Planned Parenthood!"

"I should have known better about lots of things."

I waved the apology away. "You were a kid," I said. "Kids are idiots."

"Actually," Duncan pointed out, "adults are idiots, too."

"Agreed," I said, pointing at him. "The entire human race is wall-to-wall idiots."

I looked back to Dave. "Anyway," I said. "Apology accepted."

"Awesome." He held out his fist for a bump.

I couldn't think of any response but to go ahead and bump it.

Then Duncan piped up. "Big night, huh? The boy becomes a man? *Mazel tov,* by the way."

Dave nodded. "It's a little crazy at the moment, because our party motivator canceled. Stomach flu."

"Party motivator?" I asked.

"It's a person who comes to parties and gets all the kids dancing. They're especially useful at bar mitzvahs, which are packed with awkward middle schoolers. And grandparents. And no booze."

Duncan nudged me. "*No booze.* You owe me a beer."

Dave gestured at the room of uncomfortable children. "Painful," he said.

I took in the sight. "So the party motivator helps the kids relax?"

Dave nodded. "We kind of put all our eggs in the party motivator basket. You know, some people rent a cruise ship or hire the Bulls cheerleaders. But we went for the party motivator."

"Who has the stomach flu," Duncan confirmed.

"Darcy's freaking out," Dave said with an eye roll. "She's been on the cell phone for twenty minutes trying to get a replacement."

As he said it, Darcy walked up, cell phone to her ear, in a lavender suit.

"Here she is now," Dave said, but she shushed him.

We all waited for her to wrap up her conversation. When she did, she turned to Dave. "They're all booked. There's nobody. In the entire city. I knew this was going to happen."

"Darce," Dave said then. "Look who's here."

She looked at Duncan first, and when he did not register, she turned to me. I did. "Helen!" she said, coming in for a hug.

I hugged her back. It was fine.

"I'm glad you made it," she said, not letting go.

"Me, too," I said.

Then she pulled back. "I am so sorry that Dave was such a dick to you in high school."

I squinted at her. It had actually felt like much more of a betrayal from her. I guess in some ways you expect more of a girlfriend than a boyfriend. "He wasn't the only one."

"We still feel terrible about it." The "we" seemed a little

passive-aggressive. "We'd love to take you to lunch and apologize properly."

I put my hands out in a *stop* motion. I could not think of anything in the universe I'd want to do less than spend an entire lunch listening to Dave and Darcy apologize. "No need."

She leaned in. "I can't believe he took back your corsage. I didn't even know about that until later."

"The corsage really was the least of it, actually."

"Of course, I played a role, too," Darcy added.

Suddenly, Duncan jumped in. "An X-rated role, if the rumors are true." Then he wiggled his eyebrows at Dave. "Am I right, buddy?"

There it was. I loved him.

Darcy stood up straighter. "And who is this?"

"This is my little brother, Duncan."

Darcy squinted like she was peering back into the mists of her memory. "The little brother who used to light your tampons on fire?"

"Oh, God," Duncan said, leaning his head back at the memory. "That was awesome."

"Yes," I answered, ignoring him. "But he turned out to be—" I looked for the word.

"*Excellenté,*" Duncan offered.

"That's right," I said, meeting his eyes and giving him a nod.

Another pause, and we tried to fill it by glancing around at the room. It was, indeed, entirely filled with seventh graders. And the elderly. I couldn't help but notice how both groups looked as if they'd been zipped into their bodies like Halloween costumes. But it was sweet, too, how carefully they'd all dressed in suits and dresses. The boys had clip-ons, and some of the girls even had patent-leather Mary Janes. I felt so sorry for them. I wouldn't be thirteen again for a kingdom. The dance floor was like a pulsing black hole. The disco ball spun above nothing and the string lights flashed around emptiness. Kids on one side, old people on the other. There was no getting around it. It was Titanically bad.

Then an idea hit me. "Darcy," I said, without really thinking it through. "You're a great dancer. Maybe you could motivate them."

She shook her head. "No, no. I'm the mom. Do you know how embarrassing moms are? If I tried to do that, it would literally kill my child. He would expire from humiliation."

Hadn't thought about that.

But Darcy was eyeing me now, like my idea had sparked a better idea.

"What?" I said.

"You are also a great dancer," she said, her grim expression lifting on a wave of new hope.

"Oh, no—"

"They have no idea who you are!" Her eyebrows were up now. Her eyes were bright.

"No, no—"

"You're young!"

"I'm three months older than you."

"But you *seem* young! You haven't been aged by breastfeeding and carpools! You've got that crazy hairdo. You could totally pass for a cool person!"

Duncan leaned in. "She *is* actually a cool person."

"Thanks, pal," I said.

"We'd pay you!" Darcy offered.

"I don't want you to pay me."

"It's three hundred bucks," Dave said.

"We'll double it!" Darcy said. "Oh, please!" She started jumping up and down and suddenly looked, again, like the friend I'd loved all those years ago. "This is the worst bar mitzvah ever. It will literally go into the *Guinness Book* if you don't save it. You're the only one who can!"

I shook my head. I was good at dancing—in certain circumstances. With friends. When I was relaxed. Not in a room full of strangers. I could feel my usual shyness clamping down.

"Don't you remember the dance parties we used to have in tenth grade? We'd crank up the music in the attic playroom and go crazy? Try to remember what that felt like. Think! It's the nineties, and real life is still a lifetime away. And even though my dad's going to bang on the attic floor with his nine iron and tell us to keep it down, we don't care."

I did remember. It was truly a lifetime ago, but I remembered.

"I'm not that girl anymore," I said, shaking my head. "I don't even know any dances." Unless you counted the "Cupid Shuffle." But I'd never even heard the real song.

"Make them up!" Darcy said. "They don't know any, either."

But I shook my head. "I can't. I'm sorry, I just can't."

Darcy swallowed in resignation as her face resumed its look of pinched misery. "Of course. I shouldn't have asked."

She *shouldn't* have asked.

"Well," Dave said, after a bit, ready to move on. "Thanks so much for coming. You really do look a lot better than you did in high school."

I frowned. "Thank you."

Then it was Darcy's turn, but she was already turning back to her phone. "Next time you're in town, let's get coffee."

"Great idea," I said, though we both knew we'd never do it.

They came in for a final hug, one after the other.

And then we were done. I was free to go. I'd made my appearance, faced my past, seen that shiny bald head of Dave's—and now I could go home to bed.

I looked over at Duncan. "Ready to go?"

He nodded. "I can't believe she asked you to do that!"

"Me, neither."

"What was she thinking?"

I shook my head. "She's just a mom trying to help her kid."

"Of course," Duncan said then, "though if you *had* been in the mood to do it—not for her sake, of course, but for your own—I happen to be an awesome dancer."

I looked over. "You are?"

As if in answer to the question, the DJ started playing the "Cupid Shuffle." I didn't recognize it at first, but when I did, I turned around to eye the empty dance floor.

"Helen?" Duncan asked.

"I know this dance," I said.

Watching me, Duncan suddenly knew what I was thinking, and he broke into a grin. Then he waggled his eyebrows at me. "Is it time to get funky, Lady H?"

I gave in with a shrug, like, *Oh, what the hell.*

For years after that whole prom-night debacle with Dave and Darcy, I'd fantasized about revenge. We'd all coincidentally wind up on a cruise, for example, and it would sink, and I'd sincerely try to row the lifeboat to them in time, but the sharks would catch their scent, and despite my valiant efforts, I'd be forced to watch them torn limb from limb.

I didn't have to rescue them tonight. I didn't even have to try. I had every legitimate reason in the world to abandon this sinking ship and just go the hell home. But I had a funny little epiphany on the edge of that dance floor. I really did love to dance. And if I could do it with only sticks and stones for music with people named Caveman and Caboose, I could just as well do it here.

That's how I wound up striding out into the middle of that empty floor, all alone, doing a dance I'd never even heard the music to, using my arms to beckon the kids and the grandparents to come out and join me. None of them did, but soon Duncan showed up to hand me a wireless mic.

"Hey, everybody," I said, my voice suddenly so loud I even startled myself. Everyone turned in my direction, including Dave and Darcy. At the sight, Darcy dropped her phone hand from her ear. "I'm, um, *Big Sister,* and this is my partner—" I turned to Duncan.

"Bilbo Baggins," he said.

I covered the mic and gave him a look, like, *What the hell?* "No. You can't be Bilbo Baggins."

I started again. "And this is my partner, D-Dog. We're here to teach you some dances, so get on over to the floor. Where's Sean Hoffman, by the way?"

At that, a non-bald thirteen-year-old version of my high school boyfriend raised his hand.

"Well, that apple didn't fall far from the tree! *Mazel tov,* Sean! Get on down here. And bring some friends. Or grandparents."

Sean Hoffman was nothing if not obedient.

"Where are the ladies?" I said into the mic. "Girls, get down here!"

A grandmother came out and gave me a big thumbs-up.

"Okay, friends. Easiest dance in the world. Seriously. When the song says 'to the right,' take a step to the right. When it says 'to the left,' take a step to the left. What do you think you're going to do when it says 'now kick'?"

The kids stared at me blankly.

I pressed the mic up to my mouth. "What are you going to do when the song says 'kick'?" I demanded.

"Kick?" Sean answered at last.

I pointed. "Correct! A hundred points!" That was the moment when

I found a groove. I was a teacher, after all. I might not know much, but I knew more than these kittens. I knew how to give a lesson. Age thirteen was still age thirteen, and everybody had to start somewhere. I scanned the crowd. More kids were starting to come down. Safety in numbers. Thank God the song was catchy.

I started. Duncan joined me. We had the DJ play the song three more times, and by the end, almost everybody had the hang of it. The kids were relaxing. We'd crossed the terror threshold. For them—and for me, too.

"Now, we change it up," I said, as I finally gave the okay to change the song. "And D-Dog is going to demonstrate. This is the Step-Clap. You step to the side, and when you bring your feet together, you clap. Then go the other way. It's the building block of dancing." From the Step-Clap, we moved on to the Spin, the Wiggle, the Booty-Shake, the John Travolta, the Figure Eight, and the Ooch. I made them all up on the spot. It was dance improv, and I was good, but Duncan was better. We wound up taking turns, and his contributions were the Umbrella, the Bullet-Train, the Honky Tonk, the Marilyn Monroe, the Slip-N-Slide, the Do-Nut, the Banana Peel, and the Talk to the Hand.

Here's the thing. They bought it. They accepted our authority. They believed we were party motivators. Hell, we almost believed it ourselves. Pretty soon, even the grandparents were out on the floor. Including, suddenly, out of nowhere, Grandma GiGi, in a fabulous red pantsuit.

"What are you doing here?" I shouted, when I got close enough.

"I was invited," she said, not losing the beat. "With a plus-one."

"Why were you invited?" I asked.

"They love me!" she said. "I went to their wedding, too."

I stopped dancing. "You went to their wedding?"

GiGi waved a finger at me, doing her own little version of the Oh No You Didn't.

"You went to the wedding of my cheating boyfriend and lying best friend?"

She shrugged. "They were nice kids."

"Not to me, they weren't!"

"You can't still be mad about that, can you?"

Of course I could still be mad! They had wronged me! Terribly! I had the right to be mad for eternity, if I wanted to. But that's when it hit me that I just didn't want to.

That didn't let her off the hook, though.

"I'm retroactively mad," I said. "You snuck to their wedding without telling me! And you didn't tell me you were coming here, either."

"You wouldn't have liked it," she said.

"Damn straight I wouldn't have liked it!"

She blew a kiss at me. "Life is messy, darling."

"But didn't you know you would see me here?"

"I was betting that you'd chicken out."

"But I didn't!"

Grandma GiGi smiled at me like she was very proud and nodded. "That's right, sweet girl. Be brave. Nothing good ever came from cowering." Then she spun off into the Tornado, where she literally bumped into an old gentleman in a yellow bow tie, and I watched him take her in his arms and lead her away.

Everybody was dancing. Suddenly, it was *Soul Train* in there. The room was *getting down*. They didn't need me anymore. My work was done. And just like that, I was ready to go. I waved down Duncan and pointed at my watch. He was in the middle of the floor, rocking it out like a madman, and he held up his hand to say, *Five more minutes*.

But I shook my head. "I'm going!" I shouted at him. Then I pointed at GiGi. "Catch a ride with GiGi!"

"Okay!" he shouted, and gave the thumbs-up. Then before I could turn away, he shouted, "Hey! Promise me something!"

"What?"

"Never call me anything but D-Dog again!"

I pointed my finger guns at him. "Done!"

He was going to stay. He was living it up at a bar mitzvah full of strangers, and a month ago, I would have found a way to use it against him. But, of course, a month ago, he wouldn't have even been here with me at all.

I thought about stopping at Dave and Darcy's table on my way out so they could thank me and tell me how truly magnificent I was, but then I decided I didn't need to hear it. I hadn't done it for them, after all. Plus, I liked the idea of disappearing into the night like some party-motivating superhero.

But as I walked away from the dance floor, the music throbbing behind me, I felt that familiar ache of isolation taking over again. Where was I going now? What was I headed back to? The music seemed to fade as the sounds of all those strangers laughing and talking rose. I didn't belong here, which would have been okay if I'd been able to tell myself there was somewhere else—anywhere else—that I did belong. The rest of the night stretched ahead of me like an isolation chamber. I'd head to the elevator alone, ride it down alone, walk through the lobby and the parking garage alone, drive my car alone back to GiGi's place, undress in my teenage bedroom alone, and then climb into bed. Alone.

I felt a squeeze in my throat like I might cry. I leaned forward and walked faster toward the exit, bracing against my own future as if it were a cold winter wind. I wanted to get myself out of there before Dave or Darcy caught a glimpse of me in any state other than triumph.

That's almost how I remember it: a bright warm party with a crowd on the dance floor united by the disco ball and the DJ—and me, walking away from it, as I always seemed to walk away from everything that could offer comfort or joy or belonging. I know I was wearing a pink party dress in the moment, but in my memory, as I fled the room, it's like an image superimposed from some other scene: a girl in a threadbare winter coat and scarf, cradling her arms for warmth, pushing through a swirling blizzard, head down and chilled through. It was time to pick myself up again. It was time to promise myself that I'd wake up in the morning and put my life back together—better and stronger this time, wiser for all the struggle. It was time, again, to stare the future down and say *Bring it on.*

But I couldn't. It felt like I'd been pushing my way through this same endless blizzard my whole life. And now, at last, I was too damned cold and too tired to go on.

But I did go on, of course. I kept my eyes on the floor and wove my way around tables and party guests. The exit wasn't that far. Maybe I'd feel better once I'd made it out of the room.

Before I could, though, I ran smack into someone's chest with a muffled *thump.* It could easily have been a grandpa on a walker or a seventh grader with food in his braces, but it wasn't. It was Jake.

My Jake. The Jake who had gone to Colorado. With his Windy.

I froze. There he was again, in his cool glasses, all clean-shaven. He wore an oxford shirt and a skinny hipster tie. I'd never seen him in a tie, not even at my wedding, and he looked put-together and grown-up. And handsomer than I remembered, which was overkill, really, because his plain-old regular handsome was more than enough.

After colliding with his chest, I stepped back fast, almost as if I'd bounced off, and he caught my shoulders with his hands. And I swear: That's when the blizzard stopped. The gray sky cleared in an instant to a crisp midnight blue and the blustery wind slowed to stillness. In reality, there must have been dance music blaring all around us. But I don't remember a sound.

The two of us stood frozen like that for a second, eyes locked on each other. My brain was spinning. There were so many reasons he couldn't possibly be standing there.

At last, he gave a little smile. "Hey, Holdup."

I said the first nickname that came to mind: "Hey, Honey Badger."

Just then, he seemed to notice that he was still clutching my shoulders. He let go with a start and stepped back. "You look amazing."

I looked down at my pink party dress. No threadbare coat, after all. I shook my head and looked back up. "What are you doing here?"

"Grandma GiGi brought me. As her plus-one."

"You came with GiGi?"

He nodded. "Nice dance moves, by the way."

"You saw that?"

He shrugged. "My favorite is the Beverly Hilbilly."

I shook my head. "Why are you here?"

"Well," Jake said, "first of all, Duncan left a panicked message on my phone, filling me in on the whole Pickle debacle."

"We've worked that out," I said.

"He was actually afraid that he might not live to see the morning."

I turned back toward the dance floor, which afforded a clear view of Duncan dancing like Animal from the Muppets. "As you can see, I've spared his life."

"So then I stopped by the house to check on him, and I found Grandma GiGi all gussied up. She invited me to be her date because her original plus-one had to get emergency bypass surgery."

In the hallway behind him, the elevator dinged and a whole load of grandparents filed out.

"Also," he added, "I'm staying here. At the hotel. I snagged a room on the way in."

"At this hotel?"

He nodded.

"You can't afford a room here," I said.

"Sure, I can."

"Not if you don't have any money."

"What makes you think I don't have any money?"

"Because you had to beg a ride to Wyoming."

He thought about it. "Those were extenuating circumstances," he said.

"You seemed broke. You're not broke?"

He shook his head. "I'm not broke. My mom left me a nest egg."

My brain was on overload. "But you said you were short on cash."

"I probably was. At the moment."

What were we talking about? Had he answered my question? "So," I said, to sum up, "that's why you're here tonight? You came home to save my brother's life, rented a room in this fancy hotel, and decided to go on a date with my grandmother?"

Jake met my eyes. "Not in that order, but yes."

"Okay," I said. I was waiting for something more, some kind of indication that I was somewhere—anywhere at all—in his thoughts, the way he was in mine.

But nothing.

And then, at last, I got sick of waiting. If I meant something to him he'd have said so by now. He would have told me with the same ease he applied to everything. I took a step back. It was useless, hoping and longing. There was no possible anticipation in it—only torture. I'd had enough. My poor, tired heart couldn't take anymore.

Behind him, outside the ballroom entrance and across the hallway, the elevator dinged and opened again just as I felt the sting in my chest that comes right before you start to cry.

"I've got to go," I said. At that moment I wanted nothing more than to make it to that elevator just as the doors slid closed behind me—with Jake on the other side.

But Jake followed. "Hey!"

I kept walking, but he caught up and grabbed my elbow before I made it, and the elevator closed and slid away without me.

"Where are you going?" Jake demanded.

I turned and he saw the tears in my eyes. "Anywhere but here."

He frowned. "What's going on?"

I really don't know why I told him the truth. Other than maybe I suspected that he already knew. I stood up taller and tried to be brave. My hands were shaking—hell, my whole body was—and I stuffed them in my pockets in fists. Then, taking a deep breath and looking up at the hallway ceiling to restrain the tears, I said, "When I saw you just now, I thought for a second that you'd come back for me."

I locked my gaze on the acoustical tiles above. I knew that the minute I looked down, the drops were going to spill over.

When Jake spoke next, his voice was softer. "I did come back for you."

I lowered my eyes at that. Tears fell as predicted, and, with them, I let out a little sob. "You did?" I lifted a shaky hand to wipe under my eyes.

Jake nodded.

"Why didn't you say that before?" I demanded.

His voice was as tender as I'd ever heard it. "I wasn't done," he said with a shrug.

With that, he took a step closer, put his arms around me, and rested his chin on my head. I pressed the side of my face against his lapel, and we stood there for I don't know how long. Long enough, though, for that same elevator to ding open, discharge another crowd of party guests, close, and disappear again.

"The night of the banquet," he went on after a while, "after you left, Windy put the moves on me."

"So?"

"So then we had to have a discussion."

I held still. "Why?"

"Because she *liked me*."

I stepped back to gape at him. "Of course she liked you! You guys were a couple!"

Jake had been about to say something, but that stopped him. He frowned and shoved his hands in his pockets. "We were not a couple."

"Yes, you were."

"I think I would know."

"You were a couple! A perfect couple! You both have summer homes in Maine and like peanut butter, or something. You almost proposed marriage to her at Painted Meadow. I myself personally saw you making out at the trailhead during Hugh's evac."

Jake winced. "You saw that."

"I saw it. And it was a hell of a kiss."

"But it wasn't a real kiss."

"It looked pretty real."

"It wasn't a *kiss* kiss."

"I don't care," I said. "It doesn't matter."

"It matters to me."

I looked away.

"It was Truth or Dare," he said. "She got dared to kiss me three different times during that dumb game, but she took rain checks."

"You can't take rain checks."

"Windy can. And then, on the hike, she told me that she wanted to combine them. Rather than three quick kisses, she just wanted one giant smooch."

"Well," I said. "You sure gave it to her."

"Yeah, well. I said I would."

"Why are you telling me this?"

"So you'll know what really happened." He ran a hand through his hair. "And I'm never playing Truth or Dare again, by the way."

I lifted my eyebrows. "You kissed every girl on the trip that night."

I wanted him to say no, but he shrugged. "Probably. I lost count."

I flared my nostrils at him. "The corpse of our kisses wasn't even cold."

"To be clear, those kisses never happened. If you recall, we were complete strangers by then. At your insistence."

"So? Did I run around kissing everybody in town?"

"I don't know. Maybe."

"No. I did not. I sat alone feeling miserable, like a normal person."

"At first, it was just typical Truth or Dare. But then all the girls started daring each other to kiss me. Only me. That's when it snowballed."

"So you kissed them all against your will?"

"Kind of. In a way. You can't kiss one and then not kiss them all."

"Sure, you can! You absolutely can."

He shrugged. "Once I got going, it was actually a pretty good distraction."

"Distraction from what?"

He met my eyes. "You."

I didn't know how to react to that, so I turned and pressed the elevator call button, just to have something to do.

After a minute, Jake asked, "You thought I was dating Windy?"

I turned back. "Everybody thought you were dating Windy. They were planning your hipster-bohemian wilderness wedding, for God's sake."

"Were you jealous?"

The elevator dinged then, and the doors opened. I went ahead and got on. Jake followed. But neither of us thought to press a floor number.

"Everybody was jealous!" I answered. "You got *infinity* Heartbreaker points for that. How is it possible you didn't know she liked you?"

"I did kind of know. But I thought it was just a time-killing, nothing-better-to-do thing."

"No," I said, mad now for Windy's sake. "It was a just-found-my-future-husband thing."

Jake looked around then, seeming to notice for the first time that we were in the elevator. "Where are we going, by the way?" he asked.

I pushed the LOBBY button. "Down," I said.

He shrugged. "Once I figured out her deal, I told her I didn't like her like that."

I felt protective. "You didn't 'like her like that'? What's not to like? She's adorable! And awesome! And wise beyond her years! Every single guy on this trip had a thing for Windy. She picks you and you don't want her? Doesn't that seem a little ungrateful?"

"I didn't ask her to pick me."

I pushed the LOBBY button again.

But the elevator wasn't going anywhere. I pushed it a bunch of times. We still didn't move. Then I pressed the OPEN DOORS button, but the doors didn't open. "I think we're trapped in this elevator," I said.

"Good," Jake said.

I frowned at him. "Not good."

"Now you're stuck with me," Jake said.

"I was stuck with you before."

His eyes crinkled at that. "Really?"

But I peered at him. "What about Windy? I can't figure you out. Is it a dopamine addiction?"

"Why are we talking about Windy?"

"Do you only want what you can't have?"

"I don't *only* want what I can't have."

"Because my ex-husband was like that, and it is no way to go through life. Count your blessings! Be satisfied with what life gives you!"

"I'm *trying*!" he burst out then, slamming his palm against the wall of the elevator. Just as he did, the elevator dropped about six inches.

In the seconds that followed, we both stayed frozen, crouched down, waiting for it to happen again. It didn't.

"That was weird," I whispered.

"Did I cause that?" Jake whispered back.

"Maybe it was a coincidence."

Now the elevator had his attention. He reached out slowly to press the OPEN DOORS button, but the doors didn't open. He pressed the LOBBY button, but we didn't move. He pressed all the buttons at once, but nothing happened. So then he pressed the alarm.

A voice came through the loudspeaker. "Do you need help?"

"We seem to be stuck in the elevator," he said.

"Uh-oh," the voice said.

I looked at Jake. "Did he just say 'uh-oh'?"

"Sounded like it."

Then the voice came back. "Sir, we're very sorry. We thought it was fixed. Someone will be there shortly to pry open the doors."

"How shortly?" Jake asked, but the voice was gone.

Silently, Jake took a step back to brace himself against the wall behind him.

I stepped back against my own wall. "What does that mean?" I asked. "*We thought it was fixed?*" An image of a ropelike cable frayed down to a thread popped into my mind.

Jake shook his head.

"What do we do now?" I asked.

"I guess we wait. And stay very still."

"And try not to hit the walls."

I studied the floor then. And Jake studied me.

"So Windy left for Colorado," I finally said, not looking up.

"She was pretty mad," he said.

"And what did you do then?"

"I kicked around with Beckett for a little while. He lives in Riverton, so that's not too far. Did you know he's in a reggae band?"

"That raises more questions than it answers."

"Turns out, a guy in the band restores vintage Land Rovers. He rebuilds them from scratch. He's got a barn full, all for sale. So I bought one."

"You *bought* a vintage Land Rover?"

He nodded. "In Riverton. It's orange."

"That must be a heck of a nest egg."

Jake shrugged.

"So you lost your ride, but you bought a car," I said. "Why aren't you in Denver?"

"That's what I've been trying to tell you."

I glanced at the elevator panel. "Okay. Let's hear it."

"Well," Jake said, "I'd stopped for the night on my way to Denver when my phone rang."

"Who called?"

"You did."

I shook my head. "I didn't call you."

He nodded. "You did."

I shook again. "I really didn't."

"You didn't call me on purpose," he said.

Then it hit me. My eyes got wide. "Not—"

He gave one nod. "A pocket dial."

"That fucking phone."

"Yep."

"Please tell me it was just static."

"Nope."

"What was it, then? Tell me!"

"It was you. Singing."

That had been after dinner. I'd been washing the dishes. I'd been singing with that particular kind of abandon you only ever use when nobody's listening. I squeezed my eyes closed and smacked my head against the elevator wall.

"Careful," Jake said, looking around like I might jog us loose.

"How long did this go on?"

"A good, long time."

I put a hand over my eyes. "Was I off-key?"

"Often. But in a cute way."

I peeked out.

"At first, it was 'Proud Mary.' But then you couldn't really hit those high notes, so you downshifted to like, a whole medley of things. Some Dean Martin. The Beatles. Earth, Wind & Fire. At one point, were you doing Weird Al Yankovic?"

I stood up a little straighter for authority. "Okay, 'Eat It' is a better song than 'Beat It.'"

He tilted his head to contradict me.

"'Get yourself an egg and beat it'? Come on. That's genius."

He shrugged.

I frowned. "You shouldn't have eavesdropped like that. You should have hung up."

"I couldn't hang up. It was too awesome."

I gave him a look, like *Please.*

"I seriously couldn't hang up. I didn't want to hang up. I realized I would rather listen to you than do just about anything else in the world. I realized that even if you can't stand me, and even if you deserve someone a thousand times better—and healthier—and even if the only decent thing to do was leave you alone, I had no choice but to come after you. Next morning, my Land Rover just kind of drove itself back home."

I paused. "What about the whales?"

"I'll still make it. It's not for three days."

"You're going to drive back to Denver?"

"Sure. In a day or two. But I needed to talk to you first."

Above our heads, the elevator made a kind of low groaning noise. We both looked up until it stopped. I pressed back a little harder against the wall.

"I had it all planned out. I even practiced. I was going to say it as soon as I saw you—but then, when I actually saw you, when you were actually right there, I chickened out."

"You never chicken out," I said.

He shrugged. "Once in a lifetime, I do."

"What did you need to tell me?"

His voice was quiet. "You already know."

My voice was almost a whisper. "Say it, then."

He took a deep breath. "I was going to say: I never liked Windy. There was nobody on that trip I thought about or worried about or wanted to be anywhere near but you."

I held very still.

"I don't have a problem with wanting things I can't have. I have a problem with wanting you. In particular. You are my problem. It's not a dopamine addiction, it's a Helen addiction. And I cannot seem to kick it." He paused. "I've had a thing for you for *six years*. You literally did not even know I was in the room, and you were married on top of that. There was no way I could even, like, ask you to coffee. But I made the best of it. I was fine."

"Good," I said, glad to hear he was fine.

"But then, you got divorced. Do you remember that day I helped you get your new sofa up to your apartment? Two flights of stairs?"

I thought back. No. Wait— Yes! He had helped me do that. "Where was Duncan that day?"

Jake pointed at me. "Duncan was in class. I didn't even tell him I was coming over."

"You didn't?"

He shook his head. "I was going to confess everything—starting with the day I met you and ending with that very moment. Do you have any idea what I wanted to do to you on that sofa?"

I shook my head. Then the day came back to me. "I was a total basket case that day."

He nodded. "You cried the whole time I was there."

I thought back. "So not the best time for a declaration of passion."

He shook his head. "Nope. But I was going to try again. I was going to ask you out before somebody else got you first. But then, before I could, I went to get a pair of glasses, and found out instead that I was going blind."

I looked down. "So you never tried again."

"Everything changed after that."

"Not for sure, though."

"No. I wasn't sure until just before Wyoming. There were some stages of grief to get through—some denial, some bargaining. And there were many tests to find out how bad it really was. But I didn't even think about asking you out after that. You didn't even like me with twenty/twenty."

"You know I don't care about all that, don't you?"

He shook his head. "Once I knew for sure, I couldn't breathe. I couldn't eat. My whole future was literally disappearing. Everything I'd ever wanted—to be a doctor, to have a bunch of kids, to learn to scuba dive—it was all gone. That was the day before you showed up at the party with Pickle."

He paused.

"What?"

He looked up at the ceiling. "I had a plane ticket out to Wyoming when I saw you that night. I was supposed to fly out in two days. But once I saw you, two days was too long to wait."

"You had a plane ticket?"

He met my eyes, and nodded.

"You said you didn't." He'd said Duncan had offered him a ride.

He nodded. "That's right."

"Why?"

He shook his head. "I just had this crazy feeling like you could save me."

I realized I'd been holding in my breath and finally let it out. "I can't even save myself."

"But you did. You have."

I shook my head.

"Longing for you gave me something to hope for. Even when it was hopeless."

"It didn't have to be hopeless," I said.

"Would you have wanted me to trick you into bed?"

"Why didn't you just tell me?"

He shook his head like he didn't know, himself. "Sometime in the next few years, my eyes will go dark. All the light will go out of the world. That's a fact, and nothing can change it. If I were a better person, I'd leave you alone. But I can't—I'm sorry, I just *can't*. That's really why I'm here. To say that to you. To be brave at last and say that."

It was all wrong that we were on opposite sides of an elevator at that moment. When a guy tells you something like that, you should be in arms' reach, at the very least. To hell with the elevator, I thought.

But just then, as if in response, the elevator dropped again. A foot? Two feet? The floor literally dropped from under us, and then we dropped, too, and then we hit the floor, both landing facedown on the carpet.

As soon as he could, Jake commando-crawled over to me. "Are you okay?"

I nodded. "Are we going to die now?"

"No," Jake said. "We're just going to stay trapped for a while between floors fourteen and twelve."

"What happened to thirteen?"

"There is no thirteen."

"The floor above twelve isn't thirteen?"

"It is," he said, "but they don't call it that."

"Why not?"

"Don't you know this? Everybody knows this! Because of bad luck."

"So the fourteenth floor is the thirteenth floor."

"No," he said. "The thirteenth floor just doesn't exist. And that's a good thing, because we need all the luck we can get right now."

We stayed like that for a minute, listening for a calming voice over the speaker, or for the sound of firemen prying the door open. Some— any—noise from the outside world. Which turned out, instead, to be my cell phone ringing.

As I inched my hand across the floor toward my purse to grab it, I said, "Maybe it's the hotel. You know, with elevator information."

"And they'd have your cell number because?"

Good point. It wasn't the hotel. It was Mike.

I turned it off.

Jake watched Mike's picture on the screen go blank. "You're just going to turn it off?" Jake asked.

I nodded.

"Aren't you curious why he's calling?"

"I know why he's calling."

"Why?"

"To beg me to come back."

"You don't want to be begged?"

I shook my head the tiniest bit. "Not by him."

Jake narrowed his eyes, all flirty. "Who do you want to be begged by?"

But I just smiled.

"So," Jake said, watching me. "I've just confessed how horribly I love you."

I nodded.

"What do you think of all that?"

Here, dangling above our deaths, it didn't seem like a good idea to be coy. So I just looked into Jake's eyes and said, in what felt like slow motion, "I love you horribly, too."

He shook his head in amazement. "But how? When did that happen?"

I thought about it. "It might, actually, have started when you almost peed in that Evian bottle."

He smiled and gave a nod. "Works every time."

"Or," I went on, "it might have been when you spelled the word 'lascivious.' Or when you forgot to dry off your collarbone and just left all those droplets of water. Or when you fell during the bear hang."

"These are the things that work with women?"

"Or," I went on, thinking, "it might have been how you kept rescuing me from Beckett, even when I didn't deserve it. Or how tender your hands were when you bandaged my knee. Or the way you do the right, brave, kind-hearted thing in every situation, no matter what. Or maybe it's just the way that I always, invariably, feel happier when I'm near you."

"I thought you hated me."

"I did hate you. In that way you hate people you're in love with."

"On the trip, too?"

I nodded.

"That whole time?"

I nodded.

"You sure hid it well."

"I thought you liked Windy."

"Even when I mauled you down by the stream?"

"I thought we were cheating on Windy. Which I felt hugely guilty about."

"I thought you were giving me a pity kiss."

I shook my head.

He applied all this new information to the memory of that kiss. "If I'd known you didn't hate me, I would have done a better job."

"You did a fairly heart-shattering job, as it was."

Jake looked at me in amazement. "You don't hate me."

"Just the opposite, in fact."

"So if I kissed you again, you wouldn't mind?"

"I wouldn't mind," I said. "But we're about to die, so you better get after it."

With that, he kissed me again. No tricks. No games. Just him, and me, like nothing else could ever matter, on the carpet in a broken elevator beside a hotel floor that didn't exist.

✳

Epilogue

Every story has to have a beginning and an end. Looking back, I could have begun it anywhere, or lingered on anything. I could have started it on the day I met Mike, for example, and ended it on the day I left him. I could have begun with the day we lost Nathan, and ended on the day we almost lost my mother. I could have lingered on sorrows. I could have painted the portrait of a crumbling marriage, or a family drowned by grief. It's all there.

But that's not the story I want to tell. Those aren't the moments in my life I want to dwell on. They happened. They mattered. They left their marks. But the things we remember are what we hold on to, and what we hold on to becomes the story of our lives. We only get one story. And I am determined to make mine a good one.

After all, life will hand each one of us our fair share of despair and loss and suffering—and then some. That's certain. But just as certain: It will also give us slices of chocolate cake, and sunny, seventy-two-degree days, and breezes that rustle the trees. Good things are so easy to overlook, but that doesn't make them any less *there*. A forgotten song will come on the radio. A stranger will help you change a flat. A lady walking by will love your red scarf. A mistake will turn out to be a blessing. An old friend will forgive you. A new friend will make you laugh.

And so, given every moment I could choose from, I end my story here, in the elevator, with the memory that I always turn to when I need to think about happiness and remember what it feels like. It's the image I'm most likely to reach for when I'm daydreaming. Or when I can't sleep. I carry it with me like a love poem tucked into my bra. I don't even have to read it anymore, I've looked at it so many times. But I read it anyway and let my eyes caress all the details that might otherwise disappear. It's so hard to look back on a moment without remembering all the other moments it led to, but sometimes I try. I close my eyes and see the two of us, so breathless at the start of our life together.

Here's what I know now that those two don't: There's heartbreak to come, and sadness, and trouble. But no matter what, we'll face every hard thing better together than we would apart. Every single one.

But we don't know that in the memory. In the memory, we hear a set of clanks outside the doors, some scraping, a few metallic bangs— and the elevator doors open. We're several feet lower than floor level, and we look up to see three firefighters—and a hallway full of middle schoolers—peering down at the two of us tangled together on the floor.

The firefighters clear the crowd back and lower a ladder down.

"Everybody okay in there?" a fireman asks.

"We're fine," I say.

"We're great," Jake says.

"We've locked the car in place," the firefighter says. "It's safe to climb out."

As I climb up into the lobby, I see the whole crowd. Dave and Darcy are there, and Grandma GiGi and her new gentleman friend in the bow tie. Duncan, too, who's rolled up his shirtsleeves and popped his collar. He whoops for me and then shouts a special "Attaboy, J-Town!" for Jake.

Then the crowd bursts into cheers. Jake helps me up, and we wave and take a bow. Duncan cups his hands and shouts over the noise, "Kiss her, buddy! You've earned it!"—and I barely have time to register the shocked expressions all around before Jake gives a quick salute with one hand and reaches out with the other to pull me in for a kiss so full and luxurious that the whole room falls silent, or seems to. I don't think at that moment about all the seventh graders looking on, or the fact that my brother and grandmother are watching, or even that Dave and Darcy are right there, taking it all in like they're at the movies. Nope. I can't think. About anything. All I can do is feel Jake's warm mouth and his hand behind my neck until everything else fades away. Maybe wanting something can't be the same as having it. And maybe getting what you want doesn't make you happy. But I'll tell you something: If the emotion flooding my body in this exquisite moment isn't happiness, I couldn't possibly tell you what is.

By the time Jake pulls back, looks into my eyes, and says, "That was okay, right?" all I can do is nod.

The next half hour is a blur. Somehow, the crowd disperses, the EMT pronounces us both unharmed, and the concierge offers Jake 50 percent off his room rate. Not that Jake needs it, apparently.

Speaking of Jake's room, it's on the seventh floor. Lucky seven.

That's where we go next, at last, leaving everyone else far behind.

Except, of course, we take the stairs.

Acknowledgments

Because my cute husband got the dedication this time around, my first thank-you must go to my awesome mom, Deborah Detering, who is really just a fountain of patience, support, babysitting, and carpool driving. She is my go-to person for processing anything, whether real-life or fiction, and she also happens to be my personal hero. Thanks, Mom! I will always try to pay all that goodness forward.

Also, huge thanks to my awesome husband, Gordon, who always makes everything more fun. Thank you for being so darned funny, for always seeing the best in everyone, and for taking such good care of me and the kids and the pup!

Much gratitude to my fantastic agent, Helen Breitwieser, whose name I love, and my two editors at St. Martin's Press—first Kate Ottaviano, and now the very charming Brenda Copeland. I'm truly grateful to Jen Enderlin, Laura Chasen, and all the good people at St. Martin's Press for their help and enthusiasm.

Also sending a hearty shout-out to my dear childhood friend—and almost-sister, at this point—Katherine Weber. So thankful, Kath, for your brainstorming help, enthusiasm, and encouragement.

Two nonfiction books that I was reading for fun the summer I wrote *Happiness for Beginners* made their way into the story and helped shape it. Many of the character Windy's thoughts about dogs—in particular, both the question of how one of man's worst animal enemies could have evolved into "man's best friend," and the idea of "survival of the friendliest"—were informed by the fascinating and highly readable book *The Genius of Dogs: How Dogs Are Smarter Than You Think,* by Brian Hare and Vanessa Woods. Windy also gleaned a lot of her wisdom about happiness, and what it is, and how to approach it, from a very thoughtful book by Richard O'Connor called *Happy at Last: The Thinking Person's Guide to Finding Joy.* Windy's idea of appreciating Three Good Things every day came from that book.

Thanks also to my family, just for being awesome! My dad, Bill Pannill. My sisters, Shelley Stein and Lizzie Fletcher. And always, always: my sweet-hearted, lovable, absolutely yummy children, Anna and Thomas.